THE AMBER KEEPER

OTHER TITLES BY FREDA LIGHTFOOT

Historical Sagas

Lakeland Lily

The Bobbin Girls

The Favourite Child

Kitty Little

For All Our Tomorrows

Gracie's Sin

Daisy's Secret

Ruby McBride

Dancing on Deansgate

Watch for the Talleyman

Polly Pride

Polly's War

House of Angels

Angels at War

The Promise

My Lady Deceiver

The Luckpenny Series

Luckpenny Land

Wishing Water

Larkrigg Fell

Poorhouse Lane Series

The Girl from Poorhouse Lane

The Woman from Heartbreak House

Champion Street Market Series

Putting On The Style

Fools Fall In Love

That'll Be The Day

Candy Kisses

Who's Sorry Now

Lonely Teardrops

Women's Contemporary Fiction

Trapped

Historical Romances

Madeiran Legacy

Whispering Shadows

Rhapsody Creek

Proud Alliance

Outrageous Fortune

Biographical Historicals

Hostage Queen

Reluctant Queen

The Queen and the Courtesan

The Duchess of Drury Lane

Lady of Passion

THE AMBER KEEPER

Freda Lightfoot

This is a work of fiction. Names, characters, organizations, places, events, and incidents are either products of the author's imagination or are used fictitiously.

Published by Lake Union Publishing, Seattle

www.apub.com

ISBN-13: 9781477826157
ISBN-10: 1477826157

Cover design by bürosüd° München, www.buerosued.de

Library of Congress Control Number: 2014941656

Printed in the United States of America

To David and my family,
who are always there for me.

PROLOGUE
1919

My snow-boots were worn through so that I walked on the ice that coated the rough mountain path, the soles of my feet numb with cold. Gasps of breath formed frozen crystals on those parts of my nose and cheeks not protected by scarf and fur hat. I had long since lost my small pony, the poor animal having bolted home in terror when the guns started, although whether she'd ever arrived is doubtful.

Home, if that is what you can call the house in which I had resided for so many years, no longer existed. It was but a shell of its former glory. I remembered how the darkness of the night seemed to press in upon me, almost as if I were back within those prison walls. I had closed my mind to the horrors I'd left behind, attempted to set aside my fears about those loved ones dear to my heart who had vanished from my life. Instead, I'd fixed my weary gaze on the heels of my guide trudging ahead of me, knowing that if I was to survive, I must stay focused. This was my last chance to get out of Russia.

We walked for days, through ice, snow and blizzard, sustaining ourselves with hunks of none-too-clean stale bread, and with nothing to wet our palette but sucking on icicles. When, hours later, we staggered into a cave, my knees gave way and I fell to the ground, weak with gratitude. I remember feeling a huge relief that at least I could rest for a while, thankful to be out of the bitter wind. The last two nights – or was it three? – we'd slept in the open, not even daring to light a fire in case the Bolsheviks should spot it and come searching. Curling myself thankfully into a corner, rubbing my hands and feet in an effort to stave off frostbite, I pulled up my collar, tucked my knapsack beside me and told myself firmly that I must not fall asleep. I was afraid I might never wake again, due to the fierce cold.

But despite my best efforts I must have fallen asleep instantly out of sheer exhaustion, for I knew nothing more till I was woken by a shaft of daylight filtering into the cave at dawn, and some strange sound that had alerted me. I sat up abruptly, looking around for my guide. He was nowhere to be seen. The man to whom I'd paid an exorbitant sum, every last kopek I possessed, had deserted me. I was quite alone. But as the sound of horses' hooves clattering over rocks penetrated my befuddled brain, I realised I was about to experience some unwelcome company.

ONE
1963

It wasn't until the crowds on the station platform began to clear that she saw him, a gaunt figure in a dark suit emerging like a ghost out of the steam. She stood frozen with grief and resentment as the Windermere train disgorged its passengers, heard the long hoot from its whistle and the slow grind of gears as it began to chug slowly out of the station again. Battling against the urge to jump back on board and return to Paris, anything rather than face the inevitable recriminations, Abigail felt as if this were very much the end of the line for herself as well as the train. She looked about her at the familiar scenery where pockets of snow still lingered on the mountain tops, the spring sunshine lending the frosted peaks a brilliant clarity, while the coolness of the breeze entirely suited her mood. She breathed in the clear air, as sharp and heady as champagne, and reminded herself that this was home. This was where her heart lay.

He came towards her not exactly with arms outstretched, as she had hoped, but with one hand raised in greeting and what might be evidence of a slight smile on his stiff lips.

'Abigail, there you are, at last.'

'Pops, it's good to be home.' A bleakness opened up inside her, giving the lie to her words. She hoped he might gather her into his arms as he'd used to do when she was a small child, but he made no move to do so. For years she'd dreamed of a reunion, but not for one moment had Abbie imagined it would be under such circumstances. She'd had ample time since the day she'd left home to reflect on how she could perhaps have handled things better. How wise we all are in retrospect. Unfortunately it was not possible to go back and change the past: one could only move on into a new future.

Grasping hold of her child's hand she took a tentative step forward, as if echoing the thought. All too aware of the awkwardness between them she planted a kiss on each cool cheek in typical French fashion, but as he made no response, she stepped quickly back. It was almost as if they were strangers.

'We rather expected you yesterday.' His stilted tone sounded very like a reprimand.

'I'm sorry, I missed the train.' Deliberately. But she didn't tell him that.

'We'd almost given up hope.'

'Oh, you should never give up hope, Dad. Sometimes it's the only currency we have left.' The quip was meant to lessen the tension between them. It failed miserably, although she hadn't risked using her pet name for him this time.

Somewhere she could hear a tinny transistor radio playing *Please, Please Me*, and squeals of happiness at more joyous reunions taking place around them, which made Abigail feel even worse. At one time they would have engaged in jokey banter, perhaps about her Beatnik-style stripy jumper, or the fact she still couldn't control her long, unruly dark hair despite the black beret she'd pulled down over it. 'Get your hair cut, girl,' he'd used to say in his sergeant major's voice, and she would laugh and remind him she wasn't one of his army recruits, and the war was long over. There were no such jokes today.

Taking a breath and drawing the child to her side, she said, 'This is Aimée, my daughter. She's been longing to meet you.'

'And I you,' Tom Myers politely remarked, bending a little to take a small hand in his and give it a little shake. But even the child recognised the insincerity of his words, saying nothing as she leaned shyly against her mother. Abbie smoothed her daughter's soft curls in a comforting gesture.

What had she expected? Forgiveness, or that they could take up as if nothing had happened? In all these long years of separation, communication between her and her parents had been almost nil since the letter she'd sent when first she'd arrived in Paris, announcing she had no intention of returning to finish her studies. The few she'd written since had rarely been acknowledged. Had she dreamed that one day Kate would turn into the loving, caring mother she'd always longed for? That would never happen now. The opportunity for reconciliation between them was gone forever.

~

The drive to Carreckwater took longer than Abbie remembered, which was a pity as she and Aimée were both desperate for their beds, having spent a night sleeping rough at the Gare du Nord when they'd missed the train, or rather allowed it to leave without them. Fortunately they were able to close their eyes and nod off a little in the back seat of the car, the child's head resting on her breast, warm and comforting, smelling sweetly of flowers and the doughnut she'd eaten earlier. Beyond a few polite comments about the weather, the journey was almost entirely silent, which was something of a relief.

Later, with Aimée asleep even before she was tucked into the small bed next to her mother's old room up in the eaves, Abbie couldn't resist the luxury of a long bath. The hot water and lavender oil were deliciously refreshing after the long journey and the tepid showers she was used to in the Paris apartment. Unfortunately, it proved to be a bad mistake to lie soaking too long, as her mind conjured up the hopes and dreams she'd indulged in the last time she'd used this bathroom, the night before she and Eduard had run off together. And of their parting row just a few days ago when her whole life seemed to collapse. Tears filled her eyes at the prospect of never seeing him again, just when she needed him most.

Why had he let her down so badly? Didn't he love her? Had she failed to make him happy? Briskly rubbing herself dry, Abbie closed her mind to such hurtful memories. Her decision was made. Now she must learn to live with it and move forward, her first task being to attempt some sort of reconciliation with her father.

She chose a sensible knee-length dress in a soft caramel wool. Her father was a conservative man who still clung to old traditions and etiquette, so her black stirrup trousers and fake leopard-skin top would not meet with his approval. She did, however, daringly dab on a little green eye shadow which suited the brown eyes she'd inherited from her mother, a touch of mascara and pale pink lipstick. She even dutifully pinned up her hair into a French pleat. Then, pinching her cheeks to restore some colour to her somewhat pallid complexion, she proceeded down the wide staircase to the dining room.

The feel of the highly polished banister rail beneath her hand, the creak of the old floorboards, the very smell of the oak-panelled walls and ancient furniture somehow warmed her heart. She'd forgotten quite how much she missed this old house. From the outside Carreck Place appeared rather bland and square, fronting a wide lawn, but inside was quite a different story. There was an ageless charm to the house that Abbie had always loved. She half expected to see a Christmas tree standing in the hall and a huge fire blazing in the drawing room, and hear the sound of merry chatter from the many guests her mother had loved to gather about her.

The dining table this evening was set for only two, the meal taken largely in silence. Not that she managed to eat much of the freshly caught trout prepared by Mrs Brixton, the housekeeper. Abbie's appetite seemed non-existent, despite the fact that she had barely eaten a thing on the long journey. Finally pushing away her untouched dessert, she accompanied her father to the library for coffee. Reality could no longer be ignored.

Abbie cleared her throat. 'Tell me how it happened. Who found her?'

There was a long pause in which her father stared into the empty grate. Abbie shivered. It was cold in the library, a brisk March wind rattling the shutters, yet it hadn't crossed his mind to order a welcoming fire to be lit for her return. Even so, the chill came not from the room itself but from the shock and anger that still reverberated within him.

Abbie had almost given up hope of receiving an answer to her question when finally her father began to speak, his tone carefully controlled, almost matter-of-fact. 'I'd spent the afternoon walking over Loughrigg, since it was a Saturday, then called at the shop on the way home. Linda, the assistant, was unpacking a delivery of cabochons from the wholesalers and told me that Kate hadn't been in. She'd taken quite a few days off recently as trade is often quiet at this time of year, so I wasn't too concerned. Not till I arrived home at almost seven o'clock and found the house in complete darkness . . .' Tom Myers paused to glance at his daughter. 'You know how she loved to have all the lights blazing.'

Abbie nodded, feeling the tears start to blur her vision. 'And Rachmaninoff blaring away. Where was Mrs Brixton?'

'She'd been given the day off, apparently, or so I learned later.'

Heavy silence fell again and this time Abbie did nothing to encourage him to break it, suddenly unwilling to hear the conclusion to this story, even though she knew the ending, having been bluntly informed over the phone by her brother. It came anyway.

'I found her hanging from the top banister rail. She must have been there some time.'

The horror of it all was suddenly too much and Abbie ran from the room to throw up what little she'd managed to eat at dinner down the cloakroom lavatory. She felt hot and cold all at the same time and couldn't seem to stop shaking. Ever since she'd received the news of her mother's suicide, Abbie had felt beset by a strange numbness, as if she were somehow detached from events. She'd gone about the business of packing her bags, booking a seat on the train, making the necessary arrangements to leave as if watching herself through frosted glass. Now, having rinsed the foul taste from her mouth and bathed her face in cold water, she finally allowed the flood of tears to come.

What on earth would make her mother take her own life? What terrible depths of despair had she sunk to, and, more to the point – why? Was living here in beautiful Lakeland so impossibly awful? She'd run a successful business, had a loving husband, and her precious son and grandchildren lived not too far away, so what could possibly have made life so unbearable?

Returning to the library she found a small glass of brandy standing waiting for her on the coffee table. Casting her father a glance of gratitude, she took a sip, welcoming the spread of its warmth within. After a moment she said, 'I still can't quite believe this has happened. Why would she do such a thing?'

He looked at her, his glance chilling. 'Need you ask?'

Something inside Abbie began to shrivel up. It had taken months to reclaim her self-esteem following the trauma of running away from home all those years ago, and within a few hours of returning she could feel it rapidly diminishing yet again. She strived to hang on to it, for she was no longer a rebellious teenager, but a woman of twenty-five with a child of her own. 'Are you implying that this is in some way my fault?'

'You were ever obstinate, completely oblivious to whatever your mother asked of you.'

'Perhaps because she asked too much, expecting me to behave in a way that would put her in a good light, with no consideration for what I might want. She wasn't an easy woman to please.'

Her father's face tightened with a mixture of anguish and fury. 'You know full well that she wanted only the best for you. It wasn't easy for her, being adopted.'

Emotion blocked her throat and tears again threatened. 'I'm sorry, Dad, but I don't understand. Why did she have all those hang-ups when Gran absolutely adored her? And what did *I* do that was so terrible?'

'You broke your mother's heart, Abigail, by taking off into the unknown with that ne'er-do-well.'

Abbie's heart contracted at these words. She really had no wish to discuss her failed love life with her father at this stage. Maybe she'd talk to Gran later. Lifting her chin, she held fast to her pride. 'Actually, Eduard was the love of my life.' Or so it had seemed at the age of barely eighteen. The fact that he was well into his thirties at the time, and married, hadn't troubled her in the slightest.

It occurred to Abbie that perhaps she really wasn't any good at relationships. It was certainly true that there'd been no closeness with her mother during her adolescent and teenage years, nor had they seen eye-to-eye on the future Kate had planned for her. There'd been no easy mother–daughter rapport between them at that time. Now there never would be. Was this where foolish rebellion had taken her – to be forever scarred by guilt?

Even so, Abbie longed to challenge her father's accusation by asking why, if it were true that she was the cause of her mother's alleged broken heart, it had taken Kate seven years for her to act upon it. Yet how could she do that when he was so desperately upset and grieving?

'When is the funeral?' she asked instead, tactfully changing the subject.

'Tomorrow. I was beginning to think you'd miss it. Robert and Fay will be here first thing with the children, although of course the little ones will not attend. You'd never believe how Carrie has grown, no longer a baby but a lively toddler of eighteen months, and young Jonathon starts school soon.'

Abbie quickly bent her head to rummage in her tote-bag for a hanky, unwilling for her father to witness the pain she felt at hearing the pride in his voice, and the way he smiled as he mentioned his grandchildren. It was an emotion he'd never expressed over her own daughter, and there'd been no smile for her lovely Aimée.

Their own relationship had been warm and loving once, full of jokes and camaraderie, even if he'd often expressed a resigned despair at her determination to speak her own mind and do her own thing. Everything had been fine between them until that final split with her mother.

Of course, there'd been much more to that than a disagreement over a boyfriend. The fact that Kate wouldn't consider taking her into the business, holding up Robert as a prime example of success as if Abbie weren't capable of such a thing, had hurt badly. Why hadn't her mother trusted and respected her enough to want to work with her? Nothing Abbie did, no matter how hard she tried, would make Kate change her mind. Then to also lose the respect and consideration of her father had been a pain too great to bear.

Now she dreaded the reunion with her brother. How he'd preened himself, making out he was the favourite, and the clever one as well, as he always came top of the class. Meeting his wife for the first time when Abbie hadn't even been invited to their wedding, or been told about his children, was going to be difficult. Worse, Abbie would have to look Robert in the face knowing that all her family's dire predictions had been proved correct. She had indeed made a complete mess of her life. Not that any of this should matter now, as there were more important things to worry about, and other people grieving besides herself. Yet somehow it did.

Dabbing at her tears, she tucked the hanky away again. 'How's Gran?' Kate's relationship with her adoptive mother hadn't always been close. At seventy-one Millie was still a feisty, lively lady who believed in living life to the full. Losing her only daughter, however, could easily destroy that wonderful spirit in her.

'As well as one might expect,' Tom said, with a resigned sigh. 'You'll see her tomorrow.'

Abbie could hardly wait, for in the circumstances her homecoming was going to be far more problematic than her worst fears.

TWO

Clouds hung heavy over the crags and fells as rain drizzled down on a miserably cold March day, as it generally does at funerals. It had taken over two weeks to reach this stage, with a post-mortem and inquest to be dealt with before the coroner was able to release the body for burial. Now Abbie stood holding her grandmother's arm at the graveside, marvelling at how composed she was, but then she'd always been a strong woman, a no-nonsense sort of person who never made a fuss. What she must be suffering inside was no doubt a different story.

The vicar gave a long address about how much Kate Myers had generously contributed to the church and community in her role as secretary of the Mothers' Union and Treasurer of the Women's Institute, and by serving on the committee of the local Dr. Barnardo's Home.

Abbie knew nothing of this part of her mother's life, and despite herself was deeply impressed. It was astonishing that Kate could manage to be so involved in such matters on top of running the family hand-made jewellery business. How sad, though, that it should take her death to reveal this charitable side of her nature.

Yet if she'd cared for children so much, why had she never shown any interest in meeting her own granddaughter?

The presence of the children in fact brought a welcome blast of fresh air and gentle laughter into the sombre household as people gathered for the usual wake. Ignorant of the circumstances that had brought the family together, young Jonathon chattered away twenty to the dozen, telling anyone prepared to listen how excited he was to be starting school after Easter. Eighteen-month-old Carrie didn't sit still for a second, happily poking into corners, emptying ladies' handbags and pulling open every drawer and cupboard door she could get her small chubby fists on. When her mother took her upstairs to put her down for her afternoon nap, she happily scattered Johnson's baby powder all over the bathroom floor. Abbie laughingly cleaned it up while Fay attempted to put a nappy on the toddler, now indulging in a screaming tantrum.

'Oh, she's coming up to the terrible twos. I remember it well. Aimée was just the same. Fortunately at six she's now an absolute treasure.'

Skilfully folding and pinning the terry-towel nappy in place, Fay said, 'But something of an embarrassment still, I should imagine.'

'Why would she be? She's the joy of my life.'

'I mean since your daughter is – well – what she is . . .'

Abbie instantly sobered. 'You mean illegitimate?'

Robert chose that moment to appear at the bedroom door. 'Don't attempt to deny it. I see no wedding ring in evidence. Admit it, Abbie, you've screwed up big time, and Ma has paid the price.'

His words stunned her into silence for a whole half minute. Abbie had been mildly startled by the sight of her brother after all this time, looking much older than his twenty-eight years. There was already the odd fleck of grey in his brown hair, and he'd developed quite a paunch and signs of a double chin. Clearly, all those smart lunches he must attend as a successful accountant were beginning to have an effect. But his sense of self-importance was as evident as ever.

Fay hastily pulled a pair of frilly plastic panties over the nappy, then shooed brother and sister out of the room so that she could settle Carrie for her nap. Robert and Abbie stood facing each other out on the landing with expressions as dark as thunder.

'So you start on me the minute I arrive. Nice to see you too. Thanks for that, brother dear. Bit unfair, don't you think, to blame me when I've been living away from home for *seven years*!'

'You can't deny you were responsible for her unhappiness.'

'Oh, change the record, please,' Abbie responded, keeping her voice low so as not to disturb little Carrie, or reveal how upset she was. 'Why would Mum suddenly decide *now* that she can no longer live with the shame of my scandalous teenage behaviour, *after all this time*?'

'Mother had become increasingly depressed recently, dwelling on the past a great deal. A visit from you might have cheered her. Even the odd letter would have helped.'

'Shows how much you know! I did write, loads in the beginning, but as my letters were generally ignored I gave up in the end. Mum had my address, yet I can't recall her ever using it.' Tears were choking her throat, which Abbie desperately strived to hold in check, not wishing her brother to see how badly his words had affected her.

Robert moved a step closer, dark eyes narrowed, mouth tight with anger as he hovered almost threateningly over her. 'Your trouble is that you never accept responsibility for anything. You're far too wrapped up in your own wishes and desires to consider the effect your decisions might have upon anyone else.'

A flush of crimson crept up Abbie's cheeks, although out of fury rather than guilt. 'That is *not* true! You know I tried my hardest to please Mum. She simply wasn't interested to hear what I wanted from life, wouldn't even let me help in the business, although I wanted to for years. But no, my working in a shop wasn't good enough for her. I had to go to university, then presumably marry a rich company accountant and become an obedient middle-class wife with two-point-four children.'

'Instead you ran off with that piece of garbage and managed to break Mother's heart by having a bastard child. No wonder she rejected you.'

Abbie very much doubted he felt the stinging slap she gave to his arrogant fat face, but it certainly made her feel better.

~

Later that afternoon, seeing that the strain of the day was beginning to take its toll, Abbie walked her grandmother home to the lodge house which stood at the entrance to Carreck Place.

'Would you like me to stay for a while?' she asked, putting on the kettle for a cup of tea, as if they hadn't drunk enough already on this endlessly sad day.

'That would be lovely, but then I need a little time alone, if you don't mind.'

Abbie kissed her papery cheek. 'Don't blame yourself, Gran. My mother was never an easy woman.'

'I know that only too well,' she said, sinking into her chair with a heavy sigh. 'Nor must you blame yourself either, my darling.'

'Easier said than done, since everyone else seems to.' The kettle boiled, which allowed Abbie to turn away and fuss over brewing the tea and place Gran's favourite porcelain tea cups on to a silver tray. She had ever been a lady of high standards. 'I know Mum didn't have an easy start in life, being adopted and all that, but it hurts that she rejected Aimée so completely. Why was that?'

Millie Nabokov gave a sad little smile as she accepted the cup of tea Abbie offered her. 'Once Kate had taken a stance she always found it hard to retract. Strangely, she very nearly made the same mistake herself.'

'Really? I never knew that.' Abbie sat down opposite her grandmother, eager to know more.

'Except in her case it was all about rushing into a hasty marriage. It must have been about 1934. I well remember the scent of wild garlic and bluebells in the air as we sat together on an old bench beneath the copse of silver birch down by the lake, a shaft of spring sunshine warming my face. Kate was asking about my time in Russia when she suddenly announced, with great excitement in her voice, that Eric had asked her to marry him and that she'd said yes. She thought it so romantic that he'd gone down on one knee to propose. She was seventeen at the time. I, of course, was quite shocked, and not at all in favour.'

'Oh dear. That wouldn't go down well.'

'No, sadly it didn't. Eric was a fine young man, but I told her friendship is one thing, marriage quite another matter entirely. I considered her far too young to even understand the meaning of love, let alone contemplate such a commitment.'

Abbie gave a wry smile. 'Yet you never judged me when I ran off at almost the same age, already pregnant with Aimée, nor in any of your lovely letters since.'

'I know, my darling, but it's a different world now.' The old lady's brow puckered slightly. 'Although I have wondered about the tone of your recent letters. You are happy, aren't you?' she gently asked, taking a sip of tea.

Abbie took a steadying breath then gave a sad shake of her head. 'I'm afraid not.' She'd tried so hard not to worry her grandmother with the truth, putting on a brave face, but now seemed a good time to admit to it at last, Millie being the one person in the world right now she felt comfortable with. 'A while ago I discovered that Eduard had lied to me, that he never had divorced his wife. I kept on hoping he'd get round to it because I still loved him, and for Aimée's sake. Then, when I found out that his wife was pregnant again, I finally had the sense to kick him out.'

'Oh my darling, I'm so sorry. We all make mistakes, but it's how we deal with the consequences that show our true worth, and you are young enough to start again.'

How pragmatic and sensible her grandmother was, but then Abbie had always felt able to talk to her. They, at least, had regularly kept in touch, and she was deeply grateful for her support over the years. Her grandmother continued with her tale, as if set on blaming herself for her daughter's death.

'Unfortunately, Kate found it difficult to forgive me for my lack of approval, and I'm afraid a distance grew between us which lingered for some time. She was stubborn in that respect, something with which you are all too familiar, Abbie. She said it was as if all the security she'd taken for granted had slipped from her grasp. Which was a great sadness to me, as it had been hard won. Yet I, too, remember being rather foolish at that age,' she conceded with a smile. 'Very much a young woman with a mind of my own. My rash decisions led me into a world quite beyond my comprehension.'

'To Russia, in fact,' Abbie put in. 'I always think it's so cool that you lived there, even if you've never talked much about it. I'd love to hear more about your life at that time, Gran. The revolution must have been utterly terrifying. How on earth did you cope?'

A sadness once again clouded her grandmother's eyes, and Abbie instantly regretted her request. She was on her feet in a second. 'But that's definitely a conversation for another time, not today. I shall leave you in peace for now. Is there anything you'd like me to do for you before I go?

Assured that there wasn't, Abbie quietly took her leave, promising to call again the next day.

After her granddaughter had gone, Millie sat for some time swamped by grief, her mind slipping back to that far distant time in 1934, the day Kate had started asking difficult questions about her time in Russia. Their relationship had gone so terribly wrong after that, despite all her efforts to protect her beloved daughter and give her the love she deserved. Now Kate was dead. Was there something more she could have done to save her? Had she failed her in some way? The image of Kate as a young child was almost too painful to bear, the loss Millie felt far beyond tears.

But she must stay strong, as an unexpected death could tear a family apart. Tom was eaten up by anger, Robert in his usual fret about practicalities, and poor Abbie blaming herself. Perhaps the moment had come to speak of the past, and reveal all.

THREE

It was the following morning, the breakfast dishes not yet cleared, when her father asked Abbie how long she was planning to stay. Aware of her daughter seated beside her with all the alert curiosity of her six years, instead of answering him Abbie turned to Aimée with a smile. 'Why don't you go and explore the garden, sweetie? You'll find a swing in the orchard, if it's still there. You'll enjoy that, but stay close to the house. No going near the lake.'

'Ooh, yes, Mummy, can I?

'Why don't you go too?' Robert said, addressing his son.

Brother and sister exchanged a quick glance, as if both remembering a time when they too had happily played together. Could they ever achieve such a relaxed state again? Abbie wondered.

It took mere seconds for the sound of scampering feet to disappear, followed by the slam of the front door, leaving eighteen-month-old Carrie screaming her frustration that she couldn't go with them. Fay lifted the baby out of the high chair. 'I'll take her for a walk in her pushchair, while you talk.'

Robert nodded, and as Mrs Brixton appeared at the dining room door to clear away breakfast, it was agreed to adjourn to the library. Saying nothing, Abbie quietly followed them, watching with a flicker of curiosity as her father went straight to his desk, quickly gathered up some documents and tucked them away in a drawer. When he finally turned his enquiring gaze upon her, she asked the one question that had been turning over in her head ever since she arrived.

'So what's going to happen to the business? I've no wish to upset you, Dad, but I was wondering who was going to run it now that Mum is no longer . . .'

He glared at her sternly from behind his spectacles, as if the very mention of his late wife's death was anathema to him. But then he seemed to push back his shoulders and steady himself. 'I'm afraid we have some difficult decisions to make.'

'Didn't Mother leave a will?' Robert enquired, a question that provoked yet a further glower of disapproval from his father, as if this too was out of bounds.

'Indeed she did, and left everything to me, naturally.'

'Of course, only she did once promise there would be a small legacy for me, even if Abbie was still out of favour.'

'I think you must have misunderstood her,' their father snapped, making it very clear this was not a subject he wished to discuss.

'But she was very specific about that, saying she'd never neglect me. I can't believe Mother hasn't kept her word.'

Abbie gave a snort at her brother's arrogance. 'That's all you care about – money! Ever your obsession.'

'Not at all, but I do have a family to keep.'

'So do I, in case you haven't noticed.'

Tom Myers silenced his children's squabbling by raising one hand, palm outwards. 'I assure you there were no legacies of any kind, so let that be an end of the matter. The problem is that this place costs a small fortune in upkeep, and investments and savings are not what they were.'

'What are you saying Dad – that we're land rich but cash poor? We surely can't be too hard up with a house and estate of this size, plus the business, of course. Didn't Ma leave you any money?'

Her father's face turned crimson with anger. 'Have I not made myself abundantly clear? I have no wish to discuss your mother's will.'

'The subject is normally considered relevant, following a funeral,' Robert persisted. 'Can we see it please?'

'No, you damn well can't!'

Their father's reaction to this perfectly reasonable request was so strong that Abbie frowned, examining his flushed face with some concern. 'Is there something you're not telling us, Dad?'

'Why would there be?' he blustered, which left her even more troubled. 'The only thing you need to know is that the business has not been doing too well of late.'

Abbie's eyes widened in surprise. 'Really? I thought custom-made jewellery was increasingly popular. Precious Dreams has been doing well ever since Gran started the business almost forty years ago. So what's gone wrong?'

'I'm afraid your mother rather lost interest in recent years, worn down by . . . events. She quite lost heart, not having been herself for some time, as you are only too aware.'

There it was again, the insinuation that Abbie was to blame for her mother's depressed state of mind. 'I wasn't aware of that, actually, Dad,' she gently reminded him. 'How would I be if nobody wrote and told me?'

'Or if you never asked.'

As an awkward silence began to develop, Robert intervened. 'We should sell the shop to help pay for the upkeep of Carreck Place.'

'I think that's the answer, yes.'

'Very sensible.'

'*No*!' Abbie cried, jumping to her feet. 'Please don't do that.'

They both looked at her in surprise. 'Why ever not?' her father said. 'It's the obvious solution.'

Abbie took a breath to steady herself as she sank back into the chair. 'Look, the truth is that Eduard and I, we . . . well, we've split up, so there's no reason for me to return to Paris. You know I've always been fascinated by the business, the workshop side of it more than the retail. Jewellery is an art form, just as much as painting a landscape is, and I'd love to be more involved. If Mum hadn't been so set against the idea I would have taken a course or something when I left school.'

Robert's laugh was sardonic. 'So leaving home had nothing to do with your lusting after a Frenchman, or becoming pregnant? Stop making excuses, or trying to make out it was Ma's fault, when we all know that was not the case.'

Abbie could feel her cheeks growing warm, although whether with anger or embarrassment was hard to judge. 'I'm not claiming to be entirely innocent. I freely admit I behaved somewhat rashly, but I was in love. Surely it's time to forgive me for that youthful indiscretion?'

She turned to her father, blinking back a blur of tears. 'The point is I have a child to raise, alone, so I need to earn a living. I'm prepared to work hard, and would absolutely love the opportunity to turn the business around and make it successful once more. Please allow me that chance, Pops,' she said, risking using her pet name for him once more in the hope that her father might still nurture some love for her in his heart, if not the much-longed-for forgiveness. Perhaps he did, for she saw how his gaze softened and warmed towards her.

Robert, however, was typically scathing. 'What absolute rubbish! You're hopeless, an untidy, irresponsible, disorganised mess.'

Abbie stiffened, feeling again that familiar burning resentment against the way her brother always put her down, which had forever marred their relationship. Robert never believed anyone else's opinion mattered half so much as his own, that no one could be as clever as him, or even worth listening to.

'Thank you for the accolade. However, it may have escaped your notice that I am no longer a foolish teenager. I've learned a few lessons about life, and business, these last seven years. As a matter of fact, I worked in a small, rather classy boutique in Paris, which is the fashion capital of the world, in case you didn't know, so I'm not entirely ignorant.'

Ignoring her completely, Robert addressed his father, a curl of derision to his upper lip. 'Don't listen to her, Dad. Sell it. Property is fetching a high price right now, and we could use the money to maintain Carreck Place, which is far more important.'

'Because you'll inherit it one day? That couldn't possibly have any bearing on your opinion, by any chance?' Abbie challenged him. 'You want a legacy *plus* the house. Nice!'

'I've already made it clear I have absolutely no wish to discuss these matters right now,' their father calmly informed them, raising both hands this time in a gesture of despair. 'The shop is a separate issue and I suggest you leave me to consider Abigail's proposal in private. I will let you know my decision when I'm good and ready.'

'Thank you,' Abbie said with a smile of appreciation, feeling again that small kernel of the connection they'd once enjoyed. 'I agree, this isn't the moment for dividing the spoils since Mum is hardly cold in her grave,' she added, giving her brother a fierce glare.

Even Robert didn't dare argue further, knowing how grief was taking its toll upon their father. But as he quietly closed the library door behind them both, he couldn't resist one last dig. 'Who the hell do you think you are, the prodigal daughter? You stay away for years, then imagine you can just walk back and claim a wad of cash. Even if Dad is soft enough to let you have a go at running the business for a while, it doesn't alter the fact that *you* are the reason

Mum took her own life. The blame for her death lies entirely on *your* conscience.'

So saying, he strode away in a cold fury.

ண

Feeling sick to her stomach, Abbie went in search of her daughter, finding some relief from her distress in seeing how pretty and happy Aimée looked pushing Jonathon on the swing, gently bossing him and showing off her extra year.

'Why don't we pack a picnic and go for a ramble over the Langdales?' Abbie suggested. 'Or we could walk around Rydal Water and visit the cave. I'm sure Grandpa would lend us the old Ford. Which would you prefer?'

'The cave, the cave,' yelled Jonathon.

Fay appeared with a wriggling Carrie desperate to escape the confines of her pushchair. 'Can we come too?' her sister-in-law asked, her tone revealing her own eagerness to escape for a while.

'Maybe a walk around Rydal is too long for the little ones. It would take at least a couple of hours. I know – how about a sail in a steam yacht on Coniston Water, just like in the story of *Swallows and Amazons*?'

'Yes, yes!' the children all yelled, even little Carrie who hadn't the first idea what she was shouting about. And so it was decided.

ண

The two women enjoyed the relaxing drive over Little Langdale and Tarn Hows with its spectacular views of Wetherlam and Coniston Old Man, glad of a welcome break from the gloom of the tragedy and funeral. The weather, too, was kind, a sparkling spring day with the smell of fresh new grass and sunshine in the air, perfect for a sail.

It proved to be a delightful adventure which the children loved, Jonathon and Aimée pretending to be Captain John and First Mate Susan, as they were allowed to have a go at steering by the friendly boatman. And they loved seeing Peel Island, named Wildcat Island in the book where the five Walker children set up their camp.

'Apparently the author, Arthur Ransome, also spent time in Russia, just like Gran,' Abbie commented, as she and Fay sat together in the cabin of the small boat, enjoying a sail on the tranquil lake. 'He worked as a foreign correspondent during the revolution, so must have been there at the same time as the young Millie, and became something of a spy. Although he was rather on the side of the Bolsheviks, I believe, which Gran was not. At least, I don't think so.'

Fay said, 'Goodness, I never knew that about your grandmother. What on earth was she doing in Russia?'

'I'm not entirely certain, as she rarely speaks of it.' Privately, Abbie was hoping to persuade her otherwise. There surely came a moment when it was time to pass information on to your family. There were things she wanted to ask about her mother too, and about the will which had clearly upset her father for some reason.

Could matters be quite that bad? The upkeep of Carreck Place was no doubt quite expensive, although the house no longer employed the number of staff it once had in its heyday. And it wasn't as if there was a mortgage to pay on the property. Nor, so far as she was aware, did her father have any debts. He'd always been a most prudent man. Her mother, too, could not have been classed as a spendthrift, her wardrobe being that of a countrywoman who preferred tweeds and pearls, and spent her free time outdoors in the garden or walking over the fells when she wasn't working. She'd never been one for rich furs, or even jewels, despite her selling many gems of great value in her shop.

But laying the blame for her mother's death on her own youthful rebellion was deeply hurtful and entirely unfair. Abbie hoped her father would soon come round to that point of view, too, even if her brother persisted with the accusation.

'So what's eating Robert? He seems even more strung out than usual, blaming me for everything, when it was more likely worry over finance that drove my mother to the edge.'

Fay cast her a sympathetic glance. 'Oh dear, I'm sorry if he's being a bit prissy.'

'Don't worry, I'm used to him. He always did like to lord it over me. Not that I ever paid much attention to his elder brother lectures,' Abbie added with a chuckle.

Fay smiled. 'He did complain that you never listened to a word he said.'

'I did now and then, if it was advice worth listening to.' She laughed. 'But we do both tend to get on our high horses if we don't agree on something. It's the way it's always been between us, and I'll admit I'm a bit uptight myself at the moment.'

'I'm not surprised. Look, it's none of my business, but don't be too hard on him. He's a good husband, and an excellent father to our children, but he's having some problems of his own right now. He'd been hoping for a partnership this year. Sadly, it hasn't yet materialised, so he's a bit stressed out.'

'No reason to take his disappointment out on me, though, is there? I absolutely refuse to be held responsible for my mother's death, and Robert has no right to make such an accusation.'

'I'm sure he didn't mean it quite as it sounded,' Fay insisted, clearly determined to defend her husband.

Abbie was pleased that the trip had at least given her an opportunity to get to know her sister-in-law a little better. She hadn't quite made up her mind about Fay. One minute she seemed quite a gentle creature, and certainly a caring, devoted mother, but then she would come out with some caustic remark, such as the one about Aimée's parentage, which was deeply hurtful. It was perfectly natural, of course, that she would take her husband's side. Even so her next words surprised Abbie.

'He'd been worrying about Kate's state of mind for some time, and wishing you were here.'

'Really?'

'Oh yes. He did miss having you around.'

Abbie reminded herself that they hadn't always been at loggerheads, even if sibling rivalry had got the better of them at times. Making no further comment, she took out her copy of the book and read a passage for the children, the one where the Walker children, sailing in their boat *Swallow*, meet the Blackett family pretending to be pirates as they sailed the *Amazon*.

'You'll have to read them the rest of the story now,' laughed Fay, as Abbie closed the book with a snap to huge moans all around.

'It'll be a pleasure.'

The boat docked, and as Aimée begged for an ice cream, with Jonathon acting as echo to her request, difficult family issues were temporarily shelved in favour of a pleasant afternoon by the lake.

FOUR

Abbie felt a sudden hopelessness overwhelm her as she sat gazing out of her bedroom window, her transistor radio playing Andy Williams singing *Can't Get Used To Losing You,* which was exactly how she felt right now. To lose her mother just when she needed her most, needed that much-longed-for reconciliation, was more than she could bear. How cruel life was at times. If only she possessed her grandmother's strength. She watched the whooper swans preparing to leave Carreckwater for their summer breeding grounds on the Arctic tundra. How far those beautiful birds must have to travel, and to a region even colder than this one. Rather as Millie had done when she'd sailed to Russia.

The thought reminded Abbie of her promise to visit her grandmother yesterday, which she'd failed to do since they'd arrived home quite late following their afternoon on Coniston Water. Now, leaving Aimée in the care of Mrs Brixton, who was happy for the little girl to help her make some scones for tea, she set off for the lodge house.

As she strolled along, marvelling at the display of daffodils that lined the stony path, the answer was quite clear in her head what she must do. She needed to investigate the true cause of what had destroyed her mother, and which now threatened to ruin her relationship with the rest of her family. She must find out more about Kate's background, in particular her deprived early childhood before she was adopted, and her allegedly troubled teenage years. Perhaps then she might understand, and be able to work out why her mother's life had gone so badly wrong that she had seen no other solution but to end it.

Abbie found her grandmother sitting in the small conservatory at the back of the lodge. It faced southeast so was something of a sun trap at this time of the morning, even on a cool day in late March. A book lay open on the old woman's lap but she wasn't reading it; rather, she was gazing out upon the garden, a shuttered look on her face. Abbie thought how lovely she still was, with her high cheekbones and scarcely any wrinkles. A tray of coffee rested on the table beside her. Abbie helped herself to a cup and quietly took the chair beside her, smiling when her grandmother put out a hand to give hers a warm squeeze.

'Sorry I didn't manage to call yesterday, Gran, only we took the children out on Coniston Water for a treat.'

'Good for you. Cheer you all up, I expect.'

'Indeed it did.' Abbie sipped her coffee as the two lapsed into a comfortable silence, watching a house martin flying frantically to and fro as it gathered material for its nest. 'Do you remember us once climbing Coniston Old Man, just the three of us, with me moaning about the long walk all the way up, and Mum gently urging me on?'

Millie smiled. 'Then when we neared the summit you set off at a run and beat us all.'

'She gave me a badge for winning, one she made herself out of slate with "star performer" carved on it. I've still got it. What fun we had back then.'

Both women lapsed into silence for a moment as they recalled happier days, then Abbie gave a little sigh. 'I still can't get my head around why Mum would do this. It's quite beyond my comprehension. But then she was never easy to understand.'

'It's true she was rather a complicated person, a bit screwed up, as you young people would say. But then she had a lot to deal with, not knowing exactly who she was, for one thing.'

'That must have been awful for her.'

'I'm afraid it did trouble her greatly.'

Abbie tried to recall when first she'd learned that her mother had been adopted, perhaps when she was being something of a problem during her own teen years. Kate had told her that she considered herself fortunate to have enjoyed a good upbringing with loving parents, which included being privately educated at a local girls' school, when she could so easily have suffered a deprived childhood confined in an orphanage. She said just the memory of that cold, unfeeling place gave her the shivers. Growing up here in the small village of Carreckwater, situated as it was in a wooded valley in the heart of Lakeland, had been utterly delightful, not to mention living in this beautiful house on the shores of the lake. Kate had declared that she'd a great deal to be thankful for.

So why had all that optimism disappeared?

Not knowing who her birth mother was must surely have haunted Kate. No doubt some foolish girl who had got herself into trouble, abandoned her child and simply walked away. Not a pleasant thought. It had never crossed her own mind for a moment to give up Aimée, no matter what. Of course, the girl might well have been forced into giving up her baby, as was often the case in those days.

Abbie's head teemed with questions and she longed to know more about her mother's origins. But was her grandmother up to such a discussion, grieving as she was right now? On the other hand, perhaps talking about her daughter might bring her some comfort. Abbie decided to take the risk, and to stop the moment Millie appeared weary.

'When you said Mum felt as if all the security she'd taken for granted was slipping from her grasp, why did you say it was hard won?'

'Because she spent her early years in an orphanage, which left her with a justifiable sense of insecurity.'

'Where was it, this orphanage?'

'Pursey Street in Stepney, London.'

'Goodness, that's some distance from the Lakes. Why choose that one?'

'I can't quite recall. It's all so long ago.'

'So when did you return to England, exactly? You've never said.'

'Some time in the early twenties, I think.'

Abbie could tell that Millie was being deliberately vague, but couldn't work out why. Something was going on that she didn't quite understand. Why had Millie adopted a child at such a young age? Surely at the time she'd still have been young enough to expect to have children of her own one day? Not that any had ever come, so perhaps she'd known that she couldn't. But that was not a question she dared ask. 'Was it something that happened during the revolution that made you decide to adopt a child? Did you see children starving in the streets? Was that the reason?'

She couldn't help but wonder what terrible events had happened back then to make Millie so unwilling to recall the past. Like her mother before her, Abbie had tried on numerous occasions to persuade her grandmother to talk about her time in Russia, and how she came to go out there in the first place. But only rarely would some snippet of the young Millie's early life emerge, after which she would clam up, folding her lips into a tightly compressed line as if she'd divulged some dreadful secret.

When no response came, Abbie smiled. 'Mum always wondered why you chose her, a skinny five-year-old prone to sulks and tantrums. She put the decision down to your kind and generous heart, which must be right.'

'Why would I not choose her, when she looked so sweet?' There was the softness of love in her tone, which proved the truth of this belief. 'So tell me about your day on Coniston Water with the children. Did you take them for a sail?'

The subject, as ever, was closed.

Stifling a sigh, Abbie went on to describe the *Swallows and Amazons* games they'd played on the boat, and visiting Wild Cat Island. 'It's a book that I loved as a child. Do you remember how Mum used to let us dress up as pirates and camp out by the lake overnight? Robert always wanted to be Captain Flint, of course, but Mum loved to play that role herself. She was such fun back then.'

Millie smiled. 'And you were Titty, the one who found the sea chest.'

'Oh, my goodness, yes, the missing treasure that Mum would hide some place, and I'd think myself so clever if I succeeded, always anxious to beat Robert to it.'

As they chuckled over shared memories, she decided to try a different tack. 'Mum told me you were once in service as a nursemaid in some grand house or other. Is that really true, Gran, and if so, where was it?'

Millie turned to smile at her, grey eyes twinkling with a mischievous delight. 'It was here.'

Abbie let out a startled gasp. 'Here? You don't mean this house, Carreck Place?'

'I do.'

'Goodness, are you saying that you were once actually *employed* here? But that's incredible! How could you start off as a nursemaid and end up as mistress? Lady of the manor, no less.'

Millie chuckled. 'Life is full of twists and turns with many surprises along the way. Although I've never actually thought of myself as lady of the manor, or mistress of Carreck Place, since strictly speaking it was never mine. Nor ever Kate's, for that matter.'

'So it was my grandfather's, was it?' Abbie was almost crowing with delight, itching to hear more of this fascinating revelation.

'That's not quite what I meant. The fact of the matter is, my darling, the property does not belong to our family at all. Never has, not now, not ever. We only have the right to live here.'

Abbie stared at her grandmother in a state of stunned disbelief. 'Are you saying that one day we may have to *leave* Carreck Place?' Abbie's heart almost stopped beating at the thought. It was a horrifying prospect, one she would never have contemplated happening, not in a thousand years.

Millie met her granddaughter's gaze unflinching. 'That is exactly what I'm saying, yes.'

'I don't understand. I always believed that Carreck Place had been in our family for generations.'

'I'm afraid not.'

'Oh, but I love this house with a passion.'

Millie squeezed her hand, sympathetic as always to her granddaughter's feelings. 'I know, darling, me too, but there it is.'

'And Robert fully expects to inherit.'

'He may well do so, if that is what Kate decided, although it is by no means certain. Having said that, I very much doubt the family will ever be asked to leave, even though your mother is no longer with us, since there's no one to . . .' She paused, frowning thoughtfully as if reflecting upon the possibility. 'No one left who's likely to claim it. I hope,' she concluded. 'I confess I would like to see out my remaining years here, if it is possible to do so. But that all rather depends on what your mother left in her will.'

'She didn't confide in you, then?'

Millie shook her head, smiling sadly. 'Never.'

Abbie had a sudden vision of her father quickly stowing away papers in a drawer, his prickly response to her brother's probing questions, and his concern over finance and whether or not he would need to sell the shop. 'Are you suggesting there might be some sort of problem? Dad does seem to be worrying quite a bit about money, seems to think we're in danger of losing our home through lack of funds. But why? Are we going bankrupt or something? Is it something to do with Mum's will? What's going on, and why won't he tell us?'

Millie sighed. 'As I say, I was not privy to my daughter's financial situation, but Kate was only too aware that she did not own Carreck Place, that she held only a lifetime lease on the property. However, I dare say this might have come as something of a surprise to Tom.'

Abbie felt as if her head was spinning as she struggled to come to terms with what her grandmother was telling her. 'You mean Mum kept this fact a *secret* from Dad for all these years? Why on earth would she do such a thing?' Keeping secrets was beginning to look like a family trait.

Millie frowned, looking oddly pensive. 'To explain would have opened up a veritable Pandora's box. One we preferred to keep firmly closed.'

'I have to say, Gran, now might be a good time to open it, otherwise there could be mayhem.' Abbie patiently waited while Millie considered the matter, her thoughts in turmoil. 'So who does own this house, if not us?' she gently enquired.

'Carreck Place was originally part of the estate of Lord Rumsley, who employed me as nursemaid to his children. I was very happy here, but then my life changed forever in the autumn of 1911 when I first met Olga Belinsky.'

'Olga Belinsky? Who on earth was she?'

'A Russian countess.'

'Goodness, that must have been amazing. I never realised you'd had such an important job, but then I know nothing about your time in Russia. So what was it like working for the aristocracy during the revolution?'

'Some things are best forgotten.'

Her grandfather, Anton Nabokov, who sadly had died when Abbie was around eleven or twelve, had been the same. For all he'd been Russian born and bred, only once did she hear him mention the Fatherland, as he called it, and then only to say how thankful he was they had got away when they did.

She could well understand her grandparents' relief at escaping the horrors of the revolution, which must have been utterly terrifying. Yet Abbie was increasingly convinced there was more to her grandmother's silence than revulsion over the assassination of the Romanovs, and possibly many of their aristocratic friends.

But this was the first piece of information her grandmother had volunteered in years. 'Tell me about this Countess. What was she like?'

'She was a manipulative madam, entirely selfish, wanting everything for herself, and completely profligate, with not the first idea of the value of money. Our relationship was fraught with problems from the start – challenging but interesting, you might say.' She gave a harsh little laugh at the recollection. 'Her callous disregard for others should have warned me to stay well clear of her. Unfortunately I was young and somewhat headstrong at the time, if a little naïve and easily flattered.'

'Gran, please, I want to know all about her. Where and when did you meet? Please start from the very beginning.'

'Then we'll need a fresh pot of coffee. It's a long story.'

FIVE

1911

It all began on one of those perfect sunny days in early September, the glorious russet, amber and gold of the Lakeland woodlands reflected in the still waters of the lake. Sheep dozed in the soft shadows and the only sounds to be heard were the cooing of wood pigeons, the lap and splash of water and the happy gurgles of childish laughter. A bright yellow sun warmed the lake and the children hadn't been able to resist putting on their bathing suits for a swim while the adults dozed in their deck chairs, or sipped Pimms as they quietly chatted.

Inside the house was a very different story, Carreck Place a veritable maelstrom of activity. I hadn't seen it so busy since the party to celebrate King George V's coronation in June. Maids bustled back and forth, any undercurrent of panic and concern they might be suffering quelled by long experience as they efficiently went about their many tasks. Lord and Lady Rumsley's special guests, their aristocratic Russian cousins, Count Vasiliy Belinsky and his wife Countess Olga, had been staying for some weeks, and the climax of their visit was to be a grand dinner and ball held that evening.

The kitchens had been out of bounds for days. I always felt a great pity for the scullery maids, poor little devils, their hands red raw from scouring saucepans and scrubbing dishes all day long. I'd done my share of such chores, having started my career as a scullery maid at fourteen, then moved on to kitchen and parlour maid before deciding that I hated housework. It had seemed natural for me to go into service, as my French mother was a lady's maid and my father a gardener for Lord Lonsdale. When the opportunity came to take this job, I grabbed at the chance, as I adore children. I also lived in hope that such a position would allow me to travel with the family, which had ever been a dream of mine.

The footmen had spent hours polishing the family silver, now set out on a pristine white damask tablecloth together with a centrepiece of yellow roses from the garden. The long dining table was laid following the carefully arranged seating plan devised by her ladyship, ably assisted by the housekeeper. Precedence was of paramount importance, particularly since Count Belinsky was connected to Russian royalty, being a distant cousin of the Tsar. But then who should sit next to whom was always a veritable minefield. House parties of this nature were notorious for illicit affairs, which must naturally be kept discreet. Whenever there was any doubt, Jepson the butler would decide, as he knew better than most who were lovers or social adversaries, and in either case needed to be kept well apart.

The efficiency of the entire operation was due primarily to the butler's skills; he looked almost regal himself in his best black tail coat with gold buttons, starched white shirt, collar and cravat. Even the menservants were resplendent in their finest livery, and, as I'd passed through the servants' hall earlier that afternoon, I couldn't help but giggle at how ridiculous they looked in their brown breeches and yellow and white striped waistcoats, like creatures from another age.

'Is it me you think so funny?' Liam, one of the footmen had asked, catching me around the waist to pull me into his arms.

I didn't struggle to free myself or protest too much, as I rather liked Liam. He was a fine, handsome young Irishman, and his attentions to me, a naïve young girl of almost nineteen, were really most flattering. 'You look as if you should be in the village pantomime,' I teased.

'Aw, and there's me thinking I was the bees' knees in this get-up. Don't I at least deserve a kiss for looking so smart?'

I pecked a quick kiss on to his cheek, except that he moved at the last moment so that it landed full upon his mouth by mistake.

'What's going on here?' The butler's commanding voice rocked Liam back on his heels, and sent me fleeing from the room, only too happy to escape.

Fortunately, none of these frantic preparations were any of my concern. My task as nursemaid was simply to look after the children: Miss Phyllis and Master Robin, plus the two Russian offspring who were currently occupying the nursery during their stay.

Serge, aged eight, seemed to have a great deal to say for himself. 'My full name is Serge Vasilovich Belinsky,' he'd proudly announced when first he was brought to the schoolroom to meet me. 'My second name comes from my father, a tradition you don't have in England, I believe.' Spoken with some contempt for our failure in this respect. A fine nobleman in the making, I thought.

His younger sister Irina, aged six, was a sensitive child who cried a great deal. She gave me a shy little smile then hastily began to tidy her hair as she noticed her mother frowning at her.

I loved my job and delighted in supervising the children on that sunny afternoon, first with a game of hide and seek, then serving them a picnic of egg and cress sandwiches, sponge fingers and home-made lemonade. The two boys tried their hand at fishing, without much success, and the little girls enjoyed paddling, and giggled a great deal, instant friends with only a year between them.

'Keep to the edges, Miss Phyllis. The lake quickly becomes quite deep further in,' I called, ever aware of my responsibility, and she was but five years old. When a cool wind sprang up I decided to take them indoors for their afternoon nap. I, at least, was ready for a rest.

'Come along, children. Let me dry you off, then we'll go indoors for some hot chocolate and a siesta.' This brought forth a series of groans, and, laughing, I picked little Miss Phyllis up out of the water to carry her wriggling like a giggly worm, if worms ever do giggle, back to the rug, where I began to rub her down with a towel.

'*Mamochka*, I want to learn to sail,' Serge called to his mother. In the centre of the lake cruised a small boat in which Countess Olga was reclining in the sun, her footman rowing slowly back and forth so as not to disturb her rest too much.

'Perhaps tomorrow, Master Serge,' I called to him. 'It's growing quite chilly now. Time for you to get dry and have something warm to drink.'

Lazily turning her head, the Countess smiled at her son. 'Swim out to me if you wish, my darling,' she called. 'I am here for you, as always.'

'I want to come too,' shouted Irina, and before I could stop them both children had flung themselves into the water, each desperate to out-swim the other and be first to reach the boat and their darling mother.

I was on my feet in a second, watching anxiously, itching to call out that it was too far for them to swim, too deep in that part of the lake, but how could I when the Countess had already defied me? They were, after all, her children.

Serge reached the boat easily to grasp the side, ready to haul himself aboard. His mother clapped her hands in delight, and there was a wide grin of triumph on his young face. I almost sighed with relief until I suddenly noticed that he was holding something under the water, a great splashing and bubbling going on all around. He glanced down at whatever it was, and laughed out loud. Shock hit me like a hammer blow to the chest when I realised that it was his little sister, Irina.

'Master Serge, what are you doing? Let her go this minute!'

Leaving little Phyllis on the rug, I raced down the grassy bank and plunged into the water, still fully clothed in my nursemaid's uniform. Fortunately I'd been taught to swim by my own father. No child, he'd said, should live in the Lake District and not be able to swim. I reached the boat in seconds to snatch the girl up in my arms. For one terrible moment I thought I was too late as her tiny face appeared ashen, with no sign of life. Then she took a great gasp of air before bursting into tears.

'Didn't you see that he was holding her under the water?' I shouted at the Countess, without a thought to good manners or my lowly status. 'Your daughter could have drowned.'

She gazed at me wide-eyed for a moment, and then laughed. 'Nonsense! Irina should have had more sense than to try and swim so far. My darling son was rescuing her. She's a silly little girl, always fussing, and foolishly jealous of her brother.'

I stared at the Countess in open-mouthed astonishment, my feet furiously paddling in an effort to stay afloat as I clutched the child tightly in my arms. How could this woman be so blind as to not see the truth of the incident? I'd noticed before how the Countess always gave preference to her son, but what kind of mother cared so little for her daughter that she would make no effort to save her from obvious drowning?

But what could I say? I was a young girl, a mere servant, and she a fine aristocratic lady, married to my master's cousin. I knew full well that any accusation I made against the Countess, or her precious son, would only result in my being given notice for rudeness to an honoured guest, not to mention overstepping my position.

'My little hero,' she was saying, hugging and kissing the boy as she helped him into the boat beside her.

I became aware of Irina's skinny arms clinging tightly about my neck, her small body shivering against mine. My own feet were likewise beginning to feel the numbing effects of the cold water, my long skirt tangling about my legs. It was never safe to linger in the lake for more than a few moments so, turning about, I swam for the shore, the child tucked safely under one arm.

That was my first confrontation with Countess Olga, but it would not be the last.

~

Later that evening, while the assistant nursemaid served the children their suppers, I stole a moment to have a word with Liam, quickly telling him of what had occurred.

'The bitch,' he said, in his blunt Irish way. 'Does the woman have no feelings, save for herself?'

'It would seem not,' I agreed.

We were tucked behind an outhouse in a shadowy corner of the kitchen yard, and Liam wasted no time in taking advantage of the growing darkness to steal a few kisses. Not that I objected too much, as the very touch of his lips set ripples of excitement soaring through my veins. I was, as I say, young and impressionable.

'I can't linger, I'm afraid,' he apologised between kisses. 'Or Mr Jepson will have my guts for garters. Can I mebbe see you later?'

Timing for these functions was of the essence. It was essential that everyone be seated ten minutes or so before the main guests of honour arrived, particularly if, as in this case, they were connected with royalty. Mr Jepson naturally did his utmost to ensure the meal was not kept waiting too long, or there would be even greater panic and mayhem in the kitchen if trays were brought up too soon and food left to go cold in the serving room. None of this effort was fully appreciated by either Lord and Lady Rumsley or their guests, but rather taken for granted.

I knew that Liam, along with all the other footmen, including many extras hired especially for the occasion, would be rushed off their feet throughout the evening. He would not only be serving dinner but later providing snacks and drinks, constantly supplying new packs of cards for the gamblers, calling for carriages, and fetching jugs of hot water or night caps for those who were staying overnight, entirely at the beck and call of the hundred or more guests.

'I very much doubt it will be possible to see you later, Liam. You'll be busy and I must stay with the children.'

'Aw, couldn't you sneak away for a half hour at least? I'll wait for you at the back of the summer house the minute everyone has gone.'

'It'll be nearly dawn by then.' But I was starting to waver.

'Naw,' he said. 'Midnight or just after should be fine.'

I giggled at his optimism but after another exciting, long-drawn-out kiss that left me breathless, he strode quickly away before I had time to object further.

The kitchen being awash with steaming dishes and harassed chefs, also specially hired for the occasion, I carefully avoided the chaos and hurried up the back stairs, already worrying about the prospect of a midnight rendezvous. I was quite fond of Liam, as a friend, but had no real wish for our relationship to go beyond a few chaste kisses. Even at eighteen my ambitions lay in quite a different direction to marriage.

~

I was in the process of putting the younger children to bed, preparing to read them a story, when the Countess strolled into the nursery. Miss Irina instantly sat up, bright-eyed, in her bed, eager for her mother to notice her. Instead the Countess went to sit by her son, who was playing a game of chess with Master Robin.

'Are you winning, my darling?' she asked.

'Of course. He's hopeless.'

'Poor little Robin, not quite the bright young heir your father had hoped for, then?' she said with mocking humour.

I saw how the boy's face flushed with silent anger at this jibe, but catching my warning glance he managed to hold his tongue. The Countess watched the game for a moment, making a few suggestions and laughing loudly when her son swooped to capture Master Robin's queen.

'Checkmate!'

'What a star player you are, my love,' she cried, ruffling his curls.

I felt so sorry for Master Robin, who was furiously trying to salvage yet another lost game to a boy two years younger than himself, and with a witness to add to his humiliation. Behind me I heard a small sigh from where the Countess's small daughter sat patiently waiting for her mother to pay her some attention. Filled with a rush of pity for her, too, I recklessly stepped forward and bobbed a curtsey.

'Your ladyship, I was about to read a story to Miss Irina, but I wondered if perhaps you would prefer to do that yourself. She was rather upset by the incident at the lake earlier, and I'm sure she'd love to have you sit with her for a while.'

The Countess half turned in her chair to give me a cool assessing glare. 'How long have you been working at Carreck Place, girl?'

'Six months.'

'You are clearly diligent in your duties.'

'Thank you, your ladyship.' Yet something in the tone of voice, and the steely narrowing of her charcoal eyes, told me this remark was not necessarily meant as a compliment. She was, without doubt, a beautiful woman with lustrous dark hair, porcelain white skin and a shapely, voluptuous figure. Her gown of cream Brussels lace was exquisite, and every part of her – hair, throat, wrists, hands, as well as the gown itself – was ablaze with diamonds and sapphires. She presented an awesome figure, and it occurred to me that reminding any mother, let alone a countess, of her duties was definitely not part of my remit.

Countess Olga rose, towering over me by several inches, and my confidence evaporated still further. 'Irina is a simple child with not an ounce of common sense in her, though I will concede that her behaviour has improved lately under your care. But then, that is what you are paid for,' she informed me in imperious tones, making me feel smaller than ever. 'However, perhaps you still have much to learn with regard to knowing your own station in life.'

I could feel a heat burning my cheeks. 'I humbly apologise ma'am, if I gave any offence by my outburst. It was but a moment of panic. I feared Miss Irina was about to drown.'

'A mistaken and overly dramatic reaction on your part. The children were playing a game, that is all.'

I glanced up, meeting the cool impassiveness of her gaze, and knew she read in my eyes that I did not for a moment believe so. 'It was a game which could well have ended with your child's death,' I calmly informed her, the words coming from my foolish mouth without pause for thought. Oh dear, why must I always speak my mind? Now I'd be certain to lose my place, instantly dismissed for insubordination.

Her dark eyes widened in surprise at my insolence, as well they might, yet there was a mocking triumph there too, as if it pleased her to have irritated me enough to make me step out of line yet again. 'You are an expert with children, are you, girl?'

'I certainly know how to take care of them better than many parents, who seem to have little time for their children,' I agreed with a slight toss of my head, thinking I might as well be hung for a sheep as a lamb.

She actually laughed out loud at that, as if I'd made some sort of witty remark. 'I dare say you might be right, yet I believe on that occasion you were far *too* diligent in your duties.'

Fortunately, I was spared from making a greater fool of myself by the dinner gong, which sounded at eight o'clock every evening, a signal for guests to assemble in the beautiful oak-panelled drawing room for cocktails. The Countess at once made her leisurely way to the door in a rustle of silken skirts, spine rigid, head held high and a condescending smile playing about her shapely lips. Her bearing clearly implied her conviction that she'd won the argument as easily as her son had demolished Master Robin on the chess board. 'We shall say no more on the matter. It was, as you suggest, no doubt simply your foolish panic. I'm sure you will know better next time.'

I quickly stifled a sigh of relief that I would keep my job, while secretly hoping there never would be a next time. Then I watched in stunned disbelief as the Countess swept from the nursery, not even offering her daughter so much as a backward glance let alone a goodnight kiss.

Thank goodness, I thought, that the woman would be leaving by the end of the month and I'd never be obliged to cross swords with her ever again.

How wrong I was.

SIX

At midnight, as arranged, I slipped out through a side door and started up the path to the summer house, a shawl wrapped about my shoulders against the chill of an autumn evening. There were still a few stalwarts playing blackjack in the salon, a group of men in the billiard room, and others enjoying a nightcap in the conservatory, but most of the guests were leaving. I could hear the clatter of horses' hooves and the bustle of carriages causing the usual traffic jams as they made their way down the long drive. The linkmen were swinging their lanterns as they whistled up the next, no doubt having filled the time waiting in the cold with a nip or two of whisky to keep warm. Drivers and linkmen were notorious for their drinking.

Liam was waiting for me behind the summer house, as promised, sheltering beneath an old ash tree as a drizzle of rain started. 'I thought you were never coming,' he complained.

'Sorry, I fell asleep,' I explained, and avoiding his eager kisses launched into the tale of my latest encounter with her ladyship. 'I could hardly believe how callous and cruel that woman is to her own child. Why would her son be so precious to her, while she totally ignores her little daughter? The poor child obviously feels unloved and dreadfully bullied. It is so sad. Even Master Robin was embarrassed to find himself the butt of the Countess's sarcasm.'

It was clear Liam wasn't listening, far more concerned with nuzzling into my neck, kissing the curl of my ear, and running his hands up and down my back. 'You're becoming obsessed with that woman,' he protested, 'when there are much more interesting things we could be doing.'

As the rain began falling harder he pulled me inside the small building, laughing as he brushed the dampness from my hair. Built in Georgian times of slate and stone, the summer house was a favourite picnic spot on inclement days. It boasted one large room with a fireplace, and behind this a small kitchen area used for preparing food, and which the gardener had adapted for flower arranging. It was here that Liam dragged me, a private spot where we couldn't be seen.

'We really shouldn't be here,' I protested, already beginning to regret ever having agreed to meet him, and experiencing a sudden longing for the warmth of my bed. It had been a long day, with another early start in the morning. 'What if someone should come?'

'Why should anyone come when they're all going home in their fine carriages?' His kisses grew more urgent as he smoothed a hand over my hip, letting it creep up to my waist. I caught it just before it reached my breast.

'Please behave, Liam. I'm not that sort of girl.'

'You showed no objection to my kisses earlier,' he reminded me, persisting in his attempts of seduction by pushing back my shawl and beginning to unfasten the buttons of my blouse. I slapped his hand away.

'Stop that! Allowing you to kiss me was obviously a foolish mistake on my part. Please let go of me.'

He only laughed at my protests and started on the next button. 'You know that you love it really. You're as mad about me as I am about you. Don't you think we make a lovely couple?'

'No I don't, and we aren't in any way a couple.' Despite my desperate attempts to stop him, his fumbling efforts with the buttons of my uniform were beginning to pay dividends as my blouse yawned open. Pushing him away with both hands, I finally managed to free myself, quite breathless with the effort. 'I'm not sure what you were expecting by asking me to meet you here, but I think this relationship is in danger of going much too far, too quickly. I absolutely refuse to be taken advantage of.'

'I wasn't taking advantage, Millie, I adore you, you know I do. I love everything about you: your lovely eyes as soft and grey as summer storm clouds, your gorgeous neat little figure,' he murmured, his gaze flicking appreciatively over my breasts. Then, as if recognising his mistake, he prudently smoothed his hands over my wayward curls. 'And your long fair hair that I'd love to see fly free instead of coiled into a plait on top of your lovely head.'

Fearing he was about to start undoing that too, I took a step back, attempting to restore order to my uniform. 'You have to stop this now, Liam.'

'Why must I?' he said, pulling me close once more to trail his lips along the curve of my throat. 'I swear I'll make an honest woman of you just as soon as I can. You know I'd ask you to be my wife this very minute, if I could afford it.'

Half laughing at this declaration, I gave him a firm shove. 'And if you did such a crazy thing, I would refuse.'

'What?' He gazed at me open-mouthed, as if not for a moment could he imagine any girl refusing him.

'The fact is, Liam, I'm happy to be your friend but I don't love you, and I'm not in the least interested in getting married. I'm far too young. Besides, I have other plans.' I hoped there would come a time when I would relish having a man to love me, and to experience the meaning of true desire, but that was some years off so far as I was concerned.

'What sort of plans?' he asked, not looking at all pleased as I tied my shawl in a firm knot across my breast.

'Oh, quite ambitious ones actually: to educate myself a little more, for a start. I'm reading *Stories of King Arthur* by U. W. Cutler at the moment. Great fun, you should try it. Then one day I hope to get a better job and improve my station in life, most of all to travel and see the world.' I could feel that familiar kernel of excitement start up inside at the thought. 'That's what I've always dreamed of. Wouldn't you like to better yourself?'

It was clear from the expression of disbelief on his handsome face that the thought had never occurred to him. He thrust back his shoulders as if reasserting his pride. 'I'm actually quite happy the way I am, and plenty of girls would be glad of an offer of marriage from me.'

I stifled a giggle. 'I'm sure there are any number. You're a fine looking man, a prize for any young woman, but not for me, I'm afraid. I value your friendship Liam, but it would be unfair to continue seeing you, feeling as I do.'

'Then it's your loss,' he said with a casual shrug, the dark scowl on his face telling quite a different story. He half turned, as if about to swagger away, when there came the unmistakable sound of grunts and gasps from the other room. We both froze.

'Quick,' Liam hissed. 'Under the bench.'

We dropped to our knees to shuffle out of sight, fear and fury in equal measure cascading through me, making my limbs shake, only too aware that if we were discovered here together, we would both lose our positions.

Liam nudged me with his elbow, grinning from ear to ear as he pointed to a broken plank in the wall. Through the gaping hole we had a clear view of the main room in the summer house. Sprawled on the floor on a carefully spread cloak, in the most undignified position possible, lay the Countess. She had her legs wrapped about the waist of a man as he pleasured her, his trousers drooping around his ankles. I stared at the pair in dawning horror. I could see only his bare backside, but I would have recognised those trousers anywhere. It was my master, Lord Rumsley.

In that moment of appalled recognition I must have gasped out loud, for Countess Olga's head turned towards me, her amused gaze meeting mine.

~

I spent the next few days trying not to think of what I had witnessed, concentrating on teaching young Serge to ride a pony, polishing the skills he'd been practising for some weeks now. The Count was apparently an expert with horses but his son had refused to learn, afraid he might fail and disappoint his father. Master Robin, however, was most proficient at riding, so Serge had felt bound to try as he had no wish to be outshone. There remained a strong rivalry between the two boys.

The two little girls had not joined us, choosing instead to spend the morning learning how to stitch a sampler with the assistant nursemaid. Such activities seemed to suit them very well, and even Miss Irina had seemed calmer and more content of late. For my part, I was more than happy for someone else to take on the teaching of such domestic skills, being enough of a tomboy to much prefer riding to sewing.

'*Croire en soi*,' I said, urging Serge to believe in himself. '*Avoir le courage*.' I generally spoke to the Russian children in French, since they were each far more fluent in the language than they were in English – quite common among Russian aristocracy, it seemed.

'*Gardez votre dos droit*,' I called, urging him to sit up straight as he rode the pony around the ring. I was happily applauding his success, telling him he would soon be skilled enough to take out on a proper ride, when the Countess's voice interrupted me.

'I did not know you spoke French, girl.'

I quickly bobbed a curtsey, my heart almost turning over as I feared she would be certain to ask what I had been doing in the summer house that night. On the other hand, she might well choose that act of folly on my part as a means to bully me into silence. Not that I would say a word to a living soul: discretion was essential in a servant. We are expected to be deaf, dumb and blind so far as the antics of our masters and mistresses are concerned. But she had no reason to trust me.

'My mother is French,' I politely explained. 'So naturally I am bilingual.'

'Really? Well, I'm impressed. Not only with your skill with language but your ability to bring calm to my fractious daughter, and, it seems, finally persuade my son to ride. Quite an achievement in itself.'

'Perhaps that is because I put no pressure on him, but simply made it fun. I also try to give Miss Irina the attention she needs,' I replied, as usual unable to keep my opinions to myself.

'Is this yet another piece of advice on parenting?' she remarked caustically. 'You are certainly a young lady with a great deal to say for herself, as well as a knack for always being around when least expected.'

This last comment was an obvious reference to the incident in the summer house and, silently berating myself for my loose tongue, I quickly stepped out of her way as she strode over to congratulate her son, privately vowing to keep my lips buttoned in future.

The very next day I was astonished to be called to the drawing room where the Countess and Lady Rumsley were taking tea.

'Ah, Millie, there you are. I have the pleasure to inform you that Countess Olga has offered you a job.'

I stared at my employer, dumbstruck with shock, so that it was several seconds before I could take in a word of what the Countess was saying.

'. . . I was hoping to persuade you to accompany us back to Russia,' she finished. 'I'm very impressed with the way you have handled my naughty children, as well as your facility with French. I am also naturally keen to improve the children's knowledge of English, and their manners, of course. I feel you would be the ideal person for the task.'

My mistress smiled kindly at my stunned expression, answering for me as I was still quite unable to respond. 'I know Millie is most grateful for the offer, if rather shy and surprised. We shall naturally be sorry to lose you, Millie, but this is an opportunity you can hardly afford to pass by.'

'I am indeed most grateful, y-your ladyship,' I stuttered, not quite able to believe my ears. All my life I had longed to travel, and here I was being offered the chance. How could I refuse such an amazing opportunity? It was a dream come true.

SEVEN

I'd forgotten that you could speak French,' Abbie said, smiling.

'*Bien sur. Est votre français améliorant?*'

'*Plutôt bien.*'

Having the language in common seemed to somehow emphasise their closeness, and they chatted for a little while in French, Abbie first teasing her about Liam, then talking about her work in the Paris boutique. 'I felt very ignorant as a young girl myself when I started out, with so much to learn, not least the language. Thankfully, my employer, Marisa, was most helpful. But what a dreadful woman the Countess sounds.'

Millie laughed. 'She was indeed.'

'You were unlucky, Gran, whereas Marisa became a dear friend. I really must ring her and explain I've decided to stay on.'

Her grandmother's eyes softened. 'I'm so glad. I shall enjoy having you around.'

'How would you feel about my becoming involved in the business that you and Grandpa started?'

'Immensely proud.'

Abbie pulled a wry face. 'Dad might think differently.'

'Oh, I'm sure he could be persuaded, given time. Don't give up hope.'

'Bless you, Gran. What would I do without you? And now that I know how you came to go to Russia, I'm itching to hear what it was like, and how you felt being so far from home.'

'Rather cold, I seem to remember,' chuckled Millie, then waved her away. 'Enough for now, my darling. It's time for my nap. I'll tell you more when you come again.'

It was what her grandmother was not telling her that frustrated and intrigued Abbie the most, but the following day being a Monday, she decided it was time to pay a visit to the shop. Fay had promised to mind Aimée for the morning, although later in the day Abbie intended to set about securing her daughter a place in the village school. Excitement was growing inside her, although when she'd announced her plans for the day at breakfast, her father had instantly objected.

'What possible good will that do? You aren't up to running a business.'

'How do you know that, Dad, unless you give me the chance to try? I'm not five years old any longer, or a silly teenager.'

'I'm well aware of that, but it needs a skilled professional to bring it back into profit, not some dreamy amateur.'

'Nor am I an amateur,' Abbie said, determined to remain calm and maintain confidence in herself. 'As I've already explained, I have many years of experience in the fashion industry.'

Robert smirked. 'You should go back to Paris, then, to sell frocks. You certainly don't belong here.'

Unwilling to let her brother see how hurt she was by this cutting remark, Abbie dismissed the comment with a shrug. 'It would seem that none of us rightly belongs here, or so Gran tells me.'

'What nonsense are you talking now?' Robert laughed.

Her father, she noticed, had turned ashen, his mouth set in a grim line. 'Whatever Millie has been saying is not to be taken too seriously. She's an old lady and her memory is slipping.'

'She's as sharp as ever, although admittedly I haven't heard anywhere near the whole story yet. Hopefully, she'll tell me more later, and eventually come to how and why our family have been allowed to live here, even though we don't actually own Carreck Place.'

Robert erupted in fury. 'Now you've gone completely off your head.'

Abbie folded her napkin and quietly got to her feet, but it was her father to whom she addressed her reply. 'I think you'd better explain to Robert what you recently discovered in Mum's will, don't you? In the meantime, I shall attempt to work out what needs to be done to improve the business. I'll take the old Ford, if that's okay, Dad.'

A heated argument had begun between the pair of them long before she reached the door, but Abbie didn't pause to listen as she walked determinedly away.

She parked the car close to St Margaret's Churchyard, then walked up the crooked stone steps on past the Marina Hotel along Carndale Road, a gift shop that provided summer visitors with cheap souvenirs, an estate agent, a string of other small shops including a smart art gallery and a charming little café, to finally arrive at Precious Dreams. A bell clanged as she pushed open the door and went inside, to be met by a smiling young girl standing behind the counter.

'Good morning madam. Can I help?' she politely enquired.

'I'm Abigail Myers, Kate's daughter. You must be Linda.'

'Oh, how lovely to meet you,' the girl cried, instantly shaking the hand Abbie proffered by way of welcome. She was small with flicked-up blonde hair, huge blue eyes with what must be false eyelashes and beautifully manicured fingernails. She was dressed in a smart navy sheath dress with a nipped-in waist and short matching jacket. Abbie was suitably impressed. She felt quite drab by comparison in the grey two-piece suit she'd chosen to wear, wishing to appear businesslike.

'Have you worked here long?' she asked a few minutes later as they sat drinking coffee.

'Three years, ever since I left school,' Linda told her. 'I'll be eighteen next month. I love it, and your mother taught me a great deal about jewellery, although I still have a lot to learn.'

A woman wandered in, looked at a few brooches and necklaces, shook her head with a smile and walked out again.

Linda gave an apologetic little shrug. 'We are rather quiet just now. Trade is not good. I spend much of my time polishing and cleaning the jewellery.'

Abbie glanced about at the locked glass cases displaying a variety of beautifully made costume jewellery set with abalone, lapis lazuli, mother-of-pearl, turquoise, opal, malachite and other precious stones. There was quite a bit of gold and silver in evidence, and what might even be a selection of diamond, ruby and sapphire rings and earrings. 'It all looks lovely. What about the workshop? Could I take a look in there?'

'Oh, it's pretty neglected, I'm afraid,' Linda said. Pulling aside a curtain, she led the way through a surprisingly large stock room, with mainly empty shelves, to a small workshop beyond. 'Nothing much happens in here any more. Your mother rather lost interest.'

The entire premises were more spacious than she remembered, but the workshop was as stark and empty as the stock room. The benches and work tables were bare, dust had settled over the polishing and cutting tools, and cobwebs hung from the ceiling. 'It is a bit depressing, isn't it?'

'I'm afraid so. Mrs Myers didn't think it worth her while to design our own pieces any more. Much easier to buy in, she said.'

'But then you just get the same kind of jewellery that everyone else is selling, instead of something original.'

'She believed that wasn't important, that most people buy jewellery for its value in terms of price or carats, or how shiny and precious it is. Mrs Myers said that a fine piece of jewellery was an investment.'

Abbie smiled. 'An artist might disagree and say it can be much more than that. A lovely piece of jewellery should make a statement, reflect the personality of the wearer, a fashion or style. And since we're now in the sixties we should be appealing to the young, as they are the ones with the money and the desire to look good. We need to offer jewellery that is bright and elaborate, extravagant, even brash. Lots of jingly bracelets and dangly earrings, polished and faceted beads, brooches, pendants and rings in the shape of flowers, stars, butterflies, preferably in garish colours or with lots of sparkle.'

The young girl's gaze was alight with interest as she took in the enthusiasm evident in Abbie's voice. 'Oh, I do so agree. Look how elegant Jacqueline Kennedy is. I'd love to look like her. She's so stylish.'

Abbie smiled. 'I rather think you do already, particularly in that outfit,' she said, and laughed as the girl blushed quite prettily. 'The fact is, Linda, as you will have guessed, profits are down, so something needs to be done, and soon. We must strive to attract a wider market, to create a brand that will appeal to a wider audience. Jewellery is big business right now, and I believe that with a little effort we could do so much better. I do hope you'll be willing to help me achieve this.'

Blue eyes shining, Linda was eagerly nodding. 'Oh yes, I'd love to.'

'Good, then I shall begin by giving the workshop a good spring clean, then check the equipment and stores. Meanwhile, if you could get any paperwork and stock lists together, I'll take them away with me to look at later. Precious Dreams, I hope, could be the answer to my dream too.'

~

After a busy morning Abbie collected Aimée and treated the little girl to her favourite lunch of beans on toast in the little café, while she enjoyed a tuna sandwich and a welcome cup of tea. Later they fed the ducks on the lake with some of the leftover toast crumbs, then called in at the village school where a few of the teachers were busy preparing for the new term that started in two days' time.

'I'm afraid she's much better at French than English,' Abbie explained to the headmistress. 'So her reading isn't too good, but she's bright enough so I'm hoping she'll soon catch up.'

'I'm sure she will, and you never know we might pick up a little French from her. We're delighted to welcome you to St Margaret's, Aimée. Mrs Sanderson here will be your teacher.' As the lady in question took Aimée away to show her the classroom she would occupy, the headmistress placed a gentle hand on Abbie's arm. 'My condolences, Miss Myers, over your loss. Kate was a lovely lady, and will be a sore loss to the community.'

Tears choked Abbie's throat, as always at any expression of sympathy. 'I've been surprised to hear how involved she became with church groups, the WI and so on,' she finally managed, a slight tremor in her voice.

'Oh goodness, yes, very much so. And there wasn't a day went by without her visiting several old ladies who live alone in the

Victorian villas on the Parade that circles the perimeter of the lake. She was a lovely lady with a soft heart.'

Abbie pondered these words as she drove home past those very houses, wondering why other people's view of her mother was so very different from her own. But then a teenager's opinion must surely be loaded with personal issues. Kate had been appalled when Abbie had asked if she might join the business.

'But why can't I? I love art and jewellery, and designing things. Can't I do a course or something?'

'You should get yourself a degree,' she'd insisted. 'Or perhaps a teaching qualification.'

Abbie had laughed. 'I think you're mixing me up with someone else's daughter. I'm no academic and I don't believe teaching is really me.'

'I rather thought you'd say that, so I've booked you in for a secretarial course in Manchester.'

'What? You'd no right to do such a thing, not without speaking to me first.'

'I have every right. I'm your mother.'

'Ah, so this is about power, is it? You just want to keep the jewellery business all to yourself.' Abbie had felt a hot anger bubbling inside her. 'You really don't care what I do so long as I'm as far away from here as possible, do you? Well, don't worry, I'll make sure of that.'

Kate had gone deathly pale. 'Don't say such things. Of course it's not about power, and I don't want you to go away forever. I want only what's best for you.'

'Best for yourself, you mean.' At just seventeen and hopelessly in love, Abbie hadn't been prepared to admit that she'd only thought of joining the jewellery business because she couldn't think what else she'd like to do with her life, although a passion for art and fashion did seem to be growing in her. Throughout the summer she'd been helping in the bar of a local hotel while she tried to make up her mind what to do next. It was here that she'd met Eduard, and fallen in love, hoping to persuade him to stay on in the Lake District. But if there was no job for her here, Abbie could see no reason for either of them to remain. 'No doubt sharing the profits with me is much less fun than putting it all into your own pocket.'

Kate had given a harsh little laugh at that remark. 'There aren't many profits to share.'

'Don't lie.'

'I'm not lying, Abigail. Things are not always as rosy as you might think. Life can be quite complicated at times.'

'Well, you can stop worrying about me. I am one complication you can forget. Keep the business all to yourself if that's what you want. See if I care. I have other plans, which do not include a secretarial course in Manchester,' she'd responded, with typical teenage rebellion.

'And what might they be, might I ask?'

She'd looked her mother full in the face, heart pounding, as she'd answered with a deliberate casualness. 'As a matter of fact, I'm planning on getting married.'

There'd been a stunned silence for all of five seconds before Kate had burst out laughing. 'Goodness, now where have I heard that before?' At the time, Abbie hadn't understood this remark. Now of course she saw how Kate was thinking of her own history. 'And who is the lucky bridegroom?'

'Eduard Grimont. He's the new French chef at the Ring of Bells.'

'Don't talk ridiculous. You're only seventeen. Why on earth would you wish to marry so young, let alone someone you've only just met?'

'Because I'm pregnant with his child.' At which point, Abbie had stormed off before her mother could respond.

Too late now to regret having told her so bluntly, or leaving home before she'd had time to properly get to know her mother as an adult. Now her thoughts sadly returned to the issue most troubling her. What had possessed Kate, so happily engrossed in the community, to end it all in that terrible way? Abbie could only hope that her grandmother's story would eventually throw some light upon the mystery.

~

The moment they arrived at Carreck Place, Aimée rushed off to tell her cousin Jonathon her news. In her excitement she nearly bumped into Fay, who was on her way out with the pushchair just as Aimée charged through the door. Abbie apologised and explained.

'Ah, well it seems they'll be attending the same school. Robert has decided we are not to return to our flat in Windermere, but will stay on for a while here in Carreckwater so that your father won't be lonely.'

'How very generous of him,' Abbie drily remarked, not sure whether this news pleased her or not. She rather liked Fay, despite her lack of tact at times. Her brother, however, was a different matter. What a chicken-head he was, always ready to stir up trouble. 'Then he and I had better agree upon some sort of truce.'

Fay gave a little giggle. 'I'll see if I can persuade him.'

Determined to waste no time worrying over her foolish and arrogant brother, Abbie went straight to the lodge to see her grandmother, and over a most welcome cup of tea happily related the details of her day, including her sketchy plans for the shop.

'I feel filled with guilt at separating Aimée from her father,' she said, smiling as she watched her daughter pushing her young cousin on the swing. 'They have a good relationship, and I've no wish to destroy it.'

'Isn't that why you stayed with Eduard so long?' her grandmother asked softly.

'Maybe. Guilt, jealousy, a longing for love, foolish hope – just a mass of emotions warring with each other. It wasn't easy.'

'Nor will being a single parent be easy.'

'I realise that, and do worry about whether I'll cope,' Abbie ruefully admitted.

'Of course you will. You're stronger than you give yourself credit for, and you enjoy a close relationship with your daughter.'

Abbie smiled. 'She is a sweetie, isn't she? Let's hope she settles into her new school okay. Thankfully she and young Jonathon seem already to be good friends. As for myself, I must learn to toughen up and follow my dream.'

'As did I,' Millie agreed.

'So what made you decide to accept her offer, disliking the Countess as you did?'

'Good question. Ambition. The optimism of youth. A desire to see the world. Who knows?'

'Oh, do tell. What happened next?'

Millie laughed. 'All right, where was I? Ah yes, I was about to embark upon my new life.'

EIGHT

The day I sailed for Russia was in mid-November and my parents, who'd raised no great objections to my decision, came to see me off. My mother, however, had been devastated by the thought of not seeing me again for what might be years.

'I shall write every week,' I promised, giving her a comforting hug, far too excited at the prospect of the adventure that lay ahead to fully appreciate her concern.

They stood on the quayside at Hull, and I watched as she wept in my father's arms, their image shrinking before my eyes as the ship slid slowly out to sea. It was in that moment of farewell that for the first time I felt a small nudge of fear. Despite my dream to travel I had never been further than visiting an old aunt in Leeds. As I frantically waved goodbye to my beloved parents, reality dawned. Russia was a foreign land, thousands of miles from home, where I wouldn't know a soul. I would also be responsible for two young children when I was little more than a child myself. What madness had possessed me to accept such a position?

A voice at my elbow interrupted my troubled thoughts. 'Is this your first trip?'

I looked into the smiling face of a plump young woman not much older than myself. Her red-brown hair was largely obscured by a wide-brimmed hat, although wisps of it escaped to flutter around pale round cheeks, and fringed lively brown eyes. I returned her smile with a wobbly one of my own as I wiped away my tears. 'I'm afraid it is, and I was unprepared for the depth of emotion I would feel at leaving home.'

'It isn't easy. I remember almost jumping ship the first time I did it. Ruth Stubbins,' she said, offering a hand for me to shake.

I gladly accepted it and introduced myself, feeling very much in need of a friend just then. 'It's not your first trip, then?'

'Goodness no, I'm an old hand at this lark now, having spent almost five years as a governess in Russia. I take it that's what you're going out to do?'

'I am, with Count and Countess Belinsky.'

She nodded. 'English governesses are very popular in Russia, and at least the pay is better than what we might expect to receive in service in England. Are you a good sailor?'

'I have no idea. I've never sailed in a boat bigger than the steam yachts on Lake Windermere. I confess to being rather worried about that.'

Laughing, she tucked her arm into mine, giving it a reassuring squeeze. 'Come on, let's find our cabins. I'm sure you'll be fine.'

As it turned out I was very far from fine, at least for the first twenty-four hours or so. After that the wind calmed down somewhat and the ship didn't pitch and toss quite so badly, which meant my sickness gradually abated.

Fortunately, I was not responsible for the children during the journey as they were with the Count and Countess, so I was free to spend much of my time with Ruth, and we were soon firm friends. We watched in awe as dolphins followed the ship, cheered at the first glimpse of land, and marvelled at the beautiful vista of mountains and forests. But I was unprepared for how bitterly cold it became when we entered the Baltic. I put on every warm garment I possessed, yet it still wasn't enough.

But if I'd thought that was cold, I soon learned the true meaning of the word as we approached St Petersburg. I saw small boats trapped in the ice, icebreakers moving back and forth as they attempted to free them. Our own ship cut through with relative ease, and my new friend kindly lent me a winter coat, which she called a *shuba*. It was well worn but far warmer than my own. And with my bout of sea-sickness long forgotten I felt a mix of excitement and nervousness at the first sight of this beautiful city.

'Now we have to face Customs,' she warned. 'Just be polite and do as they say.'

'But how will I know what they say since I don't speak a word of Russian?' I asked in alarm as we gathered our luggage and prepared to disembark.

'Don't worry, I'll help.'

The customs officials were indeed most vigilant and while allowing in the packets of flower and vegetable seeds I'd brought with me, plus fruitcake, playing cards and picture puzzles, they seemed to object to my books, save for a bible, which was most upsetting. I became almost frantic as I watched them take the books from me: *Little Lord Fauntleroy* and *Little Women. A Christmas Carol* by Dickens and several others that I'd brought to help the children learn English.

Ruth began to babble to them in this mystifying language. I heard her mention the name Belinsky, which seemed to give them pause, and after a few more exchanges, the books were returned to my luggage. I breathed a sigh of relief, hugely impressed by my new friend's fluency in the language.

'Don't worry,' she said, as we were finally allowed through. 'They are always nervous of written material in case it is political propaganda. Censorship is rife here. However, I explained they were children's books, and that you were employed by Count Belinsky.'

I thanked her most humbly and was sad when the Countess approached to tell me it was time to go and we were obliged to part company. 'Say goodbye to your friend now, Dowthwaite. Our carriage is waiting.'

'I'll see you soon, as arranged,' Ruth whispered in my ear, giving me a quick hug. She had told me of the British and American Chapel which she attended in her free time. The church apparently provided a welcome social life for British expatriates in the city, including governesses.

'You'll make plenty of friends there, Millie. I think of it as my home away from home,' she'd explained. It was a comforting thought. Then I climbed into the carriage and settled myself next to the children. My new life had begun.

The family apartment was set in a grand building of impressive proportions fronting one of the canals behind the Winter Palace. It must have been some eight or nine stories high, from basement to attic windows, although I didn't have time to count them as I helped the children out of the carriage. Perhaps I would be living up in the roof, in the attics, I thought. We were met at the door by a man known as the *dvornik*, or concierge, whose task was to protect the residents from unwelcome guests. He seemed to know the Belinskys well and rushed to open carriage doors and help unload luggage, bobbing and bowing the entire time.

Ignoring the mounting pile of boxes and trunks in the street, the Countess sailed past, striking the *dvornik* with her muff when he didn't move quickly enough to open the great doors for her.

I offered him a sympathetic smile as I followed in her wake, to which he responded with a huge wink. The Count, I noticed, thanked the fellow most graciously and slipped him a kopek or two. This proved to be a telling indication of life in the Belinsky household.

As was the case at Carreck Place when Lord and Lady Rumsley arrived home after a long absence, the entrance hall was lined with servants. I was introduced first to Mrs Grempel, the housekeeper, a hollow-eyed, stiff-backed woman of lean proportions who I soon learned loved nothing better than to engage in tittle-tattle. Anton, the French chef, came next, in his starched white cap. At first sight he appeared very full of himself but later proved to possess a delightful sense of humour, often having me in fits of laughter as he mimicked his mistress. There followed what seemed to be a whole tribe of maids and footmen, the entire household controlled by a very stern-looking butler known as Gusev.

'Last but no means least is *Nyanushki*,' Countess Olga informed me. 'She looked after me as a child before caring for my own children. Now that they are too old to need a nanny she acts as companion to my mother, and is still very much a part of our family.'

Klara Kovalsky, although she rarely used her full name, was plump and comfortable, wore her grey hair in a tight bun at the back of her chunky neck, and was more often than not to be found sitting in a corner knitting an endless succession of socks or scarves. I shook her hand and gave her a warm smile, hoping we could be friends. She gazed back at me blank-eyed.

'Where is *Maman*?' the Countess asked, speaking in French, perhaps for my benefit.

'Madame has not been well today, milady. But hopes to be more herself tomorrow.'

'Not hitting the vodka again, I trust,' she remarked sourly.

The old nanny protested. 'Not at all. Merely a slight headache.' The Countess appeared unconvinced, and, judging by the way the other woman avoided her probing gaze, I suspected she might have good reason.

It was Nanny, or *Nyanushki* as I must learn to call her, who showed me to my room, which was not in the attics as it turned out.

'The family occupies the entire east wing of the building,' she informed me, panting a little as she bustled me into a lift, or elevator as she called it, carrying one of my bags while I carried the other. My trunk was to be delivered later by a footman. 'The views of the city from the upper floors, you'll find, are magnificent.'

'Does the Countess's mother live here too?' I asked, as the engine cranked up and we slowly began to ascend.

'She does. Her name is Raisa Ilyinsky, although I tend to call her Madame, and the children call her *Babushka,* of course, the Russian name for grandmother.'

'I look forward to meeting her. And does she have a problem with drink as the Countess seemed to be suggesting?'

Nyanushki shook her head quite vehemently. 'Her only problem is with her daughter.'

I thought it wise to ask no further questions.

My room was right at the end of the passage, small but clean with little more than a single bed and a cupboard but perfectly adequate. I was greatly impressed with the apartment as a whole. It was vast enough to hold fifteen bedrooms, or so Klara informed me, in addition to the usual dressing rooms, study, drawing room, library, dining-room, kitchen quarters and so on.

'I hadn't expected the Belinskys to live in a flat,' I confessed as she pulled back the curtains to let in more light. 'I rather thought they would own a grand mansion on the River Neva.'

'Many people in St Petersburg live in flats, even princes, although they often have the choice of living in a palace too. Nor is this the Belinskys' only property. As well as this large apartment block, some of which they let out, they also own an estate in the country which we often visit at weekends, and for some weeks in the summer.'

'I shall look forward to that. I'll miss not having easy access to the outdoors as was the case at Carreck Place.' A wave of homesickness hit me as I thought of strolling by the lake and pottering in the rock garden, of rambling the three miles from Ambleside to Kirkstone Pass along a road accurately called The Struggle on my days off. The stirring cry of a lone curlew and clash of a stags' antlers at tupping time, the sweet woody scent of heather. Why had I never appreciated how fortunate I was to live in such a beautiful place? Here I would need to walk down several flights of stairs, or take the elevator before I could catch a breath of fresh air. Even the windows were tightly sealed against the cold. I felt suddenly claustrophobic, and home seemed very far away.

'You're very young,' *Nyanushki* was saying, critically assessing my youthful appearance although I felt I'd aged ten years during the long journey, being rather tired and bleary-eyed, and strangely disoriented.

'I do have several years' experience in service,' I said, in an attempt to reassure her, 'if admittedly only a few months of that spent caring for children. I trust you'll be able to fill me in on what I need to know.'

'Hmm, I may have to if you're to keep her ladyship happy. We used to have a French governess here so I'm familiar with that language, but you'll need to quickly learn Russian.'

'Perhaps you will help me with that too?' I asked.

She considered this, arms folded across her cushioned bosom. 'And would you in return help me to improve my English?'

'I'd be honoured.'

She gave me a sudden wide grin, revealing yellowed crooked teeth, accompanied by a brisk nod of her round head. Perhaps I had made a friend after all.

~

Little time was allowed for me to unpack and settle in, let alone rest, before a maid came knocking at my bedroom door to announce that I'd been called to the Countess's boudoir to receive my instructions. I quickly washed my face in cold water from the jug, tidied my flyaway hair and hurried after her. The Countess was tapping her nails in impatience as I entered.

'Ah, there you are. I engaged you, Dowthwaite, because of your ability to speak French. Nevertheless you are here primarily to teach my children English, and help them acquire good English manners.'

'I understand, your ladyship.'

'Mornings and early afternoons you will give French and English lessons. Irina will also require drawing and sewing lessons. She already has a tutor who teaches her the pianoforte. Serge is learning to play the violin.'

I was privately quaking at the responsibilities facing me. Was I, a nineteen-year-old girl with very little education, even up to the task? Yet I knew I must appear confident, and be far more polite and humble towards the Countess than in our earlier encounters.

'Will the children be allowed time for play, since they are both so young?' I enquired politely.

'Serge will have time each afternoon to fish and sail, and enjoy other sports considered suitable for a young gentleman. And they can both skate, of course.'

Oh dear, I thought. Yet something else I would need to learn. 'I wonder if perhaps Nanny might help with teaching sewing as it is not one of my strengths?'

She frowned, rather disapprovingly. 'You will have to ask her, but you must work hard to improve your skills.'

'Of course, your ladyship,' I murmured, meekly bobbing a curtsey.

I believed she was about to dismiss me and half turned to go, but she stayed me with a flick of her hand.

'You will be aware of the close links between Russian and English royalty. Tsar Nicholas was of course the nephew of Edward VII and is cousin to your new King George V, whom he resembles to such a degree they could easily pass for brothers. This means there is a passion for all things English amongst the more liberal-minded aristocrats. But do not imagine everyone feels that way. Certainly the conservative types don't. My husband, fortunately, is one of the more liberal-minded gentlemen, and is keen for his son to adopt the finest of English education and manners. It will be your task to provide that.'

'I shall do my best to fulfil his wishes, your ladyship.'

'It will also be your responsibility to plan the schoolroom in true English style: a new toy cupboard, book shelves, whatever you think appropriate.'

'I shall set about devising a plan forthwith,' I agreed, secretly finding the idea quite daunting, although I could at least use the schoolroom at Carreck Place as a model.

'You will also be required to find someone able to carry out the work. I sacked our latest carpenter for incompetence.'

I shivered at the prospect of suffering a similar fate, but merely gave a compliant nod.

'My son must look the part of a young gentleman, which is why I purchased several new items of clothing for him while we were in England. Please see that the clothes are properly taken care of.' She gave a fond smile at this, but I couldn't fail to notice that she made no mention of Irina.

NINE

My first day was spent largely unpacking all the goods brought from England, which illustrated just how spoiled the children were, as the many boxes and trunks were stuffed with a variety of expensive clothes and toys. For Serge a model railway, toy steam engine, bats, balls, tops and whips, lead soldiers and clockwork toys by the score. For Irina there were skipping ropes, a pretty china doll and a tiny dolls' house complete with miniature furniture. The little girl was thrilled.

'Thank goodness she wasn't ignored completely,' I whispered to *Nyanushki*, who scowled and quietly hushed me. She was right, of course. I really must learn to guard my tongue.

I began at once to draw up a list of requirements to refurbish what was actually a rather drab schoolroom with only a small table, two chairs and an old box far too small for the toys. A new look would be no bad thing, but a considerable amount of work would need to be done to meet the Countess's high standards, and time was of the essence.

The next afternoon was cold and damp, and both children protested vehemently when I insisted that a walk was necessary despite the inclement weather. 'We English believe that fresh air is good for you, as is plenty of exercise. But we'll keep it short today as it looks about to rain.'

Nyanushki came with us to make sure I didn't get lost, and we took a turn about Alexandrvovsky Park, the children grumbling and dragging their feet the entire time.

'Can you skate?' *Nyanushki* asked. I pulled a rueful face, making her laugh.

'You'll soon learn. I'm sure the children will help teach you.'

Noticing the smirk on Serge's face I rather thought he would look upon this deficiency as an opportunity for making me look stupid. He may have been only eight years old, but he was a wilful boy with a defiant streak in him.

Later, I took the children, dressed in their best, down to tea with the Count and Countess, as instructed, urging them to be good in the hope they would not embarrass me. No sooner had I taken my seat than a large metal tea urn was set before me and, overcome with panic, I realised that I was about to embarrass myself.

'I assume you've operated a samovar before?' the Countess asked with a knowing smile.

I'd never seen one in my life before. Fortunately, there was a certain familiarity about the tap from which the hot water must flow, if not the way the tea pot sat on top of the vessel to keep warm. It rather reminded me of the tea urn used by the Women's Bright Hour at our local chapel, except that, nestling in a space below this one, I could see the glowing red of charcoal that kept the water hot, and hear it hiss and spit as it simmered gently within.

Turning the tap, I poured the scalding water into the tea pot, serving the tea with only the slightest tremor in my hands. The children sat stiffly in their seats, Irina's small greedy eyes firmly fixed on a plate of lemon wafers. I knew the children must wait to be offered something to eat so I gave her a stern glance, warning her to be patient.

Serge quietly slid under the table and began to unfasten the laces of my boots and tie them together so that my feet were linked. I glanced anxiously at the Countess, worrying she might have noticed and wondering if I should chastise the boy. But on seeing what he was doing she began to chuckle. 'Serge does so love a practical joke.'

Paying no attention to the antics of his son, the Count was talking about his day which had apparently been even more wearing than usual. 'The Tsar and Tsarina are in temporary residence at the Winter Palace, instead of hiding away at Tsarskoe Selo, which must be a good thing. Unfortunately, Nicky is as obsessed with petty rules of etiquette as ever, insisting people stand in the proper order of hierarchy. Obeying correct protocol and deportment, and using the right dishes for his bread and butter, seems to be far more important to him than the problems of the nation.'

The Count bit into a small sandwich, accepting the tiny porcelain plate the Countess quickly handed to him without a murmur.

'The fact that peasants are still suffering abject poverty, and the working class possess few rights and constantly go on strike in a frustrated effort to better their lot, seems to pass him by. His desk was yet again littered with reports and papers I very much doubt he has troubled even to read.' He gave a little shake of the head in despair.

'Did he listen to you?' Countess Olga asked, reaching for a slice of cake.

'Oh, he always listens,' her husband said. 'Most politely. Whether he acts upon my advice is quite another matter. He is far too much under the thumb of his bullying uncles.'

'And that cold fish of a wife of his, who spends all her time knitting scarves and crocheting silly shawls.'

'Those are for the poor, and she isn't a cold unfeeling person at all. The Tsarina is simply shy, very sensitive to the needs of others and a devoted mother.'

Countess Olga gave a snort of disdain, which I did not wonder at since no one could lay such an accusation upon her. While taking great care not to appear to be listening, since servants are supposed to be deaf, dumb and blind, I was silently miming to Serge, attempting to persuade him to sit back in his chair.

The Count continued with his complaints, oblivious to this pantomime, or else politely ignoring it. 'I am most fond of my cousin as he is a fine gentleman, a quiet man of honour who takes his role very seriously. But Nicky is incapable of making up his mind on anything, save for his conviction that liberal reform would be a recipe for disaster for Russia, and that as God's ambassador on Earth he is the only one capable of resolving the problems.' Stopping to take a breath, he smiled at his wife. 'But enough of all that. What about your own day, my love?'

'Much of it was spent choosing and being measured for a white satin gown for the coming candlelit ball at the Winter Palace,' she told him with a sigh, as if this proved her day had been far more trying than his.

I let out a small sigh of my own as Serge slid back into his seat with a self-satisfied grin on his face, while worrying what else he had been up to down there, so I didn't at first hear when the Count spoke to me.

'Pay attention, Dowthwaite,' the Countess snapped, and he politely repeated his question. 'I hope you are settling in well?'

'Oh, yes, thank you, I'm most comfortable,' I hastened to assure him. Smiling, I took a sip of China tea which smelt strongly of wood-smoke but was hot and delicious, most welcome after my own busy day. I watched astonished as the Count poured some of his into the saucer and drank from that.

'Old habits die hard,' he laughed.

The Countess suddenly slammed her own cup down in her saucer. 'What have you got in your mouth, child?'

Startled, I turned to look at Irina, whose mouth was indeed bulging with food, eyes wide and rapidly filling with tears. It was not difficult to work out what had happened. The plate of lemon wafers was half empty.

'Stand in the corner at once with your hands on your head, you greedy little madam,' her mother ordered. 'Sometimes I think this child was born with the devil inside her.'

'Nonsense,' chuckled her father. 'Just look at her, a perfect little angel with those innocent blue eyes and curly locks.'

'She is not in the least innocent. Do as I say, child, before I think of a worse punishment for you.'

Irina shuffled off to do as she was bid, her mouth too full of biscuit to permit any argument. The Countess then turned her ire on me. 'I am seeing little evidence so far of any benefit at all in employing you.'

I was stunned into silence by this attack. How could she allow her son to crawl about under the tea table carrying out his 'practical jokes' without a word of disapproval, while the moment little Irina did something wrong she was banished from the table? The Count quietly took another sip of tea from his saucer, then smiled at his wife. 'My love, Miss Dowthwaite has been with us only a few days. You must give her time.'

'Tush! If she cannot perform her duties efficiently then she is of no use to me and will have to go.'

I felt something quake inside me as I wondered where exactly I might be expected to go. Then a voice from the corner suddenly shouted, 'There, I've finished it, Papa, can I have another?' At which point the Count burst out laughing.

'Come here, my poppet.' He held out his arms and to my complete astonishment Irina ran into them to be lovingly nestled on her father's lap. The Countess continued to simmer and glower in silent fury, clearly knowing better than to intervene between father and daughter. I was simply delighted that someone at least loved this child, whether she be angel or devil.

Before the first week was out I was convinced that my new job would be even more difficult than I'd feared. The children seemed to be constantly squabbling and up to mischief, sliding down the banister, rolling about the floor fighting over some toy or other, punching each other and pulling hair, or ringing the bell to call a servant to fetch some item they were perfectly capable of finding for themselves, as I gently pointed out.

'It is your task to tidy your toys away at the end of the day,' at which they gave me a look of utter disbelief and walked away, leaving me no option but to do the job myself. Which reminded me that the children still had nowhere properly to store their toys, and, as instructed, I really must start making plans to improve the schoolroom.

'Do you know of a carpenter we could employ to build a toy cupboard?' I asked *Nyanushki*, but she only shook her head.

'No one the Countess would consider worthy.'

The Countess also insisted that the children were provided with a good English diet, including such dishes as rice pudding, baked apples and lots of vegetables. Serge was quite tall, thin and wiry. Irina was short for her age and rather plump. She had golden-blonde hair, a slightly freckled complexion, a round chin and somewhat podgy cheeks. Not at all the beauty her mother might have hoped for, but she was an affectionate child and very generous with her hugs and kisses. I wrote out a diet sheet for Anton the French chef, hoping it would help Irina to grow without putting on too much weight. But she did have a bad habit of sneaking down to the kitchen to beg one of the kitchen maids for a biscuit.

One morning I gave the children porridge, which Irina ate in sulky silence. Serge threw his dish upside down on the floor. 'I want cake, not this mush.'

Aware of *Nyanushki* sitting in the corner knitting one of her many scarves, I made no comment. In any case, engaging in an argument about the unsuitability of cake for breakfast at this delicate stage in my relationship with the boy was not a good idea. I mopped up the mess and gave him the boiled eggs and toast I'd already prepared, nestling the eggs in a napkin which I was assured was the Russian way.

'You haven't cut off the tops for me.'

I quietly did so with the spoon, slipping the egg into a small glass for him to eat.

'And why is my toast cut into strips?' he complained.

'In England we call these soldiers, which you can dip into the yolk.' He tried out my suggestion and must have enjoyed the result as he ate the rest of his breakfast without further protest. Maintaining her sulky silence, Irina began to play with her new doll, taking off its nightdress to pull on a frock. She was struggling to fasten the buttons when Serge suddenly snatched the doll from her and yanked off one of its arms. The little girl screamed, then rushed to her bedroom in floods of tears.

'Oh, Master Serge, that was naughty,' I cried, picking up the doll to see if I could repair it. 'You must go at once to apologise to your sister.'

'Won't!' and he stubbornly folded his arms across his narrow chest.

'I think you will.'

He glared at me. 'You can't make me.' His small eyes glittered with such anger that I was struck dumb. Master Robin and Miss Phyllis had been easy to deal with, so affectionate and loving. In that moment I felt completely inadequate, without the experience necessary to deal with such wilful disobedience. 'Would you like it if Irina smashed your new train set?' I softly asked.

'She wouldn't dare! And don't think *you* can tell me what to do. If I so wish it, your job here won't last five minutes. I can get rid of you as easily as I did Mademoiselle.' Then as if to prove his point he began to empty the milk jug on to the floor in the wake of the porridge, followed by the orange juice, egg shells and contents of the jam pot. I started to protest but *Nyanushki* put a gentle hand of restraint on my arm, and gave a little shake of her head as if warning me against taking further action. With a big grin on his face, Serge marched off to play with his train. Swallowing my anger and heart beating like a drum, I began to mop up the mess, feeling very much as if this small boy had declared war.

Each evening the children were expected to take dinner with their parents. I too was expected to attend, something of a trial as I found it embarrassing to have my chair pulled out for me and to be waited upon by the white-gloved butler as if I were a member of the family. It was so very different from the life I had led at Carreck Place. But it was good for the children to be included in such an occasion in what was evidently a very cosseted and sheltered life. Even so it came as something of a shock to discover that they were quite incapable of dressing themselves.

Nyanushki and I helped Irina, and Serge was assisted by a man-servant in the privacy of his bedroom. Irina would put up her arms for *Nyanushki* to slip the dress over her head, making no attempt to do up the buttons, or to put on her stockings and patent leather shoes. Not for a moment had it occurred to me that they would be completely helpless without assistance.

'Perhaps a few more skills need to be learned here,' I quietly suggested, pointing out this failing.

Nyanushki blinked in surprise. 'Indeed not! No lady is expected to do a thing for herself when she has a maid who can do it for her. Nor any gentleman either, save perhaps for the Count who takes rather a different outlook, being so very practical. I'll admit there's nothing his lordship likes better than to help in the garden whenever we are in the country, whereas most aristocrats would not demean themselves with such peasant-type activities.'

'I'm delighted to hear it.' I was beginning to be increasingly intrigued by this man who would be paying my wages, and looking forward to getting to know him better.

When the children stood before me ready for inspection, I was instantly perturbed by the expression on Serge's face, recognising the signs of further rebellion.

'How very fine you look,' I said, anxious to calm him as he twitched and tugged at his new clothes. He was dressed like any well-to-do young English boy, in a smart green tweed suit with Norfolk jacket and knickerbockers.

I smiled with relief as he preened himself at the compliment, but then Irina started to giggle. 'You look very silly, Serge.'

Her brother glowered at her. 'So do you in that fluffy pink frock with that big green sash and stupid hair ribbon.'

'It's better than your soppy tie and big collar,' she shouted back.

Serge instantly started tugging at the tie, trying to take it off, at the same time attempting to ease the stiff Eton collar.

'Please don't do that, Master Serge.' I hastily put out my hands to stop him, but he slapped them away.

'Don't like it. Won't wear it!'

I half glanced at *Nyanushki*, again wondering how best to deal with such outright disobedience. She gave a resigned little shrug as if she'd seen this many times before. 'I'm afraid they do tend to become rather quarrelsome when shut up too long in this flat. What would you like to wear, then, my lovely boy?' she asked.

'Don't care! Not this,' he yelled, and snatching up *Nyanushki*'s sewing scissors he chopped off the tie just below the knot. Then as his sister burst out laughing he quickly turned on her and chopped off the ribbon, together with a chunk of her hair.

Irina screamed, instantly falling to the floor to drum her heels in a fit of hysterics. Terrified that the Countess might hear this dreadful noise I rushed to pick her up and quieten her. Overwhelmed by a sense of failure at not having guessed his intent, matters went from bad to worse as despite my begging her to hush, her hysterics continued unabated.

Then *Nyanushki* spoke in a calm, firm voice. 'If you don't stop this noise at once, Miss Irina, I shall have to call Mama, and you know what she will do.'

Silence followed this threat as Irina instantly stopped screaming. Rubbing the tears from her eyes she got slowly to her feet, making no further protest as I retied her hair, carefully disguising the missing lock. *Nyanushki* fetched Serge a new tie, and even he appeared chastened despite his glum expression.

'What would the Countess do?' I asked *Nyanushki* in a whisper.

'Fasten up their naughty mouths with sticky tape,' she softly replied, sliding her plump fingers over her lips to demonstrate.

I was horrified. 'But they would not be able to eat, let alone speak.'

'Indeed not. That is the point. The children live in fear of this punishment, although there are worse.'

Recalling the incident over afternoon tea I dreaded to think what further punishments the Countess could inflict upon her children, particularly on Irina. 'I have an idea,' I quickly announced, anxious to calm their fears and stop the tears and sulks. 'If we get ready quickly I'll teach you how to sing *Pop Goes the Weasel* and *Diddle Diddle Dumpling*. I love silly rhymes, don't you?'

'Ooh, yes please,' Irina said, and we had a jolly sing-song, Serge particularly enjoying *I Went to the Animal Fair*, which we sang in French.

One afternoon after taking the children out for their daily walk, I returned to the schoolroom to find Ruth taking tea with *Nyanushki*. 'Oh, how lovely to see you,' I cried, giving my new friend a warm hug.

'I thought I'd call to see if you'd settled in all right, and if I could help in any way,' she told me.

'Why don't you take your friend to your room to talk? I'll look after the children for a while.'

'Thank you, *Nyanushki*,' I said, with heartfelt gratitude.

It was such a relief to have some time in private, to be able to share my concerns over the recent squabbles and misbehaviour and how inadequate I felt at dealing with the children.

'According to *Nyanushki*, the last governess took such a dislike to Serge that she deprived him of his food and half starved him,' I said. 'No wonder he's such a trial, the poor boy doesn't trust anyone. Even his own mother is either over-indulging him, or encouraging him to play silly practical jokes.' I finished by telling Ruth what had happened back home at Carreckwater when he'd almost drowned Irina in the lake.

She was shocked. 'It is important to set out your rules and acceptable standards of behaviour from the start. But it shouldn't be necessary to impose dreadful punishments. A little talk, perhaps, or sent to bed for a rest until they recover from their tantrum.'

'Quite. It seems to be mainly Irina who suffers. The child was made to stand in the corner with her hands on her head at tea the other day. She might have been there for ages had her father not intervened,' and we were soon both laughing as I told the tale.

'I'm sure matters will improve. They're just testing you. Anyway, the real reason I called was to offer to help you buy the right clothes. Winter is coming and you can't wear that old *shuba* of mine for church or the theatre. It's an absolute disgrace. We really should go shopping. Then I'll introduce you to the British and American chapel.'

'Oh, that would be lovely.'

Nyanushki agreed to sit with the children the following afternoon, and the outing was duly arranged.

My new job had not begun well, due largely to my lack of experience. But I realised that if I was to hold on to it, and protect the children from their bully of a mother, I would need to quickly improve.

TEN

It felt wonderful to be out and about discovering the delights of this beautiful city of canals, rivers, islands and bridges, with its well-deserved title of 'Venice of the North'. Ruth took me to see St Isaac's Cathedral with its classical pillars and golden dome, and then we made our way to the Palace Square, or Dvortsovaya Ploshad, dominated by the magnificence of the Winter Palace, before entering the Nevsky Prospekt. This seemed to be the very heart of the city, a busy thoroughfare with impressive architecture, amazing statues, street artists and any number of fascinating shops.

'I'm already growing quite fond of the children,' I told Ruth as we strolled along arm in arm, 'particularly Irina, despite their naughtiness at times. But it's good to enjoy a little adult company for a change, and be free of the worry and responsibility of them for an hour or two.'

'I know the feeling,' she laughed.

I bought a new warm coat, complete with hood and fur lined, although with cony, not beaver; a pair of woollen trousers that fastened underfoot; and beautiful beige felt *Valenki* boots that came right up to the knee.

'They are so soft and warm,' I said, hugely impressed.

'You can wear them indoors to keep warm on cold winter days, or when outside you can slip a pair of galoshes or rubber boots on top to keep out the wet. You'll find this particularly necessary when the thaw begins.' The shop assistant hurried away to fetch me a pair of those too.

Ruth next insisted I buy a large packet of envelopes, and carefully wrote out my new address in Russian on one of them. 'Now you can copy that address on to all the other envelopes and send them home for your parents to use.'

'Wonderful! You have been so kind to me.' We were standing on a bridge overlooking the canal, admiring the golden cupola of a nearby church glittering in the bright sunlight. This beautiful city with its gilt spires, blue and green domes and white houses had proved to be beyond my expectations. I was beginning to grow quite fond of Russia.

'We ex-pats must stick together. Speaking of which, we've just time to pay a quick visit to the British and American Chapel.'

It was a typically plain Congregational-type building, very spacious with simple wooden pews where I could imagine ladies sitting very properly for Sunday service in their best hats. And as Ruth had explained, it was not simply a place of worship, but very much a social club.

'It provides evening classes, a library, picnics, a chess club, a choir and many other cultural activities. I'm usually here every Sunday morning and on Wednesday afternoons, as today, when we governesses get together to enjoy tea and a gossip.'

And there they all were, a dozen or so young women gathered in the vestibule area, all welcoming me with smiles, and lots of hugs and kisses. As they quickly took my coat and settled me into a chair with a cup of tea and a bun, I instantly felt as if I was among friends.

'No picnics at this time of year, sadly, but there are one or two concerts lined up. Even the odd bridge night. And the Christmas party, of course. Plenty of fun to look forward to,' a blonde-haired young woman who introduced herself as Ivy, assured me.

'Are you musical? If so then don't bother to join the choir as it seems to be a requirement that members should not be able to sing,' another warned.

Everyone laughed, seeming to think this highly amusing.

'I doubt I shall have much time to join anything. The Countess and the children keep me pretty busy.'

'Oh, do make sure you get it written down what time off you are to be allowed.'

'And when you are to be paid,' another girl added. 'Employers in financial difficulties can put off paying your wages, which isn't right at all.'

'The Belinskys are definitely not in any financial difficulties,' I hastened to assure them. 'I'm sure everything will be fine, once I've settled into a routine. But first I have to organise the refurbishment of the schoolroom.' I went on to explain how the Countess wanted it to be in English style, so more advice followed on how best to achieve this in Russia. The most useful information came from Ruth.

'I can certainly recommend a good carpenter to build the toy cupboard and everything you need. Stefan attends here regularly as his own mother came over last century to work as a governess herself for a Russian factory owner. She eventually married one of the employees. He's bilingual and feels very much a part of the English community. He might well be around this afternoon. We'll go and look for him after we've had tea.'

I set down my cup and saucer. 'Perhaps we should look now as I really should be getting back.'

We found the young man in question and Ruth quickly explained my need for a good carpenter. He was tall and lean with well-muscled shoulders, red-brown hair and only the finest bristle of a moustache on his upper lip, rather than the heavy beard that was considered fashionable. I thought him rather good-looking.

'So you work for Count Belinsky? Interesting. He is said to have considerable influence with the Tsar.'

'That's not what I've heard.' I remembered the conversation over afternoon tea when the Count had spoken of the bullying uncles.

'Oh, so he tells you his secrets, does he?'

'That's not what I meant.'

'Ah, so you were listening in to a conversation? That's interesting too.'

My cheeks grew warm, and, noticing my embarrassment, he laughed out loud. But I could hardly deny it to be true.

'Stop teasing her, Stefan.' Ruth chided him. 'We all hear things we shouldn't. It's part of life in service, as you well know. And Count Belinsky is a very important minister.'

'He's certainly that,' he agreed. 'Although whether I'm prepared to work for a member of the rich aristocracy is open to question.'

The man was beginning to irritate me but, stiffening my resolve, I looked him straight in the eye. They were a fascinating greeny-blue, sparkling brightly as if he was finding this entire conversation hugely entertaining. 'It's the Countess who has ordered this work, but if you're not interested then I'm sure I can find another carpenter, equally good.'

'I very much doubt that. I'm the best there is.'

'Oh, and do you have any references to that effect?' I must have sounded rather haughty, for he laughed all the more.

'I can provide any number, should they be necessary.'

'It is not *I* who will require it, but her ladyship may well demand assurance of your . . .'

'. . . competence? Can it even be in doubt?'

I almost wanted to slap his arrogant face, and was grateful when Ruth again intervened with a chuckle. 'Do behave, Stefan. Millie is only doing her job as well as she can, otherwise she might lose it.'

He sobered instantly and, giving a little bow of the head, agreed to come round to the Belinskys' flat the very next day to discuss what was required. I was glad to make my escape. But there was something about the way his eyes followed me as I left the building that set my heart beating just a little faster.

~

The next morning, shortly after breakfast, I was summoned by the Countess to her boudoir. I knocked politely on the door, waiting for almost ten minutes before receiving permission to enter.

She coldly looked me over with a narrowing of her dark eyes. 'It was brought to my attention that you went out yesterday, without permission.'

'O-oh, I didn't realise that was a requirement,' I stammered, realising at once my mistake.

'You do nothing without my agreement. Is that understood? You are certainly not employed to dawdle with this new friend of yours.'

'I beg your pardon, your ladyship, I will remember that in future.' I fell silent, lost in a maelstrom of self-doubt and guilt. Then, dipping a curtsey, I folded my hands neatly at my waist and began a pre-rehearsed speech. 'With regard to my time off, milady, such details were not properly settled when we were in Carreckwater, so perhaps we should discuss the matter now.' What was it about this independent streak of mine that always led me into trouble?

'You will be available for my children at all times. Once they are in bed and asleep then you are free to occupy yourself as you wish, or simply go to bed.'

This gave me pause. 'I'm sorry, milady, I don't quite understand. So when is my day off, exactly?'

'I may agree to grant you a free afternoon, perhaps a few months from now when you've proved yourself. Time off needs to be earned.'

'But that cannot be right,' I protested, beginning to feel very slightly cross. 'I sincerely apologise for making the mistake of going shopping, albeit for a few essential items, without permission. I did, however, arrange for *Nyanushki* to look after the children, and every employed person deserves some respite in the form of a day off.'

Her lovely dark eyes widened at my temerity in daring to challenge her. 'You are under *my* rule here and will do as I say.'

My heart sank to my new boots. How very naïve of me not to settle such matters before I even accepted the Countess's offer of employment. Had I been flattered, or too eager for the opportunity to travel to properly protect myself? It was rather late in the day to be thinking of the right questions now. Nevertheless, I was determined to stand up for myself and not be bullied. 'I came to work for you in all good faith, your ladyship. I trusted you, not for a moment thinking you would let me down and deny me my rights.'

'How dare you suggest such a thing! What rights can you possibly have when you are little better than a peasant?'

I almost gasped out loud at this, though wisely held my shock in check, attempting to maintain my dignity as I carefully responded. 'I know my rights because my parents too were in service, but in no way could they be classed as peasants.'

She gave a little shrug of her shoulders, elegantly draped in a peignoir, as if my background were of no account or interest to her. 'If you're not satisfied, you could always find employment elsewhere, assuming I were to provide you with the necessary reference.'

'I'm sure I'd find no difficulty in securing a new position,' I rather recklessly remarked. What was I thinking of? This wasn't England,

and apart from Ruth I knew not a soul, couldn't even speak the language, so how could I simply walk away if the terms weren't right? Yet I bravely stuck to my point. 'I already have an excellent reference, from Lady Rumsley. However, I hope that won't be necessary since I'm quite sure we can come to an acceptable agreement, if only for the sake of the children. Speaking of the children, while visiting the British and American chapel yesterday I was introduced to a good carpenter. He will be calling later today to receive instruction on what is required for the schoolroom. Would your ladyship wish to be present?'

Her silence now almost froze me more than the Baltic winds, but then she suddenly put back her head and laughed out loud, a brittle sound with little humour in it, but nonetheless a relief.

'Indeed not. That is your job, as I have already informed you. I have better things to do with my time.'

'As you wish, milady. Can we agree, then, that I have Wednesday afternoons off so that I might meet up with the other British governesses at the British and American chapel? And perhaps every other Sunday?'

She let out a heavy sigh. 'Very well. That will do for the present.' And with a wave of her hand, she dismissed me.

I dipped a curtsey, thankful that in the end common sense had prevailed. But as I quietly closed the door I felt no sense of triumph at this apparent success. Countess Belinsky was the kind of autocrat who would not easily tolerate a challenge to her authority, not without some form of redress.

~

'I'm delighted that I won the issue over a day off as I need to be relieved of duties every now and then,' I said to *Nyanushki*. 'Once I've got the children to bed, I'm usually exhausted.'

'I could do with a bit more rest myself. The children do at least go to bed early, unlike Madame. She loves a good story and when her eyes tire of reading she falls into bed and hands the book over to me. I'm often reading to her till after two in the morning and I'm fair worn out. But while she can sleep in till midday, I still have to be up by six to help the Countess dress, since she has no lady's maid at present. How many pairs of hands do I have, I wonder? Nowhere near enough.'

I laughed out loud, giving the old nanny a warm hug. 'Then let me help. Some nights you can read to the children and go to bed early, and I'll sit up with Madame.'

Nyanushki readily agreed to this arrangement, and I too would be glad of a change of activity.

Raisa Ilyinsky, the Countess's mother, or *Babushka* as the children affectionately called her, lived very independently, spending her evenings quietly with little company besides the old nanny and the occasional visit from a friend. There were none of the silk draperies or gilt framing so beloved by her daughter in the dowager's rooms. Her part of the flat was very simply furnished in chintz with maroon brocade curtains, cosy and comfortable, almost English in style save for a collection of Fabergé eggs. She would sit reading long into the evening by the light of a spirit lamp that stood on a round mahogany table she always kept at her side.

On my first visit I offered to read *Jane Eyre*. 'It's quite a favourite of mine and I thought you might enjoy it too, Madame.'

'I'm sure I shall. I'm also fond of Dickens. Did you bring any of those with you?'

'I have *The Old Curiosity Shop*, and *David Copperfield*.'

This news brought forth a beaming smile. 'Lovely. I think our tastes will prove to be quite similar. Sadly, many of my friends are no longer with us, so I shall enjoy your company. It will make a pleasant change from Klara's moans and groans.' This comment was softened with a little chuckle, as if to make it clear she was quite fond of her old companion. 'Are you settling in all right?'

I kept my expression bland as I assured the old lady that I was most content in my new position.

'I'm relieved to hear it. My daughter can be a difficult woman. She always was a handful, even as a small child. What of your own childhood?'

I explained that my mother was French, and that a busy lady's maid she worked long hours, as did my father acting as chauffeur for Lord Lonsdale. 'I was often left in my grandmother's care. She was an old fashioned Methodist with very firm ideas of what was right and proper, but I enjoyed a most happy childhood. I do hope to provide that same love and support for Master Serge and Miss Irina.'

'I'm sure you will, dear girl, but do not make the mistake of spoiling them. Children need proper boundaries set. Olga too spent a great deal of time being cared for by others and I made the mistake of spoiling her out of guilt, feeling I was neglecting her. It may surprise you to know that even aristocrats have duties and responsibilities they do not always welcome.'

'Oh, I'm sure you do,' I hastened to say.

'I acted as lady-in-waiting for the Tsar's mother, Maria Feodorovna, for many years. There were dozens of us but it was demanding work. Oh, but how I loved to see the Cossacks lead the Empress down the long gallery in her full Russian costume with red velvet and gold train, ablaze with jewels, her maids of honour all dressed in pale blue velvet. Even the room itself glittered with gold, lined with glorious works of art and vases filled with flowers.' She was looking quite misty-eyed at the memory. 'The splendour of old Russia was a sight to see.'

'It must have been quite magnificent.'

'I even accompanied the Empress to England on one occasion when she visited her sister Princess Alexandra, who married your

King Edward VII. It was lovely to see the two sisters delighting in each other's company. They remain close to this day.'

'Is that how you learned your perfect English?'

Babushka smiled. 'I'm flattered by the compliment, but yes, I suppose it must be. Maria Feodorovna was a Danish princess called Dagmar, who was originally to marry her husband's brother. Tragically, he died and she and Sasha, which is what she called Alexander, grew close as they both grieved for the loss of the young man they both adored. Then they fell in love and married, very much in keeping with their parents' wishes.'

'How romantic.'

'Oh, it was indeed. She even changed her religion for him. They were ever a devoted couple but their children, Nicholas and his siblings, were raised some distance from the court and St Petersburg. It was an isolated childhood with little in the way of culture or high society, which is probably why the Tsar still prefers a quiet life in the country.'

'Is that a bad thing?' I asked, fascinated by what she was telling me.

'In some respects perhaps not, yet it would have benefited Nicky to be a little more cosmopolitan, and more aware of how many of his subjects depend upon the land for their living, struggle to pay their taxes and are not even literate.'

'It is not always a good thing to spoil children, I agree,' I said, thinking of Serge. 'Although you cannot spoil them with too much love, only in how you present it, I suppose.'

'Maria Feodorovna was devoted to her children but made the mistake of secluding them in a sheltered world where they saw few people beyond servants and their precious pets. Alexander too adored his children but again was over-protective, insisting upon a strict routine that never allowed them to gain confidence or think for themselves. As a consequence Nicholas was never properly prepared for the task fate assigned him following his father's death. Bringing children up in the real world is vital, do you not think?'

I nodded. 'I'm sure you're right, Madame. Do I understand that you are advising me to be firm with Serge and Irina, but also to provide them with wide experiences and a good education?'

'That is exactly what I'm saying, dear girl. I believe we made the same mistake with Olga, partly because she was our only surviving child, three having died within months of their birth.'

'Oh, I'm so sorry. That must have been hard to bear.'

'It made us spoil her dreadfully. My darling husband was so rich he simply allowed our beautiful daughter to have whatever she desired. In retrospect, it was not such a good idea, as greed and desire often overtake common sense, certainly in Olga's case. We were delighted when she set her sights on the Count, believing it to be a love match, but it was his title she'd fallen in love with, and his wealth.' The old lady gave a long-drawn out sigh. 'Now history is repeating itself with Serge, although so far as Irina is concerned, a little more attention would not come amiss.'

I could hardly believe that she'd actually admitted the Countess's affection for her daughter was somewhat lacking, but I made no comment.

Leaning closer, the old lady whispered, 'Serge is a practical joker, rather like the Tsar's younger brother George. Do keep a close watch on the boy in case he gets up to his tricks.'

I gave a wry smile. 'I've learned to do that already.'

'Excellent. Then I think you'll do well, dear girl. Now if you would make me a cup of hot chocolate we'll settle down with *Jane Eyre*. Oh, and do call me *Babushka*. I much prefer it to Madame.'

Spending an evening with the dowager had taught me a great deal, and given a much-needed boost to my confidence.

ELEVEN

Stefan the carpenter came, as promised, and I showed him the shabby state of the schoolroom, the overflowing toy box and toys scattered about the floor. 'As you can see, it is rather urgent as we have nowhere to put anything. The children also need a desk each, and shelves for the books I brought out for them to read.'

'Very well, I'll start tomorrow.'

'Oh, that would be wonderful, Mr . . . ?'

He grinned, his eyes holding mine for a moment longer than quite seemly, that familiar challenge sparking in their green-grey depths. 'Kovalsky, but I thought we'd agreed that you can call me Stefan.'

Once again I felt my cheeks start to burn, this time for no good reason, and I turned away to pretend to tidy a pile of books, not wishing him to see how he affected me. 'I would be most appreciative of your help in this matter – Stefan – although I should warn you that the Countess demands only the best.'

'Which I can provide. Is that the plan?'

I was acutely aware of his closeness as he came to bend over the little sketches I'd made of the furniture I'd like, and the plans I'd drawn up for the schoolroom. 'The Countess insists it must be in the English style.'

'May I take these away with me?'

'Of course.' As I handed them to him, his fingers accidentally brushed against mine and something jolted inside me. What on earth was happening? 'The schoolroom could do with a coat of paint,' I rushed on to say, desperately attempting to catch my breath, which seemed to be coming in shallow little gasps. 'I don't suppose you . . .'

'What colour would you like?' he asked, busily making notes.

I suggested green panelling with a cream trim, and he also agreed to lay new linoleum. 'It would be so much easier to keep clean, and better for the children when they are playing.'

Once all the details had been agreed upon, I directed him to speak to the butler, who had the final word on such arrangements. I still wasn't convinced Stefan would fulfil his promise or be as good as he claimed, but as I set about the usual morning lessons I felt a strange curl of excitement within.

To my amazement, when I walked into the schoolroom at eight o'clock the following morning, he was already at work building a large cupboard where the toys could be kept on full display. I was hugely impressed and said as much. 'Goodness, when did you start to make that? It looks half done already.'

'I worked all night on it as you seemed to be in a hurry.'

'I can see it becoming a veritable showpiece. Far more capacious and stylish than anything I have seen in England, but still a very English style, as I asked. It's wonderful.'

'Stefan is a fine craftsman,' *Nyanushki* remarked, coming up behind us, holding a child in each hand. 'And most reliable and efficient. I remember your mother well, son. Haven't seen her for a while. How is she these days?'

He turned to smile sadly at the old nanny. 'She passed away, never having quite recovered from the death of my father. Her life wasn't the same without him.'

'Ah, I'm sorry to hear that, although not surprised in the circumstances. I remember they made the perfect couple. He was a most kind-hearted man, a stalwart at fighting for what was right, and your mother was his greatest supporter. You didn't follow in his footsteps, then?'

'Working in a factory was not for me.'

'So how did you acquire your skills as a carpenter?' I asked, suddenly curious to know more about this young man's background.

'Hard work and good training. Carpenter, handyman, gardener and general dogsbody at your service,' he said, giving a mocking salute.

Nyanushki smiled. 'Your mother once told me that as well as being very practical, you were also a brilliant artist.'

'I'm afraid my mother was somewhat prejudiced where my talents are concerned. Besides, I know my place. Earning an honest crust in this country is never easy so it wouldn't do to get above myself, now, would it?'

He didn't seem to be the kind of man who would 'know his place,' but there was something in his tone that warned me not to pursue the subject. 'Perhaps you could bring some of your pictures to show the children,' I suggested, smiling when, predictably, Serge pulled a face and Irina eagerly nodded.

'Ooh, yes please, I like painting,' the little girl said.

'They aren't for public viewing,' he said. Turning away, he continued to plane and smooth the wooden shelves and cupboard doors.

'You surely don't look at showing them to the children in quite that light,' I protested. 'A demonstration of your painting skills would be wonderful for their education.'

It was as if I hadn't spoken. Completely ignoring me, he carried on working, making no response. I thought this rather rude, but could see little more than the back of his head as he crouched low. Neither his face nor his hair were visible as he wore a slouch cap pulled well down. I longed for him to glance up and agree to my suggestion, not simply for the sake of Serge and Irina but because the desire in me to see that smile in his eyes again was strong.

Making a little tutting sound, *Nyanushki* began to usher them away. 'Come along, we must leave Stefan to his work. We'd better keep the children out of his hair for the next day or so.'

'Oh, yes, of course. Quite right, *Nyanushki*.' I quickly pulled my straying thoughts back to the reality of my job. 'Put on your warm coats, children. We can practise our English conversation while we enjoy a walk, and learn the name of trees and flowers. Then you can play with your toys for a little while in your bedrooms. When Stefan has finished the schoolroom, you can both help *Nyanushki* and me to clean it up and arrange everything just how you like it,' I said, in a brisk no-nonsense voice.

Serge scowled. 'That's a servant's job.'

'Possibly, Master Serge, but it is *your* schoolroom, so *your* responsibility too,' I insisted, remembering my conversation with *Babushka*. 'We shall start lessons first thing on Monday morning.'

I caught Stefan's smile as I shooed them away, and wondered what it was about me that amused him so.

For once the children did not protest about a walk, even though there were feathery snowflakes starting to fall. Perhaps they were secretly looking forward to having a new schoolroom, in which case I might be doing something right after all.

Before the end of the week the cupboard and book shelves were complete, the cherry wood polished to perfection and two school desks with tip-up seats provided for the children to work. The panelled walls had been painted in green and silver, much finer than cream, with new green linoleum in place, as requested. The schoolroom looked wonderful, even better than the plans I had given him.

'You're right' I said to *Nyanushki.* 'Stefan is both reliable and efficient.'

'No one would dare to be anything less in this household,' she commented drily.

But despite my reservations about his attitude, I felt a little sad that the work was done, and privately hoped I might see him again soon at the British and American chapel.

~

The first English lessons began, as promised, on Monday morning with my introducing the children to a game of Snap, using named pictures to help them learn words. We played at identifying some of their favourite toys and possessions, to which I'd attached labels to help the children remember the English names. I then helped them build the words with small wooden tiles upon which I'd painted the English alphabet. Irina joined in with great enthusiasm, smiling and laughing with delight whenever she successfully built a word to match the one on the label. As expected, Serge remained obstinate and grumpy.

'Why should I care what the word is in English? I'm Russian.'

'Because your mama and papa wish you to learn the language,' I gently explained in my careful French. 'You're a clever boy, Master Serge, so you won't find it too difficult.' I'd quickly discovered that he responded well to flattery.

I was helping Irina set out the letters for 'doll' when the Countess walked in. I instantly leapt to my feet, as required. 'Don't mind me,' she said, settling herself into a chair. 'I shall sit here and watch.'

As she had not given permission for me to be seated, I remained standing, feeling suddenly nervous. I handed Serge the b for 'ball,' watching as he searched for the A among the tiles on the table. Eventually he found it and lined it up with the first.

'Well done. Now look for an L,' I told him.

'Is that all you're doing, playing games?' the Countess asked, her tone deeply scathing. 'Shouldn't you be teaching them nouns and verbs?'

Turning to her with a smile, I tried to explain. 'Grammar, at this stage, would not be appropriate. Vocabulary first, and conversation, are far more valuable in picking up a language. We can come to grammar later. That is how my mother taught me.'

'You will surely give them some translations to do?'

'Not yet, your ladyship. That would be far too boring and difficult for children this young, even if they were skilled at writing, which Irina isn't yet. I believe learning should be fun if it is to be effective.'

'A schoolroom is for education, not fun and games,' she snapped.

'I think it can be both.' She glowered at me but I did not back down, and merely continued helping the children. 'Ah, you're nearly there, Irina. Now you need another L, as does Serge. We always have two at the end of "ball," and at the end of "doll." That's it, well done!'

Irina beamed. 'Look Mama, I've done it,' she cried, clapping her little hands to celebrate her achievement.

'I've done my word too,' Serge said, and looked to his mother for her approval, which he quickly received.

'Well done, son,' she said with pride in her voice, then addressing me continued, 'You will bring them down to dinner this evening as usual. However, I shall expect more scholarly lessons in future.' After which caustic remark she left, with not a word of praise for her little daughter.

My heart ached with pity at seeing the devastation on Irina's chubby little face. She seemed to shrivel into herself whenever her mother rejected her. Serge did his usual smirk of self-satisfaction. Something would have to be done about the harsh way the

Countess treated her daughter, although exactly what, I hadn't the first idea.

Later that same morning the Count also visited the schoolroom, but this time when I leapt to my feet he waved me back to my chair with a big smile. Then to my great surprise and delight he settled himself on the floor beside Irina and joined in her game of matching names to pictures.

'This looks like fun. Can I play?' he asked. 'Oh, and how clever you are, Irina, to know that this word says "elephant." That's quite a big word for such a little girl.'

Looking into her father's face with open adoration, Irina's round cheeks flushed pink with pleasure. Even Serge preened himself with pride when his father admired a short poem he had copied out in English, asking him to read it aloud, which the boy did with perfect diction.

'You seem to be making good progress with my children,' the Count said, smiling up at me with pride in his voice.

'That is because they are clever children,' I said, pretending not to notice his son's look of surprise and pleasure at the compliment.

'How very kind of you to say so.'

I recalled what *Babushka* had revealed about her daughter's reasons for marrying the Count: lured by his title and wealth. All too aware of the rumours that she was currently engaged in a sordid affair with the gardener, and not forgetting the misdemeanours I'd once been unfortunate enough to witness at first hand, I was filled with sadness that she should commit such cruel betrayals of this kind and thoughtful man.

~

As the weeks went by I became increasingly fond of *Babushka*, as I now thought of her, and loved spending time with her. She would always ask after the children, who visited their grandmother regularly, and was an increasing support to me, quite taking me under her wing. I would read from the classics, and she would fill me in on Russian history, although some of it was less than pleasant. One evening she told me about the afternoon of March 13, 1881 when Tsar Alexander II had been assassinated outside the Winter Palace by revolutionaries.

'He was attending a military review when a bomb was thrown at his carriage. It caused limited damage to the vehicle but killed a number of innocent bystanders. Ignoring his own safety and all sensible advice, he climbed out, anxious to assist the injured. Tragically, one of the revolutionaries then threw another bomb, shattering his legs. The poor man died of his injuries a short time later.'

'Oh, how dreadful, and what a very courageous man,' I said, shocked.

'His son, Alexander III, became Emperor next with Maria Feodorovna as his Empress, reigning until his death in 1894. Their son Nicholas, our present Tsar, was intent on marrying Princess Alix of Hesse, whom he loved deeply. Unfortunately, neither parent was in favour, in particular his mother.

'Why, what did she have against her?' I asked, much preferring these glimpses into family history, love and romance.

'She insisted the girl was not up to the task, far too shy and withdrawn, and there may have been some truth in that. She was also a granddaughter of Queen Victoria, largely brought up by Her Majesty, and I suspect that Maria Feodorovna was fearful of losing influence over her son if the girl had such a powerful relative behind her. However, as her darling Sasha was at death's door at the time, she gave in. Nicky married his beloved Alix and the pair are still utterly besotted with each other. Whether the Tsarina has yet gained the approval of her mother-in-law is another matter entirely,' *Babushka* finished with a chuckle. 'Have you gained my daughter's approval yet?'

I smiled. 'That is a question you must ask her.'

'I just might one day, when she's in a good mood,' she said. Grinning like old friends, we returned to our current novel, *Wuthering Heights*.

~

Over the coming days and weeks Countess Olga continued to call unannounced during lessons, clearly checking up on me. I was always required to stand whenever she entered the room, and rarely given permission to sit while she was present. Nor was I allowed to address her ladyship unless she spoke to me first, a rule I found extremely hard to keep. But I took the view that as my employer she had the right to inspect me, so tried not to let her presence trouble me too much. Besides which, the children were always on their best behaviour whenever their mother was around. When one day Serge read a short passage from *Little Lord Fauntleroy*, the Countess was so pleased she actually congratulated me.

'Well done, Dowthwaite. You seem to be making progress at last. I look forward to hearing Irina read something from the book next time.'

The little girl flushed bright crimson, being far from that stage, but then she was but six years old. 'We'll find something more appropriate for Miss Irina,' I said with a smile and, giving the child a fresh sheet of paper, set her to writing a little story of her own, which she so loved to do. With both children settled at their tasks I dutifully escorted the Countess to the door, managing for once to keep my opinions to myself.

It was as I opened it to show her out that she took me completely by surprise with her next remark. 'Ah, Dowthwaite, do you remember that young carpenter, Stefan? He did such a fine job and as I've been obliged to sack my current gardener-cum-handyman, for reasons we won't go into, I've decided to offer him a permanent position in the household. Would you please inform him of that fact.'

'Oh!' Completely lost for words, and too secretly thrilled to think of a sensible reply, I merely nodded as she turned on her heel and strode away. But a strange excitement lit within me at the prospect of seeing him more regularly.

TWELVE

Abbie had been listening, entranced, to young Millie's tale, pleased that her grandmother seemed to be enjoying her reminiscences of Russia far more than Abbie had expected. But as the old lady fell silent, perhaps drifting off to sleep, she kissed her goodnight and took her leave. Fascinating as it was, Abbie felt no nearer to discovering the facts about her mother's past. She was rapidly coming to the conclusion that she needed to find other sources of information, rather than simply replying upon Millie.

The following afternoon Abbie devoted entirely to searching through Kate's things, hoping to find letters, a diary, even a photograph or two, anything to throw light on her early years. She found the experience immensely difficult. Just the smell of her mother's perfume that still permeated her clothes brought a fresh flood of tears. Then she discovered every letter and postcard Abbie had ever written to her, more in fact than she remembered sending. But there they all were, carefully tied up in a ribbon and stored in an old handkerchief box, including the announcement of Aimée's birth. So Mum *had* cared after all. Then why had she kept her at such a distance? Why couldn't she allow herself to forgive? Abbie was overwhelmed with regret. It didn't make sense. Oh, what a terrible waste! If only she could turn back the clock.

Her father walked into the bedroom at just that moment. 'What the hell do you think you're doing?' The very tone of his voice revealed the depth of his anger at this intrusion.

Abbie went and put her arms about him. 'Dad, I know it's hard but someone has to clear away Mum's stuff. I thought I'd spare you the pain.'

Looking into her face and seeing her tears, his own expression desolate, he put his arms about her and gave Abbie a gentle hug. It was a good feeling, the closest they'd been in years. Then, turning on his heels, he walked out again, clearly quite unable to speak.

Abbie continued with her self-imposed task, with less enthusiasm but still hoping to discover something of interest. Was Kate's resentment and odd behaviour all bound up with her difficult past? Had her real mother given birth at the orphanage? Or had she abandoned her child on the doorstep? And who had chosen her name? Was that Millie, or perhaps the matron? There must be some information somewhere about her time at Pursey Street Orphanage. Abbie found nothing.

Fay came to help later, and it took the rest of the afternoon for the pair of them to clear everything, setting aside personal mementoes for each member of the family to choose from. Abbie tucked the letters into her pocket.

'I'll take these boxes to the charity shop first thing tomorrow, if you like,' her sister-in-law offered.

'Thanks, and could you mind Aimée for me tomorrow and drop me off at the station on your way? There's something I need to do before getting down to work at the jewellery shop, preferably without the fuss of explaining it all to Dad and Robert.'

'Of course. No problem.'

Pursey Street Orphanage was every bit as grim as Kate had described, a Victorian gothic-style building of grey stone surrounded by a high wall, shut off from the world behind a pair of huge iron gates kept permanently locked. A group of giggling girls with bouffant hair and mini-skirts came swinging by, happily mimicking Lesley Gore as they sang *It's My Party* at the tops of their voices. Had they any idea, Abbie wondered, what it must have felt like to be incarcerated in such a place? No chance of any parties there. How Kate must have longed to slip through those gates and escape. Even as a small child her mother would have felt imprisoned and unloved, until that glorious day when Millie had arrived and taken her at once into her arms.

The train journey had been long and tiring, so it was almost midday when she'd arrived in Stepney. And as she faced an equally long return journey home, Abbie knew she couldn't afford to linger too long.

The classrooms Abbie glimpsed as she was led along a passage were quite brightly painted, the walls covered in posters and pictures done by the children, not at all as bleak and bare as they must have been when her mother had been here. Kate had spoken of having no toys to play with, instead an endless list of chores to keep the children occupied and out of mischief. When not in lessons, she'd had to mop the bathroom floor, scrub pans and peel vegetables, or even pick stones from the fields around. There were never any visitors for her on a Sunday afternoon, nor any presents under the big tree that stood in the hall at Christmas, save for an orange and a few nuts stuffed into an old stocking. The only item she could rightly call her own had been a small bible, given to each child by Dimwitty, the cold, unfeeling woman who Kate said should never have been put in charge of young children. But the woman now facing Abbie across the desk was much younger, and actually smiling. She really looked most kind.

'How can I help you, Miss Myers?

Abbie cleared her throat, suddenly nervous of what she might discover, now that she was actually here. She quickly explained that her mother had spent her early years at the orphanage but had recently died, and that she wanted to see the place for herself and learn more about her origins. 'I wondered if you could help,' she added.

It was plain from the woman's expression of gentle compassion that she'd heard this request countless times before. 'Things have improved a great deal since your mother's time, I'm glad to say. In today's modern world we no longer consider single parenthood with quite the disapproval of our forebears, and orphanages are quickly going out of fashion. We do our best to give the children we accommodate all the love they need, and a happy childhood. When was your mother resident here, exactly?'

Abbie gave details of her mother's age, which was the only information she had. 'But who was her birth mother? That's what I'd love to know, or any clue to help me track her down.'

'We can certainly look through our records, although I cannot guarantee we'll find anything of value. Very often we have no information at all about a child taken into our care.'

'You mean if she was left abandoned?'

The woman smiled sympathetically. 'Let us hope that is not how it was in your mother's case. One moment please, while I fetch the register.'

Abbie sat with her hands tightly clasped in her lap, with no sound other than the slow beat of her heart as she patiently waited. Kate had once stated that she couldn't have loved Millie more if she had been her real mother, yet had often spoken of her regret about the distance between them at times. Abbie now realised that may have initially been caused by Kate's desire to rush headlong into marriage at seventeen, quite against Gran's wishes. Abbie was hard-pressed to know whose side to take on that one.

Yet years after this quarrel over a marriage that never did take place, a slight awkwardness between mother and daughter had been evident from time to time. Abbie herself had witnessed their unease on numerous occasions, often when they were talking about the jewellery business. She'd rather assumed that Millie had found it hard to step down and allow her daughter to take over, which she could well understand having now visited the shop. But sometimes their disagreements would be over nothing that she could quite put her finger on, or the conversation would cease the moment she entered the room.

That being the case, why had Kate made no effort to find out who her birth mother was? Or had she found the answer and kept it to herself because of the pain it might cause Millie?

It seemed to take forever before the woman returned; the book, Abbie noticed, was already open at the appropriate page.

'She arrived in January 1920, and was judged to be around two or two and a half years old at the time.'

Abbie was surprised. '1920? Two years old?'

'Unfortunately we can't prove her age accurately as there are no documents recorded, no birth certificate or identification of any sort.'

'I assumed she must have been brought here as a baby.'

'That is not always the case. Sometimes a young mother struggles to cope alone for some time before being forced to admit defeat and give up her child, usually out of poverty.'

'Did her mother bring her to the orphanage, then? And do you know who she was?'

'It is recorded that Kate was brought by a young woman.'

'Who?' Abbie felt the first stirrings of hope.

'I'm afraid I'm not at liberty to reveal her identity, not without asking her first.'

'But will you do that, and then let me know who she is?'

'I will tell her of your enquiry, assuming she's still alive and I can find her. But it will be up to her to contact you.'

'Oh, yes, I see.' Hope instantly died, for it was unlikely the mother would agree to reveal her identity after all these years of silence. 'So what about Kate's own name? Who chose that?'

'She apparently wore a label pinned to her coat. But no surname.'

Did this mean she was illegitimate? Of course she was, but Abbie had known that already. Which meant she was no nearer to finding out who Kate's birth parents were. A great sadness filled her, and deep sympathy for her mother. Struggling with her emotions she tried to think of more questions to ask. No birth certificate, no identification, nothing but a name. 'Did she have nothing at all with her when she arrived?'

'I don't believe so.' The woman put on her spectacles to examine the register more closely. 'Ah, yes, there is something mentioned here. She was apparently carrying a small bundle.'

Abbie's heart leapt. 'Really? What was in it? Was it returned to her when Kate left?' Her mind was already turning over possibilities of searching the attics.

The woman looked apologetic. 'It says here that it was offered to her adoptive mother, Mrs Nabokov, but she declined to take it.'

Abbie stared at the matron in complete disbelief. 'Declined to take it? Why would Gran do such a thing? This was an important part of my mother's life, the only item she possessed.'

'Perhaps she wished the child to put the past behind her and start afresh.'

That would be so typical of Millie, as Abbie knew only too well. The past was very much a closed book to her grandmother. She took a steadying breath. 'I don't suppose by any chance you still have it, this parcel?'

The woman was already on her feet and calling for her assistant. Turning back to Abbie, she gave an encouraging smile. 'Miss Aspen is rigorous at keeping the children's belongings safe, for just such occasions as these. I'm sure she won't have let us down this time, either.'

Nor had she. Ten minutes later Abbie was walking away from Pursey Street Orphanage clutching the precious parcel to her breast. At last she might have found the evidence she'd been seeking to shed some light on her mother's true identity.

~

She did not risk opening the bundle until she was safely home in the privacy of her room. Sitting on her bed, she gently unwrapped it. Inside she found a baby's shawl, and inside that what seemed to be a neatly folded item of clothing.

Abbie shook out the shawl, seeing nothing remarkable about it, since it was the same as a thousand others, hand-knitted in a soft cream wool. Next, she unfolded what appeared to be a christening gown in embroidered cream satin. The very quality of the fabric told her it was expensive. This unknown birth mother had clearly not come from a poor family. There was no sign of poverty here. But family disapproval might have been the issue. What on earth had happened to this desolate young mother who had been forced to relinquish her child? Frowning slightly, she spread out the gown to view it better.

'My goodness, it is quite beautiful,' she murmured to herself.

Abbie smoothed her hands over the silky fabric, marvelling at the skill of the embroidery threaded with tiny seed pearls on the quilted bodice. Then her fingers paused as she felt something hard and solid, a small lump of something stitched inside. What could it be? She had to know. Fetching a pair of sharp scissors from her sewing basket, she carefully unpicked the stitches – and then stared in disbelief at what fell into the palm of her hand.

~

Is this what I think it is, Gran?' Abbie held out the jewel, startled to see the colour drain from her grandmother's face. She had chosen a moment when they were alone, this time walking by the lake on a bright April day, a troop of ducks waddling behind in the hope of a crust or two. 'There's no chain attached, but I believe it must be a pendant.'

There followed a long stunned silence. 'I – It's Baltic amber. Extremely valuable.'

'That's what I thought.'

'This isn't stocked in the shop, so where did you get it?'

'Gran, don't be hurt or offended, but I went to Pursey Street Orphanage yesterday.'

For a moment Abbie thought Millie might be about to faint and, quickly taking her arm she helped her to sit on a nearby bench. Even then she seemed to be having trouble catching her breath and Abbie was filled with guilt for having revealed this news so crudely. She was thankful her father was out fishing; otherwise he would have been furious with her for upsetting poor Millie at this time.

'Should I fetch you a glass of water?'

'No, it's all right. I'll be fine in a moment. Are you saying that you went all the way to London? What on earth possessed you to do such a thing?'

'I wanted to find out more about Mum – who she was – and if something in her past caused her to do this terrible thing to herself. You can surely understand that?'

'And what did you discover?'

'Very little. She was two or two and a half, apparently, when she was taken to the orphanage, and not a baby at all. Did you know that?'

Millie said nothing, still looking utterly bemused by this sudden revelation that her granddaughter had been investigating her adopted daughter's birth.

'Anyway, nothing more is known about her. There was no identification of any kind save for the fact that she had a name label pinned to her coat. But the matron did give me a bundle of baby clothes, which Kate was carrying the day she was admitted. I found this pendant stitched inside the bodice. You say it is valuable?'

Millie cleared her throat. 'Amber is a resin from trees that grew millions of years ago, many of which are now extinct. As the sticky substance ran down to earth it often caught up fragments of plants and insects which were trapped in the amber resin. It was then washed away by storms and later deposited in small chunks like pebbles on the shoreline of the sea. Baltic amber is at least fifty million years old, and very precious.'

Abbie was stunned by this information; fifty million years was a length of time quite beyond her comprehension. Then she saw a single tear roll down her grandmother's cheek. Millie was staring at the pendant almost in disbelief, white to the lips as she smoothed a finger over the stone, which was as yellow as butterscotch and shaped like a teardrop itself. The jewel did indeed have the skeletal remains of a dragonfly embalmed within that Abbie hadn't recognised as such until it had been explained to her. She put an arm about her grandmother's shoulders, about to offer a few words of apology over upsetting her, when she was abruptly interrupted.

'What's going on here?'

Abbie started in dismay at the sound of her father's voice as he strode towards them, fishing tackle in hand and a now-familiar anger clouding his face. Guilt once again suffused her. 'Dad, I'm so sorry. I really didn't mean to make Gran cry, only I just needed to understand.'

'Understand what?'

'It's all right,' Millie put in, dabbing at her tears and attempting to regain some composure. 'The fault is entirely mine. I daresay

Abigail has every right to ask questions of me, and of the orphanage if she so wishes.'

'The orphanage?' Tom dropped his rod and line to the ground with a clatter. 'What about the orphanage?'

'I visited it yesterday, Dad, to ask about Mum.'

There was a slight pause and then, ignoring his daughter completely, he asked of Millie, 'What sort of questions?'

'Perfectly normal ones about who her mother was, and when she was left at the orphanage. The kind of questions Kate herself asked, and now Abigail, as we knew she would one day. It's just that I'm not sure I'm able to give her the answers she needs. I've told her all I can.'

'But it's not enough, Gran.' Abbie looked at her grandmother with a mix of anguish and sympathy in her gaze. 'What is this big secret you won't talk about? I know there must be one. I can sense it. I'm curious to know why you went all the way to London seeking a child when you could easily have gone down the road to Kendal, or to Preston, where there must have been any number of children just longing to be adopted. It doesn't make sense. Does the reason you chose London lie in what happened back in Russia? I believe they could be connected. If I'm right, then please tell me what happened back then, during the revolution.'

Millie looked helplessly at her. 'We suffered agonies. It was a difficult time and I'd really rather not talk about it.'

'Leave your grandmother alone. Can't you see you're upsetting her?'

There were tears in Abbie's eyes now, and oh, she was so tired of crying. She wanted her life to be bright and normal again. She thought of the young girls she'd seen dancing and singing along the road in Stepney, having a blast. How she longed to have some fun in her own life again after all the trauma and disappointment she'd suffered. She fully intended to achieve that dream, no matter how difficult it might be.

'Can't you see that I'm desperately upset by Mum's death?' she cried. 'You're all piling the blame for her suicide on to *me*! Doesn't anyone care about *my* feelings? I loved her too, you know, even if you don't love me any more, Dad.'

Her father looked devastated by this remark. 'Abbie, don't say such a dreadful thing. Of course I love you.'

'Well, you show little sign of it.'

Her grandmother put her arms about her. 'I'm so sorry, my darling. I know this must be very upsetting for you. It's just that some things are . . .'

'. . . best forgotten. How many times I've heard you say that.' Abbie ran her hands through her hair, tugging her wayward curls to one side in a gesture of exasperation. 'I'm sorry, but avoiding the truth doesn't help one bit. If you were simply appeasing your conscience by taking in a poor child when you'd seen so many die in the revolution, then why not say so? That's perfectly reasonable, although it still doesn't explain why you went all the way to Stepney to find one.'

'It wasn't quite like that. You've got it all wrong.' Tears were raining down Millie's cheeks by this time and Tom was patting her shoulder, trying to offer comfort.

'Hush now! Abbie has no idea what she is asking of you. She doesn't understand. How can she?'

'Then explain it to me so that I will understand. *What is the problem*?'

It was then that the answer came to her, and Abbie felt her whole body jerk with shock. 'Of course, why didn't I see it before? The answer lies in this pendant.' She picked up the jewel, turning it over in her hands, feeling its cool smoothness. 'You could start, Gran, by explaining how there came to be Baltic amber stitched into Kate's baby clothes when she was supposedly born here in England.'

'Baltic amber?' her father murmured.

'Sewn into the bodice of Mum's baby gown, which was tucked inside the bundle she was apparently carrying when she arrived at Pursey Street orphanage aged two or two and a half.'

'Ah!' he said, and exchanged a long, silent glance with her grandmother. 'Perhaps it is time that you did indeed tell the whole story, Millie.'

'But . . .'

'No more buts, dear lady. As Abbie says, she does have a right to know, and hard as it may be for you to recall the difficulties of that time, you are the only one who can tell it.'

THIRTEEN

Everything changed when Stefan came to work for the Countess. The first sign of spring began to show itself in a melting of the ice on the River Neva, although there was still plenty of snow around. The Count decided a visit to the family's country estate was called for. A few servants had gone on ahead to prepare the house for the family, leaving the rest of the staff behind in St Petersburg. We travelled by train and made the remainder of the journey from the station by sledge. This was a new experience for me so I was unprepared for the speed at which the sledge swished through the powdery snow, pulled by a high-trotting grey mare.

I felt secretly thrilled and oddly nervous to be seated up front beside Stefan, although 'bounced' might be a more appropriate word. *Nyanushki* sat behind with the children. *Babushka* was with the Count and Countess. We were all well wrapped up in *shubas*, leggings and fur hats beneath huge bearskin rugs. I was deeply conscious of Stefan's closeness, finding it hard to concentrate on the road ahead as I'd much rather gaze upon the handsome set of his angular features.

Stefan had barely spoken to me since joining us. Even when I'd given him the Countess's request he'd merely nodded and said,

'As her ladyship demands,' without even a thank you or any sign of gratitude. Why he fascinated me as he did, I had no idea, as he seemed an extremely rude young man.

For something to say to fill the uneasy silence between us I remarked upon the several small wooden sheds that littered the snow-covered hills and meadows around.

'What kind of animals are kept in those?' I casually asked, thinking of the cow byres back home.

'Those are log houses where the peasants live,' Stefan coldly informed me.

I flushed with embarrassment at my mistake and hastily apologised. 'I beg your pardon. I didn't realise.'

His smile was sardonic, with little sign of forgiveness at my ignorance. I had such mixed feelings about this man. I loved his smiles and occasional display of charm, yet there was something about him that felt almost dangerous. I forced myself to concentrate on what he was saying.

'Peasants were granted their freedom and citizenship during the rule of Tsar Alexander II. Unfortunately, many were simply turned out to fend for themselves, without any land from which they could earn their living and enjoy that freedom. This has bred a long-festering resentment which led to the failed revolution of 1905, and very likely the recent assassination.'

My reaction to this was one of horror. 'Oh, no, not another assassination? *Babushka* had told me about the bomb that killed Alexander II, but that was in the last century, a long time ago.' I felt so ignorant on the subject of Russian politics. An innocent abroad, indeed.

'Prime Minister Stolypin was shot dead at the opera last September. It wasn't the first attempt upon his life. He always wore body armour and had guards to protect him against the revolutionaries, but it wasn't enough to save him.'

'How dreadful!' I was at a loss as to what else to say, aware of a certain pragmatic quality in his tone, almost as if he thought the poor man deserved this terrible fate. 'Why did they kill him?'

'Stolypin had planned to bring in land reform to allow peasants to buy land, hoping to win back their loyalty to the Tsar. The middle classes and aristocracy did not agree. Also, back in 1905 Tsar Nicholas had allowed the formation of the Duma as an advisory elected body, with an agreement to grant it more legislative powers once it became established. Unfortunately, His Imperial Highness has not abided by that promise, apparently reluctant to relinquish any of his power which he believes to be God given.'

A harsh bitterness had crept into his voice, and judging from Stefan's earlier reluctance to work for the Count, I began to wonder if he was actually in sympathy with these so-called revolutionaries. 'So are you saying the Prime Minister's plans weren't working because some peasants couldn't afford to buy land?'

He did smile at me then, as if pleased I was listening, which quite warmed my heart. 'In a way the reforms caused yet more repression by dismantling agricultural communes. Thousands of people were executed or put into penal servitude when they protested. Stolypin even objected to trade unions. Their rights were being ignored. Whether his so-called reforms were for good or ill, nothing will come of them now.'

'I see.' I wasn't entirely sure that I did see at all. But could that possibly be a note of satisfaction I detected in his voice? Surely no one would be pleased at the death of someone in such circumstances, even a politician who was apparently failing to deliver his promises? A little shiver went down my spine as I realised there must be much more to this story than Stefan was admitting. 'Thank you for explaining this to me. I knew nothing of such matters, and might well have thought twice about coming to Russia if I had.'

His gaze was searching as he looked at me, as if memorising every feature. 'Then I'm glad you didn't know,' he quietly remarked, 'or I would never have had the pleasure of meeting you.'

Slightly unnerved by the soft intimacy of his words, I quickly turned away to look with fresh eyes upon what still appeared to be very like the cow byres we have in the Lake District. I felt a great pity for their occupants, who seemed to be treated little better than animals.

The Belinsky home, by contrast, was fabulous with a palatial grandeur, classical columns and a double flight of granite steps leading up to the magnificent entrance. Inside it was a picture of polished parquetry floors, crystal chandeliers, marble, mosaic tiles and gilt-framed furniture. The turquoise-painted walls of the main drawing room were adorned with delicate plaster figures, vases, dados and corbels. It was perfectly evident that the level of Count Vasiliy Belinsky's riches was far beyond my comprehension.

Was it this contrast between rich and poor that explained Stefan's harsh attitude towards the aristocracy, or was there more to it than that? I felt decidedly uncertain about his part in all the political goings-on he'd mentioned, and a strange reluctance to question him further on the subject. I had a great deal still to learn, not only about Russia, but also about Stefan himself.

I thoroughly enjoyed that first weekend in the country and had great fun tobogganing with the children as it reminded me so much of home. Every winter at the first sight of snow we would borrow one of my mother's big tea trays and go off sledging down Benthwaite Crag. I certainly knew how to keep my head down and hold on tight when going round corners. Skating, however, was a skill I had never acquired as my father had always been rather nervous about how long the ice would remain solid on the lake.

'Russia is different. The ice lasts for months,' Stefan assured me as he set about finding me a pair of skates that fit. Snow was falling even as I ventured out onto the ice for the first time. Both children, even little Irina, were surprisingly skilled but though I was eager to learn and join in the fun, laughing along with them whenever I took a tumble, I cautiously kept to the edges of the frozen river.

Little by little I became more confident and steadier on my feet. I didn't even mind the icy air whistling around me as I cautiously ventured a little further out onto the ice, although I did tug my fur hat closer about my ears.

'I'll have to leave you to it now,' Stefan called. 'I must go and feed the hens, and see to the horses. Just take things slowly.'

'Don't worry, I'll be fine.' But as I half turned to speak to him, my feet did a crazy little dance, flipped from beneath me and down I went again. 'Oh dear, spoke too soon. I certainly won't be training for the Russian figure skating championship,' I laughed.

Irina came swishing over to help me to my feet. 'You can hold my hand, *Baryshnya*, if you like. I'll help you.'

The children, and the other servants, always addressed me as *Baryshnya* – Miss – which made me feel slightly distanced from them. But then being a governess seemed to set me in a class of my own, which wasn't always easy. Was that why I valued this growing friendship between Stefan and myself so much? I wondered. Or did I miss the kind of flattering attention I used to get from Liam? It certainly couldn't be anything more than that, as he was not an easy man to get to know.

'Thank you. That is so kind of you, Irina.' I was growing very fond of this lovely little girl, who had the sweetest nature. Not at all like her brother. Together we skated very gently to and fro, Irina helping me to practise my turns and stops. Sometimes these worked quite well but at other times I would get in a dreadful muddle and end up skimming the ice on my bottom yet again.

'Don't worry, *Baryshnya*, it gets easier,' she assured me, giggling as she dusted the snow from my coat once more.

'I'll take your word for it,' I sighed, beginning to feel decidedly sore in various departments of my anatomy.

'Take no notice of her. I'll show you how it should be done,' Serge said, circling around me, a great grin on his face. Then, grabbing my wrist, he started to drag me further out on to the ice.

'Stop it, Master Serge, that's far enough,' I protested, but he didn't seem to be listening.

'You need more space to skate properly. It's no good hugging the bank. Keep going. That's right. Come on – faster, faster.'

My feet were flipping along like mad things, gaining momentum and moving as if of their own volition. I could feel myself losing control and fear shot through me like an icy sword. 'That's far enough Master Serge. Take me back at once, *please*!' I shouted.

To be fair, he did pay heed to the panic in my voice, and perhaps thinking better of this naughty prank, began to slow his pace and turn for the shore, which was a huge relief to me. I was thankful, too, that he maintained his tight hold on my wrist. I could see Irina standing with her hands pressed to her mouth in dismay, anxiously awaiting my safe return. We'd almost reached her when Serge suddenly let go, and flinging up his hands, went into a little skid and skated right in front of me so that we collided.

The impact on my shoulder sent me spinning out of control, heading towards the bank at great speed. Quite unable to do anything to stop myself, I cannoned into a ridge of snow and then bounced back onto the ice, where I heard a terrifying cracking sound. I fully expected to fall through to the icy water beneath. Fortunately, I was saved by a tree root that stuck out into the frozen river. I hung on to it like a life-line, which is exactly what it was.

Puffs of my gasping breath misted the air about me, and I was so relieved to be at least lying still that it wasn't until Irina reached me and cried out in horror that I realised one leg had indeed crashed through the ice. I couldn't even feel it.

She quickly pulled the leg out and, small as she was, started to drag me to the shore, all the while shouting at the top of her voice. '*Help*! *Help*! Serge, run for help quickly. *Baryshnya* is hurt.'

'Don't worry, I'm fine,' I assured her, though my head was still spinning and I was so cold I could hardly feel any part of me, let alone one wet leg.

I could hear voices as people came running: Stefan with a couple of footmen, who together dragged me clear of the ice. But it was only after they had carried me safely inside and Stefan had rushed to fetch a towel to rub my leg dry that I understood the reason for Irina's panic. As he pulled off my boot, it seemed frostbite was already setting in, and while at first I felt nothing, later as my foot began to thaw out the pain was beyond description. Never had I known such agony. I felt certain I would not survive it and just wanted to lie down and weep, or rather yell, but Stefan refused to allow me to do that.

'You must keep moving. Walk up and down, constantly. You'll need to keep exercising that foot for days to get the circulation going properly,' he insisted, not letting me sit still for a moment. 'How did the accident happen? Why didn't you stay close to the edge, as I told you?'

I darted a glance at Serge, who stood silently watching the efforts to save my foot. As he lifted his head to meet my gaze, I knew instantly that the 'accident' had been nothing of the sort. The tell-tale light of guilt in his dark eyes told me it had been entirely deliberate. He had fully intended for me to crash through the ice. That being the case, one frostbitten foot was nothing compared to what might have happened.

'Well?' Stefan repeated. 'Why did you skate out so far on your first attempt?'

I gave a pathetic little smile. 'Because I'm a silly young girl. But don't worry, I've learned my lesson. I shall take much better care in future.' This last remark was directed not at Stefan but at quite another person altogether.

~

Following the incident on the ice, Serge issued another of his furious little threats. 'If you tell Papa that it was me who knocked you over, I'll say you lied and have you dismissed.'

I smiled down at him, feeling so sorry for this insecure little boy, thoroughly spoiled by his mother but feeling very much a failure in the eyes of his father, whom he was clearly desperate to impress. Did the Count deliberately ignore Serge in order to punish his wife for being so hard on Irina? What a pair they were. 'I can't think what you mean, Master Serge. My feet were quite beyond my control. It was an accident, certainly no fault of yours. Let's forget about it, shall we?'

'You aren't going to tell Papa, then?'

'Of course not. Why would I? You and I are friends, aren't we? Why would you want to hurt me?'

There was disbelief and what might have been gratitude in his startled gaze. Nothing further was said on the subject and I kept my expression carefully bland.

Babushka had also accompanied us to the country, and sent a message with *Nyanushki* asking if I was well enough to continue with our occasional reading sessions.

'I'm pleased Madame is here. It will be good for her to have a change of scene. And don't worry, I'll be glad of a sit-down after all this exercise for my foot. In any case, I'm very fond of the old lady and love spending time with her.'

The first evening I spent with her, reading *The Old Curiosity Shop*, which seemed to be one of her favourites, she was more interested in hearing about my 'accident' and if my foot had recovered.

'It's fine,' I assured her. 'Despite my foolish incompetence.'

Her brow creased in a doubtful little frown. 'Was Serge involved in any way? As we know, my grandson does have a somewhat roguish sense of humour.'

He does indeed, I thought. A streak of mischief I neither understood, nor, with my limited experience, was able to control. I had hoped to win him round through friendship, but appeared to have left myself even more vulnerable to his naughty tricks. Nevertheless, I assured *Babushka* that her grandson was not involved, crossing my fingers against the lie, determined to give the boy a chance. 'I will admit that I haven't found him an easy child, despite your helpful suggestions. Do you have any more advice on how best to deal with him?'

'Don't give in to his demands. He twists his foolish mother round his clever little finger, doing exactly as he pleases, knowing she will never reprove him. It does the boy no good at all. A firm hand is what he needs if he is not to grow up as manipulative and selfish as she.'

I was astonished by the bitter candour of these remarks; she was surprisingly critical of her daughter, but took care not to show it. 'I do try to be firm, but the boy has a mind of his own,' I said.

'I'm afraid he does, and of course he is very jealous of his little sister, believing their father pays her far too much attention.'

'I did wonder about that. It's a great pity brother and sister can't get along better.' Refilling the old lady's tea cup, I chose my next words with care, making them sound light and frivolous. 'She does seem to be her daddy's girl. Whereas I do sometimes think that the Countess would have preferred another boy rather than a girl.'

She looked at me then with the kind of expression my own mother would have described as inscrutable. 'There are times when a child is not welcome no matter what its gender,' she said.

I frowned, in my innocence not fully understanding what she could mean. 'How sad for the Countess not to have wanted any more children, when Miss Irina is so sweet.'

'Some matters are best not investigated too closely.'

Inclining my head in polite acknowledgement, I returned to *The Old Curiosity Shop* and continued reading. Whatever secret she was hiding, the old lady obviously had no intention of sharing it.

FOURTEEN

I had so much to tell Ruth the next time I attended the British and American chapel. 'I'm not sure I like your friend Stefan very much,' I said as we sipped tea and ate slices of seed cake. 'He seems rather militant.'

She gave a little shrug. 'He certainly has a different view of life than we do, but then he has good reason to.'

'Really? Why is that?'

'For one thing, he's Russian, and we're English. How can we possibly understand how he feels about things, however sympathetic we might be to his cause?'

'What cause would that be, exactly?'

She rolled her eyes. 'Don't expect *me* to explain. Ask Stefan if you're really interested.'

I thought about this for a while as Ruth joined in the general chat with the other British governesses. I assumed she meant defending the poor, which seemed a rather risky pursuit judging by what he'd told me. I did sometimes see what might be termed peasants attempting to board a tram, only to be pushed off again by the conductor, claiming they were drunk when they were obviously only fatigued. On one occasion it had been a woman with a child in her arms and I suddenly found myself leaping to my feet, telling the conductor in my bad Russian that the woman was with me. I even paid her fare, for which she was most grateful.

But how involved was Stefan? Just because he sympathised with their plight didn't make him a revolutionary. Or did it?

Interrupting my thoughts, Ruth whispered in my ear. 'In point of fact I rather think you like him more than you care to admit. I've seen your expression when he's around. Your whole face lights up, and you can't take your eyes off him.'

'That's simply not true,' I hissed under my breath, but she only laughed. Were my feelings so transparent? I felt instantly ashamed of nursing secret desires for this good-looking but complex man.

'Actually, I think he's rather taken with you, too. What would you say if he were to ask you out?' she teased.

'Don't be silly. It isn't worth considering. I have enough to worry about with my new job without adding further complications to my life. I've certainly no time for romance or to allow myself to be flattered by charming young men.'

'So you do think him charming, then?'

I blushed. 'That's not what I meant. In fact, he's the absolute opposite at times. I'm saying that keeping the Countess happy takes all my time and energy. She is not an easy woman to please. Can we change the subject, please?'

Our visits to the country estate became more regular after that, and the Countess would frequently send me on some errand or other in search of the impossible. She made no allowance for the fact that in the country it was but a tiny village shop, that I couldn't just pop along to the Nevsky Prospekt. One afternoon she sent me on just such a wild goose chase for a particular type of expensive chocolate. When I returned with something entirely different, she reacted with a childish show of temper.

'This isn't what I asked for,' she shouted. 'I don't care for biscuits.'

'I'm sorry, your ladyship, but the chocolate you requested is not stocked in the village shop.'

'Then you must insist that they *do* stock it,' she snapped.

'I hardly think that likely as no one else in the community could afford to buy such expensive chocolate.'

She gave me a frosty glare, took a bite, grimaced, then held out the half-eaten biscuit to me. 'You bought it, you eat it.'

'No thank you, your ladyship.'

'Do as I say. Eat it!'

I drew myself up to my full height, slight though it was beside hers. 'You have already bitten into it, so why would I want to?'

'What you *want* is beside the point. *I* am your *mistress*, and you'll do as I say.' The fierceness of her tone, and the precision with which she uttered these words left me no choice. I took the biscuit from her hand and ate it, even though it near choked me. She smiled in triumph. As I turned to leave, determined to go before I said something I'd be sure to regret, she issued yet another order.

'Send Stefan to me. At once.'

'I'm afraid he's out, milady, probably exercising the horses.' In truth I'd no idea where he was, but I'd noticed that he would often disappear unexpectedly, whether into town or country, sometimes for hours at a time. Where he went or what he did, I had no idea.

'Well, he shouldn't be with the horses, not at this time of day. I need him *now*!'

'I will pass on your order when next I see him, but I have no idea when he will return.'

Her eyes narrowed and her fury escalated to such an extent that her normally pale face turned bright crimson. I fully expected her to threaten to sack him the moment he did appear, but instead she turned her wrath upon me. 'You're lying, Dowthwaite, no doubt because you've taken a shine to him yourself, and you know how he loves nothing more than to make himself available to *me*.'

I struggled to hide my shock at these words as I met the chill of her triumphant smile. Was she implying that Stefan was her latest lover? Surely not. Yet he was very good-looking, and there was no doubt she was not a faithful wife to her ever-patient husband. Wasn't the gardener Stefan replaced once her lover, until she dismissed him?

Later, when I related this conversation to Stefan, and asked him point-blank if it were true, he vehemently shook his head.

'Absolute nonsense! I'll admit the Countess has me constantly at her beck and call, acting as her personal chauffeur and footman, as well as handyman and general gardener. Today she wanted nothing more than for me to take her a tray of tea, for heaven's sake, as if I were her personal servant.'

'But that's what you are, Stefan,' I reminded him, wondering why she hadn't asked me to fetch the tea, yet knowing she'd flaunted this supposed liaison with Stefan to make me jealous, presumably as a form of petty revenge for my alleged failure to buy her the chocolate. To my great irritation, she had succeeded.

We were keeping our voices low as the children and I helped him to feed the hens, as they so loved to do. Even Serge would happily collect eggs and fill the water troughs.

'We are all at her beck and call,' I quietly pointed out. 'Even *Nyanushki* complains about being given far too many jobs – caring for *Babushka*, helping with the children, and even acting as the Countess's lady's maid while her regular one is away. Her Ladyship is very demanding.'

'And such a drama queen, always making a fuss and screaming at the Count for some alleged failure on his part. He simply walks away when he's heard enough while she throws priceless porcelain vases after his retreating figure. Why he puts up with her I cannot imagine.' Stefan shook his head in disbelief as I scooped out the old straw and replaced it with fresh, fascinated despite myself and wondering how he'd managed to learn so much about her.

'She does love to mock people and make their lives a misery, even *Babushka*, who really is a dear old lady who makes no fuss at all. Unlike her gentle mother, the Countess is completely profligate, with no idea of the value of money. So where were you this morning when you were absent without leave?' I asked.

'I don't believe I have to answer to her every demand,' he said, neatly avoiding my question. Then he leaned close to whisper his next words, his warm breath tickling my ear. 'I have discovered why she dislikes the little girl.'

'Really?'

Half-glancing over his shoulder, Stefan pulled me to one side, out of the children's hearing. 'Irina is not her daughter at all. She is the child of the Count's mistress, a woman he once wished to marry but was forbidden to do so by his parents.'

I stared at him in stunned surprise. So this was the subject *Babushka* had not wished to examine too closely, or at least was determined to keep secret, since she must know the truth of it. 'How do you know?'

'I pick up a lot of gossip in the kitchen among the other servants.'

'Would that explain why she is not faithful to the Count?'

'Oh, she was never that. It was an arranged marriage based on politics, land and money, not love in any shape or form. Even on their honeymoon, if you can call it that, she was apparently engaged in an affair with the groom. The story goes that the Count tried to make the marriage work, but soon grew tired of her antics and returned to his first love. Irina was the result.'

'Hence the reason Countess Olga resents her so much. Poor little Irina.' I looked across at the child, hunkered down chatting to a hen as if it were her best friend. 'How very sad. She is such a little sweetie who surely deserves a good mother to love her.'

Stefan gave my shoulder a gentle squeeze. 'Any love that child gets can only come from you, and her father, of course.'

Blinking back a sudden rush of tears as I recalled *Babushka* hinting at the very same thing, I nodded. 'You're right, and I'll see that she does. Thank you, Stefan.'

His hand slid down my back to my waist, sending a little shiver of longing through me at his touch. 'Love is important in life, don't you think?'

I looked up into his face, saw how his eyes scanned mine before focusing on my mouth. 'I think I'd better take the children inside now to get them ready for lunch,' I said with a smile, and beat a hasty retreat, quite forgetting that he still hadn't answered my earlier question.

~

'Why are you leaving us, *Baryshnya*?' Little Irina was sitting up in bed gazing up at me, her blue eyes filling with tears.

I quickly hunkered down to gather her in my arms. 'I'm not leaving. Wherever did you get that idea from?'

'*Mamochka* says you can't stay in this house another minute.'

I frowned, wondering what on earth I'd done wrong now, and whether the Countess really was about to hand me my notice. I felt sick at the thought. Despite the difficulties in pleasing her, I was growing so fond of her children that the thought of losing them was extremely painful, if rather unprofessional. Surely it couldn't simply be that she saw me as a rival for Stefan's attention and wanted him all to herself? Wasn't that what she'd accused me of?

'How do you know all this, Miss Irina? Have you been listening at doors again?' I knew her for a secretive child, who loved to hide under tables or behind doors to listen in on grown-up conversation.

Putting her hand to her mouth to stifle a giggle, the little girl nodded. 'I was under Papa's desk. He'd been playing a game with me after tea, and then *Mamochka* marched in and he whispered to me to hide. So I did. Papa was very cross and said he would make sure you stayed. He knows that you love us, you see. You do love us, don't you, *Baryshnya*?'

'Of course I do, sweetheart.'

'Even Serge?'

'I love both of you equally, and I love this job, so I have no intention of leaving. Not unless I have to,' I quietly added.

She put her arms about my neck and gave me a warm hug. She smelled of the lavender oil that had been in her bath water, and the jam she'd eaten with her scone at supper. 'I love you too, *Baryshnya*. You will stay, won't you? I don't want you to leave.'

'Neither do I.' The voice from the door of the schoolroom caught me by surprise as it was Serge, and this was the last remark I would have expected from him. He sauntered in, hands in pockets attempting to appear unconcerned and quite casual, but there was a tightness about his young face which was very telling. 'I don't go in for all this love stuff like my silly sister, but starting over again with another governess would be a nuisance.'

'Yes,' I agreed quite seriously. 'I can see that it would be, Master Serge. I do hope you won't feel it necessary to do so.'

He looked up at me then, a growing boy almost as tall as me. 'I hope so too.'

'Then I think we all understand each other,' I said, smiling at them both. 'Shall we play a game of Snap before bedtime?'

'Ooh, yes please,' Irina cried and Serge quickly brought the cards.

~

Thankfully, nothing more was said about my leaving and, despite my rather inauspicious start, visiting the country came to be a genuine pleasure, a regular event over the coming months. I did, however, continue to keep a watchful eye on Serge in case he tried any more of his little tricks, taking careful heed of *Babushka's* advice, but his behaviour seemed much improved. Perhaps our truce since the incident on the ice was truly working. Each day I would take the children down to the village, little more than a huddle of miserable little huts, but they did so love to visit the tiny shop to buy themselves some sweets or biscuits. Not that it had much of interest on sale – mainly black bread, strings of sausages and a few essential household items and cleaning products.

Stefan would drive us in the cart and, despite my reservations, I couldn't help but begin to share his concern for the very evident signs of poverty I saw all around. 'The peasants are having a hard time of it, yet the Tsar doesn't even seem to notice, let alone care,' he grumbled.

'Perhaps he does, but is having difficulties putting things right. Poverty is not an easy problem to resolve.'

'I can't believe that.'

'Why are you so anti-aristocracy? I've always enjoyed working for the gentry, and but for them, you and I would both be without a job. Isn't it good that they at least provide employment?'

'It depends upon what terms, and how much they try to lord it over us.'

I laughed. 'I freely admit I have to bite my tongue on occasion over remarks the Countess makes. She did rather um and ah over whether I should be allowed an afternoon off when I first arrived. But I stood my ground and won in the end.'

He looked at me with new admiration in his eyes. 'Good for you. So when you dine with the Count and Countess each evening, do you ever hear anything of interest that might give the working classes hope?'

I frowned, as I still recalled the argument we'd had when first we'd met. 'I'm not a spy, so stop asking me such questions. In any case, what is there to hear? By all accounts the Tsar and Tsarina live a quiet life in the country with very little formality. Even the servants are apparently instructed to call their daughters by their first name, and not use their titles, which seems quite democratic to me, or so *Babushka* tells me.'

Stefan snorted his disdain. 'Merely putting on a show, in my opinion, safe in their cloistered world. His Imperial Highness has little idea of how real people live, that many are attempting to become better educated and demanding more from life. He has ignored their valiant efforts to improve their lot for years.'

'So what was it that happened back in 1905?' I quietly asked, feeling the need to better understand Stefan's point of view.

He was silent for a long time, hunched over the reins, his face and expression hidden by his collar and slouch cap. Only the *clip-clop* of the horse's hooves, and the innocent chatter of the children behind us, could be heard in the silence that followed. Stefan didn't speak until they were inside the village shop, happily choosing their sweets while we stood waiting for them at the door.

'A party of workers gathered in the streets of St Petersburg, asking with all due respect for their working conditions to be improved. It would include an eight-hour day and a decent level of pay. Many of the demonstrators were women and children, their numbers quickly growing into the thousands, but all very calm and well organised. Then it went horribly wrong.'

'Why? Didn't the Tsar agree to listen to their concerns?'

'The Tsar and Tsarina were absent. As so often happens, they were at Tsarskoe Selo, where it is considered safer for them to be kept hidden behind wire fences and an army of protectors. Back in St Petersburg, someone panicked at the size of the demonstration and ordered the guards to open fire to dispense the crowds. They did so, not over the heads of the crowd as they have done in the past but into their midst. Over two hundred people were killed that day, including my father.'

He paused, overcome by emotion, and I gazed upon him in horror. 'Oh, Stefan, how terrible! I am so sorry.'

After a moment he continued more slowly with his tale, keeping his voice low so that passers-by could not overhear. 'Those who fled from the massacre were hunted down and killed by the Cossacks and mounted guards. Bloody Sunday indeed,' he said, bitterness harsh in his tone. 'My father was found some streets away, so must have run for his life. But even he, fit as he was, could not outrun a galloping horse. If only the Tsar had been present at the Winter Palace and agreed to meet with the deputation, then everything would have been different. Now he faces an almost impossible task regaining the loyalty of the working classes.'

'I should think so,' I conceded. 'Even though he clearly did not give the order, as he was not in St Petersburg at the time. Do you know who did?'

'Rumours were rife but it's not certain. Certainly a grand duke was assassinated by the revolutionaries some weeks later by way of retaliation, so maybe it was him. There's little doubt that it was one of the Tsar's autocratic relatives. I had other things to worry about at the time. Losing my father destroyed my mother, while I could only watch helplessly as she faded away and died of grief. I'd just turned seventeen and went a bit off the rails for a while. It's an impressionable age. Even now the anger created in me that day still churns within.'

'I'm sure it does.' My heart went out to him in sympathy. I longed to put my arms about him, but didn't dare risk it, not in this public place.

At length he asked, 'I don't suppose the Count has ever said if the Tsar is yet willing to improve the lot of the workers?'

Sighing, I shook my head. 'No more questions, Stefan, please. What would *I* know? I'm a simple country girl from Westmorland who never understood politics in England, so attempting to get to grips with it here is a lost cause.'

'As is Russia in many respects,' Stefan murmured.

'I don't believe that for a moment.' Reaching for his hand as it gripped the horse whip he was flicking against his thigh, I gave it a little squeeze, the nearest I dared offer by way of comfort. 'Don't upset yourself by talking about this any more. Let it go.'

He looked into my eyes and, taking a deep breath in an effort to regain control over his emotions, gave me a little smile. 'You're right. There must be more interesting things you and I could talk about, not least the way you stand up to the Countess. I rather admire that brave spirit in you.'

I gave a little grimace. 'I do have a very bad habit of speaking my mind. My father says I should try to engage my brain before I open my mouth.'

He laughed out loud, and the atmosphere between us lightened considerably. 'You've also risen to the challenge of dealing with those spoiled children without losing your temper,' he said in a soft whisper as he lifted Irina back into the cart, applauding as Serge jumped in without asking for assistance. Clicking the reins to urge the old horse to walk on, he said in a low voice. 'I think even young Master Serge is falling under your spell.'

I thought about this for a moment and smiled. 'You may be right. Certainly our relationship has improved of late.'

'That's because you have an undeniable charm, Millie. May I call you Millie? And you are looking particularly fine today in that pretty blue gown. I like the way your hair is tied into a braid on top of your head, as tidy and well-organised as you are yourself, although I'd love to see it flow loose and free on occasion. You too, for that matter.'

My cheeks were flushing bright pink at these compliments, remembering that Liam had once said something of the sort about my hair. But I wasn't interested in Liam now. I loved the way Stefan was looking at me in that teasing way he had. I could scent the delicious maleness of him, feel the pressure of his hard thigh against mine. 'Perhaps it would be safer to stick to politics after all,' I said, and we both laughed.

How could I have imagined for one moment that he was involved with the revolutionaries? It pleased me that he meandered home at a slow pace, as I was greatly enjoying his company.

FIFTEEN

A flicker of spring sunshine broke through the clouds as Abbie drove down the leafy lanes towards town, her mind still turning over her grandmother's story, filled with admiration at her courage in handling such a tricky situation with a young, clearly disturbed young boy. How brave she was, but also vulnerable when it came to Stefan's charm. She smiled. So now it was her turn to step into her grandmother's shoes and prove she, too, was up to a challenge.

Abbie looked about her with a sigh of pleasure, enchanted as always by the wildness of Scafell and Hardknot where once whole troops of Roman soldiers would march from nearby Ambleside to the port of Ravenglass on their route to Ireland. Now these fells were the haunt of enthusiasts who walked for pleasure and who, with Easter now over, were already filling the streets of Carreckwater with the clatter of their boots and bulging rucksacks.

Parking the old Ford by St Margaret's church, Abbie delivered Aimée to school with lots of encouraging hugs and assurances that she'd be there to pick her up at three o'clock.

'Why didn't Jonathon come with us?' the little girl asked, as she lingered uncertainly at the school gate, holding rather tightly to Abbie's hand.

'Aunty Fay wanted to bring him herself, since, like you, this is his first day. In future she and I will probably take turns. Will that be all right with you?'

Aimée nodded. 'I like Cousin Jonathon. I wish he was here now. I don't know anyone, and they don't speak French.'

'You'll soon make new friends, darling, and it's not a bad thing to be able to speak two languages.'

The child looked up at her mother, wide-eyed. 'Will Daddy be coming soon? I miss him.'

Abbie hunkered down to her height, feeling that familiar tightening sensation in her throat. 'Me too, and I'm sure he'll come to see you as soon as he can,' she said, secretly hoping he would do no such thing. Not yet anyway, not until she felt more settled and in control of her emotions. After that, they would surely be able to come to some satisfactory arrangement whereby Aimée could visit him for holidays. 'We must both be very brave as we start our new life. I'll be here at the gate for you, sweetheart, on the dot of three.' As she gave her daughter another hug her new teacher, Mrs Sanderson, suddenly appeared.

'Hello Aimée, everyone is so looking forward to meeting you. Few of our pupils have met anyone who can speak French before, and are really excited. I suspect they'll make quite a fuss of you. Shall we go and meet them?'

With a quick glance at Abbie, who smiled her encouragement, Aimée took the teacher's hand and went off quite happily.

Giving a sigh of relief, Abbie didn't move until Aimée had turned and waved before entering her new classroom. It was going to be all right, she told herself firmly. We'll survive.

But instead of hurrying along Carndale Road straight to the shop, she found herself taking a detour through Fairfield Park on to the Parade. As she strolled along past the band stand and up the incline by the tall Victorian villas, Abbie recalled how the teacher had said Kate would often visit old ladies who lived here. How astonishing that she was such a stalwart of the community. Abbie's own memory of her mother was entirely different, of a woman with a closed past who believed she alone knew what was right for her daughter.

Following the row in which Kate had told her of the secretarial course she'd booked without her permission, and Abbie had even more bluntly announced her pregnancy, there had been the expected recriminations later. It was the kind of argument no family should ever have, one she preferred not to think about now, realising how her parents had probably been right all along. She had been impetuous and naïve, far too trusting.

Not that she had thought so at the time. Abbie had run to Eduard the very next afternoon meeting him at their special place in the woods as they did every day, and she'd poured out to him all the terrible things that had been said. 'They aren't in the least interested in my happiness, or yours,' she'd sobbed, falling into his arms in despair. 'Not even when I told them about the child.'

Eduard had gone very still. 'Child! What are you saying Abbie?'

She'd beamed cheerfully up at him, loving the startled expression of surprise in his dear sweet face. 'I'm pregnant, didn't I tell you?' she teased, knowing she'd deliberately put off telling him, nervous of his reaction.

'How far gone are you?' he'd quietly asked.

'About three months, I think, though I really should see a doctor to be sure. Mum and Dad are definitely *not* happy people. Sooo old-fashioned. Oh, but *I* am, *darling* Eduard. I couldn't be more thrilled,' she'd cried, flinging her arms about his neck and hugging him tight.

It was true that she'd felt a certain guilt at the hurt and disappointment she'd seen in her parents' reaction. Even worse when they'd learned that Eduard was actually married, and entirely without sympathy for his plight of being saddled with a woman he no longer loved.

'It won't take long for your divorce to come through, will it?' she'd asked. Back then she'd believed implicitly in her lover. 'It's nearly my birthday, they'll surely give permission once I turn eighteen, but what if they don't?'

'I can wait, no matter how long it takes,' Eduard had blithely assured her, putting a comforting arm about her shoulders, although his expression still revealed his shock at the news.

'You may grow tired of waiting if it takes till I'm twenty-one,' Abbie had pouted. 'Or find someone else.'

'Never!' As if to prove his devotion he'd given her a long lingering kiss, if not quite as passionate as usual it had still made her tremble with longing. 'I'm sure your parents will come round, given time.'

'But we don't *have* time.' Abbie had found it impossible to imagine a life without Eduard. She'd seen him as her soul-mate, and as his kisses had deepened and grown more demanding, filling her with a need she'd never experienced quite so strongly before, she knew in her heart that he must love her.

The day they'd left for Paris her father had done his utmost to make Abbie change her mind, insisting that Eduard never would marry her.

How tragic that he'd been proved right.

Now she gazed up at the bay windows, arched doorways and wrought iron balconies of this fine row of houses, built by the rich cotton magnates of the last century. She heard a door bang as an elderly man came out of one, nodding politely as he passed her. Presumably they were now divided into flats but the old folk who occupied them must become quite lonely stuck up here at the edge of town. Perhaps she should make enquiries about taking over her mother's charitable task?

But then Abbie remembered she'd have more than enough to occupy her getting the business back on its feet. Spinning on her heel she hurried back down the Parade and along Carndale Road, realising she was going to be late, which wouldn't do at all on her first morning.

~

Abbie sat in the newly cleaned workshop wondering where to begin. All the plans she'd secretly made over the last few weeks seemed to have vanished, leaving her mind blank and panic creeping over her again.

It was all very well to boast about her experience in the Parisian fashion industry to her father, and insist she could turn the jewellery business around, but quite another matter to actually do it. Marisa had been most conciliatory and supportive when she'd rung to say she wouldn't be returning to Paris. Abbie had also made a point for thanking her ex-employer for the excellent training she'd received while working in the boutique. Since then she'd spent hours studying the accounts, which showed that profits were well down, and either expenses were up or her mother was over-indulging herself as far more money was drawn out than came in. Kate obviously did lose interest as she'd never seemed to replace the stock she sold, merely spent the money.

The overdraft as a consequence was worryingly large, which meant that one of Abbie's first tasks was to talk to the bank manager. She'd made an appointment for later in the week, not a prospect she looked forward to. As Abbie had no money of her own to invest in the business she'd need to request a further loan. She was beginning to wonder if she was right to even attempt to save the shop. It could already be too late.

Linda placed a mug of black coffee beside her, together with a sheath of papers. 'I've completed a stock check, which I thought might be useful. Didn't take long, I'm afraid, as we don't have anywhere near the quantity or variety of jewellery we once had.'

Abbie took the list from her. 'Thanks, that's great. I shall have a good nose around, if that's okay.'

'Feel free, it's your shop.'

Actually, it wasn't, but Abbie decided against mentioning the family dispute which showed no signs of ending. Robert had followed her out that morning, arguing furiously as she'd helped Aimée into the car and started the engine, coldly reminding her that the business had to be sold.

'Not if I can help it.'

'Saving this house is more important than a stupid jewellery shop.'

'Says who?' And she'd driven off leaving him shouting to himself.

Abbie spent the next hour going through drawers and cabinets. As Linda had warned there were not so many precious gems as she remembered, but still some lovely pieces. In addition to the jewellery, she came across a set of drawers containing lengths of silk and velvet, lining fabric, quilted cotton and even some gold leaf.

'Now what could I do with these?' she wondered. Fingering the fabric, and remembering the huge variety of beads and Swarovski crystals she'd seen tucked away in boxes, the answer came to her. She would make a selection of evening purses. Later, she might even try a design studded with cabochons, or patterned with gold leaf.

Abbie's excitement mounted as she set about finding the right tools for the task: round nose pliers, a pot of special glue and sewing materials. She might also need rings to attach a handle or strap, zips or press studs, but she could buy those later from the craft shop in Ambleside. The future was suddenly looking brighter as her optimism reasserted itself.

Time flew by as she drew out patterns, chose a selection of flat smooth beads that wouldn't catch on a person's clothing and began to play about with a design. She nursed a memory of her mother working at this very table, setting stones, making earrings, perhaps even creating bags like this. What had happened to turn her into a depressive and cause her to lose interest in what had once been her own precious dream? Tears pricked the backs of her eyes as she smoothed out a piece of fabric together with a layer of silk lining beneath, then carefully cut it into the correct shape using the pattern she'd made.

Abbie enjoyed arranging various swirls and loops with the beads, matching colours and shapes. Once she was satisfied with the design she began to stitch each bead on to the silk.

While nibbling a sandwich and sipping her third cup of coffee of the day she began to pick out some of the Swarovski crystals. She chose topaz and clear crystal, creating a design with a butterfly in pale jonquil yellow as the centre piece. Attaching the flat crystals upon the tiny dabs of craft glue she made with the aid of a toothpick was not easy, but seemed to work. Abbie became so engrossed that she was startled when Linda popped her head round the door to remind her it was almost time to pick up Aimée.

'Oh, my goodness, so it is. Must dash. I'll finish these tomorrow.'

'They're looking good,' Linda said, admiring the shine of sapphire and turquoise beads against the black silk, and I love the crystal butterfly. I think we have some pink mini shells too somewhere. You might be able to do something with those. I'll see if I can find them. You're really very clever.'

Abbie was pulling on her coat and grabbing her bag, fearful of letting her daughter down on her first day. 'Not really, and these still have to be made up into evening purses yet. There's a lot to learn but it's fun.'

Her first day at Precious Dreams had proved to be both exciting and nerve-wracking. Aimée too was excited about her new school, and the pair of them sang *Puff the Magic Dragon* all the way home in the car. This was to be their future. Didn't she owe it to her daughter to make a success of the business, if only for disrupting her life by walking out on her father whom Aimée adored? And the last thing she wanted was another lecture from her brother.

~

Abbie successfully managed to persuade the bank manager to extend the overdraft, if not by quite as much as she'd hoped. Nothing further had been said by her father about selling the business, but Abbie had decided it was time to approach the subject. One evening, having read Aimée a few pages from *The Cat in the Hat*, delighting in hearing her daughter recite some of her favourite phrases, she tucked her into bed and gave her a kiss, then went in search of her father to try one more time to gain his support. She found him, as expected, in the library, where he often retired at this time of night to read the paper.

Giving a quick tap on the door she pushed it open without waiting for a response. 'Hi Dad, can I have a quick word?'

Setting the paper aside with some reluctance, he nodded. Abbie pulled up a chair then placed the butterfly purse gently on his lap. 'I made that the other day. Mum used to make stuff like this, remember? So I thought I'd have a go too. What do you think?'

He stared at it, his expression pained as if he couldn't bear to be reminded of happier times, then quietly he handed it back. 'If you think making a few evening purses will get the business out of trouble you're living in cloud-cuckoo land.'

'I have other plans as well, if you'd like to hear them, such as stocking local jewellery and making some of my own.'

'But do you have any money to invest in it?'

'Not at present, no, but . . .'

'Well then, why risk further debts? We have enough of those already, largely because of that dratted business.'

Knowing her father's anger was largely born of his loss didn't make it any easier to deal with. 'Yes, but *why*?' she softly asked. 'Where have all these alleged debts come from?'

'Does it matter? Life. Eating. Living. Paying for the upkeep of this grand house. What's important is that the shop failed to deliver so it must go, *otherwise we'll lose everything.* You cannot deny reality.'

Abbie felt a deep nostalgia for those long-ago days when she'd been able to turn to her father, certain of his loving support. Now she lived in hope that she could win him round through effort and ultimate success. 'Look, it's almost the start of the tourist season and Carreckwater, like Ambleside and Windermere, is becoming increasingly busy. Please allow me at least the summer to prove myself before you make the decision to sell.'

He met her gaze unflinching. 'Robert is the accountant in this family and he believes selling that property is the only sensible solution.' Tom Myers rubbed a weary hand over his face. 'We have no choice in the matter if we are to save Carreck Place. Even if we don't actually own the house, we still need to maintain it for as long as we're allowed to live here.'

'I'm sure he exaggerates the problem, and there must be other options.'

'I'm sorry if this is causing you anguish, but you'd be far better off finding yourself a proper job.'

Abbie gasped. 'The jewellery shop *is* a proper job, and with good prospects.'

'In what respect? If your mother couldn't make it pay, why do you imagine you can?'

'Mum had grown weary of the business for some reason, but I'm young and enthusiastic, and I believe I have the energy and talent to succeed.'

He almost smiled at that. 'I admire your spirit, Abigail, but I'm not sure you've earned the right.'

She gave a brittle little laugh. 'For goodness sake, you can't keep on punishing me forever. I'm still your daughter, and if you do still love me . . .'

'Of course I do, haven't I said as much?

Taking his large square hand between her own she gave it a gentle squeeze. 'Then prove it. Please Pops, give me a chance. I love you too, and want so much to make you proud of me again, as well as do right by my own daughter.'

Tears filled his eyes as his gaze softened, but it took a while before the answer came. 'Very well, you have the summer to give these plans of yours a try.'

SIXTEEN

The next weeks flew by in a whirl of hard work and optimism. She spent hours every evening studying sales figures, worrying over what she dare risk buying as she juggled payments so as not to go over the agreed limit. Abbie and Linda completely reorganised the layout of the shop, setting the counters along each side instead of the previous somewhat haphazard approach which had just looked cluttered. Display cabinets and the two shop windows were completely transformed, given a far more exciting and modern appearance, each one themed by colour, style or content.

One whole section of a wall was lined with rails upon which were displayed a range of fun and funky fashion jewellery: ceramic poodle and peacock pendants, bunny rabbit and owl brooches, and butterfly, daisy and pansy earrings in tangerine, shocking pink, lemon yellow and lime green. Not only would they be certain to appeal to the summer visitors, but brighten the entire shop.

'And sales are up,' Abbie announced to Linda on a whoop of joy. 'Maybe we're on the right track at last.'

'You've performed wonders in just a few weeks.'

'I'd love to buy in some Greek and Indian, Art Nouveau and stained glass jewellery which is becoming fashionable, but I have to be a bit cautious not to buy too much at once.'

'Quite right. You don't want to take any unnecessary risks. Let's hope for a busy summer. Oh, and I sold another evening purse today. They're proving to be quite popular and selling steadily.'

'Excellent!' They would need a good tourist season if they were to have any chance of saving the business, but they'd made a good start. Abbie was thrilled with progress so far. Everything was going smoothly at last. Aimée had settled into her new school, taken there each day with Cousin Jonathon either by herself or Aunty Fay. Abbie had recently installed a small black and white TV in the stockroom where the two children would happily watch *Noggin the Nog* or *Blue Peter* if she needed to work a little later, although she always made sure they were home by five.

This was her day for the school run and she was carefully keeping an eye on the clock as she worked on a new design. Abbie was using a template to apply gold leaf to a piece of black silk, which she hoped to make up into a beautiful clutch purse, when there came a tap on the door.

As Linda never troubled to knock, she leaped from her stool, thinking she'd forgotten the time and it must be Joan Sanderson. Aimée's teacher had brought her daughter once before when Abbie was held up by a customer on Linda's day off. She was very kind and helpful in that respect, and was becoming quite a good friend. But on opening the door she came face to face with a stranger, a man in his late twenties or early thirties, looking decidedly hassled.

'Hi, sorry I'm late. I know the appointment was for two o'clock but I got held up by traffic. Andrew Baxter.'

Abbie politely shook the proffered hand, frowning in puzzlement. 'What appointment would that be, exactly? I haven't the first idea what you're talking about.'

He gave a grunt of annoyance. 'Oh, for goodness' sake. Are you saying Elaine didn't let you know I was coming?'

'Elaine?'

'The agent,' he answered impatiently, as if he really shouldn't need to explain.

Abbie considered this in thoughtful silence for some seconds. The man, she noticed, was tall, lean but muscular, with cropped dark brown hair rather spikily cut, piercing grey eyes, angular chin and a wide mouth that wasn't doing much smiling right now. 'Would that be the estate agent just along the road here?'

'For someone wishing to sell their business, you don't seem to be quite up to speed,' he commented, rather caustically in Abbie's opinion.

Only the slight raising of her eyebrows revealed her irritation. 'That might be because it isn't for sale.'

He glared at her, eyes darkening like storm clouds. 'What are you saying – that you've taken it off the market, that I've wasted my time driving all this way from Dumfries for no reason?'

Abbie tried a smile, hoping to soothe his growing temper. 'Actually, it was never on the market, not so far as I was concerned, although my brother might believe otherwise.'

'So this is a family feud?'

'You could call it that. I recommend you vent your wrath upon him. But do please come in and I'll put the kettle on. You must be worn out after such a long journey.'

'I don't have time for tea parties. Is this shop for sale or not?'

'Not,' she said, again attempting an apologetic little smile. It didn't work.

'Well, thanks for nothing,' he roared as he stormed out, slamming the door behind him.

'Goodness,' Linda said. 'And which northeast wind blew him in?'

'A Scottish one. Well, Elaine the estate agent, apparently, thanks to my brother. To be fair, he has driven a long way for no reason, as he was at pains to point out. Robert neglected to inform me that he'd put the shop on the market, despite Dad's agreement to allow me the summer to prove myself, let alone that someone was actually coming to view it.' She gave a little sigh, as if trying to calm her own temper. 'Believe me, he won't get away with it. I shall call on Elaine the estate agent right now, before I pick up Aimée, and make sure we don't have any more unpleasant viewers barging in.'

Linda went to the door to look down the road. 'I think he's gone in the Ring of Bells for a consoling drink.' Then turning to Abbie with a teasing smile in her eyes, she said. 'He was rather good-looking, though, wasn't he?'

Abbie blinked, then laughed. 'Absolutely gorgeous.'

That evening Abbie went at once to speak to her father, briefly explaining what had happened. His response was not encouraging. 'I very much doubt the property will sell quickly, so there's nothing lost in putting it on the market.'

'But I thought we had an agreement. So why is Robert being allowed to undermine my efforts, and without any discussion with me? You know full well I've been working my socks off these last weeks trying to get the business back on track, with some success, by the way.'

'Go back to your job in Paris, Abbie.' Her brother's voice from the door brought her swirling about, fresh anger erupting inside.

'Don't you *ever* presume to tell me what to do, or send prospective buyers round without telling me.'

'The house is far more important, even if we don't actually own it, which I'll admit came as something of a shock. However, we are apparently entitled to live out our lives here, which I fully intend to do. My family surely has that right.'

Tom gazed thoughtfully upon his son, as if for the first time beginning to question his motivation. 'Actually, it was your mother who had the right to spend her entire life here. I didn't know that myself until I read it in her will. Whether or not that right automatically passes on to any of us is the point in question, for which I don't yet have a clear answer.'

'Why would we not? Who is there to object?'

'Since I don't know who granted her that right, I really couldn't say, although I did receive a letter from someone laying claim to the house.'

'Who the hell was that?'

'No idea. Not only did I not recognise the name, I couldn't even read it. It was simply a blurred scribble.'

Robert was instantly suspicious. 'Ah, someone trying it on, some fraudster or other.'

Tom frowned, 'You could well be right.'

Abbie wondered how a supposed fraudster could have learned that Carreck Place was not actually theirs, but more important issues were concerning her right then. 'Nor do you have the right to put the shop on the market when I've been granted this summer to make it work,' she quietly but firmly pointed out.

Robert's response was to give a snort of derision. 'You're wasting your time. Even if you had the brains to operate a business it would not resolve the problem.' His condescending attitude enraged her all the more.

Her father said nothing, his expression having gone quite blank, no doubt once more locked in his own grief. Abbie lowered her voice to a hiss, anxious not to upset him further yet quite unable to let the matter drop so far as her brother was concerned. 'If you think you can destroy my efforts as well as blame me for Mum's death, do not for one moment expect me to roll over and helplessly submit. I'm a grown woman now with a mind of my own and you can rest assured I'll fight you every inch of the way.'

Having issued this bitter remark, which hurt her almost as much as it did Robert, judging by the wide-eyed shock on his face, she walked out of the room straight into Fay, who had clearly heard everything as she hovered outside. Her sister-in-law at once took Abbie into her arms. 'Don't be upset. I'm sure he doesn't mean to sound so unfeeling.'

'But he won't even give me a chance.'

'Robert's really worried about the financial situation; that's all it is. I'll speak to him, I promise. I'll persuade him to cool it and give you some time.'

'Thanks. I'd appreciate that,' said Abbie, and the two women exchanged another hug, even as the rumble of angry voices started up again in the library.

Unable to face further dispute that evening, Abbie arranged supper for herself and Aimée to be taken in her own room up in the attics. That was obviously where she belonged, with her views of no more value than those of the servants who used to occupy these quarters, of which apparently her grandmother had been one. She knew deep inside that the courage to stand up to her brother had come from hearing Millie's story. If a nursemaid could face a revolution and end up owning a house like this, surely she too could achieve something worthwhile.

~

After a largely sleepless night, as soon as Abbie had delivered Aimée to school the next morning she called in at Kirkby's, the family solicitor, to make an appointment for later that morning. If she had a battle on her hands, then she would need all the help she could get to fight it.

When finally she arrived at the shop, a few minutes after nine o'clock, she was met at the door by Linda, smiling and winking at her in an odd sort of way.

'He's back.'

'Sorry, who's back?' Her mind still on the family row, and what she needed to ask the solicitor, Abbie wasn't picking up the blatant hints Linda was giving her.

'The would-be buyer, Andrew Baxter. He's waiting for you in the office.'

'Is he indeed? We'll see about that,' said Abbie and, metaphorically rolling up her sleeves, she marched into the back where she found the man strolling about the stockroom as if he owned the place, or soon intended to.

'If you were hoping that I'd changed my mind, then you couldn't be more wrong.'

He turned towards her to offer the ghost of a smile. 'Ah, Miss Myers, I assure you I've called only to apologise for my rudeness yesterday.'

She'd quite forgotten how incredibly handsome he was, and for a moment found herself mesmerised by the softness of his grey eyes, which seemed entirely sincere. This morning he was wearing a navy blazer and grey slacks; there was a slight stubble on his chin which seemed to add to his attractiveness. It was a long time since a man had left her tongue-tied – since that day she'd first met Eduard. Closing her mind to the thought, and reminding herself she was no longer a naïve young girl, she tartly remarked, 'How very generous of you. But as I explained yesterday, this shop is not for sale, nor will it ever be if I have any say in the matter.' Although right now, she seemed to have none at all, so how did she manage to sound so positive?

'In my defence I would say that I've had rather a difficult time in recent months with one thing and another, and my patience is at a low ebb.'

'As well as suffering from a long, tiring drive.'

'Indeed.'

She looked at him more carefully, noticing for the first time the shadows beneath his eyes indicating a lack of sleep, and the cheekbones that were perhaps rather too prominent, as if eating had also been an issue. Maybe he too had problems, as did everybody, she supposed, and was surprised to find herself experiencing a touch of sympathy for the man. 'Apology accepted. Would you like that tea now, or do you prefer coffee?'

He visibly relaxed, his smile widening which for some reason caused her to warm to him even more. 'I wondered if perhaps I might offer you lunch, or maybe dinner, as compensation for the distress I caused you.'

Slightly startled by the offer but nonetheless curious to know more about this man, she gave a little shrug. 'Okay, why not? Lunch would be lovely.'

They agreed to one o'clock at the Ring of Bells, and as Linda overheard these arrangements being made as he left, she gave a wry smile and a flicker of her eyebrows.

'Don't start,' Abbie warned. 'Or read anything into it. It's just lunch, okay?'

'Okay,' Linda repeated with a giggle, then after a slight pause. 'But he's still gorgeous.'

Abbie walked back into her office and closed the door, choosing not to answer. Men, gorgeous or otherwise, were definitely not on her wanted list right now.

~

'So what can I do for you, Miss Myers?' the solicitor politely enquired, after having offered his condolences over the loss of her mother, and enquired after her young daughter. 'She's in the same class as my son. Gary is quite taken with her, and has been showing off his new-found knowledge of a few French words.'

Abbie laughed. 'Aren't kids wonderful the way they soak everything up? Just like sponges.' *Including the unhappiness between their parents*, Abbie thought. Aimée spoke regularly to her father on the phone but did appear to be settling as she'd been much happier recently. The important task now was to provide her child with a secure future here in Lakeland.

Taking a breath, she launched into an explanation of the improvements she'd already made at the shop. 'I've spoken to the bank manager, managed to wangle an extension on the overdraft, but this season is make or break. If I manage to pay that off, or at least get it well down, then I think the business would have a good chance of surviving. Sadly, I don't have the support of my family in this enterprise. My father, urged by my brother, I believe, has put the property on the market without my agreement. So I'm in need of some advice regarding my mother's estate. I'm wondering if I have any rights at all in the matter, if there's anything I can do to persuade them not to sell. I really love the shop, and need to build a good future for my daughter.'

While she'd been talking, John Kirkby had been sifting through papers in a folder on his desk. Now he appeared to be skimming through a rather important looking document. 'Haven't you seen your mother's will?' he asked, looking up, a slight frown puckering his brow. 'She made it some years ago, but it is no less valid for that. I have it here.'

Abbie shook her head. 'My father was very much against sharing it with us. But he did say that she'd left everything to him.'

'That is correct, barring one or two legacies. It was my late father, John Kirkby senior, who drew it up for her, and no doubt advised her at the time. One of those legacies concerns the jewellery business. I shall read you what it says. '. . . *I leave my company Precious Dreams in its entirety, including the property on Carndale Road, to my daughter Abigail Myers in the hope that she will eventually make a success of something in her life and properly provide for my granddaughter.*'

Abbie sat in a state of stunned disbelief. Had she heard correctly? Could this possibly be true? 'Are you saying that the business, and the shop property itself, are *mine*, Mr Kirkby?'

'John, please, and yes, I am indeed.'

She nodded, grateful for his friendship, of which she felt in sore need right now, but was completely at a loss for words.

He gave a wry smile. 'Not set down in the kindest terms, maybe, but nonetheless your mother obviously wanted to do the decent thing by ensuring that your future would be secure.'

'Why didn't my father tell me this?'

He looked a little discomfited by the question. 'At one time the family solicitor would be expected to read the will at the funeral, or soon after. That rarely happens nowadays, and the family is assumed to all have access to it. It is the role of the executors to see that all legatees are properly informed.'

'Which he failed to do.'

'Apparently so. I do apologise. Had I known . . .'

'It's not your fault. I believe we can put the blame upon my brother's influence here. Dad is in a real mess, not thinking clearly right now. He doted on my mother, absolutely adored her, and never disagreed with anything she said or did. Not even when she threw me out of the house in my rebellious teenage years.'

'Perhaps she wished to make up for that mistake,' the solicitor softly remarked.

Abbie gave a small sigh as a single tear rolled down her cheek. 'It would be good to think so, although she didn't sound too convinced I could succeed, did she? I will, though. I'll prove whatever small amount of faith she had in me was justified. And no one will stand in my way.'

~

An hour later over a ploughman's lunch of cheese and crusty rolls at the Ring of Bells, Abbie found herself relating much of this information to Andrew Baxter. Why she was being so open and honest with a complete stranger she really couldn't say. Maybe she simply needed to pour out all her frustration and he was a good listener. He certainly hadn't interrupted, or said much at all beyond repeating his apology for his bad manners yesterday.

Finally she stopped her rant to take a breath and slice off a piece of cheese. 'Sorry, I really shouldn't be troubling you with family squabbles. It's just that it came as a shock to find that I do actually own Precious Dreams, which was deliberately kept from me.'

'I'm not surprised you're annoyed. Whoever should have informed you of this inheritance is the one at fault. No doubt you'll have some strong words to say to him, or her, on the subject.'

Abbie thought again of her father still grieving for her mother, the pain no doubt worsened by learning he might have no right to remain in the house he'd believed to be his home for their entire marriage, and all the anger drained out of her. How could she possibly go on blaming him when he was suffering enough already? Her brother, however, was another matter, and she might well have further words with him on the subject. In fact, she rather looked forward to seeing his reaction when she told him that he had no rights over the business at all, that it was hers entirely to do with as she wished. At the same time, thinking of Fay, her heart quailed at the thought. She really had no desire to create yet another row. Why couldn't the matter be resolved in a civilised fashion?

Letting out a sigh, she said, 'I shall probably say very little, and hope that it all blows over. The family is still in shock following my mother's death.'

'I see. Was it unexpected?'

'I'd really rather not talk about it, if you don't mind.' How could she when she had no understanding of why Kate would take her own life? Abbie took a bite of cheddar instead, realising she was surprisingly hungry.

Andrew Baxter was nodding, his face etched in sympathy. 'Then we'll talk of other things, shall we? Shoes and ships and sealing wax . . .'

' . . . cabbages and kings.' Abbie laughed. 'Actually, it's talk of *many* things. Okay, so tell me what you would have done with my shop, had it been for sale?'

Setting down his glass, he leaned towards her, his voice taking on a note of enthusiasm that seemed to lift her own spirits along with his. 'I run a small chain of fashion accessory shops in the borders, and I'm looking to expand into the Lake District.'

'Fashion accessories?' She paused, the bread halfway to her mouth. 'You mean jewellery and handbags, the kind I'm selling now?'

He grinned at her. 'Haven't tried jewellery yet but I sell luggage, vanity cases and handbags, scarves and hair accessories etc. I didn't see any bags in your shop, beyond those rather charming evening purses.'

Abbie felt herself blushing as if he'd paid her a compliment – perhaps he had, unknowingly. Then she was frowning as she thought about exactly what he had said. 'Presumably you'll be looking for alternative premises now, since mine aren't available?'

'As a matter of fact I've put in an offer on the shop next door,' he calmly informed her, slicing a piece of pickle to add to his bread and cheese.

'*What*? The old gifts and greeting card shop?'

'That's the one.'

'So if your offer is accepted would that mean you'll be selling bags and fashion accessories right next door? And you might well sell jewellery?'

He slanted her a wry smile. 'I'll admit that was partly the attraction of buying your business.'

'So you intend to set up in competition to me?' she snapped. Abbie was beginning to steam quietly inside, her ire heating up all over again. She wished she could bite off her own stupid tongue for having been so open and friendly when this man seemed hell-bent on putting her out of business.

'Were that to happen, and I'm not saying it will, I doubt we'd step on each other's toes too much,' he was saying. 'We'd stock different styles of jewellery, different ranges, so we'd complement each other, in a way. But actually, what I had in mind . . .'

Abbie was on her feet in a second. 'Sorry, I'm far too distressed to talk about this right now, but it rather looks as if I have another fight on my hands. So be it,' and she walked out of the pub without even finishing her lunch.

~

Abbie found her brother down by the lake fishing, as he'd so loved to do as a boy. 'We need to talk.'

'I'm sure we do, but this isn't the moment. If you make too much noise you'll scare away the fish.'

Abbie bit her lip to still whatever she'd been about to say, having heard this admonition many times in the past. She'd been so sure that she wanted to confront her brother, tell him that Precious Dreams was hers and that he had no right to try and sell it, but being here with him now she felt torn. He'd been so hurtful to her recently that telling him the truth would be so satisfying, but underneath all that, she just wanted to get along with her brother again, to try and preserve some sort of family harmony. Much as she felt the need to stand up for her rights, there was something about the way Robert sat hunched over the rod, as he had done so often as a boy, but now with his face all pinched and pale, that gave her pause over choosing the first option. Maybe his financial problems were a real worry to him; she'd no wish to cause further upset, to Fay in particular. Pulling her jacket close against a chill wind, Abbie propped herself against a jutting rock to gaze out across the lake, watching the occasional ripples form where trout or char swam. 'Never took to the sport myself.'

'That's because you don't have the patience.'

'True. I'd much rather be busy doing something than sitting still for even five minutes.'

He cast her a sideways glance, a half-smile on his face. 'You always did have itchy feet, but you were much better at climbing trees than I was. I never had a head for heights.'

Abbie chuckled. 'Do you remember falling into the lake when a branch you were scrambling along broke? Mum went demented, even though I jumped in to save you. Good job the water was shallow there, but we both ended up covered in mud and laughing, Mum too.'

'I only did it because you dared me to,' he said, laughing now at the memory, 'having swung across it yourself like the little monkey you were. But then you were smaller and lighter than me so it wasn't really a fair challenge.'

She paused at that. 'Life isn't fair, Robert.'

He looked up at her more seriously then. 'No, you're right, it isn't. It certainly wasn't for Mum, or Dad, or any of us for that matter.' He paused a moment, then added, 'I'm sorry things went wrong for you with Eduard.'

Abbie blinked, surprised by this sudden show of sympathy. 'Thanks. Kind of you to say so.'

'Maybe you'll stop and think next time before doing something stupid like getting involved with the wrong man. You might even learn to take advice for once in your life.'

Whatever response she might have made to that typical brotherly remark was fortunately prevented by the arrival of Fay carrying a tray of wine. 'I thought you might like a little refreshment before dinner,' she said, looking pleased to find the siblings engaged in what appeared to be a civilised conversation at last.

As Robert set aside his rod to kiss his wife and sat beside her on a log to drink his wine, Abbie took the glass handed to her without a word. Perhaps he was right – perhaps she shouldn't rush into anything. Things might work themselves out between her and Robert and she didn't want to upset him. Maybe now wasn't the moment to reveal that she owned the property her brother wished to sell.

SEVENTEEN

By the summer of 1914 I had been in Russia for almost three years and my efforts with the language were beginning to pay off. I wouldn't exactly call myself fluent but could get by well enough, helped by my skills in French. In early June as usual, the Count and Countess Belinsky moved out of St Petersburg to spend several weeks in the country, taking with them a dozen or more servants including grooms and coachmen, plus horses, ponies, a score of boxes, trunks and portmanteau, and even a piano for the children, occupying several carriages on the train and requiring countless wagons on arrival at the station.

This was the season of the white nights, when it never went dark. I still found it strange to be able to read outside at midnight. The gardens were bursting with lilac, the scent beguiling enough to please the most ardent town-lover, which I most certainly was not. I enjoyed every moment in the country, whether it be helping out in the dairy or walking in the surrounding forest, despite the clouds of mosquitoes that hung over the pond. I relished the gentle croak of frogs, the song of the nightingale, the tangy scent of pine.

Very much an outdoor man, the Count loved nothing more than digging and weeding his vegetable plot, nurturing his strawberries and asparagus, pruning shrubs or caring for his favourite jasmine, orchids and camellia.

The gentle rhythm of country life continued despite the worry of increasing unrest in the Balkans. Then in early July, I was sitting in the garden late one evening, relaxing with a book, when Stefan brought me the terrible news that Archduke Franz Ferdinand of Austria had been assassinated in Sarajevo, as had his beloved Duchess Sophie.

'This could bring war,' Stefan warned as he came to sit beside me on the bench.

'Oh, I do hope not. Why should it?'

'Things are far from stable. Austria is sure to retaliate upon Serbia, then Russia will feel duty bound to defend its neighbour, and who knows where that will lead?'

'You think England might become involved?'

'More likely Germany, which will take the side of Austria. It could all get very nasty.'

We sat in silence for some moments contemplating this grim news. Since the day Stefan had confided the terrible story of his father's death, I'd felt much closer to him. Perhaps because I finally understood the root of his anger. Our friendship had grown over recent months and we spent a great deal of time in each other's company, when he wasn't carrying out tasks for the Countess, that is.

She was still very demanding of his time, although Stefan continued to disappear, no doubt seeking a little time to himself. I generally suffered the brunt of her ire on those occasions as she screamed at me to tell her where he was. Stefan's absences were as much a mystery to me as to the Countess, although I didn't entirely blame him. There were occasions when I'd welcome an escape from her endless demands myself.

Now I began to think how I would feel if there was a war. Worse, if Stefan felt obliged to join up and I never saw him again.

As always I spoke my unformed thoughts out loud without pausing to consider the consequences of such frankness. 'The prospect of war, and the possibility of losing you in it, is too horrendous to contemplate.'

He gave me a searching look and when I turned to meet his gaze something inside of me seemed to flip right over. 'I don't think I should have said that,' I murmured, and he smiled.

'I'm glad you did, delighted to know that you care. You are equally precious to me, Millie.'

When his lips met mine I seemed to melt in his arms, pressing myself against the power of his body. The sweetness of his kiss stirred in me a longing for more, something I'd never before experienced. When finally we drew apart he gave a sheepish little smile. 'You must know how I feel about you.'

I was trembling as I rested my head on his chest with a little sigh of pleasure, thrilled to hear his heart pounding every bit as fast as mine. 'Then why did you never tell me?'

'Because I was afraid you might reject me. Whenever I felt the urge to try to find the right words, I would wonder why you'd even trouble to speak to a stupid chap like me. I felt unworthy of your attention, and we haven't always seen eye to eye, have we?'

'But if you *had* taken the risk, you might have been surprised.'

'Would I? Why is that?'

'Because I feel the same,' I softly admitted.

Apparently lost for words he cupped my face between his gentle hands and kissed me again, longer and deeper this time, filling me with desire. Then we were both grinning at each other like idiots, his eyes scanning my face with an expression as bemused as my own must be. 'I've adored you from the moment I first set eyes on you at the British and American chapel. I'd tell myself to behave, to not run the risk of ruining your reputation, or our friendship, but I couldn't stop thinking about you.'

'I couldn't stop thinking about you either.' Then remembering the news that had led to this revelation, I quietly added. 'I really don't want to lose you, Stefan. Please don't join up unless you are forced to.'

'I won't,' he promised, tenderly stroking back my errant curls which fell loose to my shoulders this evening, not tied up in a neat braid. 'But let's hope I'm wrong and it doesn't come to war. Then we can enjoy a happy future together.'

'Oh, Stefan.' My smile faded a little as a new thought occurred to me. 'We must take great care not to let our feelings show.'

He grimaced. 'That's true. I very much doubt the Countess would approve.'

Something like panic stirred within as I recalled how she'd accused me of wanting to keep him to myself, trying to make me jealous by hinting at an intimacy between them. 'She is a selfish woman, obsessed by the need for attention, as if her every whim must be met, every man must fawn at her feet. Were she to discover how we felt about each other I suspect she would do her utmost to destroy our happiness, possibly by dismissing one, or even both of us. That's the kind of person she is.'

'You're right, Millie. Countess Olga is an autocrat in the worst sense of the word, entirely wrapped up in herself. We must take great care not to reveal our feelings when in her presence, not even to glance at each other.' Kissing me again, he groaned. 'Oh, but that is not going to be easy.'

'Nevertheless, it is absolutely essential,' I murmured, running my fingers through his hair as I had often longed to do.

I was thankful that the bench was at least hidden behind a bank of lilac bushes, as it was some time before we drew apart that evening and went our separate ways.

It proved to be a hot, dry summer and as always the children seemed to blossom, working hard at their French and English lessons each morning so that they had plenty of time to explore. Then, after painting and piano lessons in the afternoons, we would enjoy a picnic or cruise on the river, play tennis or croquet. It reminded me very much of my time at Carreck Place. The lifestyle, however, was the absolute opposite to the kind of Spartan life most Russians enjoyed at their summer *dacha*.

Serge and I were getting along much better, although the boy could still be difficult and disruptive, as he was being today by smashing the croquet ball into the pond instead of tapping it through the little arch. He was in a temper because his mother had refused to take him out with her in the carriage. I watched the Countess drive off with the chauffeur, and couldn't help but wonder where they might be going and what they would get up to alone in the countryside. Not that it was any of my business.

Serge, however, was very much my concern and, coming to a decision, I went to see his father.

I found the Count in his office and the moment I politely knocked on the door he at once called for me to enter, so different to the Countess who always kept me waiting for as long as possible. I thought he looked rather lonely and sad, a warm breeze from the open window stirring a mass of papers on his desk. Had he been watching his wife go off with the chauffeur?

Bobbing a curtsey, I quickly launched into my request. 'Sir, your son has become rather bored with picnics and croquet, and I wondered if you had time to take him fishing.'

The Count looked startled by my suggestion. 'I very much doubt he would relish my company. He much prefers his mother's.'

'Oh, but I disagree. I know that he wants to make you proud of him.'

'Really? But would he enjoy going fishing with me?'

'I truly believe he would appreciate a more manly pursuit. He's eleven years old, growing up rapidly, sir, and rather tired of endless tea parties with Irina's dolls.'

He laughed at that, and to my great surprise and pleasure, leapt to his feet. 'Very well, I shall go and collect my fishing tackle, rods and bait. Tell him I'll be with him in ten minutes,' he said and, reaching for his hat, made a dash for the door.

'Thank you, sir,' I said, dipping a curtsey.

He paused, holding the door open. 'No, thank *you*, Millie, for the suggestion.'

It was the first time the Count had called me by my Christian name and I was flattered, but even more pleased when father and son went off happily together to fish. Serge looked quite excited as Irina and I waved them off.

'Can I go and see the cows now?' the little girl asked, as she did every single day without fail. She loved nothing more than to watch them being milked. Afterwards, she would help pour some of the spare milk into the big shiny copper cheese-maker which would be turned into Gruyère cheese.

'Why is this cow so fat, *Baryshnya*?'

'Because she's in calf,' I explained, hoping further details would not be required.

She chuckled with glee. 'Oh goody. Can I watch when it's born?'

This was a question I avoided answering, thinking it might not be appropriate for a nine-year-old child, but she visited the cow several times a day after that, and one morning on hearing a great deal of agonised mooing, was in time to see the birth. She looked at me all starry-eyed as she watched the cow lick her baby clean. 'Oh, *Baryshnya*, isn't she a clever cow? And isn't this little calf lucky to have such a kind mother?'

I gave Irina a hug and kiss. 'She's lucky to have you, too, as am I.'

The fishing expeditions became a regular event for Serge and the Count, and I began to hope that this foolish jealousy between brother and sister, not to mention the rivalry between husband and wife over the children, might begin to subside at last.

Countess Olga ran the house as if it were a royal palace and she an empress, with a litany of petty rules surely as long as those set by the Tsar. As well as decreeing that no servant was allowed to be seated in her presence, she would insist upon a footman hovering outside whichever room she was currently occupying, in case she should need to call upon him to fetch some trivial item she couldn't find, mainly because she couldn't be bothered to look for it. Sometimes the poor soul would sit there for hours, growing weary with boredom and backache, but then would be kept up half the night by her constant demands for hot milk or chocolate.

'She lacks something worthwhile to do with her time,' Stefan shrewdly remarked, in one of our quick exchanges when no one was around. We might sometimes even risk stealing a secret kiss.

It was true that Countess Olga was very much a social creature and visitors to the Belinskys' country home were rare, as it stood in a remote region surrounded by dense forest. 'She does miss her friends from town,' I agreed. 'Theatre and the opera, dinner at the select *Villa Rodé* with its champagne and caviar. I just wish she would spend more time with the children while we're in the country. But even when I bring them to her she barely permits more than a moment in her presence before ordering me to take them away. Handing out money for sweets or organising picnics is as far as she's prepared to go in her role of mother, and even that is bound up with her own selfish needs in order to keep them out of her hair.'

Stefan chuckled. 'While she's up to goodness knows what.'

'Don't even ask.'

'Wouldn't dream of it. Nothing to do with us.'

'Quite.'

'Could we meet up later, though?' he whispered, his eyes beseeching me to agree. Glancing about to make sure we were alone, I nodded before quickly returning to my duties.

Sneaking a little time together wasn't easy, which was one of the reasons I loved taking the children into the village, as Stefan always drove us in the cart. One afternoon the Countess declared her intention of accompanying us, which meant we went by carriage. Overawed by the sight of this splendid vehicle in the midst of their humble community, the villagers instantly surrounded us, begging for work or a handout. I saw peasant women with children clinging to their skirts.

'Drive on,' the Countess ordered, turning her back on their demands.

'Perhaps they are hungry,' I ventured to suggest, thinking of the twenty kopeks the children were given every single day to spend on sweets, which would probably feed a family for days.

'They are not *my* responsibility,' she hissed, 'and they smell.'

The latter was certainly true, but then soap was expensive and not a first priority if you had children to feed. I managed to slip a few kopeks into the hand of the nearest peasant woman, earning myself a glare of reproof from my mistress.

The Count's attitude was entirely different. As president of the *zemstvo* or local council, made up of land owners and businessmen, which took place every month in a local hall, the Count was very much involved in caring for the community. Decisions would be made on such matters as local taxation, education, road maintenance, agriculture and veterinary issues, as well as the running of the local hospital.

He also regularly presided over a small court in his own home, where tenants could bring their problems for his help and support. It was clear to me that he was very much respected and loved. Everything about him on these occasions seemed different. He was dignified but approachable, his demeanour very much that of the local squire who cared about his people. I loved to watch him at his duties, and on one day in particular, I couldn't help but hear the sobs of a young woman and her children crying.

Seeing me hovering at the door, the Count gave a wave of his hand, indicating I should enter. 'This woman's children are sick with hunger. Her husband has died and her father-in-law is threatening to throw her out of the house if she doesn't find paying work soon. Unfortunately, try as she might, the woman has been unable to find any. Later when the crops are ready for picking there will be plenty, but not right now. I've sent for the fellow, in order to make it very clear he cannot evict her without my permission, even if she were not his own daughter-in-law. But could you take the children to the kitchens and find them something to eat?'

'Of course. I'd be happy to do so.'

I greatly admired the way he patiently listened to their tales of woe, even though I didn't understand much of what was being said, and the way he handed out justice with every sign of fairness and compassion.

The father-in-law was interviewed and suitably chastened, and the children went happily home with full bellies and a basket of food. The stink of poverty lingered long after they'd gone but my heart went out to them. How fortunate I was to have such a good job, to be so safe and secure, and so well fed.

We ended that summer with a visit to the Crimea on the north coast of the Black Sea, a favourite with the Count and Countess, where we stayed in a large villa just outside Yalta. The Romanovs, too, loved to spend time in Livadia, their Crimean palace, a beautiful white stone building situated on the heights above the town. I believe they'd been there in the spring, but I'm not sure whether they were in residence during our own visit. Apparently the Tsar and Tsarina socialised only occasionally, preferring to use the palace as a means to escape their duties and enjoy what might pass for a normal family life.

I wish I could have said the same about the Belinskys. The Count was more often than not busy in his office, and apart from a little spoiling of her beloved son the Countess largely ignored the children, as always. The roads in the region were generally poor so she was at least obliged to curtail her passion for driving out every afternoon. Instead she lay about in the sun, looking upon the villa as a place to relax.

And it was indeed delightful. The sun shone on Yalta beach, the boulevards hummed with children accompanied by their British governesses, and the resort was as busy as ever, many people coming to nurse their tuberculosis.

All of these normal pleasures and problems paled into insignificance when at the end of July we learned that Austria had declared war on Serbia. Within hours Russia had begun to mobilize its troops to defend it, just as Stefan had predicted, and on the first day of August the Kaiser declared war on Russia.

We quickly returned to Petrograd, as we must now call it. The name had been changed because the German nature of St Petersburg had begun to offend, and *Petrograd* sounded more Slavic. At first there were few signs of preparation for war, although later we did see soldiers marching in the streets, singing as they went about their training or made their way to the mobile kitchens specially set up for them.

On my first visit to the British and American chapel the war was naturally the major topic of conversation between the British governesses, all trying to decide whether they should go home or stay in Russia.

Ruth and I hugged each other by way of comfort. 'Such bad news,' I said. 'I'd been planning a trip home. Now I suppose that will have to be put on hold for a while.'

'There are ships still available but there's always the risk of being sunk by a German warship. Even travelling by train is difficult. The one transporting Empress Maria Feodorovna, the Tsar's mother, stopped in Berlin on its journey back from England and a mob attacked it, throwing stones at the windows. She was eventually saved by the police but nonetheless ordered to leave Germany as quickly as possible, so the train returned the long way, via Denmark.'

'Oh, my goodness. I must tell *Babushka*. She will be most upset to hear that as she was once one of the Empress Mother's ladies-in-waiting.'

'Well, the episode has decided me that it's safer to stay put. In any case, it will all be over by Christmas. Everyone says so.'

'And at least England isn't involved,' I remarked in all innocence.

'I'm afraid that is no longer the case. Germany has declared war on France and sent troops to invade Belgium and Luxembourg, heading for Paris. England issued an ultimatum and when it was ignored, declared war on Germany on the fourth of August.'

'Oh no. It's all happening so fast.'

'Despite the fact most of the royal houses across Europe are related, they are all now in open conflict with each other.'

'And we governesses are caught in the middle of it.'

'I'm afraid we are.'

I wrote anxiously to my parents in the Lake District, explaining the delay in my plans and praying they would be safe. Letters from home were slow to arrive and often heavily censored, but in September I received one which said that Liam had been killed shortly after joining up. I was filled with sadness. Whatever his failings in the way he'd pretended to be in love with me in order to have his wicked way, that didn't mean that I'd disliked him. He'd been perhaps over-eager and rather too passionate, but a pleasant enough young man, and a good friend. I wrote to his parents expressing my condolences, quietly weeping at his loss, and worrying over how many more young men would lose their lives before this conflict was over.

I silently prayed that Stefan would not be one of them.

At the British and American chapel we were encouraged to start knitting socks and balaclavas, which I was happy to do under the careful instruction of *Nyanushki*, since domestic skills did not come naturally to me. Some of the other girls volunteered to help at the Red Cross. When I suggested that I might do the same, the Countess refused permission.

'I'm afraid I can't spare you, Dowthwaite. I need you here.'

'But your ladyship, this is important. If soldiers are injured there won't be enough nurses to care for them.'

'That is not my problem. Now please fetch me a glass of water. I'm thirsty.'

Stifling a sigh, I went to do her bidding, deeply frustrated that fetching the Countess a glass of water she was perfectly capable of getting for herself was perceived to be more important than nursing the wounded.

I could only hope that the belief it would all be over by Christmas was correct, as the fear that Stefan might feel the need to join up was strong in me.

Yet in a strange way the war seemed distant, a world away, and life continued very much as usual, the Belinskys appearing oblivious to events. That autumn we continued to spend the occasional weekend in the country where it was still my habit each morning to take the children out on a ride. One particular morning I was later than usual going to saddle the ponies, as I'd let the children over-sleep following a party the night before in which they'd enjoyed singing to the balalaika and been rather late going to bed.

The moment I entered the stables I froze on the spot. Stefan had his back against the wall, his hands resting loosely at the Countess's waist: there was no denying that they were kissing. I must have gasped out loud for they suddenly broke apart and she turned her blazing charcoal eyes full upon me. Stefan called out, but I didn't hear what he said as I turned on my heel and ran.

~

'Oh, my goodness, that's dreadful!' Abbie cried. 'How could he so callously betray you, and after you were becoming so close?'

A sadness came over her grandmother's face at the memory. 'I confess I was devastated at the time, utterly heartbroken, in fact.'

'I can imagine. Did he apologise, or explain?' Abbie wanted to know, entirely caught up in the emotion of the moment and feeling pretty devastated herself.

'He did make a fumbling attempt, yes. He found me one afternoon in my favourite place sitting on the bench beside the river, near to tears, deeply engrossed in my own depressed thoughts. I felt cold inside, bleak and lost. The children had been enjoying tea with their parents, from which for once I had begged to be excused, claiming I had a headache when really I was heartsick.'

'Of course you were,' Abbie said, giving her a hug.

~

'May I speak with you for a moment?' he quietly asked.

My response was cool. 'I don't believe we have anything to say.' The pain of what I had witnessed hurt more than words could express. I thought myself foolish for trusting him and believing, even for a moment, that he truly loved me. I heard him draw in a jagged breath, shuffle his feet on the rough stone path in discomfort.

'I perfectly understand why you wouldn't wish to speak to me,' he said, 'but it wasn't quite as it appeared. I did nothing. You need to know that, Millie.'

'You were kissing her.'

He tentatively sat down on the bench, not attempting to touch me or come too near, but it was too close for comfort so far as I was concerned. I was on my feet in a second and walked away, head held high, blocking my ears to his voice as he begged me to listen.

'Did he come after you?' Abbie asked, but Millie shook her head.

'I rarely saw him in the days and weeks following, but then I did make a point of avoiding him.'

'So that was it, all over between you? How sad. But at least you found out before you became too involved, I suppose.'

'Oh, that was just the start. Things became much more complicated after that.'

EIGHTEEN

I was supervising the children one morning as they practised their French verbs, about to read them an extract from Charles Kingsley's *The Water Babies* by way of reward, when I was summoned to the Countess's boudoir. The urgency of the order obliged me to send the maid who'd brought the message to run and fetch *Nyanushki* to mind the children, so it took a few moments before she arrived and I was free to obey the command.

'Why does she always choose the wrong moment?' the old nanny complained as she hurried, somewhat breathless, into the schoolroom. 'Just when I was preparing *Babushka's* lunch. I really can't be in two places at once.'

Feeling some sympathy with this, I rushed along the corridor and tapped on the Countess's door.

'Ah, Dowthwaite, there you are at last. I thought you were never coming.'

'I couldn't just leave the children alone.'

Dismissing my excuse with a flippant wave of her bejewelled hand, she made a surprising request, or rather delivered yet another unexpected order. 'I have decided that in future you will act as my lady's maid.'

I stared at her in open dismay. 'I don't understand. How can I be your maid as well as governess to your children?'

'I'm sure you'll cope. I've dismissed the girl who has been with me for some years as she keeps disappearing for long periods at a time, claiming her mother is sick.'

'I'm sorry to hear that,' I said with genuine sympathy.

'Yes, well, I need someone here every day.' Flicking back her long dark hair, the Countess handed me her brush, thus indicating my new duties were to begin immediately.

'But I have more than enough to occupy me, teaching and caring for the children,' I protested, even as I obediently began to tease the brush through her tangled curls. 'I doubt I would have the time necessary for all the extra work required. May I suggest that you hire someone else for the task, milady?'

'There isn't anyone else, certainly no one that I could trust or who has your degree of discretion. Dear Stefan is always eager to run errands for me, of course – to do anything I ask, in fact,' she said, slanting a teasing glance up at me through her mirror. 'I cannot think how I would manage without him.'

The Countess, of course, had found the incident in the stables highly amusing, and continued to make snide remarks and drop hints implying there was a great deal more she could say about their intimacy if she so wished, as she was doing now.

'But although he has his uses as a man, and the most delightful skills in those wonderfully gentle hands of his, there are some matters that require a woman's touch.'

At these provocative words I felt again that all-too-familiar stab of jealousy, although I was careful not to show it. Drawing in a breath, I answered with a determined firmness. 'The job of lady's maid would not suit me, your ladyship. You would only be disappointed.'

'You will do as you are told, Dowthwaite, without argument,' she calmly informed me, handing me a selection of emerald-encrusted pins for her hair, making it abundantly clear the matter was settled.

As I obediently clipped her curls in place with clumsy fingers, I frantically sought a way out. No solution sprang to mind. How could I refuse if I wanted to hold on to my job? Although it might make sense for me to leave, in view of how things now stood between Stefan and me, the thought of abandoning the children to this woman, particularly little Irina, didn't bear thinking about. Who would protect and love that little girl if I left?

Stifling a sigh of resignation, I gave up. 'If I agree to accept the job, at least temporarily, could you find someone else to be responsible for all the mending, needlework and laundry? As I once explained, sewing is not one of my strengths, and I will have the children to see to as well. And please don't ask *Nyanushki*, as she too has more than enough to do.'

The Countess was smiling in triumph at seeing me buckle under pressure. 'That is easily resolved. You can arrange for one of the servants to deal with such matters. But you, Dowthwaite, will be responsible for putting out the clothes I wear, usually four or five changes each day, and for keeping my jewellery in safe and proper order, including my precious collection of amber.'

I began to tremble beneath the weight of such responsibility, worrying how I was to fit in all this extra work without neglecting the children. Why was it that neither parent gave a moment's thought to the emotional needs of their son and daughter? This was not what I had bargained for when first I came to Russia, yet it seemed that I had no option but to agree. I made one last bid for freedom. 'May I think about it, your ladyship?'

'You have twenty-four hours.'

The following afternoon, it being a Wednesday, I attended the British and American chapel and wasted no time in sharing my problem with Ruth. 'I really have no wish to play lady's maid to the Countess. I've more than enough to occupy me as governess to her children, but how can I wriggle out of it?'

'You could find other employment,' Ruth suggested. 'British governesses are still in demand, and you have good references.'

'I have the one from Lady Rumsley, but the Countess has made it clear that were I to leave without her permission, she wouldn't give me one.' I frowned. 'Actually, there was a time when she seemed to want rid of me. Now she's giving me yet more work and seems anxious to keep me for some reason.' I surmised that the beautiful Olga relished being able to lord it over me that she'd won Stefan for herself. The memory of that kiss still burned a hole in my heart; I was finding the knowledge of his betrayal still hard to live with. 'Besides, the children want me to stay.'

'I'm not surprised. You've done so much for them, not least in persuading the Count to take more of an interest in his son with those fishing trips you arranged, which I'm sure Serge appreciated. They've grown fond of you over the years.'

'I'm really quite fond of them, too, even Serge in spite of his naughtiness.' I smiled, pleased that the Count often came to me now with suggestions of other activities which might meet with approval from his son. The pair did seem to be growing closer. 'And I love little Irina. In order to find new employment I might have to go as far away as Moscow, and I'd never see them again.'

I might also never see Stefan again, I thought, which despite his infidelity filled me with despair. Perhaps when I'd finally come to terms with the loss of what I'd once believed we had together, then I might be able to cope better. Right now I still clung to some vain hope that all might come right between us.

Recognising the undercurrent of emotion simmering beneath the surface, my dear friend put her arms about me and gave me a hug. 'Is there something you're not telling me?' she quietly asked. I shook my head.

'Nothing I want to talk about.'

'Perhaps you could talk to Stefan, then. I know he's very fond of you too.'

'I don't think that would be appropriate.'

Her face creased with anxiety as she instantly guessed that there had been some disagreement between us. 'Ah, well, in that case let me say that I'm always here, as your friend, should you change your mind.'

'Thank you, Ruth. It's just that I need to work this problem out for myself.'

She squeezed my hand in sympathy. 'So far as the lady's maid post is concerned, why not agree to do it until Christmas? That should surely allow the Countess ample time to find a replacement.' And having gained my agreement to this suggestion, she marched me off to the vestibule for a comforting cup of tea. 'But do take care,' she warned, handing me a scone. 'From what I hear, Countess Belinsky is a very manipulative, scheming woman who can turn nasty if she doesn't get her own way.'

'I'm well aware of that. You only have to look at the way she treats her husband by conducting a sordid liaison with Viktor the chauffeur.'

Ruth laughed. 'Ah, so it is true, then, what I hear through the grapevine?'

'She makes no secret of the fact, going off every afternoon for long mysterious drives alone with him in full view of her husband. What else could they be up to?'

'She was also apparently seen out with Dimitri Korniloff the other evening at the *Villa Rodé*.'

'That wouldn't surprise me. It's one of her favourite haunts.'

'The fellow is certainly good-looking, but a more money-grubbing, social climbing, political know-it-all would be hard to find. So if you're right about her relationship with the chauffeur, that's at least two men she's got dangling at her fingertips, and there could well be more.'

I gave a harsh little laugh. 'Oh, I'm quite certain there are.'

Noting the bitterness of my tone, Ruth considered me with sadness in her eyes. 'Oh dear. Then you have an even bigger problem than I thought.'

~

My first challenge as lady's maid came when Countess Olga began issuing instructions as I helped her dress for her usual evening out and about round town. 'Should my husband ask for me, you may inform him that I am feeling unwell and have retired to bed early. That is all you need say, and to request that he sleep in the dressing room.'

'Are you suffering from a headache, milady? Is there anything I can get you?' I politely enquired.

She gave a tutting sound of exasperation. 'Aren't you listening to me, Dowthwaite? In point of fact I'm off to see Anna Pavlova of the Imperial ballet, after which we shall dine at the Café Chantant. My escort usually hires us a box where we can indulge in champagne and caviar, among other things,' she laughed. 'Don't expect me home before midnight, perhaps not at all. All you have to do is visit my room from time to time and pretend to talk to me as if I were lying sick in my bed. Just in case the Count should be listening.'

I froze in the process of fastening her amber necklace. 'You are asking me to lie?'

She gave a wry smile as she lifted her head to meet my shocked gaze. 'I am giving you an order. Do you have a problem with that?'

My cheeks grew warm beneath the harshness of her glare. 'Of course not. Only what if the Count were to come looking for you?'

'You will not let him into my room. Is that clear?'

'Very good, your ladyship.' I concentrated on fastening the necklace, studiously battling against my natural instinct to refuse to embroil myself in her illicit affairs. But it was not my place to do so.

'No, not those earrings, foolish child. The long amber teardrops that match this pendant.'

Later, as she slipped out through a side entrance to quietly depart in the carriage with her own personal chauffeur, I couldn't deny that she looked magnificent in an emerald silk gown with a silver fox fur wrap and amber jewellery. Was she meeting Dimitri Korniloff again, I wondered, or another man entirely? Surely not Stefan, as he couldn't afford such treats, unless the Countess was paying, of course.

After she'd gone I spent an anxious night flitting between the children's rooms and the Countess's, barely snatching a wink of sleep as my fears mounted over the lie I was caught up in, as well as a deep ache inside over losing Stefan. On the third occasion, hoping against hope she might have returned early, to my dismay I found the Count about to tap on her door. I quickly hurried to his side. 'Can I be of assistance, milord?'

'Ah, Millie, there you are. I was wondering how my wife is, whether she is feeling any better.'

'I – I should think she's fast asleep by now, milord. I gave her a draught for the headache so I certainly hope so.' Even as I stumbled over the falsehood, I was terrified he might insist upon my allowing him to enter, where her empty bed would instantly reveal his wife's deception. The consequences of such a revelation would undoubtedly lose me my position, and goodness knows what else besides.

'Then I will not disturb her,' he said, taking a step back.

'I shall tell her of your concern – in the morning – when she wakes.'

'You are very good to her, Millie. I do hope my wife appreciates your loyalty.' There was something in his eyes when he said this that made me wonder if he had already guessed about the empty bed. 'But then you have a generous heart.'

'Thank you, sir.'

He considered me with a quiet thoughtfulness in his expression. 'Are you happy here, Millie? Do you ever get homesick for your family?'

'Sometimes,' I confessed. 'But I enjoy my work, and I love the children.'

He smiled. 'I know you do, but don't allow my wife to bully you too much.' As he walked away, shoulders hunched, he made a rather sad and lonely figure in his humble dressing gown, and my heart went out to him. What would this dreadful woman ask of me next?

It was, of course, impossible to avoid Stefan entirely as we lived and worked in the same apartment. Sometimes I would catch a glimpse of him hurrying along the labyrinth of corridors, or slipping in or out of the Countess's room, and then I'd dart through the nearest door to escape. There were days when I would find myself looking for him in vain, as he continued to go absent for periods of time. Was he avoiding me too? I wondered.

But then one afternoon as I walked home along the Nevsky Prospekt on my way back from the governesses' club, I saw him huddled in the corner of a coffee shop. He spotted me at the same moment and, tossing some kopeks on the table next to his untouched coffee, came rushing out.

'Don't run away, Millie. I'm desperate to speak to you and explain. Please listen.'

Unable to resist the appeal in his voice, I allowed myself to be ushered inside. With a coffee set before me, and keeping my gaze fixed on its muddy depths, I steeled myself to listen to yet more lies.

He took a breath. 'That kiss you witnessed – I do assure you that it was not instigated by me. I would never do such a thing.'

'You didn't seem to be resisting too greatly.'

'The Countess has been harassing me for months, dropping big hints that she was mine for the asking, if I played my cards right. Then on catching me alone in the stables that day, she suddenly shoved me back against the wall and flung herself upon me. I was shocked, I can tell you, but what could I do? I was at a complete loss how to handle such a delicate situation. She is my employer, after all, the Countess Belinsky no less, so pushing her away, shouting at her or telling her to leave me alone was quite out of the question. I decided to simply not respond, to endure the kiss without moving a muscle, hoping she would get the message. What would have happened had you not turned up at precisely that moment, I have no idea. But I swear to you, Millie, that I was hugely embarrassed and didn't know what the hell to do.'

Dropping his voice, he leaned across the table to take my hand, stroking my fingers one by one. 'You know full well that it's *you* I long to kiss, not Countess Olga.'

Could I possibly have been wrong to accuse him of betrayal? The Countess was fascinated by men, with a string of affairs to her credit long before this latest with the chauffeur, including the notorious occasion in the summer house with Lord Rumsley. And there was no denying that Stefan was handsome. Just looking at him made my heart sing.

I was also aware that Stefan had done his best to avoid being left alone with her, and until the incident in the stables I'd seen nothing untoward regarding his behaviour towards her.

But if he could choose between a rich and beautiful Countess or a boring little governess, which is how I saw myself, why on earth would he choose me? Could I really be certain of his sincerity? Was Stefan as innocent as he claimed?

Deep down he nursed a huge resentment towards the aristocrats over the death of his father. That being the case, it was perfectly plausible he could be seeking some sort of personal revenge by embarking upon an affair with Countess Olga. But to what end? What could he achieve by such a ploy? And if *I* did not believe in him, what right did I have to be falling in love with him, which I knew in my heart to be the case?

Perhaps I'd inadvertently allowed the Countess to ruin the special feelings growing between Stefan and me by not giving him the benefit of the doubt. I noted the anguish in his green-grey eyes, and an emotion I might once have interpreted as adoration. 'I do want to believe you, Stefan.'

'Thank heaven for that,' he said with a sigh of relief. 'I swear she is pursuing me with a vigour that is terrifying, which is why I have to keep hiding away in coffee shops.'

I found myself almost smiling. 'It's rather a nice coffee shop.'

'But you haven't touched your coffee,' he said with just a hint of his famous crooked grin.

'Neither have you.'

With one accord we each proceeded to take a sip, looking at each other across the rim of our cups, then both of us pulled a face as the coffee had long since gone cold. Stefan quickly ordered fresh cups.

'We could always find other jobs,' he said and, taking both my hands in his, lifted them to his lips to kiss each one in turn. 'Why don't we run away and start a whole new together life far from the Count and Countess? She means nothing to me. It's you that I love, Millie, and always will.'

'Oh, Stefan!' I was overwhelmed with emotion. His plea sounded entirely genuine and heartfelt. 'But the country is at war. Jobs are hard to find. From what I hear Russia can't even afford to equip its army, or provide it with sufficient ammunition. Thousands of men are being killed and I certainly don't want you to be one of them, forced to join up because you are unemployed.'

He looked deflated by this, probably knowing there was some truth in what I said. 'I may be called up anyway. In the meantime, how do I handle the Countess's advances? How do I hold her off?'

I was silent for some moments. 'I could speak to her, ask her to stop harassing you.' The words came out of my mouth of their own volition, surprising even myself as Stefan looked at me in stunned disbelief.

'Would that be wise?'

The image of a pair of legs and a bare backside came into my head. 'It might well be necessary,' I chuckled.

'She wouldn't listen. It would never work.'

'You're probably right.'

'Marry me, Millie. More than anything I long to make you my wife. I can't imagine life without you.' His arms came about me then, despite the very public nature of the coffee shop, and my heart melted with love for him.

'Oh, Stefan, at any other time I might be tempted to say yes, but we can't, not with the war and everything.'

'They say it will all be over by Christmas. We could do it then.'

I gave a little laugh, a mix of excitement and panic. 'We mustn't rush into it. I love my job, and the children, so I'm in no hurry to leave. I always was ambitious, and we're both young, so let's bide our time. Perhaps it would be best if you just kept on trying to avoid being alone with her.'

Stefan readily agreed. 'That is good advice I will do my utmost to follow, if you promise to forgive me.'

'Oh, I do. I'm sure that kiss wasn't your fault.'

We walked home together by the canal and his kisses beneath the bridges set me on fire. I never realised it was possible to love a person so much, or to feel so loved.

NINETEEN

By August 1915 the war was so bad that 450,000 Russian soldiers were being killed every month, with over a million and a half men lost in one year. Russia had won some victories over Austria, but Germany was proving too a big a force for them to defeat. I could read the papers sufficiently well by this time to understand that the country simply didn't possess the necessary resources to conduct a war, even if the politics behind it all remained something of a mystery to me.

It was a glorious summer's day and I'd been reading a long-delayed letter from home while I sat watching the children swim and splash in the river. It reminded me so much of Carreckwater that a wave of homesickness hit me. I couldn't help but worry about how my dear parents were surviving this dreadful conflict. How I longed to be with them in that moment. They wrote how Miss Phyllis and Master Robin were quickly growing up, Robin now almost fifteen. I turned to the newspaper seeking some sort of hope that the war might end soon, before he too was called up. Struggling as best I could with the Russian, in the end I tossed it aside in disgust.

'The newspaper has no solutions, just stories of political treachery. Why is that, I wonder?' Believing myself to be alone, I'd spoken my question aloud.

'It's not easy to explain, as Russia has rather a long and complicated history, but there is a growing awareness of democratic ideas brought in from the West by political activists.'

I'd been completely unaware that the Count, who loved nothing more than dabbling in his beloved garden, was close by weeding a flower bed.

Leaning on his garden hoe, he paused in his labours as he went on. 'There is also an ongoing resentment at the treatment of peasants as well as the poor conditions experienced by thousands of workers. In addition, millions of peasant farmers have been forcibly conscripted into the army, which has led to a serious shortage of manpower on the farms and a corresponding fall in food production. Prices are rising as a consequence, not least because of the relentless increase in taxes to pay for this war. But wages have failed to keep pace. The country seems to be rapidly sinking into economic depression.'

I listened, engrossed, grateful that the Count treated me with sufficient respect to take the trouble to explain all of this to me. 'It must be so painful for you to see your beloved Fatherland suffer.'

He came over to sit beside me on the grassy bank. 'I like to think that I am not entirely oblivious to my tenants' concerns.'

'I've seen with my own eyes that you are not,' I assured him.

He nodded. 'I am always grateful for your help, and your faith in me, Millie, is much appreciated. However, certain members of the aristocracy continue to live their lives oblivious to these food shortages, and to the fact that vital raw materials are becoming increasingly difficult to import.'

'Perhaps that's because, unlike the poor, they can afford to pay whatever is necessary for their food.' I hid a smile, for it was true that Countess Olga showed no inclination to allow something as boring as a war to spoil her pleasures. She never gave a thought or a care for anyone but herself – not for the soldiers dying, or her servants striving to find sufficient supplies in the shops and markets to keep up with her high standards, and certainly not for the Count, who was dealing with an increasing number of problems at the *zemstvo*.

'Will the war end soon, do you think?' I asked, feeling quite comfortable with this conversation and the growing respect between us. He was so kind it made me quite cross to think of how badly his wife treated him.

The Count gave a sad shake to his head. 'The sense of unrest is growing, Millie, not lessening. Who knows what will happen?'

By 1916 the value of the rouble had fallen substantially, causing prices to soar even higher, yet the Countess continued to ignore such trivialities as cost or availability, expecting dinner to be served at the same standard as in pre-war days. When Anton served cabbage soup and fish, on this occasion stuffed herring, for the third time in a week, she pushed her plate away in disgust.

'I need to get away,' she complained. 'Perhaps to the French Riviera. It must be years since we visited our villa there.'

'I'm afraid that is quite out of the question,' the Count calmly informed her. The children groaned their disappointment. They loved their holidays in the sun and as autumn approached, the flat was growing colder by the day.

'Why?' she snapped.

The Count tucked into his fish with gusto, but then he must have worked up quite an appetite as whenever we were in town he was back and forth to the Winter Palace throughout the day about his ministerial business. 'I am too busy for one thing.'

'Tush! We can manage perfectly well without you.'

I ate my own meal in silence, suitably deaf as required when they argued. I knew the Countess would prefer her husband to be absent, as that would allow her to embark upon yet another holiday romance while I, of course, would be left to mind the children. Not that I had any choice in the matter even if I was fast losing patience at being constantly expected to cover up her indiscretions. Two Christmases had come and gone since I'd been burdened with the extra task of acting as her lady's maid, and all hope of finding a replacement seemed to have vanished. But then with a war on I really didn't feel able to object.

The Count's words echoed my own thoughts.

'There is also, don't forget, the small issue of a war being fought in France,' he reminded her.

'We shall go nowhere near the battlefield. In any case, I'm sure the war isn't half as bad as you claim.'

'It's a great deal worse.'

'The Count is right, milady. You should stay safely at home, if only for the sake of the children,' I said, unable to keep silent any longer.

He smiled his gratitude, but his wife remained unconvinced. 'I *need* a holiday!' It was almost as if the soldiers fighting and losing their lives were doing so deliberately to annoy her.

'Don't be foolish, Olga. Millie is right: think of the children. You must put the idea right out of your mind.'

Unfortunately, once the Countess had set her heart on something, nothing would prevent her from getting it, or in this case a reasonable alternative. Since the French Riviera was out of bounds she opted instead for the Crimea. The climate was almost Mediterranean, with sea breezes that stopped it becoming unbearably hot in the summer, and was still pleasant at this time of year. The Count made no further protest, and in late September we packed our trunks and departed.

It was no surprise to discover that Countess Olga's latest lover, Dimitri Korniloff, happened to be staying nearby. Sufficiently discreet not to let the children see him, nevertheless she made no attempt to hide the fact she'd be out and about with him most days.

'What if the children should need you, milady?'

'I shall be here to take tea with them, and to see them at bedtime.'

'But you will surely wish to play with them occasionally on the beach, or go out and about with them around town?'

Her glance was disdainful. 'Tired of caring for the children too, now, are you, as well as being my personal maid?'

'Of course not, but they do like to spend time with their dear mama,' I reminded her. 'Particularly when their papa is not around.'

She strode from the room without even troubling to answer. There were times when she treated me as if I was invisible. Perhaps it would have been better if I were, instead of opening my mouth when really I shouldn't.

~

The Count joined us for Christmas, anxious to escape Petrogad himself for a while, which was just as well as he looked in need of a rest. In the city the weather was bitterly cold but here in the Crimea the winters were much milder, sheltered as we were from the worst of the bitter north winds by the mountains, although there was often snow on the higher slopes above the town. I admit to finding it all rather exciting and had great fun helping the children to make paper lanterns and home-made Christmas crackers. A tree was brought from the forest which we decorated with walnuts and chocolates wrapped in gold and silver paper. Then we fixed candles onto the lower branches where we could easily reach them. But as I had no wish to risk a fire, I set a long stick with a wet sponge fixed to the end close by, just in case.

The children hung up stockings by the chimney, and, in accordance with tradition, *Nyanushki* set an old galosh in the empty grate that would later have snow packed round it, so that the children would know when Santa Claus had been.

On the morning of Christmas Eve I took them out into the woods to collect holly, mistletoe and ivy with which to decorate the house. Such plants do not grow in the north of Russia, the climate being too severe, so it was a thrill for me to have echoes of Christmases back home in dear old England.

As the children and I wound the ivy around the banister rails, Stefan climbed the stepladder to pin up the holly and mistletoe over pictures and door frames. When he was done he called me over.

'Is that enough, do you think?' I barely had time to answer before he caught me with a kiss. The children thought this very funny and applauded loudly, roaring with laughter. I was not so amused, particularly when a voice rang out behind us in the hall.

'Ah, so this is what you two get up to when my back is turned?'

Too startled to reply, I dipped a curtsey, carefully keeping my head down so that the Countess could not see how my cheeks flamed. 'Now look what you've done,' I hissed at Stefan under my breath.

She sauntered over in that graceful way she had, looking as elegant and magnificent as ever in a gown of embroidered gold satin encrusted with pearl beads. Several strings of pearls hung about her neck over a décolletage cut daringly low. The Count and Countess were to attend a Christmas ball that evening and I have to confess I had never seen her looking more beautiful. Placing herself below the mistletoe, she glanced provocatively across at Stefan. 'Is this where I should stand for *my* Christmas kiss?' she asked.

Stefan's embarrassment was all too plain to see. A crimson stain crept up his throat and over the tightness of his jaw as he darted me a glance of appeal. Aching with sympathy for the awkward situation in which she was placing him, I clumsily attempted to intervene.

'It is snowing outside, your ladyship. If you are ready to leave now, shall I fetch your coat and fur wrap?'

She didn't even glance in my direction, keeping her gaze firmly fixed on the object of her desire, my own beloved Stefan, as she ordered me to do so. It seemed that, far from saving him, I had accidentally created the necessity to leave him alone with her. We were saved by Serge, who gave a snort of laughter.

'You wouldn't dare touch Mama.'

There was a small stunned silence as even the boy's mother did not quite know how to respond to this sharp retort from her son.

Stefan, however, was quick to take advantage. I could almost sense his relief. 'Your son is absolutely correct, your ladyship. That would be entirely out of place,' he said, and giving a little head bow, he tucked the stepladder under his arm and calmly walked away.

As I flew up the stairs to fetch fur coats, hats and wraps, I could almost feel her fury.

Yet another Christmas had passed and the war in Europe continued without any sign of peace on the horizon. Come the New Year, and weary of the extra demands upon my time and discretion from duties as lady's maid which had already lasted far longer than our agreement, I politely requested a rise.

The Countess burst out laughing, clearly amused by what she perceived as a show of impertinence. Money, as I knew only too well, meant nothing to her, but at the same time she hated handing it over to anyone else. The poor, in her opinion, could stay poor, it being no one's fault but their own that they were in that situation, and certainly no concern of hers. 'What on earth makes you imagine that you deserve a rise?'

'Because I am doing two jobs,' I reminded her. 'I am still governess to your children and also acting as your personal maid, even though we agreed the latter role was only temporary. But no attempt to find a replacement has been made, and your ladyship is fully aware that I really don't feel comfortable in the position.'

No laughter this time, only a deep and furious frown. '*I* will say when you are relieved of this duty, and I'm not in the least interested in your comfort.'

But I was determined to make my point. I sent money regularly to my parents, who I knew were carefully investing it for the time when I returned home for good. Sometimes my longing for the Lakes and my worry over my family at this difficult time were almost unbearable, despite my increasing fondness for Russia. I certainly had no intention of being taken advantage of. 'May I politely remind your ladyship that if I am to carry out both sets of duties, I should be paid accordingly.'

'I think you have an inflated idea of your own importance, Dowthwaite.'

'Then perhaps you don't really need my help, or my discretion and loyalty after all?' I rather recklessly remarked.

Countess Olga understood exactly the challenge behind these words, as her entire status and honour depended upon my silence. She was also remarkably skilled at ignoring reality and not answering difficult questions.

'Where are my pearls?' she suddenly asked, starting to rummage among the clutter on her dressing table.

Irritated by the way she'd so casually brushed aside my request for a rise, my tone was unusually brusque. 'In the safe, where they should be.' I went to fetch them. To my surprise and dismay, however, I could see no sign of them. All too aware that my mistress was somewhat careless with her jewellery, often leaving it lying about, I didn't panic too much. 'They must be here somewhere,' I said, annoyed. 'Or did you perhaps lend them to someone?'

'Of course not!'

'Do you recall putting them back in the safe after you wore them at the Christmas ball? Or did you take them off and leave them lying about?' I was searching the room as I asked these obvious questions, but having scoured every drawer, cabinet and jewellery box, and checked the safe several times more, I was obliged to admit defeat. There was no sign of the pearls anywhere.

'This is *your* fault, Dowthwaite, entirely due to your incompetence. It is *your* job to keep my jewels safe, so *you* must have lost them,' she accused me in icy tones. 'Or else you took a fancy to them yourself.'

I gasped. 'You surely aren't suggesting that *I* took them? I would *never* do such a thing. I haven't touched your pearls,' I said, hotly defending myself.

'Yet were you not attempting to blackmail me just now? So why would I not believe you capable of anything?'

There was a long telling silence in which I recognised the danger my recklessness had led me into, and how cleverly she had turned the tables on me. Keeping my expression carefully bland, I said, 'I haven't the first idea what you mean, milady, but I will continue to search for your pearls. They must be somewhere.'

Convinced of my guilt, she punished me by refusing to speak to me for the rest of that day, and the one after that, leaving little notes of instruction on her dressing table instead. And at dinner each evening, by the time it was my turn to be served, there would be no food left.

'What am I to do?' I sobbed to Stefan. 'Apart from any other consideration, I'm starving. I have to keep sneaking off to the kitchen to beg food off the chef, and Anton is wary of offending the Countess so not particularly generous. How can I convince her of my innocence? I'm quite sure she's about to sack me, if I don't die of starvation first.'

He pulled me close, pressing his lips against my forehead, making me feel so safe in his arms that I wanted to stay there forever. 'You could speak to the Count and ask for his support. Either that or find the darned things.'

'That's a good suggestion. He has never been anything but kind towards me.'

I trusted the Count, as he possessed the common sense and stability his wife lacked. I rather assumed he'd married Olga out of duty as there was little sign of love between them, a union no doubt arranged by his family since he had the title and connections, and she was a rich heiress, as *Babushka* had indicated. He must have been very young at the time, as I guessed he could only be in his thirties now. I admired him enormously, as he cared for his staff and tenants and was a good father to his children. What a dreadful waste to be a good-looking man trapped in an unhappy marriage.

As expected, he was deeply sympathetic of my plight, but with a sad shake of his head he said there was little he could do to help. 'My wife has her own way of doing things, and I rarely intervene. I'll admit she is somewhat careless with her belongings and I'm quite certain of your innocence. I'll put in a word for you, Millie, should it become necessary.'

'Thank you, sir.' I was always touched by the fact that he addressed me by my first name, and grateful for his belief in me. It seemed all I could hope for.

And then quite out of the blue the very next day Irina came running, the string of pearls dangling in her small hands. 'Look what I found, *Baryshnya*. They fell out of Serge's fishing bag when I was putting it away for him.'

The boy denied all knowledge of them with a surprisingly fierce vigour. 'I never touched *Mamochka's* pearls,' he insisted. 'I can't think how they got there. I swear I wasn't playing one of my jokes. Nor do I believe you stole them, *Baryshnya*.'

I smiled at him with gratitude, wanting to believe him. 'Thank you, Master Serge. Your faith in my innocence is wonderful to hear. It quite warms my heart. I expect the pearls simply fell into your bag by accident. We'll say no more about it.'

So was it an accident, I wondered, or yet another practical joke? Against all previous evidence of the boy's behaviour there was something genuine about Serge's passionate denial. More likely the Countess had pocketed the dratted pearls to punish me for standing up to her, and then dropped them into her son's bag. For once, though, it looked as if involving her son in her nasty little scheme of revenge had backfired.

TWENTY

In the early days of the year we returned to Petrograd. The cold snap that had descended over Christmas worsened, with huge solid banks of snow and ice blocking the roads and icicles hanging from the roof. Keeping the children happy was not easy as they soon grew grumpy and quarrelsome from being confined largely indoors, apart from the odd afternoon skating on the frozen River Neva, or playing on ice slides in the park.

While the Countess took to her bed for a rest and I set about unpacking, the Count went at once to the Winter Palace to continue with his duties. He returned later with the startling news that Rasputin had been murdered on 29th December.

'The fellow was partaking of Madeira wine and cake with Prince Yusupov and one or two of his comrades when he was allegedly poisoned.'

'Good heavens,' the Countess said. 'Are you saying the prince was responsible?'

'I am saying nothing of the sort, and neither must any of you,' he quietly warned. 'It is true that Prince Yusupov and Grand Duke Dmitry have been placed under house arrest while the matter is investigated. We must await the outcome of that, but whoever the perpetrator is, they were certainly determined to finish him off one way or another. When the poison did not have immediate effect, assuming cyanide was actually present in his food, he was shot and then thrown into the freezing River Neva, where he drowned. Whoever did it was determined to finish him off, but I believe the fellow put up quite a fight.'

The Count had gathered the entire staff together, the children already in bed, and every one of us was shocked by this horror story. We stood in silence for some moments, contemplating the ramifications of the loss of the Tsarina's favourite *staretz*, with his magnetic eyes and his amazing ability to have prevented the Tsarevitch from bleeding to death on more than one occasion.

'He was a charlatan and completely mad, so it's surely no bad thing,' the Countess remarked somewhat dismissively, as if a man's life was of no importance even if he had been a monk and an advisor to royalty. 'Foolish Alix was becoming far too obsessed with him.'

Looking grim, the Count did not disagree. 'I've noticed a shift in the public mood, though, an odd mix of expectancy and celebration in the air, as if Rasputin's death frees people in some way.'

Stefan said, 'I suppose the murder could give the would-be revolutionaries an incentive to take the power they have long craved. Why would they trust a man who believes in the divine right to rule? Or a woman who has been obsessed with a mad monk?'

'I worry about that too, Stefan.' The Count was looking seriously concerned. 'I'm afraid the Tsarina's shy, retiring nature has done her no favours. It's rather sad but not surprising that people accuse her of being aloof. Some family members have even suggested she be sent to a convent.'

'But is that quite fair?' I butted in, speaking out of turn, as always.

'Millie claims to know nothing of politics but always has an opinion on it,' Stefan put in with a wry smile.

'I know only what I've picked up by listening to *Babushka* relating her memories of her life as a lady-in-waiting at the palace, which I've found fascinating. But yes, I do think the Tsarina is unnecessarily vilified.'

The Count gave me a nod of encouragement. 'In what respect, Millie?'

Blushing with embarrassment at finding myself the object of attention, I struggled to organise my thoughts. 'People accuse her of all kinds of things, such as being a German traitor when she's clearly doing everything she can for her adopted country, like turning royal palaces into field hospitals and working for her Red Cross Certificate.' Which was more than could be said for the Countess.

'Indeed that is true. The Tsarina is seen in the hospitals most days in her white uniform, witnessing all the horrors of war first-hand without complaint.'

'And isn't she also responsible for running the country while the Tsar is away commanding military forces?'

The Count pulled a face. 'Yes, but she doesn't do it very well, unfortunately. The problem is that dear Alix, a devoted wife and mother, is far too protective of her husband. She is so determined that no member of the government should challenge his authority that she chooses ministers who are weak "yes men", whose only wish is to win favour with the Tsar, which unfortunately divides the nation even more.'

'Oh, then Stefan is right. I really don't understand politics.'

With a smile, the Count patted my shoulder. 'You at least try, dear Millie.'

I might have asked more questions but as the Countess fixed me with one of her fierce glares, I held my silence, nervous of finding myself going hungry yet again.

Over the coming days and weeks the Countess frequently complained she wasn't feeling well. She lingered in bed of a morning, and constantly called for snacks to nibble throughout the day, due to an upset tummy. She even abandoned her passion for cold baths, which she considered good for her skin, putting them on hold in favour of two hot baths a day. I most certainly ensured that the children took one each night due to the bitterly cold weather, and gave them each a warming cup of hot chocolate before tucking them into bed. I was taking Irina her drink one evening when I found the little girl crouched beside the door of her mother's boudoir.

'What are you doing there?' I gently scolded her, carefully keeping my voice low in case the Countess should hear.

The child pressed a finger to her lips to shush me. Her insecurity was such that the only reassurance she found was in secretly listening in to whatever her parents were discussing. What a little imp she was, not quite the angel her father described. 'Is *Mamochka* going away?' she whispered.

'Goodness, what nonsense is this?' But as I reached for her hand I realised that her parents were engaged in a most furious row, and making no attempt to keep their voices down.

'So what if I am having an affair with Dimitri Korniloff? What business is it of yours? You haven't been exactly innocent yourself in that regard.'

'If I broke our marriage vows it was because you rejected me from the start, destroying any trust between us from the very first day of our marriage.'

'You didn't care about me, only about pleasing your father and making him proud.'

'A task at which I clearly failed, thanks to your lies.'

The Countess's laugh rang out, as if he'd said something highly amusing. 'You should have stood up to your parents and married that foolish Mavra Obelensky. Such a tragedy that she died.'

'Stop that, Olga. Don't even mention her name.'

'I want a divorce, Vaska, and I'll do whatever it takes to get one.'

The Count mumbled something we couldn't quite catch. Quickly taking Irina's hand, I attempted to lead the child away as this really wasn't a conversation a little girl should hear. She firmly resisted. 'No, *Baryshnya*, I need to listen.'

'Come with me, *please*,' I begged, not wishing to see her hurt, and then her father's voice rang out, paralysing us both.

'Make no mistake, if you are foolish enough to run off with the fellow, your reputation and status will be in ruins, and I will cut you off without a single kopek to your name.'

'You wouldn't *dare*!'

'Don't underestimate me, Olga. I'll also make sure you lose all contact with the children, even your precious son.'

Gathering Irina into my arms I carried her quickly to bed, paying no attention to her furious wriggling. Once I'd settled her and she was sipping her hot chocolate, albeit with a sulky expression on her face, I sat beside her on the bed. 'You really shouldn't listen to the silly things grown-ups say. They can get very cross with each other at times, but it's only like you having a quarrel with Serge. It's not as bad as it sounds.'

She looked at me, a wisdom in her young eyes that was really quite alarming. 'Divorce must be a very bad thing if *Mamochka* wouldn't ever see us again. Why would she want one?'

Why indeed! I smiled reassuringly as I tucked in the blanket. 'Your dear mama probably wasn't thinking properly. Don't we all say silly things when we're cross over something? Now, which story shall we have tonight? What about *Polly, A New Fashioned Girl*? That should be fun.'

I kept reading until Irina's eyelids drooped and sleep claimed her, then left the night light burning as I quietly closed the door.

Only then did I allow myself to wonder whether the Countess really would leave the Count, and what would happen to us all if she did.

~

Relations between the couple became ever more strained, almost as icy as the weather. The word *divorce* was never mentioned again, so I could only assume that the Countess had backed down, fearful perhaps of losing her position in Russian society. I kept out of her way as much as possible, spending longer than normal at the British and American chapel with my friends.

'It will be the International Women's Day Festival in Petrograd on February twenty-third,' Ruth announced while a group of us were enjoying our usual cake and gossip. 'We often celebrate the day with a meal, or loved ones buy us flowers or send a card. In 1913 women demonstrated on the right to vote. This year there is to be a rally protesting over the high price of bread. Many textile workers, housewives and women struggling to feed their families will be taking part. Who is willing to join them?'

'We're British. Wouldn't they object? We don't have children and we're fortunate enough not to have to buy our own bread,' protested Ivy, who much preferred a quiet life.

'But that's no reason not to support our fellow sisters in their hour of need, is it? I'm willing to walk with them to protest, carry a banner or something,' Ruth pointed out.

'Me too,' I said, remembering the anguish on the peasant woman's face when the Countess had refused to give her a few kopeks to feed her children and then given her own a small fortune each day to buy sweets.

'I don't mind joining,' another girl agreed.

'Sounds like a good cause to me.'

Several more hands shot up and we were soon engrossed in writing posters with powerful messages that read, '*Our children are starving*' and '*We need to buy bread.*'

When the day came I was astonished by the numbers that turned out. There were some men present but literally hundreds of female textile workers took to the streets, waving their posters or proclaiming their message, shouting as loudly as they could. 'Bread', 'End the war!' and even, 'Down with the Autocracy!'

The women assembled at the corner of Bolshoi Prospekt and Gavanskaya Street, looking desperate, hollow-cheeked and weary, many like walking skeletons since feeding their children was a priority. I was deeply moved, filled with admiration for their courage and determination as they began to hammer on doors demanding bakers bring prices down or give them bread there and then to feed their starving children.

'We need decent wages in order to eat,' they cried.

'It's a disgrace that we can't afford to buy bread.'

'Our children are starving!'

'Are your children really starving?' I asked the woman beside me. 'I do wish I had money to help you.'

'You help just by being here, and yes, my children consider themselves fortunate if they get cabbage soup or a bit of bean stew once a day. The price of milk, butter and eggs makes buying those quite beyond my reach. Sometimes I can afford to buy a few potatoes to add to the beans.'

'And the government keeps on printing more money which pushes up prices still further, while our wages stagnate,' added her friend. 'I've been driven to picking dandelion leaves and nettles to boil into soup for my children.'

The women, wrapped in their long drab coats and scarves against the cold, walked in a mass through the streets carrying their banners between them. Although most of the snow had been cleared, it still felt icy underfoot as we followed on at the back, a small group of supporters, while onlookers cheered as the procession passed by.

'Down with the war!' someone shouted.

'Down with hunger!'

'Long live the revolution!' This latter cry came from a group of agitators who had appeared out of nowhere.

The numbers rapidly grew, the demonstration developing a momentum of its own as the women were joined by factory workers all demanding modernisation and better working conditions, which had worsened thanks to the Great War in Europe. An ever-increasing number of strikers then swept into the city centre, apparently coming from the Vyborg district and other industrial areas, even crossing the frozen River Neva, or so our fellow marchers informed us.

'I thought this protest was just about the price of bread. It's looking to be about a lot more than that now,' I murmured, as Ruth and I hooked arms to avoid being separated.

'It would seem so,' she agreed, keeping her voice low in the eerie silence that was settling all around us. 'I heard that a few days ago hundreds of workers started a strike in one of the workshops at the huge Putilov factory. They asked for a rise and demanded that some fellow-workers who had previously been sacked from their jobs be reinstated. Thousands more from the plant joined them, but the management's response was to lock everyone out. Consequently they appealed to other workers for their support, which it very much looks as if they're getting. That could prove dangerous if the authorities object.'

'I hope you're wrong,' I said, beginning to feel a sense of unease. No sooner had I spoken than mounted policemen arrived on the scene, thrusting their horses through the crowds in a brutal attempt to disperse them, swiping at people with the flats of their swords.

Yet the moment they passed through, the crowd closed up again, as solid as the ice beneath our feet.

It was scary and thrilling all at the same time. I liked the Russian people very much and my heart went out to them, the mothers and their children most of all. Serge and Irina couldn't imagine for a moment how it might feel to be hungry, let alone starving, since they were both so well fed, as their plump, rosy cheeks indicated.

I'd arranged for *Nyanushki* to take them to the Catherine Gardens on the pretext that I had lessons to prepare and needed a break. No one knew I was taking part in what had begun as a simple protest march, certainly not the Countess, or even Stefan, as I was fearful even he might have prevented me from attending. But though I wouldn't have missed it for the world, I knew that I ran a huge risk just by being here.

'I should be getting back before anyone misses me, and before things get any worse.'

'You're right,' Ruth said. 'We've done our bit. Let's get out of here.' As we started edging out of the procession we found our way blocked by yet another mounted policeman. I pulled Ruth out of the horse's path but, reaching down, he struck her across the shoulders with the flat of his sword, sending her tumbling to the ground.

'*Ruth*!'

I could barely see my dear friend in the mass of feet and horses' hooves surrounding her. It seemed to take several long, frightening moments before I managed to grab hold and hoist her to her feet. She was deathly pale, had lost her hat and was covered in snow and filth; she was so wobbly I feared she might be about to faint at any minute. Fortunately, Ivy emerged from the crowd to take her other arm and together we battled our way out of the demonstration, almost carrying her between us.

When I asked if she was all right her mumbled response was not encouraging. 'She needs to see a doctor,' I said.

'Right. Let's find a tram to the hospital,' said Ivy, steering us down a side street. Unfortunately, none were running so we were forced to walk all the way back to the British and American chapel, where Ruth was at last examined.

'Apart from some bruising she's suffered no major injuries,' the nurse informed us.

'Thank goodness for that.' I turned to Ruth. 'Were we mad to take part?'

Smiling, she shook her head, then winced at the pain. 'No, it was the right thing to do. The protest needed to be made. I'm really glad we did our bit to help. I'll be fine.'

Later, when I crept back into the flat, careful not to alert my mistress to the fact I'd been out without her permission, I felt an inner glow at having been a part of such an important demonstration. I prayed the women had successfully made their point and that emergency rations would soon be set up to help their starving families.

TWENTY-ONE

I didn't see Stefan until later that evening, having spent the time since my return rushing about trying to catch up on my usual tasks in order to make it appear as if I'd been fully occupied within doors all day. I saw to the children, attended the Countess as she prepared to go out for the evening as usual, and enjoyed a welcome glass of tea with *Nyanushki*, served with a slice of lemon, listening with only half my attention as she talked about the children's adventures in the park without enlightening her on my own.

Stefan, however, was different. I couldn't wait to tell him what I'd been up to.

He was waiting for me in the laundry room, which was where we tended to have our secret meetings when in town. He gathered me in his arms to kiss me the moment I walked in. We needed to be so careful, always on our best behaviour, that it was a relief to be able to respond without fear of being observed. My heart raced at his kisses, wanting so much more, and when we paused to take a breath we kept our fingers entwined, looking deep into each other's eyes, which said everything that words could not.

'Where have you been?' he said. 'I've been looking for you all day.'

I laughed. 'You wouldn't believe me if I told you.'

Something in my tone of voice must have alerted him. 'You were there, weren't you, at this demonstration everyone is talking about? You sneaked out of the house to watch it.'

'Actually, I took part,' I said.

'Good lord, why didn't you say you were going?'

'You might have stopped me.'

He laughed. 'You underestimate me, Millie. I'm greatly impressed. Well done!'

'I'm rather proud of myself, too,' I admitted, 'if somewhat exhausted from all the walking we did. It felt like a worthwhile thing to do, although whether we did any good by it remains to be seen. I do hope so, as children really are starving. The Tsar needs to order emergency food rations urgently.'

'I'll believe that when I see it,' Stefan muttered. 'But what about us? How much longer are we going to tie ourselves to these autocrats?'

The remainder of our precious half hour alone was spent dreaming of a future together, although the hows, whys and wherefores had yet to be decided.

A day or two later I was working with the children in the schoolroom as usual when, glancing up from his work, Serge asked, 'What's that noise?

Irina ran over to the window to look out. 'There are a lot of people, *Baryshnya*. Where are they all going?'

Joining her, I saw that she was right, and it was fairly plain where they were heading. The demonstrations had been growing daily to ever more dangerous proportions, and Stefan had told us at breakfast that Russia was now in the throes of a national strike.

Not that I explained any of this to Irina. Ushering the child back to her seat, I said in my most cheerful tones, 'They are going to an important meeting. Nothing to do with us, but I agree it is rather disruptive, so we won't do any more arithmetic today, and instead carry on with our knitting for the soldiers. Master Serge, you could write them some letters. Soldiers at the front deserve all the support they can get.'

Nyanushki and I set about helping the children with these tasks. After they were settled, I had just resumed knitting the balaclava I'd been working on for so long I'd begun to think it would never be finished, when the first shots rang out.

I froze. Poor old Nanny almost fell off her chair in shock. Irina burst into tears, and Serge looked panic-stricken.

'Who's shooting?' he yelled, rushing to the window, but I quickly pulled him away.

'Keep well clear, just in case. Stay here with *Nyanushki*,' I ordered, 'while I find out what's going on.'

I ran into the corridor, straight into Stefan, who'd come rushing to check that we were all right. 'What is it? What's happening?'

'I've no idea. I can't see anything from here.' He turned to me in frustration, his face white to the lips. 'I'm going out to investigate. I won't be long.'

'No, don't,' I cried, grabbing hold of him, and we both instinctively dropped to our knees as the terrifying sound of shooting rang out louder than ever.

We stared at each other in horror. 'Surely they wouldn't be firing their guns at the demonstrators?' I said, numb with disbelief.

'It sounds very like 1905 all over again.'

'Then you mustn't go out or the same thing could happen to you that happened to your father. Please don't risk it, I beg you, Stefan. What would I do without you if . . . ?' I choked on the words, unable to express my fears out loud. 'Wait for the Count. He's at the Winter Palace and will no doubt be able to tell us more when he gets home.'

'I *must* go. There might be something I can do to help.'

'No, Stefan, please.'

We'd been forced to raise our voices as the shooting continued, and as I argued with him the boudoir door flew open and the Countess appeared. She looked dishevelled and pale, not at all her usual elegant self, as if the noise had woken her from a deep sleep. She proceeded to rail and shout at us, demanding to know what was going on, implying the fault for disturbing her was entirely ours. She seemed to be constantly in a bad temper these days.

'It's the demonstrators, milady. Something terrible seems to be happening to them.'

Clasping her hands together, she let out a sigh of relief. 'Oh, is that all? Well, they deserve all they get, dreadful people.'

I stepped forward, ignoring Stefan's attempt to restrain me. 'How can you say such a thing? There are children starving, men and women being overworked and paid a pittance, losing their jobs, and with no money to feed their families. It's all right for you, being rich, but what if you weren't? Would you silently stand by and watch your children suffer and possibly die?'

She stared at me, eyes narrowed in cold fury, and I knew instantly that I'd made a bad mistake.

'So how do you know so much about this so-called demonstration, Dowthwaite?'

I heard Stefan's low groan, but nothing would stop me now. I remembered the sunken cheeks of the women, their hollow eyes and the fear in their voices as they cried out when the mounted police hit them. Lifting my chin with pride, I met the Countess's fierce glare. 'I was there. I heard their stories, witnessed their misery and desperation. Something needs to be done.'

The silence that followed this rash statement was profound, interrupted by the slam of the front door and the sound of the Count's footsteps hurrying up the stairs. He was calling out, asking if we were safe.

'I'll speak to you later,' she hissed.

~

The Count confirmed our worst fears, telling us that under instruction from the Tsar the soldiers had indeed opened fire. 'Nicholas was informed of the situation and the Duma begged him to order the release of emergency food supplies. 'Sadly, he declined to do so. Instead he sent a message to the police to "end the disorders in the capital by tomorrow". They valiantly attempted to obey, at some risk to their own lives, but the people ran to hide in the courtyards, returning to the streets whenever there was a pause in the shooting. In the end, more than two hundred people were killed.'

We were all dumbstruck with horror. I was thinking how easily it could have been Ruth and me, as we had merrily and wholeheartedly joined in the start of the protest just a few days ago.

'What now?' Stefan quietly asked. The Count shook his head in despair.

'This could get a great deal worse. Even now the political leaders do not grasp the true dangers, believing they are in control of the situation. Nor does the Tsar quite understand the precariousness of his own position.'

There was no sleep for us that night as, like thousands of other frightened citizens, we stayed safely behind locked doors. The Count was proved to be entirely correct: things did indeed get worse. Sickened by what they'd been obliged to do, the regiment concerned in the shooting stood down, swapping sides and becoming part of the demonstration themselves. Others followed suit.

By the first of March 170,000 soldiers had joined them. The stink of fear and decaying bodies was everywhere, as was the red flag. Prisons and police stations came under attack, the prisoners were released on to the streets, and the number of rioters exploded. Law and order had completely broken down in what was by now being dubbed a revolution.

~

The Countess wasn't in the least interested in the turmoil going on around her, even if people were dying. She was far too preoccupied in exerting her power, the eyes fixed upon mine hard and cold as she proceeded to make her displeasure about my recent actions plain. 'You will never involve yourself in such a carry-on again, do you understand?'

'I beg your pardon, milady. It's just that I considered it important. It seems that not everyone can afford food of any kind for their children, let alone the sort of fine meals we are served every day by Anton. I believed it was right to help and . . .'

'*I am not interested in what you believe*!' the Countess screamed.

'Hard as it may be for you to accept, milady, I am entitled to have opinions and a mind of my own.'

'Oh, you've made that abundantly clear, Dowthwaite, from the very start, I seem to recall.'

I almost smiled at the memory of our first disagreements back at Carreck Place. 'There we are, then. Every person has rights, even the poorest and the lowest of the low.'

'On the contrary, you do not have the right to defy my orders and go *anywhere without my permission*! Not even to this so-called chapel of yours.'

'Goodness, you surely aren't intending to hold me prisoner? With respect, milady, what I do with my free time is my choice, not yours. It was a properly organised support group for a straightforward protest march about the price of bread, and no fault of ours that the demonstration turned into something far more serious.'

'That's enough! I will take no more of your obstinate defiance. You may consider yourself dismissed herewith.'

I blinked in disbelief, this being the last thing I'd expected. I'd been quite certain I'd be able to win her round in the end. 'You can't be serious?

'Never more so. Pack your belongings and go. I will not harbour a revolutionary in my own home a moment longer than necessary.'

I gave a half-laugh. 'That's absolute nonsense. You know I am no revolutionary. As I explained, my friends and I from the British and American chapel were merely supporting mothers desperate to feed their children. What if Master Serge were starving – wouldn't you do everything you could to keep your son alive?'

'Get out!' Moving across the room at speed she pulled the bell cord to summon Gusev, the butler. 'Leave my house this instant, or I'll have you thrown out.'

Without pausing to offer my usual curtsey I turned and walked away, chin high, wanting her to see that I was not intimidated by her fury. Oh, but I was. Deep inside I was shaking with shock, and on reaching my room collapsed on to the bed. What had I done?

Within minutes Gusev was tapping on my door. 'I'm sorry, *Baryshnya*, but I am to escort you off the premises.'

I was almost in tears as the butler led me downstairs, kindly carrying my bag with barely a portion of my belongings quickly stuffed inside. I could feel everyone's gaze upon me as we passed through the back kitchen. Stefan, I noticed, was not among them, no doubt out on one of his mysterious jaunts. I couldn't even begin to guess how he would react when he returned and found me gone. Unless he was involved with the revolutionaries after all.

'I'm sorry it had to end this way, Miss Dowthwaite. You have been good for the children,' the butler kindly remarked as he opened the door. A swirl of bitter cold wind swept over us, taking my breath away. 'We'll send on your trunk when you let us have your new address.'

And where might that be? I hadn't the first idea where I was going.

Perhaps someone had called her, for the next instant I was being gathered into *Nyanushki's* arms. 'Don't leave, my dear. Let me talk to her ladyship. Whatever you're supposed to have done, I'm sure it's all a silly mistake.'

I kissed the papery soft cheek. 'I'm afraid there's nothing you can do, Klara. The Countess has decided I'm a revolutionary, so I am dismissed.' And on that shocking note I walked out of the door into the unknown.

TWENTY-TWO

'She sacked you? Just because you supported those starving mothers and children? Had the woman no heart at all?' Abbie had been enjoying an afternoon off from the shop listening to more of her grandmother's story, filled with admiration for her attendance at the demonstration but shocked by this new development.

Millie gave an ironic chuckle. 'Not that I ever discovered.'

'So you found yourself accidentally caught up with the start of the revolution and all she could think about was herself, and the fact you hadn't followed her stupid rules?'

'We didn't see it as a revolution at the time, more a demonstration and riots, but yes, I'm afraid so, as always.'

'Surely Stefan took your side and stood up for you, or did he lose his job too?'

The phone rang before her grandmother could answer that, but as Abbie picked up the receiver Millie watched how her granddaughter's face changed colour to a flush of furious pink.

'How did you get this number? Well, Marisa had no right to give it to you without checking with me first. So, what is it you want? Sorry, say that again.' A slight pause while Abbie allowed the request to be repeated. 'No, Eduard, I can't simply drop everything to do your bidding. I understand you must be missing her, but why would you care about Aimée when you'll be having another child soon, one that would never have been conceived had you remained faithful to *me?*'

'*I am her father, so I have the right to see her,*' he shouted at the top of his voice, so that even her grandmother, seated some distance away, could hear.

Abbie instantly felt ashamed. Of course he was, and Aimée adored him, so she really had no right to keep them apart. Not that she wanted to. Abbie just didn't wish to see Eduard right now. She took a calming breath. 'I'm not disputing your rights, but I can't bring Aimée back to Paris at the moment. The new school term has started and she's settling in nicely, so I really don't want her disturbed. You'll have to wait till the summer holidays.'

'If you do not come to me, I come to you.'

'Don't even consider it,' Abbie hissed furiously into the phone. Hearing his voice again had brought back a strange ache of nostalgia, yet she felt an instinctive reluctance to have her life disturbed by echoes of the past just when she too was beginning to settle, at least emotionally.

'We need to talk,' Eduard said, in his carefully enunciated English. 'We cannot do that over the phone.'

'We have nothing to talk about,' Abbie coolly responded. 'Unless, of course, you have something important to tell me, like you've actually spoken to your wife about a divorce.'

'You know I can't do that, Abigail, not while she's pregnant.'

Abbie gave a harsh little laugh, feeling nauseated that she could still fancy this man who had betrayed her so many times. 'Just as you couldn't tell her while *I* was pregnant, or at any point in the six years since. You know what your problem is, Eduard? You're a coward.'

'I have soft heart. That does not that make me a coward.'

'It does when you end up hurting people.'

'I do not want to hurt you.'

'How can you say that when you've been refusing to marry me for years?'

'I don't wish to hurt my wife, either. I love you both.'

'It doesn't work that way.'

'Come home. I miss you, Abbie.'

Her heart seemed to contract, but whether with love or pain over what their relationship might have been, was hard to decide. 'Why would I? Has anything changed since I left? Don't even bother answering that. Sorry, but I'm not interested.' And she put down the phone.

'Oh dear,' her grandmother softly remarked. 'I'm sorry, but I couldn't help overhearing much of that conversation. You do seem to be having a rough time of it at the moment, my darling.'

Abbie sank back into the chair opposite Millie, tears starting yet again which she quickly thumbed away. 'I'm still furious with him for making no effort to do as he promised.'

'And with yourself for believing in him?'

'Yes, that too. Lies, lies and more lies, that's all I've had from him. He never even asked her for a divorce. When he was absent from our apartment, as he often was, I thought he was working away, doing the catering for some event or cooking at an out-of-town hotel. Instead, it turned out he was living a double life and still sleeping with this wife. I only learned the truth when I saw her by chance at Galleries Lafayette just before Christmas, and realised she was pregnant. When I challenged him about it he admitted everything. Could hardly deny it.'

Millie gently patted her granddaughter's hand. 'Oh, my poor darling. You must have been so jealous. I know how that feels.'

'Yes, I suppose you must, with all that business between Stefan and the Countess. What a madam she was. Did she get him in the end?'

Millie seemed to be looking into some far distant place and, recognising there might still be more pain to be revealed in her grandmother's story, Abbie deliberately brightened her tone. 'Which is why I decided to stay on in the Lakes, and I'm so glad I did as I'm loving spending time with you, Gran, and listening to your stories.'

'Not to mention the wonders you are achieving with the jewellery shop. I'm so proud of you. Didn't I say how strong you are?'

Abbie smiled. 'It's your belief in me, and hearing your own story, that gives me the strength I need. And remembering how Mum used to love to work in the shop once upon a time.' Abbie would like to have said that she wanted to justify her mother's faith in leaving it to her, but she still hadn't yet confessed to her father that she knew the contents of the will. 'I've even brought in some amber pieces from a Polish firm. Not as valuable as the one we have, but I simply couldn't resist. Apparently they carve it with a sharp knife, then polish the piece and drill a hole for the chain to turn it into a pendant. Not sure I'd ever have the skill to do that job myself, but I thought I'd have a go at setting a few of the smaller stones into earrings.'

'Good for you. Amber is beautiful, likened to the sun because of its colour and clarity. There are many myths and legends attached to it, not least that it is considered to possess healing properties, often worn by children when they are teething. And significantly it is a symbol of fidelity, meant to represent everlasting love,' Millie said with a smile.

'Oh, I like that. We could do with a bit more fidelity in this world, judging by all the scandalous goings-on in this Profumo affair. What his lovely wife feels about her MP husband sleeping with a woman who is also having it off with a Russian diplomat, I dread to think. Poor woman!'

'Windmill girls, or so they think, and the dreadful scandal is having to be carefully kept from Lady Astor that her son has become an innocent victim in the affair, a scapegoat in fact, just because he allowed Stephen Ward to use a cottage on the Cliveden estate. The poor lady is losing her memory and not at all well and it could make her last days even more painful if she heard what was happening. I know someone who works for her, who says they have to keep changing channels so that she never hears the news.'

'Sometimes ignorance can be a good thing, then,' Abbie said. 'But it didn't work for me.'

~

Abbie spent the next several days working with the amber, not only making a range of earrings but slipping doughnut-shaped pieces on to silver chains to form pendants, and setting cabochons into rings and brooches. Each piece of raw amber was unique, its shape entirely natural. There were even some faceted bead-shaped pieces that Abbie threaded into bracelets and necklaces. The colours ranged from white through pale yellow, beige, gold and brown, and even blue and green, all with a varying degree of translucency. None contained the kind of inclusion that was in Kate's amber pendant, but all were still beautiful.

'They're as glamorous as diamonds and an absolute joy to work with,' she said to Linda when her assistant set a mug of coffee and a real doughnut down on the work bench beside her. 'Ooh, delicious, I'm absolutely starving. Is it calorie free?'

Linda laughed. 'Absolutely. Not that you need to worry with your slender figure. No wonder that Andrew Baxter is showing interest.'

'Stop it. You'd do better to ask yourself why. Did you know he's thinking of setting up in opposition?'

'I did hear a rumour. Will that finish us?' Linda sank onto a stool, her face grim.

'Who knows? I'm trying not to think about it. Hey, but this amber might help to create more custom. I can quite see why people love it. It warms the heart and delights the eye, is organic and fragile, and yet touches history by reaching back through the millennia. Amazing!' Abbie thought of her grandmother being held responsible for the protection of such valuable gems, even accused of stealing the Countess's pearls, and shivered at the thought.

'A treasure from a lost world,' Linda agreed, licking the jam from her own doughnut.

'Absolutely. I'm so hoping they'll sell.'

'I'm sure they will. They really are lovely. I could type out some cards giving information about its origins, myths and legends, if you like.'

'Excellent idea, and I'll make a display in the window. In Gdańsk and also in Russia before the revolution, as well as jewellery, craftsmen would use amber to create little snuff or trinket boxes, often with images of Venus, the goddess of love, or Ceres, the goddess of fertility, carved into the lid. They made candlesticks, panels and cabinets decorated with religious icons and sculptures of the Crucifixion or the Last Supper. Sadly, after the revolution, when religion was pretty well eradicated, the market died, and many artists turned to painting fairy tales on tiny lacquered boxes instead.'

'Maybe you could have a go at making a few boxes yourself.'

Abbie rolled her eyes. 'I very much doubt my skills would stretch that far, but I might try something a little more modest such as decorating a wooden trinket box with a mosaic design in amber. If I ever reach such an advanced level.'

'Don't put yourself down. It's quite evident you're an artist at heart. You have a natural flair for design.'

Leaning back in her chair to sip her coffee, and ease the tension in her arms and fingers, Abbie let out a sigh. 'The problem is I need to be a businesswoman first, Linda, if we are to survive.

You're right, I am more into design, most content doing window displays, choosing and arranging the stock, even making some of it myself. Doing accounts doesn't come naturally to me.'

'You can always pay someone else to do all of that stuff.'

'True, if I could afford it.' Abbie looked troubled as she finished off her doughnut, thinking of what would happen if she were forced to admit defeat and sell the shop after all. It didn't bear thinking about. What would she do then – go back to Paris? Never! She was here to stay, and to make a success of Precious Dreams, no matter what the effort involved. Shaking off these gloomy thoughts as she dusted sugar from her lips, Abbie smiled. 'We must make a pact to eat more doughnuts and somehow encourage more feet to walk through that door.'

Linda chuckled. 'The first is easy. As for the second, I was wondering if we should hold a launch party to officially declare the newly improved Precious Dreams open.'

'Wow, that's a good idea! We could offer wine and canapés.'

'Or frothy coffee and doughnuts.'

'And a special discount on anything bought on launch day, or maybe that entire week.'

Within minutes they'd fixed a date a couple of weeks ahead, and Linda had gone off to ring a catering firm and start writing posters to put up around town to publicise it. Pondering the expense of such an event, Abbie pulled out the latest bank statement. As she read the bottom line she heaved a sigh and pushed it quickly back into the filing cabinet. They'd just have to hope the launch party worked and brought a rush of much-needed trade.

~

It was a Saturday and Abbie was sitting eating her lunch by the lake, which she loved to do, laughing as Aimée attempted to ensure that every duck got a crust of bread. Mallards and teals were hustling each other as they searched the reedy edges of the lake for scraps, shaking their feathers in the warmth of the summer sunshine. A pair of tufted ducks came waddling across the road, holding up traffic as they too noticed food was on offer.

'The same greedy fat ones keep getting it every time,' Aimée complained. 'Go away, you bad boy. Let the others have a turn.' Raising her thin little arm, she flung the crusts as far as she could, hoping to reach the more shy ducks who were still swimming on the lake.

Andrew Baxter strolled over. 'You look as if you're having fun. Do you mind if I join you?'

'If you really want to,' Abbie coolly remarked, then could have kicked herself. 'Sorry, I didn't mean to sound rude,' she said, edging along the bench to make room for him.

He laughed. 'Actually, I was about to say the same to you. Apologies between us do seem to be turning into rather a habit.' He was wearing an open-necked shirt and jeans today, the sleeves rolled up over powerful biceps. As he sat beside her, Abbie thought he looked much more relaxed, his face touched by the sun, perhaps due to the fresh air here in Lakeland, or maybe he'd been taking walks over the fells. Linda was right: he had the kind of looks any woman would drool over. She realised he was still speaking, giving her an odd little smile, perhaps having noticed she was staring at him. Abbie found herself blushing, not something she'd done since she was a schoolgirl.

'Sorry, what did you say?' Barely having caught more than a few words, she felt obliged to ask him to repeat himself. But before he had chance to answer, Aimée came bounding over, slamming herself onto her mother's knee in a breathless, giggling rush.

'I've no bread left. Can I have an ice cream?'

'I don't think ducks eat ice cream,' Abbie teased.

'I mean for me.'

'May I buy you one?' Andrew Baxter asked.

'Ooh, yes please, can he Mummy?'

With Aimée happily eating her strawberry ice, Andrew turned back to Abbie with a smile. 'I was wondering if we could have dinner to clear the air.'

Abbie raised her eyebrows in mock surprise. 'Dinner – goodness, you're a glutton for punishment. Wasn't lunch enough for you?'

'You walked out, and rightly so. I realise I messed up so thought maybe we could start again. Allow me to introduce myself: Andrew Baxter, although friends – which I hope we'll soon be – call me Drew.'

Unable to hold back her laughter, Abbie played along and took the proffered hand for the second time. His grip was warm and firm without in any way being over-powering, going on far longer than was quite necessary before he released her hand. 'Pleased to meet you – or I would be if you weren't intent on putting me out of business.'

'That wasn't exactly what I had in mind, which is why I thought dinner might be a good idea, to allow me the opportunity to fully explain my plans.'

Choosing not to answer his question, Abbie turned away to watch her daughter chatting to the ducks as she licked her ice cream. He sighed. 'So how long have you lived in the Lakes?'

'I was brought up here, although I was living in Paris for some years until recently.'

'Really? I love France. Am I allowed to ask why you left?'

'I came back for my mother's funeral but then decided to stay. The Lake District is my home.'

He glanced about as if seeking something or someone, and then quietly asked, 'Is your husband with you? If so, I'd be happy to include him in the dinner plan.'

'There is no dinner plan, and I don't have a husband,' she tartly informed him.

'Ah, sorry. Whoops, there we go again: yet more apologies. We really must stop doing that.'

Abbie stifled a sudden urge to giggle. Could it be nerves, or because he was really being extraordinarily kind to invite a non-existent husband to join them? 'I was involved in a relationship but found he'd cheated on me, so I walked out.'

'I understand why you're feeling rather vulnerable, then,' he softly remarked. 'I can relate to that absolutely. My own marriage ended almost two years ago, and it took me quite a while to get over it, basically by working too hard.'

'Oh, I'm so sorry. Any children?'

He shook his head as he glanced across at Aimée, who'd taken off her shoes and socks and was now paddling with the ducks. 'I wasn't so fortunate.'

Abbie smiled at her daughter's antics. 'I'm rather relieved now that we never actually married, and have no regrets at leaving him, not any more. I've decided to stay in the Lakes and take on the business because I feel in need of a fresh start,' she explained, feeling she should respond a little to his kindness even if any sort of date was quite out of the question as far as she was concerned. She was done with men.

'A fresh start is an excellent idea. I, too, wish to be far away from Scotland and all the memories connected with it. The three shops my wife and I owned there have now been sold. The profits are in the process of being divided between us. The house, too.'

Abbie nodded. 'Ah, I see. So why Carreckwater?'

He slanted her a wry glance. 'It's a pretty honey-pot of a village with a thriving tourist trade, if with an odd name.'

'*Carrec* is an old Celt word for rock, which as you can see we have in plenty all around the lake, not forgetting that black knuckle-bone giant of a rock that sticks up in the middle, an island you can't actually land on.'

'Magnificent. You are very fortunate to live here. I love the place already. When I saw your business advertised I knew it was exactly what I was looking for.'

'And now that you know it isn't for sale you intend to steal all my trade anyway, and destroy it.'

'I can see it might look that way, but actually that wasn't what I had in mind.' His gaze was intense as he looked into her eyes. 'So will you allow me to explain over dinner tonight?'

Abbie stood up, brushing the crumbs of her sandwich from her lap. 'Come on Aimée, it's time we were getting back. Saturday is a busy day in the shop.' And taking her daughter's hand, she turned to go, nodding a brief farewell. 'Say goodbye to Mr Baxter.'

'Byee, Mr B,' Aimée chortled.

'And thank him for the ice cream.'

'She already has thanked me,' he said, and as mother and daughter began to walk away, he called out, 'Seven o'clock at the Ring of Bells, okay? You'll find me there this evening and every Saturday thereafter, should you feel like taking me up on the offer.'

Since she hadn't accepted his invitation, and had no intention of ever doing so, Abbie didn't trouble to answer, nor did she pause for a second as she walked away.

She might well have changed her mind later, thanks to Linda's eager encouragement, and perhaps in no small part to the warmth that emanated from Andrew Baxter, which stirred some response within her, despite her better judgement. Why would such a kind man deliberately set out to ruin her? It seemed oddly out of character, although what did she know? He was little more than a stranger.

Yet he had provoked a curiosity in her, almost a need to learn more about him.

But when she arrived back at Carreck Place she found a letter, postmarked Stepney. Abbie ripped it open, certain it was from the orphanage. Had they discovered something more about her mother? A quick glance at the letter proved this not to be the case, but the warden was forwarding a note from a Ruth Ashton, née Stubbins. Abbie skimmed it quickly then reread it more slowly, perhaps hoping she might discover some hidden secret about Kate.

Dear Miss Myers,
'. . . I recently visited the orphanage and they told me you'd come seeking information about your mother Kate. I'm so sorry to hear that she has died, and at such a young age. What a shock that must have been. I offer my sincere condolences for your loss. I've always been nervous of asking questions in the past but I've now reached an age when I thought it was worth the risk, so I wondered if you might by any chance have any information about Millie Dowthwaite? Is she still alive? I haven't seen her in years, but she was once a good friend of mine and I'd so love to meet up with her again.
Kind regards,
Ruth

Abbie took the letter straight to her grandmother, who came over all teary-eyed as she read it. Taking the old lady's hand as she sat beside her, Abbie asked the question that was burning her in mind. 'I understand that Ruth was your friend. But was she also Kate's mother?'

TWENTY-THREE

I went straight to the British and American chapel where I sent word to Ruth that I'd like to see her and she arrived within the hour, wrapping her arms about me in one of her big warm hugs. 'What a surprise. How lovely to see you.'

As I told my tale over coffee and spiced tea cakes, she began to giggle at the very idea of my being considered a revolutionary, although she quickly sobered when I revealed my predicament. 'Oh, my goodness, so now you've nowhere to stay?'

I shook my head, struggling to hold back tears. 'I keep thinking of little Irina, and Master Serge, wondering how they will cope without me, without anyone other than poor overworked *Nyanushki* to look after them.'

'The children are no longer your problem. We must let it be known that you are seeking employment. Finding you a new post won't be easy at the current time, but surely not impossible. In the meantime, I know of a hostel where you can stay. Come on, I'd best take you now as they soon get booked up.'

As we walked along arm in arm, I asked, 'How can I be sure of finding a job without a reference from the Countess, and with such an accusation hanging over my head?'

Ruth seemed to swell with anger, pressing her lips together with fresh determination. 'It's all my fault. I blame myself for suggesting you join the demonstration.'

I hotly protested. 'It wasn't your fault at all. I have absolutely no regrets, although obviously I'm relieved we didn't choose the day when the shooting took place.'

We both shuddered.

'Have you heard the latest news?' she asked. 'It's getting worse.'

I didn't respond, more concerned with my own plight than attempt to understand Russian politics. She was saying something about the Duma having formed a provisional government without a mandate, which meant nothing at all to me.

Looking at my blank expression, she went on, 'They are claiming to be so alarmed by the riots that they must act. Some people say they wish to take advantage of the situation to win more power for themselves. Alexander Kerensky, one of its leaders, has ordered that the Tsar return at once from Stavka. The story goes that on the second of March the train bringing Tsar Nicholas back to Petrograd was stopped at the Estonian border by two of the Duma's highest officials, who ordered him to abdicate. He agreed to do so, saying he had no wish to risk the lives of his people for the sake of his throne.'

I couldn't quite take this in. 'You are saying that the Tsar has abdicated? But that is awful. Who is to take his place?'

Ruth shook her head. 'No one. Three hundred years of Romanov dynasty ended that day. Tsar Nicholas apparently refused to allow his son to take the throne, even with a suitably appointed regent, as the boy would have been removed from his parents' care. I dare say the Tsar feared he might never see his son again, and being a haemophiliac he is not a healthy child. The Tsar instead named his brother, Grand Duke Michael, as his successor, but he has declined to take on the role, no doubt realising the unstable state of the monarchy. The poor man was pursued by the rioters but managed to escape.

Others were less fortunate and many aristocrats and relatives of the Romanovs have been killed.'

A jolt of fear hit me. 'Oh, my goodness, I do hope the Count will be safe.'

'I very much doubt it. As an aristocrat related to the Tsar, who also works at the Winter Palace, he's an obvious target for reprisals.' Ruth shook her head in disbelief. 'But why would you care what happens to him when he's sacked you?'

'The Count didn't sack me. It was the Countess in one of her fits of temper, which she generally recovers from, given time. He's a kind man, always very supportive in the past. I was considering asking him for my position to be restored.'

'Then ask him for his help, if you think it worthwhile, although I wouldn't bank on getting any,' Ruth warned. 'What does Stefan think of your dismissal?'

'He doesn't know yet. He'll be shocked to find me gone.'

'Write a note saying where you are and I'll see that he gets it, although it may be a few days before I can slip out again. I daren't take too much extra time off right now, with all this going on. Golly, it's a changed world. The situation is becoming so dire that some of our members are talking of returning home to England. No one feels safe any more.'

'I'm sure you're exaggerating,' I protested, deliberately putting such worries from my mind as I settled into my new quarters and started on the laborious task of writing the first of a dozen letters. I intended to hand these out to families I knew, in case one of them should be seeking a governess for their children. I could only live in hope that someone would take me on. Otherwise, I would need to start making arrangements for my return home to Carreckwater, leaving Russia and Stefan behind me.

Despite sleeping in a dormitory packed with other governesses and maids seeking temporary accommodation for one reason or another, I'd never felt more lonely in my life. I'd brought few clothes with me; my warmest coat and scarves had been left hanging behind the door in my room at the flat, as I hadn't been thinking clearly when I left – I had been hustled out of the door with some speed. Perhaps as April was approaching, and with it the first signs of spring, I could manage until Gusev sent on my trunk.

'The food is pretty dreadful here,' one girl warned. 'But eat whatever they offer you, as there's precious little of it.'

I thanked her and, despite following her advice, was soon grateful for a dry crust of bread dipped in Oxo gravy which another girl happened to have spare one evening. It wasn't that I had expected living in the hostel, or securing a new position, would be easy, but I was unprepared for the sense of utter rejection that overwhelmed me when I didn't find one.

A week went by, still with no offers of employment forthcoming. Nor had Stefan appeared even though Ruth, who visited regularly, assured me that she'd delivered the note I'd written, telling him what had happened and where I was.

'Who did you give it to?'

'I gave it to a maid at the side entrance.'

'Maybe she forgot to give it to him.' I'd been longing to see him, keeping a constant lookout as I went from door to door seeking work, so far with no luck in either respect. But even if Stefan hadn't received Ruth's letter, he must surely have noticed I wasn't around and be missing me. 'More than likely he's being kept fully occupied under the control of the Countess.'

'I'm sure he'll come when he can,' Ruth consoled me. 'The trouble is everyone is living in fear, and staying put behind locked doors. The killing is far from over.'

She was right. In the days following we learned of sailors ridding themselves of draconian commanding officers, factory foremen being beaten up and committees formed to replace them. Following what we now termed the revolution every person, whether autocrat or peasant, was classed as a citizen with equal rights, and many employers had been forced to agree to an eight-hour working day and a rise in pay, perhaps in fear of their lives. Nevertheless there was a fresh burst of optimism in the air, as people believed liberty and democracy had won the day.

'Everything is changing at an alarming rate. If you do not work the land then you have no right to own it, or such is the general cry,' Ruth said as we sat writing yet more letters of application one afternoon. 'Village communities are being reformed on that basis, and land owned by the gentry redistributed.'

'But the Count *does* work on the land. I've seen him many times digging in the vegetable plot on his estate, pruning trees and bushes, chopping logs or helping to load potatoes onto the cart that takes them to market. He's a practical man, and most supportive of his tenants. His family have owned the estate for centuries.'

'I'm afraid the respect that the gentry once enjoyed in Russia has quite gone, no matter how long their families have been around.'

'It doesn't seem fair to judge everyone by the same standards. Politically the Count is a moderate liberal, considered rather unorthodox for his class. Nor is he the social creature his wife is, tending to live rather a quiet life, by preference in the country. While she goes out gallivanting, he tends to retire early. He is not profligate with money as the Countess is, looking upon his fortune as one held in trust to help others.'

Ruth gave me a rueful smile. 'I'm sure he is all you say, Millie, and you clearly admire him a great deal to speak so fervently in his defence, but it may not be enough to save either him or his property. The new communities are taking over, ridding themselves of the elders who have been running their village or town. Even local policemen are in danger. The word is that they are intent on devolving power to themselves, even ignoring central government, which is either a good thing or a further breakdown in law and order, depending on your viewpoint. I wouldn't let on that you have this soft spot for the Count, if I were you.'

My cheeks grew warm at this piece of well-meant advice. 'I don't have a soft spot for him.'

She laughed. 'I think you do.'

~

Days later the man I really held a yearning for appeared on the hostel doorstep. As Stefan was not allowed inside, it being for women only, I grabbed my coat and we went to our favourite coffee shop on Nevsky Prospekt where we could talk in relative privacy.

'Why did it take you so long to come and see me?' I couldn't help but ask, after a welcome sip of hot coffee.

He gave me a sad smile. 'I didn't even know you'd gone at first.'

'Why, didn't you receive my note?'

'By the time I did, I couldn't get away.'

'You surely could have sneaked out, if only for half an hour or a few minutes.'

'Without her permission, as you did? Then I'd have lost my job too.'

'So you cared for your job more than me?' My disappointment at his non-appearance was beginning to turn into resentment, despite the logic in his words.

As if reading my thoughts he took my hands in his and began to kiss each fingertip in that tender way of his. As always, I melted a little inside at his touch.

'You know I would have come, Millie, given half a chance, but it just wasn't possible. The Countess kept me within her sight all day and every day, a deliberate tactic on her part to prevent me from coming to you.'

'So she hasn't forgiven me? Have you asked her to take me back?'

He looked slightly depressed by the question. 'I tried, but she really doesn't like anyone interfering in her decisions, and she's been even more moody than usual lately. In any case, why would she listen to me?'

'You know very well why: because she adores you, lusts after you.'

Stefan burst out laughing, a rather hollow sound that echoed deep in my heart, filling me with suspicion. 'Has she been pursuing you again?'

He gave a resigned sigh. 'Don't ask, Millie, it will only upset you. You are the girl I love. Always remember that.'

I felt a warmth flow through me at his words. How could I think he would let me down? He loved me, and nobody knew better than I how difficult Countess Olga could be. 'If you truly do love me, you should threaten to leave yourself if she doesn't agree to give me my job back.'

Stefan looked seriously concerned by this request and was silent for some moments before eventually giving a little nod. 'All right, but I don't hold out much hope.'

Hope was something that completely drained away in the days and weeks following. I quickly used up what little savings I'd kept by me for emergencies, and with no wages coming in I was obliged to ask my dear friend Ruth for help. She was able to offer a small loan, but I was growing increasingly desperate. If I didn't find employment soon, I would have to ask my parents to buy me a return ticket home. My adventure in Russia would be over.

Stefan managed to escape the Countess's control and visit me a few more times, but could offer no progress on my request for reinstatement. The Countess apparently refused to even discuss the matter. Close to despair, I decided to call at the flat on the pretext of asking how the children were, and if I could find the courage I'd swallow my pride and beg the Count for his help. It had to be done if I wasn't to starve.

I chose a time in the late afternoon when I knew Count Belinsky would be back from the Winter Palace and in his study dealing with estate affairs. *Nyanushki* welcomed me with open arms and a few tears, rushing to the kitchen the moment she heard I'd arrived.

'Why did you leave, and so abruptly? The children miss you so much, particularly Miss Irina, who cries every day for you.'

My heart sank at the thought of the little girl's distress, perhaps thinking I'd deliberately deserted her. 'It was not my choice. I was dismissed, Klara, you know that.'

'You should have waited. She would have come round. Her ladyship generally gets over her tantrums in time.'

'I've been gone a few weeks. Has she ever asked about me, where I am or how I'm surviving without work or wages?' My question was met with a rueful silence. I hugged the old nanny and thanked her for caring. 'Now, I need to see the Count. Is he in?'

'Oh, yes, that is a good idea. He will help you.'

My polite tap on his study door was answered at once, as always. No matter how busy he was, the Count never kept anyone waiting.

'Millie, how wonderful to see you.' The moment I entered he came striding towards me, his beaming smile so warm and welcoming I thought for a moment he might be about to envelop me in a bear hug. Fortunately, he grasped my hand instead with both of his own, his bright hazel eyes studying my face with grave concern. 'You look a bit peaky. Have you not been eating well?'

I laughed. 'I wouldn't say the food at the hostel is of the best, but I'll survive, thank you.' He patted my hand in that kind fatherly way of his. 'I've been worrying about the children and . . .'

'. . . wondering if they are managing without you? No, they ask all the time where *Baryshnya* is, and when you will be coming home. They miss you, Millie. What on earth possessed you to leave like that?'

So he had no idea. 'Didn't the Countess explain?'

He frowned and, gently leading me to a chair, invited me to sit. 'I shall order coffee and biscuits, and then you can tell me the whole story from the start.'

It was not a tale I enjoyed telling since I was obliged to admit to attending the demonstration without permission, even though the Countess had made her rules on the subject of time off clear from the start. 'I thought it would be just a simple protest march about the price of bread on International Women's Day. I need you to believe milord, that I am not in any way a revolutionary.'

At this he put back his head and laughed out loud. 'I never thought for one moment that you were, Millie, and I cannot imagine why my wife would accuse you of such.' The laughter did not last long as his brow creased with anxiety. 'There is talk that Lenin may return to Russia soon. Vladimir Ilyich Ulyanov, as he should rightly be called, has been living in Europe for some years, avoiding Russia out of fear for his own safety. But with the Tsar under arrest and the country in chaos, it is believed he may take the opportunity to return and lead the Bolsheviks to power. This would be welcomed by some sections of the populace, if not perhaps the more moderate. Whether he will succeed remains to be seen, but there is talk he is colluding with Germany.

He gave a rueful smile. 'I am aware that Russian politics is of little interest to you, dear Millie, but what I'm trying to say is that we could be moving into dangerous times, in which case I would wish to be certain that you are safe. Also, my wife is unwell, not at all herself these days for some reason. So with things the way they are, I have agreed to her taking yet another holiday. A little time out of Petrograd might be no bad thing.'

Keeping my eyes lowered, fearful they might reveal the hope that had lit within me, I responded with a smile of my own. 'I'm sure her ladyship will be delighted to hear that. She does love her holidays.'

'Indeed, so long as you are there to care for my children. You know, Millie, how very important they are to me. You will stay, won't you? Please don't disappear again: we need you. *I* need you.'

I looked up at him then, took in the untidy tangle of his brown hair as he kept running his fingers through it, and the tight line of his jaw. I'd never realised before what a very good-looking man he was, with his square intelligent face and powerful shoulder muscles, no doubt as a result of all the work I'd seen him do on the land. There was a gentleness to those hazel eyes and a caring quality about him that could not fail to touch any heart. He had certainly touched mine, as I knew that not only did I admire this man, I trusted him, perhaps with my life if what he'd just told me was true. With my own father many thousands of miles of way, I looked upon this man very much as his surrogate. Clearing my throat, I chose my next words with care. 'I would be only too happy to return to my former post, but the Countess may not agree.'

The gentle face hardened. His eyes narrowed and his wide mouth firmed with fresh resolve. 'I'm sure you are aware that my wife and I have not been getting along too well lately. Not that we could ever claim to have enjoyed a good marriage, which was one of convenience, if truth be told. I wished to marry a young woman called Mavra Obelensky, but wasn't allowed to as she had no money.'

'Oh, that is so sad. You must have loved her very much.'

'I did what I considered to be my family duty, although my efforts to please my father came to nothing. He was very much a selfish autocrat, hard on his tenants, once evicting a recently widowed woman who had three children. I vowed never to be like him.' The Count ran a hand through his hair again in a distracted sort of way, then quickly got to his feet. 'Nothing quite turned out as I'd expected, especially where my marriage was concerned. But best not to look back. Since the past cannot be changed, where is the point in dwelling upon it? I believe in accepting the cards life deals you and focusing on the future.'

'Quite right, sir, and at least you did enjoy some happiness with Mavra, however short.'

He gave me the kindest of smiles. 'I did, and thank you for listening. I still find it painful to talk about her. May I, Millie, offer you a piece of advice?'

'But of course.' I was standing before him once more, aware I shouldn't be seated in his presence if he was not. 'I would welcome any advice you could give me.'

'I may be wrong but I suspect a fondness is growing between you and Stefan. If that is the case I would advise you not to reveal this attachment to my wife. She is a jealous, vengeful woman who craves attention, with a dangerous desire to possess what she believes should rightly be hers. It is not beyond the bounds of possibility that she dismissed you in order to clear the path for her own pursuit of this young man.'

I was stunned by his words, so startled by his shrewdness and prescience that I could think of no suitable response.

He turned back to his desk, a signal our conversation was drawing to a close, and his tone became brisk. 'So far as your employment is concerned, you have my personal assurance, Millie, that my wife will make no protest whatsoever, once I have pointed out how badly she needs your assistance.'

And so it came about that I returned to the hostel only to collect my things, and by tea time I was sitting in the schoolroom with the children and *Nyanushki*, Irina cuddled up beside me and even Serge grinning from ear to ear, enjoying a wonderful celebratory reunion.

TWENTY-FOUR

'So when were you planning to tell your husband, milady?' We were on the train travelling south, occupying an upper bunk opposite each other, with Irina fast asleep beside me. I was finding sleep impossible due to loud conversations going on all around us in the overcrowded train, so I thought it as good a time as any to force my mistress to face reality.

The morning we'd left she'd sat on the edge of the bath with her head in her hands, having spent the previous half hour throwing up. 'Something must have disagreed with me. It will pass.'

'Of course, milady,' I'd politely responded, wondering how much longer she hoped to keep up the charade. I'd watched this performance for the better part of a week, and young and naïve as I was in most other matters, it was pretty clear to me what the problem was. It would explain why she'd been feeling below par lately, and was constantly in a foul mood. The moment had come to confront her with my conclusions.

My impudence was rewarded with one of her fierce glares. 'What do you know? You are but a young girl.'

'It's fairly obvious, considering the morning sickness you've suffered.'

'Well then, now you understand why I was so desperate to get away. I'm nearly five months gone so can't disguise it for much longer, and Vaska must never know, so keep your prattling mouth shut, Dowthwaite.'

I fell silent, a sensation of anger on the Count's behalf consuming me. I remembered the terrible row that had taken place between them before we left, when he'd walked into his wife's boudoir while we were packing. If he had any suspicions about the cause of her alleged illness, he gave no sign of it as he attempted to do the right thing for us all in difficult circumstances. His expression had been sombre as he'd outlined his plans.

'The entire city is in the hands of the revolutionists, including all transport. The telephone isn't working either, so I've decided to go to our country estate near Luga as I'm concerned over what might be happening to my property. I am, after all, responsible for the *zemstvo* hospital there, and the local schools. Also, with most of the men at the front it's mainly the women who have been left working the land so I must make sure they can cope. However, as agreed, you may take your holiday, Olga, if that is what you wish. France is still out of the question, so it will have to be the Crimea again. Serge will come with me.'

'*No*!' It was the most heartfelt cry I'd ever heard from her, followed by floods of tears.

The Count appeared entirely unmoved. 'Only by keeping my son with *me* can I be certain you will return. I have arranged for the carriage to be brought round at six tomorrow morning to take you to the station. I trust you can be ready by then?' He'd half glanced at me as he asked this question, knowing that most of the packing fell on my shoulders, although for once my mistress was taking a personal interest in the task, almost as if she believed she might not be returning. I'd quickly inclined my head, but before I could say a word the Countess exploded with rage.

'How dare you attempt to control me in this way! Serge is my son, and should stay safely by his mother's side.'

'This is not about his safety as he'll be perfectly fine on the estate. This is about you and me and our disastrous marriage. Were I to agree to grant you a divorce, which I'm not inclined to do as I will not allow you to steal my son from me, we can make no decisions while this current political instability continues. Nor do I want him anywhere near your lover.'

The Count didn't normally make a habit of arguing with her, generally choosing to walk away and avoid conflict, but this was one occasion when he clearly meant to stand firm. As he turned to leave she leapt at him, grabbing his sleeve to yank him around and slap his face with the flat of her hand. It was quite a crack but he showed no reaction, seemingly impervious to her bullying. 'Don't *ever* walk away when I'm speaking. Dimitri, my *lover*, would make a much better father than you ever have.'

Sadly, he shook his head. 'I may not have been the best of fathers, shut out as I was by your possessive nature and jealousy, but I hope to rectify that by spending more time with my son in future. We've been enjoying going fishing together, and thanks to Millie's efforts he has overcome his fear of horses. I intend for us to pursue other country sports, as well as involve him in the running of the estate. Take good care of Irina while you are away. See that no harm comes to her.' He looked up, including me in this plea.

'She will be well taken care of, milord,' I assured him.

'Thank you, Millie,' he said, with his ready smile.

'Damn you, Vaska. You haven't even given me sufficient funds for this holiday, although you know I am unwell and need care.'

He let out a heavy sigh. 'Money was ever your god, Olga. But you have plenty of your own money so hardly need any of mine, which I prefer to use to help people who are truly in need.'

'*I* am in need. You know that I have very little left.'

He laughed. 'That is the irritating thing about money, is it not? Once you have spent it, it has gone. I should warn you that even if I eventually give in to your demands and agree to a divorce, you would not receive a large settlement. I'd rather give away every rouble and kopek I possess than see you waste it on your fripperies and many *lovers*.'

On that startling note this time he did walk away, without a backward glance. The Countess picked up a crystal vase that was close to hand and flung it after him. It hit the closing door, smashing into a thousand shards of broken glass.

At dawn the following morning we'd set out for the station in the carriage, a trail of carts carrying the Countess's many possessions following on behind. Her mother, dear *Babushka*, chose not to accompany us, the journey being too much for the old lady. She elected instead to go with her son-in-law to the country estate, which was just as well in the circumstances. I rather suspected the old lady knew far more about her daughter's state of health than she was prepared to admit, but really had no wish to be confronted with the reality of it. *Nyanushki* also stayed behind to care for her, and for Serge too. Stefan's services, too, were required to drive the Count to the country.

So the dreadful Olga and I were alone, apart from Irina and a handful of servants. It was not a prospect that appealed, and the weeks ahead stretched before me like an empty desert.

~

If the Countess's future plans included the hope of marriage with her lover, she was soon to be disappointed. At first when we arrived in Yalta everything was as normal. The Countess went out every day, visiting her lover at his hotel and socialising with their friends. Irina and I happily occupied ourselves with lessons, playing in the gardens or on the beach, although it was a little too cold for swimming at this time of year.

But then one day she came home in a terrible temper, slamming doors, shouting and stamping her feet before bursting into tears. Yet another show of hysterics. What a madam she was. Stifling a sigh I went to fetch her a glass of vodka, which was generally required at these moments of stress. 'What is wrong now, milady? Has someone upset you?'

'He has gone.'

'Who has?

'Dimitri, who else?' she screamed as tears flowed, although they seemed to be more out of anger than genuine distress. 'I received a letter yesterday from Vaska, again insisting there would be no divorce. I showed it to Dimitri, explaining that even if my husband did finally grant me one, there would be little money.'

'Oh dear, was that wise?'

'Clearly not, as he's left me, disappeared, vanished like a puff of smoke on a cloudy day.'

'So what will you do? Where does that leave you?'

'Stuck in this awful marriage. Apparently I've little choice but to make the best of things and carry on.' And giving a loud wail, she sank down onto the Persian rug, lay on her back and began to drum her heels like a two-year-old engaging in a tantrum.

I watched her for a moment, wondering why the Count was so determined to hang on to a wife who regularly betrayed him and treated him with open contempt. Presumably for the sake of his son. 'I can see this is distressing for you, milady, but like it or not you have no choice now but to tell your husband about the baby.'

'Never! I thought I'd made myself clear on that issue.' She was on her feet in a second, tugging off her clothes and ordering me to fill her bath and bring her nightgown.

I pressed my case further as I went about these hated duties. 'You don't seem to appreciate what a good man you have for a husband, yet you continue to treat him with utter contempt.'

'Whose side are you on?'

'Why, yours, milady,' I lied. 'I have always been discreet over your affairs, exactly as you ask, but that isn't to say I approve.'

'My goodness, you could never be accused of being bashful when it comes to expressing an opinion, Dowthwaite. However, you should know that Vaska once had a mistress too.'

'I know that he hoped to marry a woman he loved before he met you, but followed his duty instead.'

She raised her eyebrows in surprise. 'Did he tell you that?'

'He did.' I scattered bath salts into the steaming water, longing to climb in myself to rest my weary limbs, but we servants were obliged to take turns with a tin bath in the laundry room, not a beautiful bathroom like this one with mirrors and tiled walls. I set her towel to warm while the Countess sank into the bath with a weary sigh.

'She was a woman with nothing to recommend her, not looks or breeding, and barely a kopek to her name, yet she foolishly imagined she could keep him all to herself out of *love*.' The Countess laughed. 'Did he also tell you that they became lovers *after* our marriage? Although by then I had closed my bedroom door to him so he really had little choice but to return to his lost love.'

'Why on earth would you close your door on such a good-looking man?' I asked, once again quite forgetting my place. Perhaps because of her anger over her lover's betrayal, she answered.

'He did not excite me. It wasn't as if I ever loved him, any more than he loved me.'

'Then why marry him?'

'What an innocent you are, Dowthwaite. Why would I not? The Count was a highly eligible bachelor, titled and rich. I really couldn't allow him to be wasted on some loose piece of baggage. It was a tragedy, I suppose, that the woman later died in that dreadful accident, and irritating when the Count stupidly adopted Irina, believing she was his.'

'Wasn't she?'

'I expect so, although we have no absolute proof.' The Countess gave a careless shrug. 'What he didn't know at the time, and still doesn't to this day, is that Serge is not.'

Something in my shocked expression must have caused her to rush to her own defence. 'What choice did I have in the circumstances? I had no option but to marry once I realised I was carrying Serge, my lover being long gone. Vaska was so trustingly innocent he believed me to be a virgin.' She laughed all the louder at this, as if she'd said something highly amusing.

I diligently continued to fold her discarded clothing, saying nothing, too stunned to take in all the implications of what she'd so casually revealed. The laughter suddenly ceased, her face darkening with displeasure. 'Not that any of that would matter now, were it not for the fact that he has run off with *my* son.'

'Why did you never come clean and tell him the truth?'

She gave me a glance of utter pity and contempt. 'I need a divorce, Dowthwaite, one in which I am granted a fair settlement. Why would he do that if he realised Serge wasn't even his son?'

As I helped her out of the bath and began to dry her with the towel, she reached for me, pinching my cheek between her sharp nails. 'And don't you think to enlighten him about my little secret, or you'll live to regret ever coming back into my employ.'

'So what do you plan to do with the baby?' I quickly changed the subject, struggling to contain my irritation at her bullying.

'Oh, I have plans,' she whispered. 'But since yet another lover has let me down, they will not include Dimitri Korniloff.' When nothing more was forthcoming it became plain that whatever these plans might be, she had no intention of sharing them with me.

'I'll go and put the kettle on, milady, for a nice cup of tea. Then you really must rest and start thinking of this baby instead of yourself.'

~

Countess Olga gave birth to a daughter at the end of August without any difficulty whatsoever, the local midwife claiming it had been the easiest delivery she'd ever attended. It was only when the child was bathed and dressed that the difficulties began. The Countess absolutely refused to hold her.

'Now come along, dear,' the midwife said in her most encouraging voice. 'This baby needs a cuddle, not to mention putting to the breast.'

'Then you'd better find it one for it's not having mine.'

The poor woman looked so shocked I quickly ushered her out of the room before a worse argument ensued. 'I'm afraid the Countess is not the maternal kind of mother. Besides, the gentry rarely breastfeed themselves. Could you perhaps recommend a wet nurse?'

'I've known plenty of her sort in my time, but yes, I'll send a wet nurse over this afternoon. We can't have the little one suffer because of that selfish madam. Is it any wonder the country is in the state it's in?' And on that chilling remark the woman hurried away, leaving me with a screaming baby.

Fortunately the wet nurse arrived within the hour, a warm-hearted woman who was undoubtedly a natural mother. She gathered the baby into her arms and had her suckling in seconds. The infant's fretful cries ceased instantly.

~

At this point Abbie could not resist interrupting. 'Are you saying that this baby was my *mother*, the daughter of the Countess?' she asked, in a voice filled with wonder.

'That is correct, my darling. Instantly abandoned and the truth of her birth kept secret.'

'For years.'

'Indeed.'

'Oh, my goodness! But why was that? Why couldn't you tell Mum the truth?'

'Out of fear of losing her. You can't take risks with a woman like the Countess.'

Abbie's heart filled with sympathy, imagining how she would feel at the prospect of losing her own child. Then very quietly she asked the question that had been bothering her from the start. 'Did Mum ever discover who her real mother was?'

'She did, yes. It was an extremely difficult time for us both.'

'I can imagine.' A silence fell in which Abbie longed to ask more questions but as she saw the tears begin to slide down her grandmother's cheeks she put her arms about the old lady and held her close. 'Perhaps that's enough for now. I think you need to rest.'

Millie pressed her handkerchief to her eyes, then patted her granddaughter's hand. 'No, I'm fine. Wouldn't you like to know how she came to be left in my care? I didn't steal her, you know.'

'I never for a moment thought you had, but yes, I would like to know how that came about.'

The next morning when I took the Countess her breakfast on a tray, she rewarded me with a smile, which I innocently interpreted as genuine gratitude.

'Thank you Millie, most kind,' she said. 'I've been thinking about my little problem and have come up with a solution.'

'What would that be, milady?' I asked politely as I helped her into a chair so that I could remake the bed, wondering how she could describe the birth of a baby that was not her husband's as a 'little problem'.

'It's perfectly simple. All we have to do is to say that the child is yours.'

I was so shocked that I almost dropped the coffee pot I was holding. 'What are you saying? You can't do that!'

'I can do anything I like, and it's the most obvious answer to my dilemma. That way Vaska will never learn the truth. Besides, it's a perfectly logical solution. You're young enough to have a baby, known to be fond of Stefan, and he would make a good father at some point in the future, no doubt.'

My instincts told me that Stefan would not welcome taking on another man's child. No man would. 'I'm sorry, milady, but I cannot agree to that. I am young, yes, young enough never to have experienced . . . a relationship with any man, so how could the baby be mine?'

She laughed. 'Who would know or care whether or not you're a virgin?'

'*I* would. Besides, I'm not prepared to be responsible for someone else's child, or to besmirch my character with such a lie. You really aren't thinking clearly, milady. I suggest you eat your breakfast and take some rest, and then you can start planning how you will explain this new arrival to your husband.'

I dutifully buttered her toast and cut the top off her egg, then with a curt bow was about to depart when she caught hold of my wrist with a grip like iron.

'You've experienced firsthand the difficulties of being unemployed. In all the weeks you were at that hostel you found no one willing to take you on, isn't that so?'

Looking into her eyes I saw at last the reason for that. She had spread the word amongst her friends that I was a revolutionary, making absolutely certain that I'd never be taken on no matter how many doors I knocked on, or how many letters of application I wrote.

There came that all too familiar glimmer of triumph in her eyes when she knew she had won. 'So, Dowthwaite, the choice is yours. Either you take charge of this infant, who is badly in need of a mother, or you face starvation yet again. I doubt you even have the funds left to buy yourself a ticket home. And this time I'll make sure that the Count leaves you to rot.'

I gazed upon her in dawning horror, realising I was trapped. Since I was virtually penniless following my last dismissal, and it would take some time to get money or a ticket from my parents, I had no option but to agree if I was to keep my job and survive. Was I in this situation because I'd supported a group of starving women, or because – more likely – she lusted after the man I hoped to marry? As I walked away, not giving her the satisfaction of entering into an argument, which she so enjoyed, I made a private vow to secretly look for another position the very moment we returned to Petrograd. I would get out of this mess, which was none of my making, one way or another.

TWENTY-FIVE

Sadly, the moment we arrived back in the city in October, it was all too evident that any chance of finding alternative employment had vanished, as the situation there had grown a great deal worse. Petrograd was cold and frosty, a damp mist hanging over the river that made us all cough and pull our fur wraps close. I'd forgotten how bitterly cold it could be at this time of year, softened as I was by Yalta's milder climate.

We soon ran into difficulties as the streets were in a state of utter mayhem, thronged with people. Here and there fighting had broken out among civilians as well as soldiers. Within minutes, the carriage that had come to collect us from the station drew to a shuddering halt, blocked by carts laden with chairs, mattresses, rugs and other possessions as the occupiers fled, presumably escaping the city for the country. Supply carts had been overturned, their loads of wood, hay, or potatoes strewn all over the street. People were grabbing what they could and running away as fast as they could, arms laden. Even shops had been looted, their windows smashed and emptied, while we sat watching the scene in numbed disbelief.

It was all too evident that the country was in even worse chaos. Petrograd was in the midst of yet another riot.

Drawing the baby close and putting my arm about Irina, who was becoming increasingly alarmed by the noise of the crowds, I felt an instinctive need to protect them both. But I could barely contain my impatience, so desperate was I to see Stefan again. My longing for him felt almost like a sickness, one that would be healed only when he gathered me in his arms once more. But I didn't even know if he would be at the flat, or still in the country with the Count.

'What is going on?' the Countess demanded of our driver.

'We can only guess, milady, as no newspapers are being printed. Some say there's another strike, and there's much talk of Cossacks and slaughter.'

A group of Polish soldiers walked by, jeering and laughing as they crossed the marketplace. The Countess called to them. 'Tell me what's happening here.'

One of the men, perhaps the captain or lieutenant, turned to her as if surprised by the question. There was no salute or clicking of heels, no mark of respect, merely a slight raising of his eyebrows in disdain. 'Haven't you heard? Lenin is staging a coup d'état. His intention is to overthrow the Provisional Government and replace it with his own party, the Bolsheviks.'

As they staggered off, very much the worse for drink, the driver added, 'Trotsky made an attempt to proclaim the Soviet Congress as the supreme power. Unfortunately many people have no wish to be ruled by the soviets. The result, milady, is civil war.'

'Oh, for goodness' sake, I'm not prepared to sit here all day in this muddle just because of some stupid battle over power,' snapped the Countess, in that tone of voice she used when life or politics had inconvenienced her.

The baby stirred in my lap, whimpering slightly, and Vera the wet nurse and I exchanged a glance of concern.

'It is nearly her feed time,' she quietly pointed out. 'Shall I take her?'

'Let's wait till she properly wakes. I'm sure she'll let us know when she's hungry,' I said, and we both chuckled, for already the little one was making her presence felt.

In the few short weeks I'd been caring for the baby, I'd fallen completely under her spell. I loved her pouting lips, perfectly formed finger nails, and the sweet baby scent of her soft skin. Her baby blue eyes had now changed to a soft brown and regarded me with studious intent. I could have sat and gazed upon her all day. Yet a part of me held back, fearful that I might grow too fond, that when her mother finally started paying attention, I would lose her.

Not that there was any sign of that happening so far. Little Katya was already three months old and still the Countess barely acknowledged her existence. I was the only the one who cared for her, with the help of Vera. I got up at night when she cried, changed her nappies, cuddled, kissed, soothed and played with her as if she were indeed my own child. I'd even chosen her name and organised her christening. Someone had to do it, and several attempts to prompt the Countess into making a decision had failed miserably.

'Do as you please. She's your child,' had been her only comment, repeated in various versions every time I mentioned the subject. Only Vera knew the truth of the baby's birth, and had been sworn to secrecy. However, I had every intention of telling Stefan. Not for a moment did I wish him to think that I had betrayed him. But I gave no indication to the Countess of this decision. That would be my secret.

'Ah, the traffic is starting to move,' cried the driver, and we all let out a sigh of relief as the journey was completed with no further delays.

The flat felt eerily empty when finally we arrived; the Count, Serge and most of the servants were still in the country. *Babushka* had returned, with *Nyanushki* in attendance, as the old lady missed city life, along with her personal doctor who helped her to deal with her arthritis. To my great relief it turned out that the two old ladies had been accompanied home on the train by Stefan, who'd acted as their protector.

I couldn't wait to see him, longing to feel his arms about me, to be welcomed home with his heart-stirring kisses, praying that his love for me would be as strong as ever. I intended to broach the subject of the baby with tact and care, explaining fully what had happened, how the Countess had given birth but immediately abandoned the child. And how she had given me no choice but to act as its mother if I was not to be sent back to the hostel or, worse, out onto the streets to starve. She cared nothing for *my* reputation, only her own. I had it all worked out in my head what I meant to say, but the moment I saw his ashen face I realised I was already too late. She had got there before me, giving her own version of events.

'Stefan . . .' I began, but he quickly silenced me.

'Not here.' Then, taking my arm, he grabbed my coat and marched me out of the building. I was almost running to keep up with him as I struggled to put it on and fasten the buttons.

'Where are you taking me?'

'Somewhere we can talk without any fear of being interrupted.'

He took me to Alexandrvovsky Garden, no more than a ten-minute walk from the flat, close to Palace Square, a distance we completed in silence. Finding a bench beside the fountain we both sat, some inches apart. There were no people around on this cold blustery day, the only sounds those of bare branches creaking in the wind, the rustle of leaves on the ground and somewhere a dog barking.

'I believe you have something to tell me,' he said, keeping his eyes on the water. The fountain was clogged with dead leaves, muddy and neglected, no water spraying out as it should. There was rubbish lying all around, evidence of the revolution we were going through with no one troubling to clean up.

Swallowing carefully, I began my carefully rehearsed explanation. 'I shouldn't really be telling you this, as I gave a promise not to speak of it to anyone, but I decided you have a right to know the truth. The baby's name is Katya, an unexpected addition to the Countess's life. Fearful of losing any possible divorce settlement she absolutely refuses to acknowledge the child and insists that I pass her off as my own. I was forced to agree if I was not to be abandoned in Yalta, dismissed without a single kopek to keep me from starvation. But I want you to know, Stefan, that she is not my daughter!'

'Whose is she, then?'

'I've just told you: she is the Countess's.'

'She warned me that you'd claim innocence and deny the child was yours.'

I let out a gasp. 'It's not *me* who denies her, it's the *Countess*! Weren't you listening to a word I said? *I* didn't give birth to her, so if that's what she told you it was a lie, at which I have to say she is an expert.'

'Who is the father? Tell me the truth.' He glared at me, the kind of look that sent a shiver down my spine, being far colder than the winds that came down from Siberia.

'You should ask that question of Countess Olga, but I'd say either Dimitri Korniloff or Viktor the chauffeur. Unless you know of any other men in her life?' My gaze was equally challenging, wishing him to understand how it felt to be doubted.

'Why would I?'

'You don't include yourself as a possible candidate then?'

'Of course not.' He sounded shocked by the suggestion.

'So, you expect me to believe in *your* innocence, swearing you are not engaged in an affair with her, even though she has implied many times that you and she are intimate. I've trusted *you* Stefan, so why can't you trust *me*?'

He shook his head. 'It's hard to believe in your innocence when I've seen the evidence of your betrayal with my own eyes.' Getting up from the bench, he began to pace to and fro, kicking stones from the path in his anger. Then, standing before me, he said, 'I'm sorry Millie, but I'm deeply disappointed in you. I thought you and I had something special. Obviously I was wrong. The Countess suspects that you've had a fling with the Count, and I can certainly vouch for your closeness to him in the weeks before you left.'

I gasped out loud at this accusation. 'What are you suggesting – that I had an affair with Count Vaska? How dare you?'

'You cannot deny that it was his influence which forced her ladyship to take you back into her employ.'

'What if it was? He is *Count Belinsky*, the person in charge. He's been like a father to me.' I was utterly horrified by the direction this conversation had taken. That dreadful woman had planted seeds of doubt and bitterness in Stefan's head that I could do nothing to dislodge.

'Why would he defend you so vehemently if he didn't have good reason?'

'Because he's a kind man, loves his children and needs me to care for them. I swear to you, Stefan, *this is not my child!*' We were standing facing each other now, almost shouting in our distress.

'The Countess insists she is, that this was the reason she took you to Yalta: so that she could protect your reputation, and the Count's too, presumably.'

'It was her *own* reputation she was protecting, not *mine*!'

'So you say, but I asked the wet nurse – Vera, is she called? She told me it was definitely you who gave birth, not the Countess.'

I let out a sigh of exasperation. 'Vera is only repeating what she's been ordered to say. Besides, she wasn't present at the birth, so can hardly claim to be a witness. Please don't tell me you'd rather take her word, and that of the Countess, than mine?'

'To be honest, I don't know who to believe, but it . . . she . . . this baby . . . has absolutely nothing to do with me.' And turning on his heels, he strode rapidly away, his furious figure quickly swallowed up behind a copse of trees.

I felt as if I'd been struck. How could Stefan think so little of me? It was devastating that the Countess had got to him first with her lies and scheming. Goodness knows what tale she'd told him. But why would Stefan choose to believe her rather than me, the woman he claimed to love? Did this mean that he didn't love me at all, that he'd been lying to me all along? Perhaps he and the Countess had indeed enjoyed an affair?

I walked slowly back to the flat alone, deeply depressed. Then picking up little Katya from her cot, I buried my face in her shawl and wept silent tears of anguish.

The shooting started as we sat eating a somewhat frugal supper, since there were few supplies in the flat. We were all terrified, fearful of what might happen next. The two maids who had accompanied us were shaking with fright and almost in tears, far too scared to risk stepping out into the yard to replenish the log baskets. The fire in the drawing room soon died and we all began to shiver with cold. There would be no undressing for any of us that night, and precious little sleep. In the end we gathered together a few mattresses and blankets and spent the night in the cellar. It seemed the safest place to be, even if the Countess did complain endlessly of discomfort and cold. Unable to sleep, she sat wreathed in blankets dictating a long list of instructions for the morrow, to which I only half listened, guessing they would be quite impossible to fulfil.

I was proved correct as the next day we heard that the Bolsheviks had set themselves in charge across the city, guarding buildings of importance, and every bridge that entered the city. They'd also taken over the telephone and telegraph offices, banks, post offices and railway stations.

Later we learned that Kerensky, a leading member of the Duma, together with several other ministers, had retreated to the Winter Palace with only a small guard as protection. The rest had either fled the city or surrendered without a fight and joined the other side.

But even if we knew nothing of all this at the time, Stefan and I saw the warships in the harbour when we ventured out in search of food, as we were obliged to do even though we were barely speaking to each other. We heard the guns firing as we cooked a stew for our dinner, which left us in no doubt that defeat was inevitable. Stefan slipped out again, seeking further news, while *Nyanushki* and I tried to distract Irina with a game of dominoes. The Countess was taking a rest in her room. As we played, the old nanny glanced at the baby asleep in her crib beside us. Then, leaning close, she whispered, 'I can see this child isn't yours. Besides, you think too well of yourself and guard your reputation, I know.'

'Thank you, Klara. I'm glad someone believes in my innocence.'

She raised her eyebrows in surprise. 'Are you saying that Stefan doesn't? Why, even a blind man could see how you feel about each other.'

Irina gave my arm a little shake to recapture my attention. 'Come on, *Baryshnya*, it's your turn.'

I postponed any further discussion until the game was over. At twelve years old Irina was rapidly growing up into a lovely young lady, but there was nothing she loved more than reading, and was soon curled up happily absorbed in her book. I spoke in quiet whispers so that Irina wouldn't hear anything she shouldn't. By the time I'd finished relating the conversation between myself and Stefan, *Nyanushki* was pink with anger.

'That is the Countess all over. She always has to win, at any price. It's been plain for some time that she wants Stefan for herself. Handsome young men are like gold nuggets to her: she must grab them all for herself.'

'I will do everything in my power to stop her from having him.'

A sad expression came over the old woman's face. 'I can understand how you must feel, but it will not be easy to stand up to her. I have been with her most of my working life and there was a time – seems hard to imagine it now – when I too was courted by a handsome young man. She offered him employment, took him to her bed, and then when she was bored, dismissed him. I never saw him again. She has a charm about her that few men can resist.'

'Oh, Klara, how dreadful!' My heart went out to her. The fact that she'd suffered the same experience somehow created an even greater bond between us.

'Don't let her win,' she whispered in my ear as I gave her a hug. 'She is the very worst kind of autocrat, and Stefan is a lovely man. You fight for him, dear.'

At that moment the object of our concern came rushing back into the schoolroom. 'The ships are firing at the Winter Palace,' Stefan cried. 'I saw Kerensky in his fancy uniform drive away in his car at great speed. I very much doubt we'll see him again.'

Leaping to my feet, I ran to him out of instinct, touching his dear face, checking his hands and arms. 'Are *you* safe?'

The gaze that rested on mine was filled with confusion and unspoken questions. 'I'm fine. It seems the entire city is now under the control of the Bolsheviks. Some are calling it the October Revolution, others a coup d'état in which Lenin has seized power with scarcely a drop of blood spilled.' Pushing my hands away, he continued, 'I'll go and inform the Countess.'

Feeling utterly rejected, I stood and watched him go to her, my heart sinking to my boots. However you cared to describe the situation, we all realised that life was never going to be the same again. Not only had Russia lost a world ruled by the Tsar, albeit one with flaws, but no one could begin to guess what we would get in its place.

As for me, I grieved for the loss of trust from the man I loved.

TWENTY-SIX

Trust is everything, Abbie thought as she watched the sun come up over Great Gable, having been at the shop since before dawn. She was filled with love and admiration for this brave woman who was her own beloved grandmother. What trauma she must have gone through, yet she had readily taken the baby to her heart, despite the effect that would have upon her own reputation. Why didn't Stefan believe in her innocence? Why should Millie trust him? Thrilled as she was to learn the truth at last about Kate's origins, she was anxious to know the answer to those questions, which brought her wandering thoughts back to her own dilemma.

Abbie remembered how at the start of their relationship she'd trusted Eduard implicitly, a feeling which had slowly dissipated over the years. Now it was gone forever. She was relieved to discover that she'd hardly thought of him at all in recent weeks, being far too busy preparing for the official opening party, now only hours away. Even her relationship with her father seemed to be slowly improving.

They'd invited the mayor, various friends and organisations in the town, and the local paper, of course, so she was hoping for a good turnout. For the umpteenth time that morning, Abbie went to check a range of rose quartz, red jasper and agate jewellery, carefully adjusted a row of copper bracelets, and then stepped back to admire her handiwork. Apart from the amber, the jewellery in the display bore a suitably local theme.

The Lake District was famous for its copper, lead and silver mines, as well as the quarrying of green slate from Honister, graphite for pencils, and various minerals including barite, calcite crystals, fluorite and quartz. Abbie had obtained some of these stones either locally or from Weardale, further north, from which she'd made bracelets, necklaces and earrings. She felt quite proud of her achievements, her only worry being whether or not they would sell.

'I'm beginning to feel a bit nervous,' Linda said, coming up behind her to tweak a few hair clips into place, although they were perfectly well displayed.

'Me too,' Abbie admitted. 'Isn't that silly? We just have to be relaxed and friendly. When are the caterers coming?' she instantly asked, defying her own words.

Linda laughed. 'They promised to be here by nine o'clock to set out the canapés and pour the wine, ready for the opening at ten, so they should be here any minute. Whoops, that's the phone.'

She was back in seconds, her face grim. 'Their car broke down just before they reached Skelwith Bridge. They're stuck in the middle of nowhere between Coniston and Ambleside, although one of them did manage to find a telephone box to ring, after walking a couple of miles. What on earth are we going to do now? It's all my fault. I should have gone for a local firm, but I chose them because they were cheaper.'

'It's nobody's fault, Linda. It's just one of those things. Look, I'll get my car and drive out to see if I can find them.'

'But we need you here, Abbie.'

'Can I help, if somebody needs picking up?' The deep throaty tones were a joy to Abbie's ears.

'Oh, yes please.' Turning quickly Abbie felt something stir inside her at the warmth of his smile as their eyes met. Despite his threat to open up next door, and she could see that work had already commenced, Andrew Baxter, or Drew as she now called him, was proving to be a difficult man to dislike. As well as kindly including her alleged husband in the invitation to dinner that time they'd met by the lake, and buying her daughter an ice cream, he'd called in at the shop almost daily since, to help with the preparations for the launch, or just for a friendly chat. Now he was offering to be their saviour in a crisis. Abbie quickly explained the problem.

'Right, do you have a map of the area?'

Linda quickly produced one and within seconds he was on his way, promising to return with the caterers, and the wine and food, as soon as possible. Abbie and Linda exchanged an anxious glance. 'He doesn't even know the area terribly well. Let's hope he finds them.'

'It's a long road but he'll surely discover them eventually. In the meantime I'll start work on plan B, just in case they don't arrive in time and we have to resort to coffee and doughnuts after all.' She shot back to the phone.

The next hour flew by in a maelstrom of activity, not least the arrival of a reporter, introducing herself as Clarinda Ratcliffe, who was keen to conduct an interview before Abbie became too distracted with customers. 'How did you feel losing your mother in such a tragic way?' was her first question, which threw Abbie completely. Pulling herself together, she replied by saying it had been a dreadful shock but now it was time to move on.

The journalist, however, had other ideas. 'I was speaking to one of the old ladies she used to visit on the Parade who says she chatted to Kate the day before she died, and that she was excitedly saving up for a trip to Russia, a long-held dream apparently. That doesn't sound like a woman contemplating suicide, does it?'

Abbie stared at the reporter, momentarily lost for words as she absorbed this new information. 'As with all fatalities of this kind, it is impossible to understand what she was thinking or feeling. But today is not the time to talk about my mother's death, if you don't mind.'

'Do you think she would have been pleased that you've taken over her business?'

'I should think so, since she left it to me in her will,' Abbie drily remarked, managing a smile. This interview hadn't started well, a real downer so far. 'I am of course aware of how well she ran Precious Dreams, just like my grandmother before her, so I'm delighted to be following in their footsteps.'

'That's interesting. So your grandmother started the business when exactly?' the reporter asked, scribbling madly in her notepad.

'Back in the twenties, and we're proud it has survived, as few family businesses do these days.' Abbie mentally blocked out the overdraft.

'It can't have been easy, and your family has not been without its troubles over the years, has it?' Clarinda Ratcliffe said with a curious little smile.

Abbie felt herself starting to quake a little inside. Surely the woman wasn't going to interrogate her on the subject of Eduard? Was it still a crime to have an illegitimate daughter? She really had no wish to have her personal life all over the local press. 'I'm sorry?' she said, feigning ignorance at the question.

'I understand that you have only recently returned from Paris where you've been living for some time?'

'Indeed, and it's good to be back home in the beautiful Lake District,' Abbie blandly remarked, telling her nothing.

The journalist continued, unfazed. 'I assume your grand-mother also loved to travel, as she went out to Russia as a governess, I believe. Is she here today? I'd love to have a word with her, too.'

'She will be calling in later. You seem to be very well informed.'

Clarinda Ratcliffe offered a faint smile, chillingly insincere. 'Since you belong to a notable family in the region, I naturally did some research before coming today. Your mother also once ran off to live on the French Riviera back in the thirties. Seems to be a family trait. Why is that, do you think?'

Abbie blinked. This was the first she'd heard that Kate had ever left home, let alone 'ran off to live on the Riviera'. Why on earth would she do that, and who did she run off with? More importantly right now, this interview was supposed to be about jewellery and the business. 'Would you like me to show you round?' Abbie asked, choosing not to go any further with this line of questioning. 'We have some wonderful jewellery here, much of it using local stones, as well as this lovely amber from Poland.' She quickly launched into a description of its healing properties, and how it was said to bring everlasting love.

'What about the fashion accessory shop that is about to open next door?' the journalist asked as Abbie was showing her the workshop, seemingly determined to focus on problems.

Abbie really had no wish to go into that either. Glancing at her watch and worrying over whether Drew had managed to find the caterers, she attempted to draw this most unpleasant interview to a close. 'You'll have to excuse me now, Miss Ratcliffe, if you don't mind, as I really must get back to my customers.' And with a smile she walked away.

The journalist scurried after her. 'But won't the competition badly affect your trade?'

With some difficulty Abbie managed to keep smiling, assuring the woman that she had absolutely no worries on that score. 'This will clearly be the part of town to come for jewellery, bags and accessories. Besides, competition is a good thing,' she said, giving the expected answer.

Moments later, to Abbie's great relief, Drew appeared at the door giving the thumbs up. The caterers came bustling in and within minutes it seemed the shop was awash with people, all chattering and laughing and drinking the wine, greatly enjoying themselves and admiring the products on display.

Abbie heaved a huge sigh of relief when finally Clarinda Ratcliffe left, though she worried slightly about what the woman might actually write up. But no matter what family skeletons were dug up by the local press, the party was proving to be a great success. And by the sound of the ringing of the newly acquired cash register, plenty was also being sold. Oh, Abbie did hope so.

Her grandmother and Fay arrived shortly after that, bringing both Jonathon and Aimée to admire the jewellery and join in the fun; baby Carrie dozed contentedly in her pushchair. Her brother, Abbie noticed, was absent, evidently having chosen not to attend despite it being a Saturday and his day off.

'Robert had to slip back to the office, rather unexpectedly,' Fay explained by way of excuse, which Abbie did not for a moment believe. 'But don't worry about Aimée; I'm taking the children to see Hill Top, the Beatrix Potter house, later, so they'll be quite happily occupied until you get home.'

'Bless you, Fay.' Abbie hugged her sister-in-law in gratitude, then turned to hug her grandmother, too. 'Thank you both for coming. You don't know how much it means to me. I really appreciate your support.'

'I'm here to offer you that, too.'

In delighted amazement, Abbie turned to kiss her father, who had suddenly appeared at her side. 'Oh, I'm so touched that you should come, Pops, knowing how anxious you've been about finding a way to save the house.'

His eyes twinkled at her in the way they used to do back in the day when she was his darling child. 'I've decided I should stop worrying and wait upon events. Something may turn up, as the saying goes, or the worst may never happen and we won't be evicted after all.'

'Excellent. So let's not worry about it unless it does.'

'Mummy, can I have one of those butterfly brooches?' Aimée pleaded, jumping up and down in excitement.

'Of course you can, darling. Let me pin it on for you. There, don't you look beautiful? You can go and look at it in the mirror.'

As the little girl rushed off to admire herself, Fay asked, 'How did your interview go?'

Abbie pulled a rueful face. 'Okay, I suppose, although not quite what I'd expected. The journalist mentioned that she'd love to talk to you about Russia, Gran, and seemed to think that Mum, too, had been interested in travel, going off to live on the Riviera when she was a girl in the thirties. Is that true?'

Millie took a second to answer, seeming to indicate this incident may have taken place during that painful period she still couldn't bring herself to talk about. 'Kate did spend a little time in France, but didn't stay long. Now do show me the amber earrings you made,' she said, and Abbie had no alternative but to drop the subject for now. But it was definitely something she would investigate further.

Later, having enjoyed the celebration and wishing her well in her new enterprise, her family departed to continue with their day out.

'Don't fret about Robert,' Fay told her as Abbie kissed them all goodbye. 'He's softening a little, and he's finally been offered that much-longed for partnership. He'll come round eventually.

Look at your father, filled with pride at your success, if still angry at what your mother did. "How could she leave me like that when we were so happy together?" he keeps saying. But he's gradually coming to terms with her death a little better now, which must be a good thing.'

'Thanks in no small part to your influence, Fay. I'm quite sure of it.'

Abbie felt a warmth inside that her family should have taken the trouble to come to the launch party, in spite of their differences and squabbles in recent months. But she still worried about what this Clarinda Ratcliffe might unearth, given her comment on her mother's wish to visit Russia. Why wouldn't Kate wish to visit, since she had been born there? But what had happened to make her give up on that long-held dream?

Glancing about at the crowd that was gradually thinning, Abbie found herself searching for Drew, feeling a sudden longing to pour out her heart to this sympathetic man. As if reading her thoughts, he was suddenly standing by her side.

'That reporter spoke to me last week about my plans for the shop next door, and I must say it was very like an interrogation,' he said. 'Personally, I didn't take to her. So how did your interview really go?'

Abbie heaved a sigh. 'She seemed to be looking for some sort of hook to hang the story on, some scandal about me. It was strange, and not particularly pleasant.'

'That's the press for you, always wanting to dig for dirt, although from my standpoint I honestly can't see how she could find anything against you,' he said with a grin.

Abbie's laugh was sardonic. 'You mean besides my notorious youth, an illegitimate child, or having a mother who committed suicide for some unknown reason, and a father and brother who blame me for her death and wish to sell this property without my consent? Oh, and a neighbouring shop apparently setting up in opposition. Not much there for a story, then.'

He frowned throughout her little rant. Then, taking her by the shoulders, he drew her gently towards him to place a kiss on each cheek. 'Think positive: you've done a splendid job. I for one am hugely impressed.'

His kisses were tender and soft, not in any way steamy or passionate, and on her cheeks, not her lips. Even so, they seemed to stir a coil of pleasure and something very like desire deep inside. Abbie slanted him a glance, struggling to read the thoughts reflected in those mysterious grey eyes, so enigmatic but undeniably sexy. She sensed his breathing quickening slightly, but there was no sign of a smile; his expression was profoundly serious.

She cleared her throat, which had gone suddenly dry. 'Thank you for having faith in me.'

'You deserve it, with your talent,' he said, admiring a display of amber earrings. 'Did you really make these?'

'I did.' They stood side by side, not touching, much as Abbie secretly longed to slip her hand into his, or have him kiss her again, properly this time. What was she thinking of? How much wine had she drunk that she'd become so aware of this man? Or had this feeling been secretly growing inside her for some time?

'We still haven't had that dinner,' he said. 'How about tonight, since it's a day of celebration?'

'I'm not sure it would be quite appropriate for business rivals to socialise, would it?' she asked, with just the trace of a smile to soften her words.

'Do we have to be rivals? Can't we just be friends, or at least business colleagues?'

Not knowing how she felt about spending an evening with this man, which might or might not be looked upon as a date, Abbie was thankful to be interrupted by a woman seeking assistance to choose a pair of mother-of-pearl earrings. It also gave her a moment to get her emotions back under control.

Andrew Baxter must have used this distraction to beat a hasty retreat, as by the time she'd gift-wrapped the earrings and found the customer a glass of wine and a pastry, he was gone. Perhaps he'd regretted that unexpected moment of intimacy.

'Thank goodness for that,' Abbie half murmured to herself, setting down her own glass and resolving not to allow another drop to pass her lips. Yet there was just the slightest twinge of disappointment that he'd left early.

Linda sidled over and whispered the total they'd taken during the day. It was a considerable sum. 'Oh, and Drew says to remind you that the invitation remains open. Now what would that be, exactly?'

Abbie's eyes twinkled as she hugged her assistant with joy at their success. 'Never you mind, but I won't be taking it up. Well done, and thanks for all your help. I would never have managed this without you, might not even have thought of the idea.'

'You're welcome. I just want Precious Dreams to survive, as I love working here with you.'

Just as the final customers of the day were preparing to leave, and a few last-minute purchases were being made, the shop bell rang yet again, bringing with it a blast of cool air as the door banged open.

'*Mon amour*! At last I find you.'

Abbie stared in horror. 'Eduard!'

TWENTY-SEVEN

'I come to say I make big mistake. I am full of remorse that I let this happen. It is all the fault of my wife. The silly woman will not let me go and I feel sorry for her. Now she have the child, and I do not even know if it is mine. She say he is, but he do not look like me.'

'So she's had a boy? Congratulations! What makes you think he's not yours?' They were sitting in The Ring of Bells, Eduard drinking a small cognac while Abbie kept safely to coffee, feeling the need for a clear head to deal with this unexpected and unwanted visit. She'd rung Fay and, asking her not to mention to Aimée yet that her father was here, explained that she would be a little later than expected. Her sister-in-law had promised to put Aimée to bed, encouraging Abbie to enjoy an evening out for once, saying she deserved it after all her hard work.

Eduard said, 'He has fair hair and my wife and I are both dark.'

'He's a baby! No doubt he also has blue eyes.'

'How you know that?'

Abbie laughed. 'Oh, Eduard, the colour of a baby's eyes and hair change as they grow. Does your wife say he's yours?'

He shrugged. 'Of course. She deny any sort of *affaire*.'

'Well then, accept it and be a good father to the boy, as you were to Aimée. And still can be, albeit it from a distance. But you are welcome to call at the house tomorrow to see her. It's Sunday, so we're home all day.'

Eduard pouted, in that sulky way he had. 'Thank you. I am lost without my lovely daughter. I come not only to see my little girl, but to take her home with me. You too. Marie will soon be my ex-wife – I swear it, *mon amour*. Then we can marry.'

Abbie didn't respond. Hadn't she heard this tale times without number over the years? All the same, as she sipped her coffee she was finding it hard not to feel a little sorry for Eduard's sense of loss, partly out of loyalty for the years they'd spent together, but mainly because of their daughter. He was still Aimée's father, and he loved her as much as she loved him.

Eduard went on talking, outlining his plan, or rather his crazy dream that they could just carry on as before. Abbie lost interest, becoming momentarily distracted from whatever he was saying as she glimpsed a familiar figure walking through the pub door and take a seat in the bay window. Perhaps the sight of Drew acted as a reminder that she was living a new life now. She set down her coffee cup with a firm click.

'Eduard, stop. It isn't going to happen. I've already explained that now isn't a good time to be uprooting Aimée, just when she's settling in to her new school. She can come and stay with you for a few weeks later in the summer. She'd like that.'

He dismissed this suggestion on a puff of cognac-scented breath. 'I want my little girl to come home for good now, and you too. Why you leave me? I not understand. What did I do to hurt you?'

'You *lied* to me.'

'*Non*!'

'You *did*, Eduard. Your promise to marry me never materialised. It finally dawned on me that my father had been right all along. You never would divorce your wife; therefore, I saw no reason to stay.'

He looked perplexed, a frown creasing his brow. 'But it is perfectly normal in France for husband to have a *maîtresse*. Did I not always love you and care for you? So what is the problem?'

How could she get it through to him that he had indeed hurt her, quite badly? It was a waste of time even talking to him. Abbie was acutely aware of Drew glancing up occasionally from the paper he was supposedly reading to watch them through narrowed eyes. Had he guessed that this was her ex-lover?

'I'm sorry, but it's over,' she said. 'I really have no wish to put myself through that anguish ever again.'

'I do not believe it. How would you manage without me?' he scoffed. 'I see little to keep you here.'

'As a matter of fact, I have a business to run now.'

He gave a puff of scathing disbelief. 'Why would you waste your life running a *shop*, when you could be my *maîtresse*? You will end up old and lonely with no one to love you.'

'That's a dreadful thing to say!'

'It is true,' he said, giving a typically Gallic shrug. 'Who would marry you now, the mother of an illegitimate child? You make good mistress, but no man would consider you for a wife.'

If Abbie had been hurt before, she was devastated now by this cruel comment. She had a great urge to slap his arrogant face. Instead she rose slowly to her feet, holding fast to her dignity. 'In actual fact I think you are the one likely to end up old and lonely, when your wife finally grows tired of your *affaires* and finds the courage to throw you out, or when you fail to persuade some other foolishly naïve woman to become your next *maîtresse*. In the meantime, I have another engagement this evening, so I'll say goodbye.'

Heart pounding with fury, Abbie picked up her bag and made her way across the crowded public house, head held high. On reaching Drew she gave him a kiss on each cheek before seating herself beside him. 'I thought I'd take up your offer of dinner after all, if that's okay?'

'You've made my day,' he said with a grin. 'Let me order you a large glass of wine, you look as if you're in need of one.'

She did not even glance up as Eduard stormed out, making heads turn as he banged the door behind him. She just kept on smiling into Drew's eyes. He was not only gorgeous, but the kindest, sweetest man she'd ever met.

~

Over a delightful meal in which they barely seemed to stop talking for more than a few seconds, no mention was made of her previously intense conversation with Eduard, nor the way she had used Drew as a means of escape. Abbie did insist upon sharing the bill, as she had no wish for him to look upon this as a date.

'May I at least drive you home? It might be advisable, considering you've had rather an over-indulgent day so far as wine is concerned,' Drew offered with a smile.

'Thank you, that would be most appreciated,' she laughed. 'I could leave my car by the church and easily collect it tomorrow.'

They drove largely in silence, a crescent moon shedding a pale light over the black humps of the mountains, the only sound that of the lapping of the lake beside the road, and the *whoo-whoo* of a wood pigeon. His closeness was having a strange effect upon her. Abbie couldn't help keep glancing at his long stretched-out legs, at the way his fingers smoothed over the steering wheel, almost as if she'd like to have them do the same to her.

When he drew to a halt in the drive of Carreck Place he turned to her, his gaze deeply intense. Then without saying a word, he pulled her into his arms and kissed her. This was no tender peck upon the cheeks but a deep, passionate kiss to which Abbie found herself completely surrendering. Desire surged through her like fire. Never, in all the years she had spent with Eduard, had a kiss ever felt so right, so perfect, as if she had been waiting for it all her life.

'I've been wanting to do that for so long,' he said, echoing her own thoughts, when eventually it ended. 'You are rather irresistible.'

Abbie stroked a finger over his mouth. 'So are you.' What was she thinking of? What had happened to her resolve not to get involved with anyone right now? But he was kissing her again and she blocked all such thoughts from her head, giving herself up to the intimacy of the moment, and the delicious churn of excitement within.

When he pulled away this time his expression was oddly serious. 'I think you know how I feel about you, Abbie. I know you're busy but I'd really like us to spend more time together, to get to know each other a bit better.'

She wanted to tell him that she'd like that too, but the memory of Eduard and how easily she'd messed up her life before was warning her to tread with caution. 'Maybe we could talk about this some other time, Drew. Right now I really must go, as I've imposed upon my sister-in-law quite enough for one day.'

'Okay, but before you do, there's something I've been trying to pluck up the courage to ask for a while now, something for you to think about.'

'Oh, and what would that be?'

Smoothing a strand of hair back from her cheek, he smiled, causing Abbie to feel almost giddy with the need to kiss him again. But she really should concentrate on what he was saying.

'I greatly admire the way you've restored and revitalised Precious Dreams in just a few months. You've done a splendid job. I can see a great future for the business, and I assure you that I will not be selling jewellery or attempting to compete with you in any way.'

She smiled up at him then, placing a light kiss on his mouth in gratitude. 'I'm delighted to hear it.'

'I did wonder, however, bearing in mind the similarity of our respective shops, if a partnership would be of any interest?'

Startled, Abbie jerked back in her seat, releasing herself from his hold. But before she had time to speak, Drew held up a hand.

'Let me explain before you shoot me down in flames. You have quite a bit of unused space at the back of your premises, as does the one next door. So why not blend both shops into one large store? We could expand into fashion, in addition to jewellery, bags and accessories, perhaps even ladies' shoes too. I believe you and I could work well together.'

Maybe they could, she thought, instinctively intrigued by the idea. Abbie looked into his face and couldn't help but wonder if she was actually falling for this lovely man. Her feelings for him had certainly grown over these last weeks. 'Are you serious?'

'Never more so. Obviously it would need to be set up on a proper legal footing, and I'd be prepared to pay you whatever is appropriate.'

'Pay?' She struggled to clear her muddled head as an ugly suspicion once more reasserted itself. 'What are you saying – that you're still determined to buy me out?'

'No, that's not what I'm saying at all. I mean that I would buy into the partnership, as you actually own the premises, rather than simply renting.' Pulling a scrap of paper from his pocket, he scribbled something on it and held it out to her. 'What do you think?'

Abbie stared at the figures, which would more than pay off the overdraft with a fair sum left over. It was a hugely tempting offer, but she felt totally bemused. Hadn't she told herself never to trust a man again? She thought about Stefan and Eduard, and how neither one had proved himself to be worthy of trust. What if Andrew Baxter was running away from debts in Scotland, or the tax man?

What if this story of his wife leaving him was as much a fiction as Eduard's, fabricated in order to gain her sympathy?

'I hardly know you.'

'Does that matter?'

'I'm not sure.'

The offer had come right out of the blue and her mind felt utterly scrambled after that kiss, not to mention all the wine she'd drunk today. Why had he chosen to bring the matter up now, when she was on too much of an emotional high to be in any fit state to judge? Was that kiss part of his plan, so that he could get his hands on Precious Dreams by whatever devious means he could? She shook her befuddled head as she gathered up her bag.

'I don't think I can quite take this in right now. It's been one hell of a day. The caterers were late, there was that dreadful interview, and then Eduard turning up and making demands. Exciting, profitable, yet a real bummer in many ways.'

'But you'll think about it.' He looked as if he might be about to kiss her again and Abbie put up her hands to stop him.

'Sorry, but in view of what I've been through in the past, I confess to being rather wary of guys who attempt to take advantage of a girl when she's at her most vulnerable.'

'Oh, lord, I'd never do that, Abbie. I thought you and I were . . .'

She didn't stop to listen to any more. Emotion suddenly overwhelmed her and before the tears flooding her eyes could start to fall, Abbie pulled open the car door and fled.

~

He rang first thing the next morning, a call Abbie felt obliged to take rather than risk her brother discovering the reason he was calling.

'I seem to be apologising yet again,' he began. 'I didn't mean to take advantage of your vulnerability. I can see that I went about things the wrong way last night, made a real mess of it, in fact. But I want you to know my feelings for you are genuine, Abbie, that if you aren't interested in a partnership you only have to say so and I'll entirely respect your decision. But I would like to see you again.'

Eduard arrived at just that moment, and as squeals of joy broke out from her daughter, Abbie put down the phone without responding. Her trust in men was at an all-time low, so she really didn't feel inclined to accept his apology, not this time.

'I made a complete fool of myself by responding to his advances so easily,' she admitted to her grandmother later as they sat in the conservatory for one of their regular heart-to-hearts. Eduard had taken Aimée out for the day and she was feeling at a particularly low ebb. 'I made myself look like a naïve idiot.'

'Don't be so hard on yourself, my darling. It sounds like a very reasonable offer to me.'

'What, because he softened me with a kiss beforehand? Very businesslike, I don't think!' Much as Abbie struggled not to dwell upon his kisses, she was finding it hard not to remember the delicious sensation of being held in his arms.

'Do you like him?' Millie asked, a soft teasing light in her eyes as she seemed to sense the melting emotion within her granddaughter.

'That's quite beside the point. I intend to focus my mind entirely upon building my own business.'

'Not all men are like Eduard. Don't let one bad apple spoil the entire barrel for you. You're a sensible, mature woman now, not a giddy teenager, so why not talk to him as such, and find out what a partnership would actually involve?'

For a brief moment Abbie was sorely tempted. It was true that he'd shown himself to be a man of wit and humour, always kind and helpful. Or maybe that, too, had all been part of his campaign? 'I don't think so. He deliberately played on my feelings in order to win me round, almost a seduction, which in my inebriated state at the time made me an easy target.' Abbie felt ashamed of herself for allowing it to happen.

'Or maybe he simply couldn't resist you, my darling, lovely as you are.'

Abbie laughed out loud at such a ridiculous notion. 'I'm a single parent with responsibilities and a shameful past. Sorry, but I don't trust him and intend to steer well clear of Andrew Baxter.'

Oh, but it wasn't easy. In the days following, sometimes she could hear him chatting to Linda while she was busy in the workshop decorating boxes with a mosaic of amber pieces. Abbie had made it very clear to her assistant that she had no wish to see him. No doubt Linda assumed this was because of the threat his shop presented, unaware there was much more to it than that. He never did intrude upon her privacy, and a part of her was almost sorry that he didn't, although whether she'd rail at him or fall into his arms, Abbie couldn't quite decide.

A few days later Linda brought her a note, which she put on the desk without a word. Only by the sad expression in her eyes did Abbie realise who it was from. She opened it with trepidation.

'*Linda tells me you're very busy so I won't disturb you, but this is just to let you know that I'm on my way back to Scotland as I need to see my wife. Maybe we can talk later. I'll give you a call.*'

Oh, how many times she'd heard those words: *I need to see my wife*. Abbie felt sick inside, surprisingly close to tears for someone who'd convinced herself that she didn't care a hoot about Andrew Baxter. And she most certainly didn't trust him. Why would she, when he'd tried to get his greedy hands on her business by pretending to fancy her? Did men never tell the truth? Oh, and why did she always find herself falling for those who claimed to be divorced, and actually weren't? Putting her head in her hands, she let the tears fall at last.

TWENTY-EIGHT

That winter of 1917–1918 was depressingly cold, and life became increasingly difficult with each passing day. None of us had any notion how we were to get through the coming months. Many banks were closed, withdrawals blocked and estates seized. We'd still had no word from the Count, which was a daily concern, although the Countess was more worried about Serge, her precious son.

Struggling to cope in the flat without them, and without the help of Gusev, Anton, Mrs Grempel and the other servants, was immensely difficult. Even more important, we were constantly hungry. One of us would go out every morning to try to buy food at a local shop, generally with little success. More often than not the answer was, 'We have not yet received permission to sell.' We never asked from whom permission was required, as it was all too plain that the Bolsheviks were now entirely in control.

A maid came home one day in great excitement claiming she'd bought a bag of coffee on the market. But when she opened it, it turned out to be a heap of musty grain and not coffee at all, not even fit to eat as it was alive with mites. Our disappointment was keen, our hunger all the more intense.

Providing the Countess with enough to eat was our chief priority, otherwise she would fall into one of her famous tantrums. Fish soup featured most often on our menu, much to her dismay, and one night we had just two small spicy balls of cabbage each. *Nyanushki* and I made sure that Irina was fed as well as possible. *Babushka*, who was old and infirm, largely confined to her bed, was also given priority. Whatever was left, often very little, was shared equally between us servants. Secretly I made sure that Stefan received a little extra, being a man with a larger appetite and the one most engaged in physical labour. Not that he noticed or appeared to appreciate anything I did for him, largely ignoring me completely.

How I missed those drives in the cart, the way we used to talk all the time, and joke and laugh together. Why couldn't he appreciate that I'd broken my promise to the Countess and told him the honest truth? What more could I say or do to convince him of my innocence?

'The problem seems to be that the railway system isn't working properly,' he told us one night as we sat with the maids and *Nyanushki* in the kitchen, chewing on a few tough crusts of dry bread dipped into the remains of a fish stew. 'The tracks are blocked or damaged as a result of large quantities of troops and supplies being moved to the battlefront, so the transporting of food has virtually ceased.'

'Then how will the Count manage to return to Petrograd if the trains aren't running?' I asked, a bad mistake judging by the tight expression that came over his face.

'I dare say he'll just have to wait a bit longer to see you, as you will him.'

'Oh, Stefan, not that again. How can I convince you that this baby is not mine? Or the Count's?' I was nursing her on my lap as we ate, and when she smiled up at me my heart contracted with love. How could it not? She was beautiful and vulnerable, the sweetest, most adorable baby in the world.

'Never, when you look at her like that.'

'Which is entirely unfair. I care for Irina and Serge too, but this little one has no one in the world to love her but me.'

'And who do *you* love?' he snapped. Thrusting back his chair, he strode rapidly away before I had the chance to respond.

'Oh dear,' *Nyanushki* softly murmured. 'It is not going to be easy to convince him.'

'What can I do?' I cried, feeling tears block my throat.

'Be patient. Men have their pride. But he'll come round in the end.'

I kissed Katya's fluff of dark hair and sighed. 'How long will that take, I wonder?' Maybe a lifetime.

~

One night as I was feeding the baby, Vera now having returned to her family, and little Katya almost weaned and content with a bottle, I heard the sound of a window being smashed. Greatly alarmed, I quickly tucked her back into her crib, grabbed my dressing gown and went in search of Stefan, my heart racing. Ever since the troubles had begun we'd all lived in a state of high anxiety, and even though Stefan and I were barely speaking, as he was the only male in the house apart from a couple of young lads who did the rough work, who else could I turn to? Fortunately, he'd heard the noise too, and we met in the servants' corridor. Stefan instantly pressed a finger to his lips, urging me to be silent, then handed me a piece of wood from the log basket.

'That's just in case you need to protect yourself,' he whispered, and with a jerk of his head indicated I should follow him.

We crept slowly down the stairs that led to the kitchen area, where we could see the soft light of a candle burning. Keeping close behind him as he moved stealthily into the kitchen, I raised the big stick in my hand in readiness to batter someone on the head if necessary.

'There's no one here,' he said, looking about in surprise.

'Then who lit the candle?'

'Someone could have left it as a marker for when they return.'

'Which means they are elsewhere in the flat. Katya!' I cried.

'Irina,' Stefan said at the same moment, and as we turned to run we exchanged a quick glance of shared fear. It was then we heard the scream.

Coming face to face with the two thieves, although we could barely see more than the outline of two figures in the dark, neither of us hesitated to set about them with our sticks. Stefan resorted to punching with his fists when his weapon was wrenched from his hand, and when my stick broke I used my feet to kick the fellow in the shins. It gave me enormous satisfaction to see him squirming on the floor and hear his cries of pain. Still fearful for Irina and little Katya, I set off at a run for the nursery. I'd gone no more than a few yards when I was hit in the back and knocked to the floor, completely winded. Within seconds the man jerked me over and was on top of me, his hands tugging at my nightgown, ripping it open at the neck. I let out a scream, quickly stifled as he clamped one hand over my mouth, half smothering me, the weight of him so overpowering that I had little hope of freeing myself.

What would have happened next is beyond question, despite my furious struggles. Fortunately I was saved, as he was dragged off me. Then Stefan was helping me back to my feet, his arms holding me tight. 'It's all right. You're safe now, thank God,' he murmured against my ear. I leaned into him, feeling the solid warmth of his beloved body, inhaling the familiar masculine scent of him that I loved so much. Our closeness was electrifying and as he moved his head to study my face I knew he was about to kiss me. How I needed that kiss, even if this wasn't exactly the right time for such intimacy.

Perhaps also realising that this wasn't the moment he quickly ended it, a half-smile of shame on his face. 'We'll talk later. We mustn't let him get away.' And as Stefan turned to give pursuit, I quickly grabbed my broken stick and followed him.

We did our best, chasing the robbers the length of the vast dark corridors and down the stairs but the two escaped, leaving a trail of goods behind in their wake. Even so, we grinned at each other, pleased with our efforts, and for the first time since we'd returned to Petrograd and he'd learned about the baby, our connection felt as strong as ever.

'You were very brave.'

'Thank you for saving me.' I silently hoped that he might kiss me again, but he mumbled something about checking on the Countess and hurried off in the direction of her bedroom, leaving me to clear up the debris. Even so, my heart was singing.

~

Arms laden with stolen goods, I found the Countess storming about her room in a rage, the worst I had seen in a long while, only this time directing her anger at Stefan. 'Why weren't you here to protect me?' She paused to jab a finger in his chest. 'Someone has taken every item from my jewellery box. My pearls and several other trinkets are missing. I heard a noise and came out to my boudoir, thinking it must be you. Instead I found those pieces of scum helping themselves to my precious possessions. *Why were you not here*?'

She carried on shouting at Stefan while I read far more into her questions than a simple quizzing on his ability to protect her. The Countess seemed to be implying she'd been expecting him. Could that be true? I stared at Stefan but all he said was, 'I'll see what else they've taken,' and dashed off, joined by the two young boys and the maids who'd been woken rather late by the racket.

I went at once to the safe and sighed with relief to find it still locked. 'At least your amber and most important pieces are still safe milady.' But sifting through the items we'd saved, mainly sheets and blankets, oddly enough, I found nothing of any value. 'No sign of any pearls here, unfortunately. Perhaps there was a third party outside, and these two dropped stuff out to them through the window.'

'It's all Stefan's fault. He promised to protect me.'

'That's not quite fair. You can hardly expect him to be everywhere, or to sleep at your door like a guard dog just in case a robber should come.'

Her lips twisted into a slight smile. 'Actually, I had quite another place in mind for him to sleep.'

I felt my cheeks start to burn, an ache in my throat as I strived to hold my emotions in check. This was not the moment to take issue with her on the way she had stolen my man, or the lies she had told him about Katya. Perhaps there never would be a good time. Could it be that they hadn't actually been lovers before, but that in retaliation for my perceived betrayal Stefan had now allowed himself to be persuaded? It really didn't bear thinking about. But hadn't he just protected and kissed me as if his love was as strong as ever? So why would I take the Countess's word and not his? But he had been anxious to get back to her, hadn't he? How confusing it all was.

'I must go to the children, milady, and make sure they are safe.'

'Send Stefan to me at once,' she cried, flinging herself down on the bed, bursting into yet another flood of tears.

Ignoring her hysterics for once, I did no such thing. Stefan was waiting for me on the landing, and I walked straight into his arms.

'I want you to know that I've never slept with her, never touched her, not since the day she assaulted me with that kiss. You must believe me, Millie.'

'I do, my love, I do.'

'Thank heaven for that.' He nestled me close on a sigh of relief.

Settling my head against the steady beat of his heart, I admitted to having suffered the occasional doubts. 'Those will soon be banished when the Countess reveals her true nature with some other trick or lie. She is the one not to be trusted.'

Fresh love surged through me as we kissed, the soft pink of dawn bathing us in a misty haze of passion. When, some moments later, we broke apart, I said, 'The question I have to ask is, do *you* believe in *me*?'

His voice now sounded somewhat sheepish and filled with guilt. 'I think I knew all along you weren't the baby's mother. But I was so eaten up with jealousy, so afraid that it might be true you'd had an affair with the Count, that I wouldn't let myself believe in your innocence.'

'And now?'

'If we can't trust each other, who can we trust?'

Smilingly resisting further kisses, I said goodnight and hurried to check on Irina and Katya, who were fast asleep, bless them. Taking them both into bed with me, I snuggled down beside them. What a joy children were, and how sweet was true love.

~

The next morning we discovered that the robbers, whoever they might be, had taken other items besides the Countess's pearls, including a good many of her clothes, a few porcelain vases and pictures, plus most of the food from the larder. I went straight to the militia to lodge a complaint. Although it was barely nine-thirty in the morning, there was a whole queue of people waiting with complaints of a similar nature, not least a priest coming to report the theft of chalices and sacred vessels from a local church.

The guards who were supposedly meant to protect the area were sitting in an office playing cards. I stood, hands on hips, looking down at them in disgust. 'Looting seems to be taking place all over the city, judging by the queue of people waiting to report a robbery, so what are you doing about it?'

They looked up at me in surprise. 'Are you accusing us of being negligent in some way?'

If the cap fits, I thought, remembering the remark my mother would often make when scolding Dad for some perceived failure on his part. A shaft of homesickness struck me in that moment. Oh, how I missed my beloved parents. Why wasn't I packing and going home like many of my friends from the British and American chapel, making my escape from the oncoming danger facing us all? The answer was plain. Stefan! How could I leave, loving him as I did?

Perhaps it was the return of Stefan's trust in me that caused me to be so reckless, but my prattling tongue ran out of control yet again. 'I'm sure there are better ways to spend your time than playing poker, or whatever it is.'

One of the men rose slowly to his feet, his manner seriously threatening. 'Perhaps you'd like to take your complaint to court, miss? Or maybe *we* should court-martial *you* for speaking so rudely to us.'

Turning on my heel, I hurried away, heart pounding with fear, realising I'd overstepped a dangerous line. One I would need to take better care to avoid in future.

~

The Count returned in early December, much to everyone's delight – save for the Countess, of course. She swept her son into her arms, ignoring her husband completely. What he had to tell us was not reassuring.

'The estate is no longer under my control. Serge and I were turned out of our own home by the local committee, obliged to live in one of the small cottages on the estate.'

'Why did you allow that to happen?' the Countess demanded, clearly shocked by such treatment. 'Couldn't you simply refuse to leave?'

'Not when a Bolshevik is pointing a gun at my son's head, no.'

She turned ashen at this, pressing Serge close to her breast, and we all fell silent as the reality of the situation was finally driven home.

'It is anarchy rather than democracy, I'm afraid. We soon ran out of food as, despite the cellar back at the house being well stocked with potatoes, and the granary full of flour, we had to bribe the peasants for the merest portion of it for our own use. They are cutting down trees for fuel; the soil lies untilled, crops have not been planted, cattle have been stolen or slaughtered to provide village feasts. The estate is in chaos.'

The Count went on to explain how many of his Romanov relatives were now under house arrest, or had likewise been deprived of their property or other possessions, their servants turned out to fend for themselves. 'A few have escaped or successfully hidden themselves away, while others have been forced to sell what little they have left to buy food, or are starving and close to death.'

'And what of the Tsar?' asked *Babushka* from her seat in the corner where she sat wrapped in blankets to keep warm.

'No one knows where the Tsar and his family are. Nicholas's first cousin, George V, offered sanctuary, but the idea was opposed by the British people and government, so what will happen next is anyone's guess. I'm afraid the Tsar's enemies will make life as difficult as possible for him.'

'We can only pray he will be safe,' the old lady said, and many voices echoed in unison of that wish.

The Count approached me just as I was shepherding the children to bed. 'May I have a quick word with you, Millie, when you have a moment?'

It was not an order, simply a request, but it wasn't difficult to guess the topic that was on his mind. I nodded, saying nothing, and as soon as the children were settled, *Nyanushki* offered to read them a story while I went to the Count's study and tapped on the door.

~

'Ah, Millie, please take a chair. I know you are busy so I won't take up too much of your time.'

'My time is yours milord. I was sorry to hear about the problems on the estate.'

'It makes for a very sad picture, not least because of the dead horses everywhere.'

'Dead horses? Why?' I asked, appalled.

'Hundreds of army horses have been brought back in an exhausted condition but there is no hay or straw to feed them on. So they die.'

'Oh, that's dreadful!'

'People too are dying, Millie. You must never forget that.'

'I beg your pardon, sir. I didn't mean to sound uncaring. It's just that I have a soft heart where animals are concerned.'

'We all do,' he conceded. 'But if you imagine we are in difficulties now, I fear it could get a great deal worse. Where the food will come from next year if no crops are planted I dread to think. However, that is not why I asked to speak to you.' His gaze softened. 'Is there something you need to tell me, Millie?'

The kindness of his smile was meant to encourage me to open my soul and confess to giving birth to an illegitimate child. Had that been true, then I'm quite sure he would have forgiven me and my job would have been safe. But I was innocent of the charge and, despite promising to keep the Countess's secret, I had no intention of telling lies on her behalf. Nor had I any wish to seek revenge for her maliciously turning Stefan against me, but I surely had the right to hold on to my dignity and reputation. Stiffening my spine I looked him straight in the eye. 'If you are referring to the baby, I'm afraid I can say nothing, not without permission.'

He was silent for several long seconds, reading the defiance in my gaze, hearing what I wasn't saying, perhaps guessing the truth from my silence. 'I presume you sought permission, and it was not granted.'

'That is correct, sir.'

He nodded and rose to his feet. 'Thank you, Millie. You may go.'

I turned to leave, but then hesitated. 'Milord, I trust you have no objection to my continuing to care for this baby?' Realising I was in danger of saying more than I should, I began again. 'I mean, is it all right for me to keep her?'

He smiled. 'If you are asking if I will insist upon you having it adopted, I assure you that won't happen. A child is in no way responsible for what its parents do. You will make a good mother, whatever the circumstances, and I certainly have no objection to you keeping her, Millie, if that is what you wish. She is fortunate to have you.'

Back in the nursery, I kissed little Katya's head as she slept. 'You are quite safe, my darling,' I said. But at the back of my mind a small voice murmured, *Unless the Countess changes her mind and reclaims you, which she is quite capable of doing simply out of revenge since Stefan has rejected her for me.*

TWENTY-NINE

It was a sad, drab Christmas that year as we all felt great trepidation and fear for the future, not only for the Tsar and his family, but for ourselves. Everyday life became increasingly difficult. We were constantly hungry, and the flat was bitterly cold as fuel too was in short supply. Sometimes we had electricity and sometimes we didn't. What little wood we did have was needed for Anton to cook on when the electricity was off, as it too often was.

A sense of defeat and depression hung over us all. The Count and Countess rarely exchanged a civil word, and while Mrs Grempel, Anton and Gusev loyally struggled on, if silently begrudging the extra work involved, many of the other servants left. The natural instinct in these precarious times was to go home to be with family and close friends. I asked myself a thousand times a day why I didn't do the same. The reasons I stayed were naturally all tied up with my feelings for Stefan, although also affected by an increasing fondness for baby Katya.

The Countess instructed Mrs Grempel to call in at a local agency and find replacement staff, which she dutifully did, despite knowing none would be found. Working for the aristocracy was no longer considered appropriate. In the end her young niece was engaged to help in the kitchen, and the chauffeur, Viktor Lytkin, brought in his brother Ivan to act as footman.

'Standards are slipping,' the Countess bitterly complained. 'We cannot be expected to manage with such a small number of servants. It's quite ridiculous.'

'I would take care not to broadcast those views too widely, if I were you,' her husband warned. 'I doubt the Bolsheviks would approve, and may well deprive us of the few we have left.'

'Obviously, you would think it best to keep silent and give in to their demands, since you are a coward.'

'I am a reasonable man who wishes to survive this revolution. What is so wrong in that?'

It was a huge relief to escape the tense atmosphere at the flat on occasion and visit Ruth and Ivy and my other friends at the British and American chapel. We all contributed bread, cake or a few biscuits whenever we could spare it, although bread was rationed at 50 grams a day, assuming you could find any in the shops. *Nyanushki* would take over the care of Katya for a few hours, with even *Babushka* happy to jiggle the baby on her lap, as they both believed I deserved a little break now and then. Serge and Irina were old enough to amuse themselves.

'I never knew what it felt like to be really hungry until now,' Ruth complained. She was beginning to look hollow-eyed and much thinner, very like the women who'd taken part in the demonstration back in February.

'What I wouldn't give for a hot dinner of roast beef and Yorkshire pudding,' Ivy said, licking her lips.

'Ooh yes, and jam roly-poly to follow,' I agreed.

'But it's nearly Christmas,' Ruth reminded us. 'So I would choose goose with chestnut stuffing, plum pudding and brandy sauce.'

'And mince pies with cream,' Ivy said.

'Stop it, please – you're making my mouth water and my tummy ache even more. Anyone want a hard biscuit?'

We all pulled a face but nobody refused to take one. Grab what food you could was very much the order of the day.

'So what about this baby you've supposedly had while you were in the Crimea?' Ivy asked, never shy of coming straight to the point.

Heaving a sigh, I desperately struggled to find the right answer. It wasn't my friends' fault, after all, that I was in this situation, and it was only natural that it should incite gossip. I decided to keep as close to the truth as I dare. Giving a little laugh, I said, 'You should never listen to rumour. As a matter of fact, I haven't had a baby. I'm looking after one for – well, as a favour to someone.'

'Ah, anyone we know?'

'I'm really not in a position to say.'

'Hm. So why you? Does this mother not have anyone else to care for her child?'

'She asked me, and I agreed to help.'

Ruth said, 'That was very brave of you, considering how gossip is bound to put the very worst connotation on it. You disappear for months on end then return wheeling a baby in a pram, who no one else in the Belinsky household is prepared to lay claim to. Folk are bound to make assumptions.'

'I can say nothing more.'

'Not even to defend your own reputation?' Ivy asked. 'Is this person too poor to keep the child, or too rich and important to acknowledge an unplanned daughter?'

These questions were getting dangerously close to the truth, so I laughingly replied, 'Ivy, you have a very fertile imagination. Why don't you write the story and we'll read it?'

This brought laughter all round and fortunately the conversation moved on to other topics, but my two friends continued to cast me curious glances throughout the afternoon. It seemed that all my worst fears were coming true. Would I lose my friends now, as I had very nearly lost the man I loved?

~

Days later, as we were about to sit down to afternoon tea, Countess Olga received the dreadful news that her lover had been arrested and killed. 'They took all his money and property and when he objected they shot him,' she sobbed. 'Poor darling Dimitri is dead!'

'You have my sincere sympathies,' the Count responded with commendable patience, considering it was his wife's ex-lover whose death she was supposedly grieving.

'Why would such a terrible thing happen?' She began to pace back and forth, wringing her hands in distress, although from her expression I suspected she was far more concerned over her own safety than the loss of her erstwhile lover. Her next words proved my guess to be entirely correct. 'Are you even certain it's safe for us to remain in Petrograd?'

'We can only hope so,' the Count said, his face sombre.

'You *hope* so? Don't you know?'

'None of us do. These are uncertain times.'

'We should all return at once to the country,' she protested.

'Where would be the point when things are equally difficult there? And there's no room for servants in that small cottage.'

She stamped her foot in fury, as a child might in a tantrum. '*Why couldn't you have been killed instead of my darling Dimitri*?'

'You might be in even greater difficulties if I had been.'

I concentrated on setting out the cups and saucers, trying not to listen.

'It was Dimitri I loved. I don't need *you*!'

'You need my money.'

'Which you are too mean to properly share,' she snapped.

The Count laughed. 'I do have a nasty habit of giving it to those most needy rather than the most greedy, don't I? But I'm surprised you still care about Korniloff, considering how he abandoned you when he discovered there was to be no divorce with a high settlement. You'll have to find yourself some other rich lover, instead of one who just happens to be handy,' he coldly remarked.

'Meaning what?'

'Wasn't that the new footman, Lytkin, I saw entering your room the other evening?'

Her cheeks flushed bright crimson, although whether with rage or embarrassment is hard to say. 'He was bringing me a cup of hot chocolate.'

'Why would you need one? I wonder. Isn't he capable of keeping you warm enough in bed?'

For once she was lost for words, and sweeping the tea cups and even the precious cake stand from the table, she stormed out the room.

Heaving a sigh, the Count gave a pragmatic shrug. 'How very fortunate that Mrs Grempel had not yet brought in the tea pot, and that the children haven't arrived. Perhaps you would help me pick everything up, Millie, since we really cannot afford to waste a crumb.' And we did just that, saying not a word about the Countess's latest fit of temper.

Sadly for me, as *Nyanushki* arrived with the children, Stefan too appeared at the door of the drawing room. The Count and I were down on our knees on the rug. Maybe Stefan couldn't quite see that we were actually picking up broken cups and bits of cake from under the tea table, for he took one look at us huddled together on the floor and quickly left, slamming the door behind him. Setting the cake stand back in place, I was overcome with worry that just when I thought all was well again between us, the situation had suddenly taken a turn for the worse.

I hurried after him to explain but he was nowhere around. As so often in the past, Stefan had done one of his disappearing tricks and we saw little of him over the next few days. And despite Christmas being over I was kept fully occupied caring for the children in difficult circumstances.

As the final days of December slipped by the Countess surprised us by announcing that she intended to hold a ball to celebrate New Year. 'I have decided we need cheering up. If we don't have enough food to feed people we can at least provide music and dancing.'

It was the most marvellous decision I'd ever heard her make. Even the Count looked pleased.

'Could she possibly be coming to terms with reality at last?' I asked of *Nyanushki*.

'We can only hope so.'

We set about making plans with eager anticipation. Finding the necessary supplies to feed all the guests she intended to invite would certainly not be easy, and vodka had disappeared from the shelves some years ago at the start of the war. But Mrs Grempel declared herself up for the challenge, and the Count assured us that he still had several bottles of champagne in the wine cellar. The few remaining servants would also be allowed to watch the dancing as reward for their loyalty. Even the children could stay up and take part in the fun. Excitement was high. And Stefan had returned.

It was a beautiful, snowy winter's night, the glitter of moonlight reflecting upon the icy river. We felt grateful that for once the electricity was working and lights blazed from every window, although we had candles at the ready since it could go off at any time. A knot of pain gathered in my throat as I watched Stefan set out the candelabra on the dining room tables. He looked so handsome, so smart and neat in his footman's uniform, his chestnut hair slicked down instead of sprouting in all directions as it usually did, particularly when he was out and about in the country. He picked up an empty log basket and went out to fill it from the much-depleted wood store in the inner courtyard.

At the same moment I spotted the Countess hovering at the end of the servants' corridor. What on earth was she doing there? Then I saw she was talking to Lytkin, the new footman. As I stood watching them walk away together I shook my head in disbelief. So this was the cause of her change of mood? The Count's suspicions had been correct. She'd come out of her sulks and tantrums because she'd acquired a new lover from among the servants. Goodness, first the chauffeur, now his brother. The woman was utterly insatiable, and none of the men she set out to seduce ever refused her, whatever rank or class they were. While I couldn't seem to hold on to the one man I loved.

Remembering *Nyanushki's* advice that I should fight for Stefan, on impulse I followed him out into the courtyard. Hearing my footsteps he looked up, his face pale in the moonlight. I longed to cup my hands about his cold cheeks and press my lips to his. Losing courage, I wrapped my arms about myself to make sure they didn't misbehave.

'You shouldn't be outside without a coat,' he scolded.

'I wanted to talk to you.'

'I think everything that needs saying between us has already been said, don't you?'

'No, I don't. I understand why you're confused because of what you imagine you saw, but . . .'

'I'm no fool, Millie. That wasn't the only time. I've seen you coming out of the Count's study on more than one occasion.'

'It isn't what you think.'

He turned away. 'Not now, Millie. Can't you see I'm busy? The guests will be arriving at any minute.'

Undeterred, I took a step forward, blocking his path so that he couldn't escape without pushing me to one side. I smelled pine on his clothes, saw the tiredness on his face and guessed he wasn't sleeping well, any more than I was. Standing close to him like this I couldn't help but remember the way he used to hold me safe in his arms, his body warm and filled with passion as it pressed against mine. I missed his kisses and those loving moments. But fearing yet another rejection, I didn't dare to touch him.

'Then later, when the guests have gone?' I asked. 'I need to explain.'

Hoisting the log basket into his arms, he avoided meeting my gaze and, pushing past me, headed back to the kitchen.

'I love you, Stefan. Don't you love me any more?'

He paused, still, with his back towards me, and didn't move for some seconds. Then, adjusting the basket on his hip, he continued into the flat without saying another word.

Pain clenched my heart. I was losing him after all. How would I survive without him?

There was little time to feel sorry for myself or pursue the matter further just then, however, as carriages and cars were already lining up outside. The ball was about to begin. The scene reminded me of Carreck Place, which right now felt like another world, long gone.

Here in Petrograd there were no scullery maids to stand all day scrubbing pans, no menservants in yellow striped waistcoats, no linkmen swinging their lanterns as they whistled up the next carriage, and no extra hired staff of any sort. Gusev the butler was giving out instructions though there were very few servants around to carry them out. As I helped Mrs Grempel, her niece, and a couple of maids lay the tables, and the footmen bring out dishes and trays, I wondered if this world might disappear altogether.

Nor was there the same calmness or clockwork efficiency so evident at Carreck Place. Here, each of us was rushing about, falling over each other in our desperation to do the work of three pairs of hands, not one. But despite all the problems, the apartment looked lovely.

The supper-room was decorated to replicate a garden, with groups of palm trees, flowering lilacs, crocuses and daffodils, all brought in specially from the country. There was even a small fountain surrounded by lotus blossoms.

Who Anton and Mrs Grempel had needed to bribe to provide the excellent repast they provided, I have no idea, but it must have been a mammoth task. All credit to them that they managed it to perfection. It may not have been as grand as the caviar and lobster dinners held in the past, but there were ample supplies of veal, ham and chicken, salad and asparagus, plus a wide selection of biscuits, cakes and jellies. It was a most substantial meal with no cabbage soup in sight.

The Count looked resplendent in evening dress, and the Countess was more beautiful than ever, if that was possible, in a white chiffon gown embroidered all over with sparkling sequins and ablaze with diamonds.

The ball was opened by a polonaise, the musical quartet entertaining us all as we carried round trays with glasses of cider, wine and champagne. The baby was asleep in her crib in the kitchen where everyone could help keep an eye on her. Serge was with his father, Irina with me.

'I could show you a few steps later, if you like,' I suggested, seeing how she looked longingly at the dance floor.

Since she was beginning to blossom into a pretty young lady I had expected her mother to show an interest in encouraging her to dance. It was a vain hope. The Countess was interested in no one but herself, certainly not this shy, neglected young girl.

She beamed up at me. 'I would like that, *Baryshnya*.'

What a sweetie she was.

Later, with the work largely done and our bellies full for once from a substantial amount of leftovers, we servants gathered together at the far corner of the ballroom. It was wonderful to gaze upon the scene: the ballroom with its pale blue marble walls interspersed with mirrors and decorated with a mosaic of gold and white flowers, its gilded doors, jasper columns, lapis lazuli vases and malachite tables was utterly breathtaking. Its magnificence was enhanced by the beauty of the ladies and handsome gentlemen dancing.

In a quiet corner Irina and I practised a few steps of the polonaise, the waltz and the tango, the pair of us giggling all the while. The temperatures outside might be plummeting to well below zero but here we were radiant with warmth, good food and wine, and a contented gathering of people all enjoying themselves. Almost a glimpse of the old Russia, of which *Babushka* had told me so much, the dowager looking very like an empress herself as she sat in state at the end of the room.

Mrs Grempel was seated beside me on a comfy chair enjoying a glass of port. Anton was becoming slightly tipsy on red wine, although I have to say he deserved it after all his hard work these last few days in preparing this feast. It was then that I became aware of the new footman, Ivan Lytkin, edging his way along behind the pillars and heading for a side door. *Now why would he do that?* I wondered. I saw him glance up at the clock on the wall, its fingers pointing to just fifteen minutes short of midnight.

Could he be tired and seeking an early night? No servant had the right to leave without the butler's permission, as these affairs rarely ended before the early hours. Footmen in particular were expected to see to the gentlemen's needs until every guest had left.

I remembered Liam explaining his routine when he was persuading me to meet him in the summer house that night. Even this fellow's brother, Viktor the chauffeur, had been pressed into service, in view of the shortage of staff, although now he'd gone outside to act as linkman for the few carriages already beginning to gather.

So where was the fellow off to?

It wasn't difficult to guess the reason.

I looked about the room for Countess Olga but could see no sign of her either – not on the dance floor, nor seated on any of the sofas, chairs or seats of all shapes and sizes that lined the walls where the dowagers sat gossiping. It wasn't like her to leave early, her dance card generally being full for the entire evening. So where could she be?

There was no doubt in my mind that it was an assignation, and really none of my business.

But where was Stefan? I hadn't seen him for some time either. My heart skipped a beat. Could she possibly be with Stefan and not the new footman at all? Had he gone with her in retaliation for the jealousy he felt over my alleged affair with the Count? The urge to sneak out and check was impossible to resist. Did he love me or my mistress? I needed to know, once and for all. If the latter, then I would waste no more time on him and begin making arrangements for the next ship home.

I found Irina sitting with her back against a pillar happily dressing her favourite doll in a corner, a selection of ball gowns, shoes and veils spread out around her. Still a child at heart, she loved nothing more than dressing the doll in fashionable Russian costume. 'Come, Miss Irina. Aren't you the lucky one? I can't remember you ever being up so late before. But now it's time for us to fetch Katya and get to bed. I'm certainly ready for mine.' In truth, once they were both settled I meant to seek an opportunity to make those vital investigations.

Irina pulled a face. 'Oh, just another few minutes, *please, Baryshnya*. I'm not in the least tired, honest.'

I laughingly exchanged a glance with *Nyanushki*. It was a special occasion, after all, and perhaps it would be better to do my spying first. 'Would you sit with Irina for a moment while I see to the baby?'

'Of course.'

Heart racing, I slipped out of a side door and ran swiftly along the back corridor, straight down to the kitchen where I found Mrs Grempel's niece minding Katya. 'Thank you so much for your help. I'll take her now. You go and enjoy the ball.'

My intention was to put the baby in her cot, then go straight to the Countess's bedroom. As her maid I surely had that right. What I would do if I found them together, perhaps in the Countess's bed, didn't bear thinking about. But even if that was the case, then at least I would know where I stood.

Wary of meeting any guests I reached the hall via the servants' private entrance, Katya in my arms. I was about to slip through the door that led to the Countess's quarters when I heard a noise behind me. I paused to listen. Was it the scratching of mice? No, more like that of a ticking clock, yet there was none in the hall so far as I could recall. I looked around to make certain, even though I knew that the grandfather clock the Countess had bought in England had been put in the library. Following the sound, I finally spotted an object tucked under a hall table. It looked like a box of some sort. As I approached, the ticking grew louder. My insides froze.

'Dear lord, surely it couldn't be . . .' But I'd read enough in the Russian papers lately not to take any chances.

I ran back to the ballroom as fast as my trembling limbs could carry me, and hurried straight to the Count. He appeared somewhat shocked to see me in such a state and with the baby clutched tight in my arms. Strictly speaking, according to etiquette I should have passed the information through Gusev the butler, but there wasn't time. Not even pausing to bob a curtsey or politely excuse myself, I grabbed Count Belinsky by the arm and dragged him away from the group of guests with whom he'd been engaged in conversation.

'Millie, what on earth . . . Is something wrong with the child?'

'No milord, I think someone has planted a bomb.'

~

I find it difficult to remember the order of events after that. Everywhere was pandemonium and the stench of raw fear. I know I felt deeply thankful that I had the baby in my arms, and when I ran back for Irina Mrs Grempel told me that *Nyanushki* had already taken her out. The entire building was quickly evacuated, people running about in total panic, searching for loved ones, falling over each other in their anxiety to escape. Serge was with his father. *Babushka* was carried out on her chair by two of the guests. I still hadn't seen Stefan or the Countess. Everyone gathered on the road and gardens outside. By this time Katya had woken up and was screaming her head off, disturbed by all the noise and panic.

I found *Nyanushki* talking to the Count and hurried over to join them. 'I'm looking for Irina. Where is she? Mrs Grempel said that you had her.'

She looked at me in alarm. 'I was just telling the Count that she was here with me a second ago, but now she's disappeared. I don't know where she's gone. Isn't she with you? She did say something about her doll.'

'Oh, no. She can't have gone back inside to look for it, can she?'

Frozen in horror, I looked back at the tall building, now safely emptied of its occupants, or so we'd thought. Then, thrusting baby Katya into *Nyanushki's* arms, I started to run towards it. Stefan emerged out of the crowd, grabbing hold of me just as I reached the door.

'Where the hell are you going? That bomb could go off at any minute.'

'It's Irina. We think she's gone back inside for her doll.'

The Count too appeared at my side in the same moment. 'You mustn't go in Millie. Leave it to me – I'll find her.'

'Where was this doll?' Stefan asked.

'In the ballroom. She was dressing it in the far corner behind the pillars where we were all standing.'

'You stay here. I'll go.' And before either the Count or I could protest, Stefan pulled open the door and rushed back into the house.

'Oh, dear God, please keep him safe,' I murmured. The Count gripped my arm as if fearful I might run after him.

'Come away, Millie, we must stand well back.' The mass of guests and servants were likewise rapidly retreating, getting as far from the building as they could. Yet still I struggled against the Count's hold, wanting to stay with Stefan, to go with him and help. In the long seconds that ticked past while we all waited, in my imagination I saw him run through the hall, race along the corridor into the ballroom where he would find Irina and . . .

It was then that the bomb went off.

THIRTY

Mass had been taken, the corpse candles lit, and now it was the burial with the priest chanting the usual prayers and people throwing dust and coins into the grave. The coffin had been made as comfortable as possible with a pillow stuffed with straw and various precious belongings set beside the small figure of the deceased, including the doll.

My heart was breaking, tears running down my cheeks unchecked. I stood beside the Countess. Her manner was cold and unfeeling, and she showed not a glimmer of regret or emotion at the loss of this child. Oh, why hadn't I kept Irina with me? If I hadn't been fussing over what Stefan was doing, I might well have done so. I'd intended to take both girls to bed, but would they have been any safer in the bedrooms, which were farther from any exit? Probably not. Debris had blocked off that section as a result of the explosion, and smoke from the resulting fire had filled the entire building. Two of the maids who chose not to stay and watch the dancing had suffocated in their beds. In the end, I did go back for Irina, battling through the mass of panic-stricken guests only to be assured that she was safely outside, as she had been until she went looking for that dratted doll.

Pressing a hand to my mouth to stifle my sobs, I glanced across at the Count. The poor man appeared on the verge of collapse, his shoulders hunched in misery, his face barely visible beneath a fur hat pulled well down over his head. It was impossible to understand the depth of his anguish. I longed to go over and comfort him, but knew it would be inappropriate, and would only irritate my mistress.

The day dragged by in a blizzard of misery. I was scarcely able to concentrate on anything other than caring for little Katya, who seemed now more precious than ever.

It was a relief when all the mourners had finally departed. The part of the east wing that had suffered the worst of the bomb damage was little more than a heap of rubble. Smoke still drifted out of the upper windows, and small pockets of fire had lingered for some days before being doused with water pumped from the canal. When and if the building would be habitable again was impossible to say. The Countess had already begun organising the removal of her precious belongings, her wardrobe and jewels being top priority.

Accommodation had been found for us in a nearby apartment further down the road. The family who used to live there had departed to their estate in the country so it had been unoccupied for some months. It smelled of damp and mice, and was quite small by comparison with the original apartment. The Count sat with his head in his hands in what had once been the library but now contained only empty book shelves, a tragic picture of a broken man. I stood by the door, as instructed, unable to get the image of Irina out of my head.

The Countess was pacing back and forth, as impatient as ever, Stefan standing before her. I assumed he'd been summoned to be thanked for his heroic bravery.

He'd emerged out of the smoke with Irina in his arms, believing he'd saved her. At first sight it was evident they'd both sustained injuries: cuts and bruises from falling masonry, and some serious burns from the fire. But worst of all, so far as Irina was concerned, was the inhalation of smoke from which she never recovered. The doctors did everything they could but to no avail. The only comfort they could offer was that the bomb had gone off so suddenly she would have been unaware of what was happening, and probably rendered instantly unconscious. Both of her legs and back were broken from the pillar falling on top of her. Had she lived, it is unlikely she would ever have walked again.

I came out of my gloomy reverie to hear the Countess say, 'We sent for you to say that we know who is to blame for this tragedy.'

Her tone was strangely condemning, with little sign of either gratitude or sympathy. Not at all what I'd expected. The Count, locked in his grief, wasn't even listening.

Stefan frowned, perhaps thinking the same. 'I'd be interested to hear who you suspect.'

'Why *you*, of course. Who else?'

I must have made some startled sound of protest, for he glanced across at me, equally stunned. 'I beg your pardon, milady, I believe I must have misheard you. I thought for a moment you were blaming me.'

'Don't try to play the innocent. We are all aware that you are a revolutionary at heart, with a driven desire to seek revenge on the aristocratic class you believe responsible for the death of your beloved father.'

I was out of my chair and at his side in a second. 'That is entirely unfair, milady. How can you accuse Stefan when he was the one who tried to save Irina?'

'It was the Count he wished to murder, not his daughter.'

'You have absolutely no proof to back up this theory.'

Ignoring me completely, she continued to coldly address Stefan. 'You've been plotting this for some time. I can guess where you go when you slip away and imagine that I don't notice your absence: to clandestine meetings with your fellow intriguers. You laid that bomb. Who else could it have been?'

He was ashen faced, white to the lips. 'You are wrong, milady. I beg you to believe me. I am innocent of the charge.'

'So you say, but you will need to prove your innocence to the police, with whom I have already spoken. They will question you on the matter first thing in the morning.'

Interrogate him, more like, and probably lock him in prison while they did so. I was utterly devastated at the prospect. Stefan and I might have our problems but not for one moment did I believe him capable of doing such a terrible thing. He might well be far more anti-gentry than I, a fervent advocate for democracy, and feel some resentment over the loss of his father, but I was quite certain he would never resort to violence. He was as much a moderate in his political views as the Count himself. Hadn't I heard the pair of them discussing the situation more than once, generally in agreement?

The Countess herself had never shown any reticence in taking revenge. She could have decided upon an alternative way to be rid of her husband, and if Stefan had indeed rejected her advances, as he once claimed, might well be happy for him take the blame. If that were the case, it would explain her meeting with Ivan Lytkin. They could have been plotting together and not involved in a romantic assignation at all. Suspicion was strong in me, every instinct telling me I was right. But how could I prove it? With the country so unstable, anyone could have laid that bomb. Why would anyone suspect her of being the guilty party? She was the Countess Belinsky, after all.

And if she had already spoken to the police, time was of the essence.

The Count had retired, taking Serge with him, as the boy was, understandably, still in a dreadful state. Baby Katya was at last asleep, *Nyanushki* nodding in a chair beside her. *Babushka* was in the adjoining room and she and I shared a consoling hug as I took her a cup of hot coffee instead of her usual chocolate.

'Don't blame yourself,' she said, shrewdly guessing the guilt I was suffering.

'I'll try not to.'

'The blame lies with whoever planted that bomb.'

'It's been a long day. No reading tonight. You must try to get some sleep.' I kissed her papery soft cheek, not wishing to explain that Stefan was the one being charged.

With everyone settled for the night I hurried downstairs to talk to him through the door of the laundry room, where he'd been locked up for the night.

'Are you all right?'

'I'll survive.'

I prayed that he would, was not prepared to consider the alternative. 'I don't believe you're guilty, not for a moment.'

'Thank you for your support, Millie.' His voice sounded hollow through the wooden panels, or perhaps from the terror he must be feeling. Once the police, or worse, the Bolsheviks arrived, he would be taken straight to the prison across at the Fortress of Saints Peter and Paul, a grim place from which few people emerged sane, if they were fortunate enough to come out at all.

'I love you, Stefan, and I know that you love me in your heart, so please stop listening to the Countess's lies. The Count and I were only picking up cake she'd tossed on the floor in one of her tantrums. There is nothing between us at all, beyond my gratitude for his support.'

'I'm sorry for being such an idiot. You're right; I do love you Millie, with every ounce of my being.'

Pressing myself against the door, I ached to see his face, to touch him, hold him, show how much I loved him. The longing to kiss him was overwhelming but the door remained locked, a wedge of solid oak between us. I couldn't reach him, couldn't get help, and soon the police would arrive and it would be too late.

An idea struck me. 'Stefan, I think I know where the keys might be. Hold on while I go and look.'

Every kitchen has a small rack or cupboard on the wall where keys are kept, so it wasn't difficult to find the hook marked 'Laundry Room'. It was empty. Of course, the Countess herself would have it on her person, and I had no wish to attempt to steal it from her. But there must be another one somewhere, possibly in the butler's pantry. The search took longer than I'd hoped but at last I found a duplicate key in the housekeeper's old room. Within seconds of fitting it in the lock, I was in Stefan's arms.

'I love you so much,' he said, after kissing me long and hard. 'And I *do* believe you when you say the baby is not yours, but the Countess's. Come, my darling, we'll leave together, this minute. We'll get as far away from this place as we can.'

'But I need my papers, and to fetch Katya. I can't leave her with a woman who doesn't care about her.'

'Then hurry. We mustn't delay a second longer than necessary.' Even as he told me this he kissed me again, as if unable to resist, and I certainly had no objection. It was then that we heard a small hiccup of laughter.

'I do seem to make a habit of interrupting you two at your love making, or perhaps you unwisely choose the wrong moment or place. Was it you who let him out of the laundry room, Dowthwaite?'

I turned to face the Countess with every scrap of dignity I possessed, desperate to hide the tremors of fear running through me. 'Why would I leave him locked up when I know him to be innocent? Those charges you made were groundless. Absolute stuff and nonsense! In fact, without too big a stretch of the imagination I could bring similar charges against you, milady. And since Russia is undergoing a revolution against the autocrats, the Bolsheviks might well choose to believe me rather than you.'

She was smiling, my words having made no impression; there was an odd twist to her lips as her eyes focused on something behind me. I half turned, just in time to see Stefan climb through the kitchen window and vanish into the night. It was then that I heard the hammering on the front door.

~

'I dare say you've heard the news?' I was sitting with the Count on a low wall by the bridge over the canal with the baby on my knee. We were watching the builders start to clear the rubble from the front of the apartment. Just across from us on the opposite bank were the onion domes of a nearby church glinting gold in the sun, a reminder of normality in a world that had been torn apart.

The Count looked at me with blank eyes, struggling to focus on what I was saying. At length he said, 'If you mean that Stefan has gone on the run to escape arrest, yes, I was sorry to hear that.'

I nodded. 'The police called first thing this morning to question and arrest him, but he escaped just in time. I want you to know milord, that Stefan was not responsible for planting that bomb. He loved Irina, and you too, as a matter of fact. He was – *is* – your greatest admirer. He would never harm a hair of your head. If anyone should say different, please don't believe a word.'

He smiled at me then. 'By "anyone", I take it you mean my wife?'

Anxious though I was to protect Stefan, I answered with care. 'I admit I find it hard to understand why she would believe him to be guilty.'

'My wife's motivation has always been difficult to fathom, save for her need for attention and money.' He paused a moment, a thoughtful expression on his face. 'And revenge. If Stefan has offended her in some way, that could be the reason.'

If the Count guessed that his wife had attempted to seduce her gardener-handyman and he had rejected her, so be it, but I wasn't about to confirm his suspicions. Silence fell as we watched a boat chug by, stirring up the icy water. Despite the bright sunshine, temperatures had not risen a great deal. The sound of a wall collapsing brought our attention back to the apartment. Staring at the devastation and the cloud of dust surrounding it, our thoughts naturally returned to Irina. The Count quietly remarked, 'She was my life.'

'I know.'

'I shall never stop loving her.'

Emotion choked my throat as I struggled to find the right words, if only it were possible. 'She adored you too, and enjoyed a good life, if sadly far too short. Always remember that. And you still have a son.' I had no intention of mentioning the Countess's claim that she'd been pregnant with Serge by another man when she married the Count. Some secrets were best kept.

'Serge is a fine young man, thanks to your efforts in dealing with those silly rebellions. Both my children have benefited from your service, as did I when you encouraged me to take more of an interest in him. I am most grateful, as it seems to have paid off. Our relationship is much improved and I shall continue to do my utmost to be a good father to the boy.'

'I'm glad. That is exactly what he needs.'

As I listened to the Count continue to sing my praises, an uncomfortable feeling began to grow inside me, for it sounded very much as if he was saying goodbye. Was he about to hand me my notice? It seemed highly likely now that Irina was lost to us and Serge was a boy of fourteen, nearly fifteen, hardly in need of a governess any longer. His next words seemed to confirm my worst fears.

'I intend to tell my wife that she may have her divorce and a settlement, if a far more modest one than she would like. Our marriage is over, has been for a long while, but now it is time to call it a day. I intend to return to my country estate. Even though it is more of a communal project now, it is where I am happiest.'

'Where will the Countess reside?' We again glanced across at the builders who were carefully stacking stone that could be reused and loading the rest of the rubble onto carts to take away.

'There are other cottages on the estate. She could have one of those. If she chooses to stay in Petrograd the apartment will eventually be restored and refurbished, and she's welcome to remain there until such time as she finds a place of her own. I hope to take Serge with me to the country, if he'll come. He seems to love it there. His inheritance will not be what it once was, but I'll find a way to make a good life for him.'

'I'm sure you will.' I paused a moment before asking the question beating in my brain. 'And what would you advise me to do, milord?'

He gave me one of his kindest smiles. 'I do know the truth about this little one,' he said, stroking Katya's head. 'I read between the lines when we last talked about her. The birth of this child is part of the reason I've called an end to our marriage. Olga is now quite beyond the pale. I'm sure she would claim she had every right to take a lover, but in my opinion none at all to give the child away. You may not be aware of this Millie, but Irina was not Olga's daughter. She was the child of my mistress Mavra, the lady I told you of.'

'I rather guessed that,' I said, making no mention of the gossip that was rife among the servants.

'I returned to her when it became abundantly clear my marriage wasn't going to work. Mavra and I were very happy together, despite the difficult circumstances, but then she died in a horrific accident.'

'What happened exactly?'

'She drowned while swimming with a group of friends in the River Neva.'

A chill rippled down my spine as I recalled a similar accident almost happening to Irina, on that lovely autumn day all those years ago at Carreckwater. 'How tragic. Did she go out too far? Who was with her at the time? Was the Countess present?'

'Oh, yes, there was a large party of us enjoying a bright day of sunshine in early spring. What went wrong is difficult to say. Perhaps the coldness of the water gave her cramp but she unexpectedly got into difficulties. No one noticed until it was too late. My wife was in a boat nearby and did what she could to help, and brought Mavra ashore. How could I not take her child, since darling Irina had been so tragically orphaned? She was my daughter too, and I'd loved her from the moment she was born, if not before.'

I could find no response to this sorry tale as thoughts and suspicions raced through my head.

'Sadly, my wife never cared for the child, which was only to be expected, I suppose. She was most neglectful, so it was a blessing when you came to work for us. Irina loved you dearly, worshipped you to such an extent that she sought to *be* like you, as young girls do.'

Tears were filling my eyes, blocking my voice. 'I loved her too. She was a sweetie.'

'A mother's love had been largely lacking in her life until you came along, but thanks to your care all that changed, and she grew in confidence daily. I know now how important it is for a child to feel loved and safe. Having lost Irina, I would hate to see this little one suffer as she did. The Countess may have given birth to her, but she is now *your* child, and you will make an excellent mother.'

'Thank you for your faith in me, milord.' A huge sense of relief swept over me, the very real fear that I might lose Katya beginning at last to dissipate.

'However, to help you cope with the inevitable expenses of raising a child, and because she is my wife's offspring, however much she might deny it, I have created a trust fund in her name to secure her future.'

'Oh, milord, I don't know what to say, or how to thank you.' I was regarding him in awe, his generosity leaving me quite speechless.

'By rights I dare say we should seek legal confirmation, adoption and so on. But in the current climate that could take years. It would be far better if you took her far away from here, somewhere safe, and I know the very place. You will recall Carreck Place, once occupied by my late cousin . . .'

'. . . late? You mean Lord Rumsley is dead?' I interrupted.

'I'm afraid so. A heart attack, I believe. His wife, son and daughter have moved to America, where they are happily residing in Boston.'

'They've left their home in the Lake District?' I could hardly believe what I was hearing. Perhaps I had assumed that nothing bad could ever happen back in England, as we seemed to be the ones suffering, caught up in a revolution. His next words took me completely by surprise.

'Lord Rumsley never actually owned Carreck Place: I did. Or rather, I provided the funds for my cousin Charles to buy it. The man was an idiot, but family, you understand? Now I wish to give it to you, or at least to the child of my foolish wife.' Kissing Katya's cheek, he smiled down at the baby. 'She deserves some recompense for being so abandoned. The house will be hers for life, and yours too, with a trust fund in her name to maintain it. What happens after that can be decided upon later, depending on which of us is still around by then.'

I was shaking my head in disbelief. 'I couldn't possibly accept it.'

'Yes, you can, for little Katya's sake.'

There were tears in my eyes now as I looked down at the baby sleeping contentedly in my arms. 'I shall do my best to be a good mother to her. I love her already more than life itself.'

'Of course you do. The house is standing empty. Go and revive it and turn it once more into a loving home. Find Stefan and take him with you.'

The Count smiled at my blushes, giving my hand a gentle pat. 'I assume you and he will get together in the end. Find him, Millie, and leave together. Don't stay in Petrograd a day longer than you need to. It isn't safe. I ask just one favour: do not tell my wife any of this, not until you are safely established in Carreckwater. Perhaps not even then. There is safety in silence.'

There was a warning note in his voice and I found myself nodding, understanding completely what he was telling me.

'Now I shall go and break the news to my wife that she is about to become a free woman.'

THIRTY-ONE

Leaving her grandmother in peace, Abbie went in search of Aimée, panicking slightly when she couldn't immediately find her.

'No sweat,' Fay said. 'She's out on the lake with your father.'

'Wow, really?'

'I suggested he make some effort to get to know his new grandchild, give her a little more attention. He looked quite surprised by my suggestion, and a little bit thoughtful, but it seems to be working. He's taken her and Jonathon out in the boat to teach them how to fish.'

'Oh, my goodness, that's wonderful!' Her thoughts at once turned to the Count and Serge doing exactly the same thing, remembering how their relationship had developed as a result, and her heart warmed with affection for her father and for her sister-in-law. 'You really are brilliant!'

Fay gave a wicked grin. 'Still not quite there with Robert, but making progress.'

'Then I suggest you give me some advice, too, on how to handle my brother. Perhaps over a glass of wine?'

The two women were happily sitting chatting, baby Carrie playing at their feet, when the fishing party returned. It was very plain to Abbie, by the way Aimée giggled as her grandfather lifted her out of the boat, then happily took his hand to come over to them, that progress was most certainly being made there. Her daughter had clearly captured his heart.

Abbie's mind was whirling. She understood now how the family came to be living in Carreck Place, and thought this might be the moment to reveal her own little secret.

'I think Mrs Brixton has some fairy cakes and orange juice waiting for you in the kitchen,' she said. And as the two children ran off, whooping with delight, she cast a sideways glance at her companion. Fay instantly picked up the message that she wanted a moment alone with her father and, announcing that Carrie too would enjoy some cake, hurried after them.

Taking a breath, Abbie turned to her father. 'Dad, I've been meaning to say that I've been to see the solicitor.'

'Ah, I rather thought you might.'

'I needed John Kirby's advice on extending the overdraft and it all came out.' Pitching her voice low and carefully non-accusatory, she asked, 'When were you planning to tell me that Mum had left me the shop and business?'

Letting out a heavy sigh, he came to sit beside her on the bench. 'It's hard to say why I put it off. I just couldn't bear to speak of it for a while. It's true that Kate had badly neglected the business in recent years and was in debt, with a large overdraft she'd never had before. But we do still have money coming in from land we let out to local farmers, which helps to maintain the house. Things aren't quite as bad as Robert made out, although I know nothing of his personal financial situation. However, your mother's decision came as something of a surprise, of which I didn't entirely approve.'

'You didn't think I deserved it, and were trying to find a way out?' Abbie softly asked.

'Maybe. I also doubted she would have made such a will had she realised what a sorry state Precious Dreams would fall into. But then I realised it wasn't my decision to make. The shop belonged to her, not to me, and as you constantly remind me, you are no longer a foolish teenager. I decided I should at least allow you the opportunity to prove yourself and hopefully restore some of the damage you did.'

Abbie inwardly cringed, instantly feeling an urge to defend herself, but before she could find the right words, a voice boomed out.

'She could never do that!'

Neither of them had heard Robert approach, and with an anxious-looking Fay at his side he stood glowering down upon them both, legs astride, arms folded across his puffed-out chest. 'Did I hear right? Are you saying that Mother left the property on Carndale Road to you?'

Abbie met her brother's glare with an apologetic little smile. 'So I've been told.'

'Why on earth would she do such a thing when you let her down so badly? It's not as if she'd forgiven you for ruining your reputation, along with that of the entire family.'

Abbie was on her feet in a second, trembling slightly as she always did whenever her brother attempted to intimidate her. But she felt her father's hand upon her arm, gently drawing her back down beside him.

'That's enough, Robert. Maybe she had forgiven Abigail, deep down, but just couldn't bring herself to admit it. The longer an estrangement lasts, the more difficult it is to bring it to a close. Perhaps the will represented a step towards that, as far as your mother was concerned. A decision we should respect.'

A small silence fell upon them all, one broken finally by Abbie herself. 'I promise I will do my utmost to justify her faith in me. But it's my life, and I have the right to make my own decisions, so I'd appreciate no more elder brother lectures, please.'

Clearing her throat and slipping an arm about her husband, for the first time Fay chose to intervene in the family feud. 'I think you appreciate that now, don't you, darling?'

Robert looked into his wife's eyes, then at his father's questioning gaze, but there was little softening of the glare he finally directed at Abbie. 'As long as you appreciate that if you fail, Dad stands to lose everything.'

And as he walked away, taking Fay with him, Abbie was grateful for the small squeeze her father gave to her hand before he rose to follow his son. But, heart pounding, she was left in no doubt that failure was not an option.

The local paper came out the following Thursday, and as expected the piece began by mentioning Kate's suicide at some length, although it did add that Abbie was still grieving for her. But any sympathy this might have provoked was destroyed by the next sentence. '*As an unmarried mother with no sign of a husband to support her, Abigail Myers is making a valiant attempt to restore a business badly neglected in recent years, no doubt due to her mother's state of depression.*'

'Was it absolutely necessary to mention my lack of marital status, let alone Mum's suicide?' Abbie groaned, as she and Linda read the article together. She wished Drew was still around, as she felt a great urge to run to him for comfort and consolation, but then remembered he wouldn't be the right person to turn to at all.

'Don't take these comments too much to heart. You are not alone. There are other single women with children out there.'

A résumé of Abbie's family history followed which hinted at a tendency of its female members to share a craving for travel.

'*Grandmother, mother and daughter have all run off to foreign lands in their youth. We can only assume that affairs of the heart were the reason for such adventures. How long Miss Abigail Myers will remain in Carreckwater will perhaps depend on what new temptations come her way.*'

'She seems to be suggesting that I could run off with another man at any time,' Abbie steamed. The piece did eventually give a brief description of the official shop opening and the members of the community who had attended the party, and concluded by warning of the possibility of a rival shop soon to open next door.

'It's so negative. Why does she paint such a bleak picture?'

Giving a sad little sigh, Linda said, 'Presumably to make a story. She barely even mentions the jewellery, or all that information you gave her about the amber. What a let-down.' At that moment the shop bell jingled and two women walked in. Linda quickly stuffed the paper out of sight to welcome them with her usual bright smile.

Later, after a surprisingly busy morning, Abbie was feeling much more relaxed. 'We've done well despite that dreadful article. Well, they do say there's no such thing as bad publicity.'

Linda gave a rueful grin. 'Attem girl, even if his lordship next door does seem to be working his socks off to open up in competition any day soon.'

'You've changed your tune.'

'I'm on your side. We'll fight him every inch of the way, right?'

'Absolutely!'

~

Abbie was collecting Aimée from school when Joan Sanderson, the little girl's teacher, came out to speak to her.

'Ah Abbie, I'm glad I caught you. I've seen that piece in the paper and wanted to say that I thought Clarinda Ratcliffe gave you rather a hard time. Not that it greatly surprises me. I don't know all the details but she and Kate didn't get on too well.'

'That dreadful woman actually knew my mother?'

'Oh yes.'

'She never said.'

'They fell out years ago, over something very silly. Kate was chosen to be secretary of the local Soroptimists instead of her. Clarinda isn't the kind of person who takes to being overlooked or ignored.'

'Neither was my mother. Oh, but that makes me feel so much better, even though it doesn't actually change the fact she put the worst possible slant on everything. Surprisingly though, trade has perked up wonderfully today.'

'Excellent, but then Miss Prickly, as she's known locally, isn't particularly well liked.' Joan Sanderson laughed, drawing Abbie to one side to avoid the crush of children rushing to meet the parents come to collect them, as well as away from anyone who might overhear. 'Clarinda Ratcliffe is the kind of gossipmonger who loves to root out the worst in people, as well as being a notorious flirt. I believe she tried it on with your father but got nowhere.'

Abbie frowned. 'I'm not surprised. There was only one woman for my dad.'

'Exactly, but that rather sealed the deal on any hope of a reconciliation between the two women. If they both happened to be at the same function, their comments to each other would be extremely barbed, almost embarrassing to listen to. Clarinda hated the fact your mother enjoyed a happy marriage, and Kate believed her rival had done her utmost to ruin it.'

Abbie was listening to all of this with great interest. 'By the sound of it, you must have known my mother rather well.'

'Oh yes, Kate and I were good friends.'

'Could we meet up for coffee some time? I'll love to talk to you and try to find out more about her, since I lost touch with my mother for all those years. For instance, do you know why she went to the Riviera?'

The teacher drew in a breath, released it on a sigh. 'I do, as a matter of fact, and it's really rather a sad tale.'

'I'd love to hear it, sometime soon if at all possible,' said Abbie and, glancing across at her daughter, happily playing tig with Jonathon, added, 'When I don't have Aimée with me, of course.'

'Perhaps tomorrow, then, when your sister-in-law collects the children and I've finished work for the week? Could you come to my house around five?'

'That would be wonderful.'

The next afternoon, leaving Linda in charge, Abbie set out for what she hoped would be a fruitful visit. Taking a detour, she turned left at Benthwaite Cross and up through St Margaret's Walk rather than face the crowds still milling around the main shopping area of Carndale Road, even at almost five o'clock. In the winter Carreckwater was a quiet, sleepy place where locals strolled about, nodding and smiling and greeting everyone they met. Now that summer had arrived there was barely room to move let alone recognise a familiar face, so Abbie was not concerned when she first heard footsteps behind her, assuming it to be one of the many tourists wandering about. But when she entered the quieter streets leading to Hazelwood Crescent where Joan lived, she was surprised to still hear the distant click of heels on the cobbles behind her.

She quickened her pace slightly. So did the footsteps. After another few yards she glanced back over her shoulder, but could see no one. Feeling rather foolish, thinking she must have imagined it, she hurried on to find Joan waiting for her on the doorstep.

'I thought I heard you coming. We don't get many visitors in these parts, thank goodness.'

Looking back along the street, a thoughtful frown puckering her brow, Abbie considered these words as Joan led her along the side of the house to where a table and chairs were set out on the back lawn. Had it just been her imagination, or was someone really following her?

'I've made some lemonade, which I thought we'd take outside to enjoy this lovely sunny day.'

'What a beautiful garden. Oh, and what a magnificent view.'

'I never grow tired of looking at it. That sprawling ridge is Loughrigg. From its summit there are even more spectacular views of the Langdale Pikes. I love to walk over there, or around the tarn that nestles beneath, particularly now in early summer when the surface is awash with water lilies. The tarn was a favourite of Wordsworth. The poet described it as being as "clear and bright as heaven".'

'I can well believe it. I hope to put in some walking myself this autumn, once the shop is less busy.'

Joan began to pour lemonade in to two glasses, adding ice from a jug. 'I'm delighted to hear business is good, despite Clarinda's vicious little piece. But let's not talk about her. Let us remember my dear friend Kate.'

Accepting a delicious slice of chocolate cake, Abbie soon forgot all about her possible stalker as she became instantly caught up in the tale Joan had to tell.

'I know you are aware that your mother was adopted, and I dare say by now you will have discovered that Countess Olga Belinsky was actually her birth mother.'

'Yes, I knew years ago that she was adopted but not where or when.' Abbie told Joan briefly of her visit to the orphanage at Stepney, and something of what her grandmother had told her.

'Well, back in 1936 when Kate was just nineteen, the Countess arrived at Carreck Place, quite out of the blue. At first Kate was delighted to see her. I suppose it was a relief to find out at last who her real mother was, and even quite exciting that she should turn out to be a countess. But I don't believe your grandmother was quite so pleased.'

'I can understand that. Apart from the fear of losing her, Millie hates to look back. It has taken months of effort on my part to drag out the story of her time in Russia and learn the information I wanted about my mother. I must say I didn't hurry her because I found it all absolutely fascinating, both tragic and touching. So how did Millie react to the Countess's sudden appearance?'

Joan sadly shook her head. 'There were many arguments, apparently, both between Kate and her mother, and between Millie and the Countess, over the way she was intruding upon their lives. She called constantly, refusing to let go, and even accused your grandmother of stealing her daughter, whom she called Katya. She threatened to tell the police that Millie had also stolen her jewellery.'

'God, that woman talked complete trash. Millie told me how she'd once been accused of stealing the Countess's pearls.'

'In this instance the Countess was referring to an amber pendant, not her pearls. Millie insisted she had no recollection of what had happened to that.'

'Ah, it must be the one I found in Mum's baby things. But do go on. What happened next?'

'The battle was really over access to Kate, and your grandmother tried to explain to her daughter that it was all lies, that the Countess had ordered Millie to claim to be her mother, as she'd refused to acknowledge the child. I think Kate found this hard to accept, which resulted in more quarrels. Then Olga offered Kate a home in the Riviera, and she agreed to go.'

'Oh, my goodness. So that was the reason she supposedly ran off?'

'I'm afraid so, and it rather broke your grandmother's heart.'

Abbie was silent for some minutes, understanding what a cruel blow this must have been for Millie. 'I can't imagine how I would feel if I lost my darling Aimée. I'm quite happy for Eduard, my ex, to have her visit from time to time, but I'd be in pieces if he tried to take her from me completely.'

Joan was nodding. 'I should think that's exactly how your grandmother felt. She'd brought Kate up as her own child from birth, and as she was unable to have any children of her own she couldn't have loved her more. Kate loved her too, but was at a rebellious age. However, she soon regretted her decision to move in with Olga, as she quickly became disillusioned. After just a few months she found herself more and more controlled and manipulated for the Countess's own selfish purposes. Kate told me she was shocked by her decadent lifestyle, her string of lovers, her profligate spending. Apparently she had learned nothing from the Russian revolution. So when Olga attempted to force her into marriage with a rich aristocrat, Kate had had enough and returned home. She'd finally realised that the woman who had been the only true loving mother to her was Millie.'

There were tears in Abbie's eyes by this time. 'Oh, thank goodness for that, although I'm not sure their relationship entirely recovered from the trauma. I can see now why there was always a slight restraint between them.'

'Indeed. They were probably nervous of reviving past hurts.'

'I really do appreciate you telling me all of this. It has helped enormously.'

'Feel free to call whenever you wish to talk. Any daughter of Kate's is a friend of mine.'

~

When she reached the church yard, Abbie was surprised to catch a glimpse of Eduard parking his car, which puzzled her as he was supposed to be taking Aimée out on a steam launch. Why would he take her home early when he'd made such a fuss of wanting to spend as much time as possible with her? The answer came to her in a flash and she marched right over.

'Are you following me?'

Eduard blinked. 'Follow you where? I thought you were at the shop, working.'

'Don't lie to me. I heard your footsteps following me earlier when I went to visit a friend.'

His lip curled in derision. 'Was that the friend I saw you with the other night? Is he your latest lover?'

'He most certainly is *not* my lover, and nor was he the friend I was visiting. All of which is irrelevant to my question. Why were you following me?'

Eduard held out both hands in a helpless little shrug. 'I can only say *non*, I was not following you. I take Aimée out for sail, then she want to go home as it too hot, so I drive her home in my rental car. Now I buy ticket at the post office for train tomorrow.'

'Train? You're going home?'

'There is nothing for me here. You have made that very clear. I like spending time with my little girl. We have enjoyed good days together and she is eager to come see me later in the summer. If you can't fly her out, I will come for her. Now it is time I go see my little boy.'

Stifling a sigh of relief, Abbie smiled. 'I'm sorry it didn't work out for us, but I do wish you well, Eduard. And please give my best wishes and congratulations to Marie on the birth of her son. Have you chosen a name yet?'

He shook his head. 'She wait for me to decide.'

'Of course.' Eduard always liked to be the one to make the decisions. Allowing him to plant a triple kiss on her cheeks in true French fashion, she stood by her car, watching as he walked away. Now she was truly free at last. But instead of the expected joy, she was swamped with sadness, for she seemed to have lost Drew as well.

~

On the Monday morning, after an oddly quiet weekend, Abbie was alone in the shop, Linda having taken a well-deserved day off. A short, stocky man in his fifties was her first customer, and Abbie offered her usual smiling welcome as husbands buying gifts for their wives were some of her best customers. But he was not smiling as he approached the counter. His expression was largely obliterated by a scraggy beard and a peaked cap pulled well down over his round head; despite the warmth of the day the collar of his navy duffle coat was turned right up. Little was visible of his face but a pair of piercing dark eyes.

'Are you Abigail Myers? I see the interview in the paper saying you take over your mother's business.' His words were not easy to distinguish, as he spoke with an accent.

'That's correct,' Abbie replied, feeling a slight twinge of unease.

'I was companion to one of the ladies your mother visited.'

'Ah, do you mean the one who spoke to her about a possible visit to Russia?' Abbie asked, remembering what the journalist had told her, but the man was shaking his head.

'I know nothing of any visit to the Fatherland.' Looking about the shop, his eyes lighted on the amber jewellery in the display cabinet. 'Ah, is that the stolen amber?'

'What are you talking about? I bought it from a company in Poland, all legal and above board.'

'No, your grandmother stole it. She owe big debt to my lady. She steal not only my lady's jewellery but also her daughter.'

Abbie had gone quite cold. 'That is absolutely not true. My grandmother is no thief.' So this man must have been a companion or servant to the Countess.

He leaned across the counter towards her, his scornful smirk revealing a row of yellow teeth, several of them chipped as if he'd been in a fight. 'I know the truth, the whole story. Your grandmother, she even get the house that should have belonged to my lady, had her husband done the right thing by her. Instead she died in penury, having lost everything. Now I need an income for having looked after your mother's mother for all these years, and the Countess instructed me on where and how to go about getting one. If you don't want your grandmother to spend time in jail, then you pay me money. I want the same as my lady was receiving from your mother: one hundred pounds a week. That is four hundred a month or I tell police.'

Abbie gasped. 'That's blackmail. Even if I was in possession of such a huge sum I wouldn't pay you a penny.'

His lip curled, eyes glittering. 'This is business. Everything you have should belong to my lady, and now to me. You tell the old woman that Ivan has not gone away and it would be wise for her to do as I say. She cannot hide forever in her beautiful panelled drawing room. I will be back in one week for the money. Make sure you have it waiting.'

THIRTY-TWO

By the end of January, the Count and Serge had left Petrograd. *Babushka* decided to remain as this was where her friends lived, and they did sometimes pay her a visit. *Nyanushki* agreed to continue as her companion as the old lady's rheumatism was getting worse and she could do little for herself.

'The poor dear might die of neglect, if I didn't stay,' *Nyanushki* whispered in an aside to me while these negotiations were taking place.

I'd heard no word from Stefan for almost two weeks, which was driving me half demented. I'd spent many hours trudging about this huge city asking people if they'd seen him, hoping for some clue as to where he might be hiding, so far to no avail. I positively haunted our favourite coffee shop, even though it rarely had any coffee to offer these days. It was most distressing that I could discover no news of him.

But if I was upset by the cards fate had dealt me, the Countess was in a veritable rage over her own. A divorce was proving to be a mixed blessing. Without her lover, or the settlement she had hoped for, its appeal had diminished somewhat. At one point she went so far as to reject the very idea.

'Why can we not stay as we are, at least until the political situation improves?'

The Count's expression as he answered her was uncompromising. 'Because things could get a whole lot worse. Besides, why would I wish to keep you as my wife? Infidelity appears to be second nature to you. I could personally name many of your lovers, although certainly not all.'

'So you would ruin my reputation?'

'I think you managed that all on your own.'

Worse, the fact that her precious son had chosen to reside with his father, and not with *her*, came as a terrible shock. 'I will not allow you to steal him from me!' she screamed at the Count.

'I would not dream of doing so. The choice is entirely his. Tell me, Serge, where do you wish to live: here in Petrograd with *Mamochka*, or with me at the estate, such as it is?'

'With you, Papa.'

She begged and pleaded with the boy, yelled and shouted at him, but he left her in no doubt over his reasons for making this choice.

'I do love you, *Mamochka*, but you are never around when I need you. You really only care about yourself, and were horrid to my little sister. How do I know that you won't get bored with me too one day? Papa and I are good friends, and I shall be a man soon so I wish to be with him. You can come and visit me any time you please, and stay in one of the cottages on the estate, so stop fussing. I'll be fine, and so will you.'

The discussion, it appeared, was over, even if her anger continued to fester.

Much as I had come to love Russia, I was growing increasingly anxious to return home to England, assuming a train or ship became available, just as soon as I could arrange the necessary papers from the Duma. I'd tried on numerous occasions with no success. At my last effort the House Committee had demanded proof of where I had been living these last six years, and who the flat belonged to, which the Countess refused to provide for fear they might come seeking payment or extra taxes of some sort. What should have been a perfectly simple procedure was turning into a nightmare.

I'd written to my parents assuring them that I was safe. But with no reply I wasn't even certain they'd received any of my letters. There would be much about Russia that I would miss if I left, not least *Nyanushki* and Ruth, but I longed to hear English voices, to see smiling happy faces, to leave all of this misery behind me. Except that I still hadn't found Stefan. Sick as I was of the difficulties in Petrograd, finding him was my number one priority, as I hoped to persuade him to come with me. I certainly had no intention of leaving without him.

Many of my friends from the British and American chapel had already gone, although not dear Ruth. She often spoke of leaving but had so far set no date to do so. She did advise me to get together some money in preparation for my own departure.

'I tried to draw out some of my savings the other day,' I told her. 'Not that I have much left, but was informed that we're only allowed to draw out one hundred roubles a week. How I'll get my hands on the money the Count has provided for me is uncertain.'

'Didn't he give you any cash?'

I looked around to make sure we were quite alone and not overheard by any wagging ears. 'Yes, as a matter of fact he did, safely stitched into a secure place. I hope!'

She rolled her eyes. 'So if anyone were to find it there, you'd have a bigger problem than just losing the money.'

We both giggled, as if it were all some sort of joke, when really it could easily turn into a life or death situation. How much money it would take to complete the long journey to England was impossible to say. I knew I needed to be prepared for any emergencies, such as bribing a guard to allow me on to a train, or to persuade someone not to rob me of my precious belongings. Problems of this sort were now quite common. Bribery seemed to be the new currency.

I let out a weary sigh. 'I need to go again and ask about my papers. All I've had so far are endless promises but no actual documents. Oh, I do wish Stefan was here to help. I really don't want to leave without him. Where can he be? Have you heard anything?'

'I haven't seen him, no,' Ruth said. A little smile lit her face, and I was instantly on the alert.

'But you've heard something?'

Now it was my friend's turn to glance nervously over her shoulder. Then she carefully dropped her voice. 'He left a message for you in my hymn book.'

'Oh, tell me where he is,' I cried. 'Why didn't he contact me directly?'

'Because he's terrified of endangering your life. Listen, he isn't far away, and wishes to see you too.' She told me the place and time, and I hugged her with joy. 'You are the best friend in the world. I don't know how I can ever repay you.'

'Just be careful. Remember, he's still a wanted man. He says you must continue to behave as normal. You must keep on trying for your papers and making the necessary arrangements to leave, and when you go to meet him, take a circuitous route, making sure no one is following you. The last thing he needs is for the Countess to find out where he is.'

'Don't worry, I'll make absolutely certain of that.'

~

It was such a joy and a relief to have Stefan's arms about me again, to kiss him and hold him and feel his heart beating against mine.

Being with him after all these weeks apart was an exquisite pain. Neither of us could speak for some time as we clung to each other beneath the shelter of a bridge down by the river, a safe distance from the centre of the city.

'Show me where you're living,' I asked him, when finally we paused to take a breath. 'I need to know in case something happens and I have to leave without you. I need to know where to contact you.'

'Nothing is going to happen and we are going to leave together, I swear it.' We both knew it was one promise he couldn't guarantee to keep. 'You weren't followed today, I trust?'

I shook my head in reassurance, for I shared his fears. 'I saw no one but an old lady selling flowers. You're quite safe, my love.'

His hideout was little more than a shack which, I was surprised to discover, was actually a studio filled with easels, oil paints and brushes. There was also a range of beautiful paintings of local landscapes and sunsets, ships and architecture, birds and animals. I gazed upon them in awe. 'This is your work?'

'It is.' He was almost blushing.

'So is this where you go when you disappear for hours? You took days off to go and paint, not to meet your revolutionary friends, as the Countess imagines.'

He grinned. 'Yes, either out in the country, or here in my studio, my secret hideaway.'

'Why didn't you tell me? Why keep it a secret?'

He shrugged, for the first time looking vulnerable, almost shy. 'My painting is very private, my secret creative world, and sharing it is difficult for me. Maybe one day, when I'm convinced I have talent.'

'Oh, you have talent, *Nyanushki* was right about that,' I said, remembering a conversation years ago when he'd first come to do the work in the schoolroom. I smiled in wonder at a picture of the blue and white pavilion at Catherine Palace, and one of a tall ship in the harbour. 'But I do wish you'd been more open about it.'

'You mean I might not be in this mess, if I had.'

I gave him a rueful smile. 'Maybe. The Countess likes to keep her own secrets, but is not approving of other people's.' I went to put my arms about him. 'May I tell her that this is what you were doing, painting? It might help to persuade her to drop all charges against you.'

'What if she doesn't, and the Bolsheviks discover where I'm living?'

'I promise I won't reveal your hideaway, or give any hint that I know where you are living.'

'It's too big a risk, Millie. They might wonder why you've never mentioned it before and start to question how you know, and where I do this painting. The Countess could make your life impossible as well as ruin mine.'

As we walked along the river bank sharing the warmth of each other's bodies, blissfully uncaring of the feathering of snow falling upon our heads as we kissed, we agreed to postpone the decision until I had my papers safely in my hand.

By the end of February the apartment was refurbished sufficiently for us to occupy a small portion of it. No one could claim it to be comfortable as it was bitterly cold, with very little fuel available. But with only us four women remaining, as even Mrs Grempel, Anton, Gusev and the other servants had all gone their separate ways, we would huddle together in the library during the day. If we were lucky we would find sufficient wood for one fire. On the days we couldn't, the Countess would order us to chop up a chair or table, and we'd burn that. Anything to keep warm. Once we ran out of wood and the cold became too much, we went to bed.

We were also starving.

Today, dinner consisted of beetroot soup and nothing else. The price of food, even if we could find any, was extortionate: seven roubles for a small pack of sugar, eight for a quarter measure of potatoes, and even rice was over three roubles the pound. We'd managed to buy some bread in previous weeks, if only the kind made from rye flour or bran. This week no bread had been given out. *Nyanushki* had attempted to bake some out of potato flour and bran. It was dreadful and made me feel quite ill.

As the winter dragged on we lived in constant fear as the apartment was frequently searched by the Bolsheviks. In the first raid they came seeking the Count and his valuables. His work at the Winter Palace and his connection with the Romanovs had not gone unnoticed. That alone put him in danger, as well as his fortune.

'If you possess gold in any shape or form, it must be given up to the new government,' the soldier informed Countess Olga.

'In view of the bomb, and the resulting fire, we have precious little of anything left,' the Countess told him in her most regal tones, which did not go down well.

Fortunately, the Count had taken his most precious possessions with him, save for his Russo-Balt black car, as they'd travelled to the country by train. He still employed Viktor the chauffeur to look after it, and the Countess still loved to drive out of an afternoon whenever petrol could be found to fill the tank. Whether the pair were still involved in a liaison was none of my concern, but the outings ended that day when the Bolsheviks spotted the car parked at the door and demanded the key. The soldiers all piled on board and drove away content.

'Damnation upon the lot of them!' the Countess raged. Then, turning to Viktor, she asked, 'Where is the carriage? Is that at least still safe?'

'Oh yes, somewhere they'd never think to look.'

'Good, then we can continue with our drives,' she said with a smile.

'I'm afraid not milady, as they have also taken the horses.'

Walking for pleasure was not something the Countess was prepared to contemplate; therefore, her afternoons were now spent confined to the apartment. Viktor, who lived in the room over the garage with his brother Ivan, continued to call regularly. *Nyanushki* and I would exchange a knowing look but say nothing as the pair of them disappeared for an hour or so to her boudoir.

At the Countess's instruction, we spent every free moment hiding her jewels in unlikely places. I stuffed some in balls of *Nyanushki's* knitting wool, stitched rows of pearls into a long pair of stays. On one occasion we sat up half the night sewing amber jewellery, sapphire and diamond brooches, and many dismounted gems into hems, collars, cuffs and corsets, and even the baby's clothes. We padded each with cotton-wool so they wouldn't press into our flesh and hurt when we wore them. Were anyone to discover this treasure and inform upon us, they would receive one-third of its value, so no one could be trusted.

Just when we were beginning to feel safe, the soldiers came again, this time looking for firearms. 'What right do you have to search the Countess's rooms? We have no weapons here.'

Perhaps it wasn't wise of me to confront them, but they merely waved a piece of paper in my face then thrust me to one side and began to pull open cupboard doors and drawers in the Count's office. They even searched the schoolroom, going through the children's old toy boxes, Irina's dolls, and Serge's box of lead soldiers. They found nothing, so turned their attention back to the living areas.

'Do I look like the kind of woman who would know how to use a pistol?' the Countess asked the captain in her most flirtatious tones, lifting up her arms and pulling back her shoulders in a gesture that revealed her cleavage. 'Let alone hide one among my children's old toys?'

I saw the lust in his eyes as he looked at her, but then she was still a beautiful woman. 'Your husband might.'

'He isn't here, so I'm all alone and unprotected.' There was a teasing note in her voice now, and as I watched her smile provocatively at him, it came to me that there must indeed be a firearm in the apartment. Were the soldiers to discover a pistol we might all end up in prison. 'It is most alarming to have men riffle through my personal belongings. Now if it were just *one* man – you, dear sir, for instance – I should have no objection. I would be happy to show you anything you wished to see.'

The captain cleared his throat, a crimson flush creeping up his throat as he took in her meaning. It was an invitation few men had resisted in the past. For once I did not condemn her, feeling nothing but admiration for her courage. Turning to his men, the captain ordered them outside, then eagerly allowed the Countess to lead him to her boudoir. I was deeply thankful that her mother was asleep in her bed and not present to witness her daughter offering herself as a bribe.

Nyanushki and I sat in silence, not even daring to exchange so much as a glance as the clock on the mantel-shelf ticked by fifteen minutes before the captain re-emerged, fastening his tunic with a small sigh of satisfaction.

The whole apartment stank for hours after the soldiers had left.

The Countess returned to the library without a word, her expression completely bland and unreadable. Later that afternoon as it began to go dark, she drew the pistol from its hiding place among the books on the shelf behind us, and for the first time ever the pair of us took a walk together and threw it in the River Neva.

~

Our spirits lifted a week or two later when we received a letter from Serge, addressed to all of us, not just his mother. He spoke of his pleasure in being in the country, of helping his father to work the land which he so loved to do.

'*We have our own vegetable patch now, although we've not much wood left. The soldiers seized what we had and did not pay for it. We have to buy it now from the peasants who take it from Papa's own forests, but there's no point in objecting. Papa thinks that come next spring the hunger could be so bad that fighting will break out between villages, so we're working hard to make ourselves as secure as possible, and be a part of the community. At least we have the goats and some milk here, and a few hens for eggs . . .*'

The letter rambled on, giving more descriptions of their farming achievements. We all read and re-read it, savouring every word, thankful to hear that Serge was cheerful, fit and well, and reasonably happy despite the difficulties. I saw the tears in the Countess's eyes and my heart filled with pity for her. Nursing little Katya on my lap, I fully understood the pain she must be suffering at the loss of her son.

'What a brave boy he is,' I said, and the Countess smiled, pleased by my compliment.

'He always was.'

'If rather fond of practical jokes as a youngster.'

'He seems to have grown out of that now, thanks to your influence, Dowthwaite. Pity you didn't have the same good effect upon Stefan.'

'I know now that he was never your lover,' I told her, feeling a sudden need to clear the air between us, perhaps because I no longer thought of myself as her servant. She wasn't even paying me any wages, her excuse being that she had no wish to draw attention to herself by attempting to draw too much money out.

Her reaction was to laugh out loud. 'It was great fun to let you think that he was. Hugely entertaining to see how worried and jealous you became.'

I shook my head in bewilderment. One minute I was in awe and admiration of this woman, and feeling genuine sympathy for her over missing her son, and the next her words filled me with fury.

'You've seen him, haven't you?' she asked, startling me so much by the question that I felt the blood drain from my face. In my foolishness I'd almost given myself away. I visited him almost every day, of course, always taking care that I wasn't being followed. 'I wish I had, but I've no idea where he is.' Turning to *Nyanushki* I said, 'I've finally made up my mind to push harder for my papers as it's long past time I went home now that I'm no longer needed here. Would you come with me this time? Obviously your Russian is so much better than mine.'

'I'd be happy to help, though I have no wish for you to leave, dear Millie. I shall be sorry to lose you.'

As we set out first thing the next morning for the consulate, the Countess was in the library with the chauffeur.

'Viktor is here early for once,' I said, pulling up my scarf against a chill wind.

'I've noticed he's here more and more. I doubt he even went home last night.'

'Ah, then we continue to turn a blind eye, do we?'

'I would recommend that we do, yes,' *Nyanushki* agreed, giving a little giggle.

It took hours of queuing and argument but finally we were successful and I returned to the flat jubilant, papers in hand.

The Countess was reclining on her sofa as she so loved to do of an afternoon. She did not even open her eyes as she spoke to me. 'Ah, Dowthwaite, I've had word today from the police about Stefan. Apparently they found him in a hideaway by the river. He was duly arrested and put in prison, and this morning he was executed. So that puts an end to him.'

THIRTY-THREE

I felt as if I had nothing left to live for. Where was the point of anything without Stefan beside me? I couldn't even begin to take in what she'd told me. How could he be dead when only yesterday he had held me in his arms under the bridge and we'd spoken again of our plans for a wonderful future together? Everything had appeared perfectly normal – the snow still feathering our hair as we kissed, the boats sliding slowly along the River Neva, the old woman selling her flowers. Now he was gone from my life forever.

I had never known such pain, both physical and mental. It gripped my heart, my chest, my entire body. Grief consumed me, and I could think of nothing but the hours, days and weeks, *years* we had spent suffering foolish jealousy, instigated by our employer. What a dreadful waste of the short time we'd been granted together. Precious moments gone forever.

'Why did we ever allow the Countess to tear us apart with her lies and tricks?' I sobbed as *Nyanushki* held me close. She said nothing, unable to find any words of comfort to offer, and merely wept along with me. 'Now, just as we'd finally overcome all the doubts and lack of trust between us, he's lost to me forever.'

And the fault could be entirely mine.

It came to me in a flash of understanding that I had indeed been followed, right from the start. 'That old lady selling flowers was probably the Countess herself. She watched us from a distance, taking note of where I went.'

Nyanushki gazed at me in dismay, tears still marring her pallid cheeks. 'No doubt she sent Viktor to inform the police, and personally took them to Stefan's hideaway.'

As the reality of what had happened sank in, it made his death all the more unbearable. 'They might never have found him but for me.'

'Don't blame yourself, dear girl. How could you have known?'

'He warned me, over and over. Yet I never even suspected an old woman selling flowers.' How would I ever be able to live with myself? I lay on my bed that night in a torrent of grief, the pain of my loss crushing my heart.

~

After a long freezing winter, one of the worst I remembered for some time, the thaw finally set in. I could see out of my bedroom window again and a river of water ran over the sill on to the floor as the ice melted. For once my breath did not mist the air, and we had no need to swathe ourselves in blankets the entire time. Even so, the Countess was not happy and began making plans.

'I loathe the discomfort of this miserable flat. It's time we left,' she calmly announced one day. 'We don't have sufficient food or heat. Having taken the car and many of my possessions, the Bolsheviks could continue to pester us for more. I see no reason to stay any longer. We should leave before they start searching our bodies for the jewellery. I was lucky on that afternoon with the captain that he was in too much of a hurry to sate his lust to bother to undress me, but he could be back at any time.'

I had considerable sympathy with this argument. Neither of us was safe from unwanted male attention. 'So where would you go?'

'To the Crimea. I have already spoken to my mother and *Nyanushki*, but they have no wish to join me as they feel too old and sick to travel. But you can come with me, Dowthwaite. Now that you have your papers, all you have to do is buy us a couple of train tickets.'

'There were only two trains going anywhere in March, so that won't be as easy as it sounds,' I said, starting to protest, but then lost interest. What did it matter where I went, now that I'd lost Stefan? The Crimea was as good a place as any until I could find a ship back to England.

It was late May before we managed to find a train going in the right direction and buy the necessary tickets. It was leaving the very next day so we had just twelve hours to prepare, although there was talk of a dispute between the Bolsheviks and the railwaymen, so the journey could be called off at the last moment. Hoping for the best, I made my farewells to Ruth and Ivy, and all my friends at the British and American chapel. I found it dreadfully hard to say goodbye to my dearest friend.

'You need to leave Petrograd too,' I warned.

'I'm hoping a ship will come soon,' Ruth agreed, 'or a train to France or Belgium, anywhere that will take me out of Russia. You aren't intending to stay in the Crimea, are you? You need to get home.'

'Oh, I will, just as soon as I can find the necessary transport to take me there. I've had no success so far, and it might be easier to find food for little Katya in the Crimea. It's as good a place as any, for now, and safer than Petrograd.' We hugged and wept a little, not least over the loss of Stefan.

'Stay strong,' she urged me. 'He wouldn't want you to give up. Go back home. Live life to the full.'

I hadn't the first idea how to begin to do that.

~

The endless packing that the Countess demanded took *Nyanushki* and me most of the night, before finally we had three trunks ready to send to the station early the next morning. My own possessions I restricted to one piece of hand baggage, leaving behind the books and other requisites for the job that I'd brought with me all those years ago, which seemed unimportant now. *Nyanushki* also packed us a small picnic hamper of food for the journey, no doubt leaving herself short. The Countess had an overnight bag, and I also had the baby to carry. I tucked my papers and passport into a small pouch that I fastened to my belt, for safety.

'It's not going to be an easy journey,' I said, wondering how on earth we were going to manage this heavy load, although fortunately Ivan was accompanying us. 'And we must wear as many clothes as possible, despite the fact it will be warm, just in case anything gets lost or stolen.'

'Don't let on that you're a countess,' Ivan warned. 'You're plain Citizen Belinsky now, don't forget. If the Bolshevists find out who you really are, they'll arrest you.'

She glared at him, affronted. 'Are you serious?'

'Never more so, my lady, just as they would have arrested the Count had he still been living in the flat when they came looking for him. And remember what happened to your friend Dimitri Korniloff.'

Her brow puckered into a thoughtful frown as she considered this for a moment, then nodded. 'You're right, Ivan. Citizen Belinsky it is.'

There were more tears as I said goodbye to *Nyanushki*. 'Thank you for being such a good friend, and a good teacher. I've learned so much from you.'

'I've learned a lot from you, too, not least how to control the children with love and fun, rather than smacks and punishment.'

We wept even more at these words, remembering our darling Irina. But it was time to leave and move on. 'I shall write to you. Take care of yourself, and of *Babushka*.'

The old lady was in tears when I went to kiss her goodbye and thank her too for her friendship and support over the years.

'If anything goes wrong and you ever need me, I shall be here,' she told me. 'Remember that.'

It was nerve-wracking when we reached the barrier at the station to see how everybody's bag was opened and searched, every individual item unfolded and examined. I dreaded the moment when our turn came. The Countess, as usual, was completely oblivious to my distress, merely instructing Ivan to put the trunks on board.

'The train has not yet arrived,' he pointed out. 'The porter says it is running two hours late.'

'And what are we supposed to do in the meantime?' she snapped.

'Sit in the waiting room along with everyone else.'

She cast one scathing glance at the crush of people inside, and declined. Citizen Belinsky by name, but still Countess by nature. We perched on the trunks on the station platform for the better part of three hours, and they were indeed searched. None of the trunks contained any jewellery, but the Countess had insisted on packing several precious items including a silver inkstand, tray, candle sticks, cruet sets, and several enamelled gold-encrusted boxes.

'What if the guards or customs officials search us and find them?' I'd asked her.

'We'll have to take our chances they won't. I absolutely refuse to leave anything of value behind for the Bolsheviks to steal.'

Fortunately, I'd managed to hide the items pretty well and the official had many other people's luggage to check so his efforts were somewhat perfunctory, constantly interrupted by questions from my mistress. In the end I suspect he was glad to escape and leave us to it.

Eventually, when we'd almost given up hope, the train steamed into the station, red-hot sparks flying from the wood fire that drove the engine. Ivan loaded the trunks into the luggage truck while we hurried along the platform searching for a carriage that might have free seats.

'We're allowed only minutes to board so let's just get on and I'll find seats later,' I urged, almost pushing the Countess up onto the step. It was not easy, as the carriages on Russian trains are much higher and broader than our English ones. 'You'll have to help,' I reminded her. 'I have the baby to carry, the picnic box, and my own heavy hand luggage.' With an irritable click of her tongue, for once she did agree to carry her own bag.

'What about Ivan?' she asked, when we found ourselves hanging on to a strap in a crush in the corridor. We could hardly breathe, there were so many people squeezed in.

'Don't worry, he'll find us.'

The train gave a jerk as it began to pull out of the station. 'Well, go and find those seats you promised, Dowthwaite. I will not spend the entire journey like this.'

Stifling a sigh, I dutifully went off to search, thankful that we were at least on our way.

~

It was a long and tiring journey, and for some reason I felt nervous throughout despite having all my papers in order and nothing suspicious in my own personal belongings. Which was just as well as searchers came on board at every station. If they saw something they disapproved of, or perhaps wanted for themselves, they took it. One man had his fur hat taken, and a poor woman lost her supper that way. Angry words would be exchanged between the railway guards and the soldiers, each calling the other by the now familiar term of 'comrade', a name I came to loathe since they were clearly anything but.

A train passed us with open trucks loaded with coffins, which sent a chill down my spine. The more I witnessed of the new Russia, the more eager I was to get home to dull old England. Crimea would be only the start of my own journey. I intended to make enquiries about trains south just the moment we arrived.

I did eventually manage to find us a seat although the carriage was stiflingly hot. Soldiers lay about all over the floor and the air stank of tobacco and unwashed bodies.

'*Nyanushki* has packed the tea pot and kettle, but we have no hot water.'

'Give me the kettle,' Ivan said. Minutes later he returned with it full and we were able to make tea. I didn't ask where he'd found the hot water, but was truly grateful. After we had eaten I fed the baby, while he and the Countess chatted. I must have dozed off for when I woke, we were pulling into another station.

'Stand by; here we go again,' I said with a weary sigh, kissing little Katya who was still asleep, bless her.

As always several people got off the train to stretch their aching limbs or buy food from the traders that haunted every station platform hoping to sell their wares.

'We too are running out of food,' said the Countess. 'Go and get some more, Dowthwaite. We've hours of travel left.'

I was surprised. 'Really? I thought there was plenty left.' I was about to open the picnic box to check, but she stopped me in that impatient way she had.

'There was nowhere near enough, particularly for Ivan, being a man. Stop arguing and be quick about it, or there'll be nothing left for you to buy.' Handing me twenty kopeks, she gave me a push, and as always I did as I was bid.

The queues were long, and Katya grew fretful as I moved slowly along the line, but I did eventually manage to buy a little bread and cheese. It cost the entire twenty kopeks, yet I considered myself fortunate as even biscuits cost twice as much as normal. It was as I was about to board that I was stopped by one of the Bolshevist officials.

'One moment,' the man said. 'We need to search you first.'

I thought of the jewels stitched into my clothing, and that of the baby, and my heart sank even as I struggled to smile and be polite. 'As you see, comrade, I have no luggage with me, save for the baby's bag. I got off the train only to buy food for myself and my child.' It would clearly not be wise to mention the fact I was servant to a countess.

'Then let me see your papers.'

I pulled them from the pouch strapped to the side of my belt, and as he read them I saw his face change. 'So you are a countess, are you?'

'What? No, of course not,' I protested.

'Don't lie, citizen. Your papers clearly state that your name is Countess Olga Belinsky, wife of Count Vasiliy Belinsky. In which case, I have to inform you that you are under arrest.'

~

The prison at the Fortress of Saints Peter and Paul, situated on Zayachy Island in Petrograd, was every bit as terrible as I had feared. Transported in a car over the Ioanovski Bridge, through the courtyard, and from there to the fortress via Peter's Gate, never had I known such fear. I was numb with terror, even more so for Katya as I held her close to my breast. Over and over I protested my innocence, explaining that I was not a countess, that it was all a mistake. I was English.

Nobody was listening, certainly not the guard who took most of my clothes and possessions from me and locked me in one of the dark and damp cells of the Troubetzkoy bastion. I tried talking to him in Russian, French and English, all to no avail. He simply ignored me.

Strangely, I felt no great surprise over the way the Countess had tricked me. It was typical of the woman I had come to know and despise. For all I admired her beauty, courage and feisty spirit, I'd been a fool ever to trust her. She cared only for herself, and would do whatever she considered necessary in order to save her own skin. The fact I had served her well for almost seven years counted for nothing. Nor did she give any consideration to the innocent child she had already rejected once.

'I shouldn't even be here,' I cried as the door clanged shut. 'I'm not who you think I am.'

The only response was the sound of his laughter as he strode away, and the clump of his boots echoing in the empty corridor.

I knew that the prison was used to hold ministers of the Tsarist government and members of Kerensky's Provisional Government. Judging by the number of people I'd seen being lined up for interrogation in the courtyard, including elegantly dressed women, most hadn't the first idea why they'd been incarcerated. There were traders charged with selling food without a permit, soldiers who had broken the rules by stealing property and selling it for themselves, and people who simply looked bewildered as if they hadn't the first idea why they were there, rather like myself. Anxiety, fatigue and fear were evident in all their troubled faces.

The first problem I encountered was lack of food. If I thought I knew what it was to feel hunger while living at the flat, it was nothing to how I suffered in prison. Feeding the prisoners did not appear to be a priority, or even a consideration. Bread was distributed by means of coupons, but comprised a mixture of buckwheat, sand, plaster and straw. Quite impossible to eat without vomiting. If you didn't have friends or family to bring food in for you, you could die of starvation and nobody would care.

I managed to persuade my jailor to bring some milk for the baby, but he offered nothing else. 'She needs more than milk. She's a growing child.'

'Nothing to do with me.'

'Please may I have paper and pen to write to a friend for help?'

He rubbed his finger and thumb together, asking for payment.

'I'll get you some money and pay you when I can.' I thought of the money and the Countess's jewels stitched inside the clothes they'd taken from me. Would I ever see them again? Although that seemed the least of my worries right then. 'Oh, and can I at least have the baby's clothes, the bag with her bottle and napkins, and her shawl and blanket? It gets cold in here.'

He brought me paper and pencil, and all of Katya's belongings, so the man must have a heart after all. I thanked him most graciously and wrote at once to *Nyanushki*. Within days a small basket of food was brought to my cell, including mashed carrot for the baby. I quickly fed Katya first for she was well past even screaming and had fallen into a sorry state of floppy inactivity which terrified me.

By then I hadn't eaten a morsel of food myself for over three days, and the very notion of eating anything made me want to throw up, not least because of the stink of urine and faeces, and the rats and other vermin. But I must eat if I was to survive and continue to protect Katya. I managed to force down some bread and water, nibbling a little at a time till eventually my feeling of sickness and the pains in my belly began to subside a little.

Thereafter a basket arrived daily, *Nyanushki* sending whatever she could spare. I was deeply grateful to my old friend who was obliged to secure a permit every day, and persuade one of the guards to deliver the food, which no doubt involved a bribe.

~

'May I see the person in charge? I need to explain why I had the wrong papers,' I asked my jailor one day, thinking that if he was kind enough to bring in my food, he would be willing to help in other ways. He made it very clear that he had no wish to involve himself with the personal problems of prisoners in any way.

We were allowed to receive letters, as well as food, but they were all opened and read. *Nyanushki* started writing in French, as it was obvious the guards could not understand that language. I doubt some of the jailors could even read Russian, but no doubt they wished to give the impression they could. *Nyanushki* wrote constantly, reassuring me that they were doing all they could to bring about my release.

'*We've explained who you really are, although we've heard nothing from the Countess. Nor has she apologised or returned your papers. But Babushka and I are determined we won't abandon you or give up the fight for your freedom. We are doing everything we can to secure your release.*'

I could only weep with gratitude for their support.

The worst of it was the monotony, the endless hours and days that dragged slowly by with nothing to occupy me but my own sad thoughts, my longing for Stefan making me sink into a pit of despair. Would this dreadful feeling of loss ever go away? I somehow doubted it. The only sounds were those of some poor soul being beaten up, or a woman screaming as she was raped by drunken soldiers. This was a worry that kept me awake night after night on the hard plank that passed for a bed. Perhaps having a baby that cried of hunger all the time put the soldiers off, but I considered myself fortunate that no one interfered with me.

One morning we were woken at dawn and ordered out of our cells. I wore only a flannel petticoat as all my other clothes had been taken from me. Even my feet were bare as I followed my fellow prisoners, numb with fear, and with no understanding of where we were going.

We were led to the Place de la Monnaie, in front of the Cathedral, where we saw that a huge trench had been dug. It was only when I noticed the heap of bodies within that it dawned on me what it was. I began to shake with terror. Was I soon to join them, along with my companions? I could hear whimpers of fear and quiet sobbing all about me. But then three soldiers were lined up before the grave and one by one they were shot and fell into the trench. When this task was completed, the guards began to fill in the grave and we were sent back to our cells.

They wished us all to know what could happen if we did not behave and do as we were told.

The day I was told I had a visitor was the best in my life. I expected it to be *Nyanushki*, who had been trying for some time to gain a permit to visit. Instead, I saw the plump cosy figure of my dear friend, her brown eyes bright with tears as I entered the small room set aside for the purpose. 'Oh, Ruth,' I cried, and she gathered me into her arms, Katya too, in one of her all-enveloping hugs.

'How are you? Are you surviving? Do you have enough food? I couldn't believe it when I heard what happened. What are you even doing here?'

I answered her questions briefly, telling her in a few words how the Countess must have swapped our papers while I slept in order to save her own skin, then tricked me into leaving the train. 'But *Nyanushki* and dear old *Babushka* are doing all they can for me, providing food and so on. They are also trying to secure my release but I hold out little hope. No one gets out of here, do they?'

'But you are English – that should be enough,' she protested. 'Except that it isn't any more. Apparently many foreigners have been taken prisoner. Look, I don't have long. They've permitted me only five minutes at the most. I leave for England tomorrow on a train and am picking up a ship from Belgium. But I didn't want to go without seeing you. What can I do for you, Millie? Name it and I'll do it.'

'Take the baby.' Without a moment's hesitation I thrust Katya into her arms.

Ruth looked down at the child, an expression of total shock on her face. 'Oh, my goodness, are you sure? I don't know anything about babies.' At that moment the door opened and the guard signalled to her that it was time to leave.

'It doesn't matter. Just feed her and love her. Take her to England and keep her safe. I can do nothing for her here. If they ever let me out then I'll come for her. If I don't . . .' I paused, my throat blocked with tears. 'Then make sure she knows that I loved her and gave her away only to keep her safe. Will you do that for me?'

'I will, Millie. I'll see that little Katya is safe and properly cared for, I promise.'

My heart ached as I watched her walk away, Katya holding out her little arms to me as if begging me not to let her go. I was led back to my cell where I collapsed on to the hard bed and wept as if my heart were broken, which indeed it was. I'd lost Stefan, and now my beloved Katya, all because of the selfish manipulations of one woman who had done far more damage to my life than the revolution itself, as far as I was concerned.

THIRTY-FOUR

'My heart bleeds for you,' Abbie said. 'I can't imagine how you coped after suffering such a loss, let alone the horrors of that prison. Meanwhile, the Countess had run off with your papers and this Ivan, who presumably was her lover.' *Not only back then, but possibly for the rest of her life*, she thought.

Abbie had come to the unwelcome conclusion that it hadn't been Eduard stalking her at all but her recent visitor, who was clearly set on blackmail. How to deal with him was causing her considerable concern. She'd been trembling by the time he'd left, partly from fear but also from fury, shaking so much that she'd had to close the shop till she'd made herself a coffee and calmed down. How she'd longed for Drew to be next door, as he had been all the previous week while she ignored him. Were he there now, Abbie would not have hesitated to run to him for help and advice. Never had she felt so terrified.

For the last hour she'd sat listening to the final part of her grandmother's story. The entire family had joined them, once the children had been put to bed, as Abbie felt everyone should be made aware of what was happening. Fay and Robert had looked slightly puzzled, but agreed to come along to listen to what she had to say, if only out of curiosity. But Abbie wished to approach recent events slowly.

Taking the old lady's hand, she gave it a gentle squeeze. 'Gran, I know that the Countess came here in the thirties when my mother was a girl. I've been talking to an old friend of hers, Joan Sanderson, and she's told me the whole sorry tale of how Kate was persuaded to go off with Olga to the Riviera. That must have upset you greatly.'

'A lot of lies were told which were difficult to refute. It was, after all, only her word against mine, and as a countess the police would be more likely to believe her rather than me.'

'Well, it seems those same lies still are being told.' As Abbie quietly revealed the recent visit from Ivan, and the threats he'd issued, which startled everyone, she watched with concern as all the colour drained from her grandmother's face. The old lady seemed to be suddenly short of breath, rubbing her chest with the palm of her hand, which caused Abbie to panic. 'Gran, what is it? Are you feeling unwell?'

'Should I call the doctor?' Fay asked, leaping up.

'No, no, I'll be all right in a moment. It's just the shock of hearing that name again. He was indeed Olga's lover, or one of them, the brother of the chauffeur who laid the bomb, a previous lover, and the man who obviously assisted her to steal my papers. I'm sure there have been plenty more since, but Ivan has remained loyal to her.'

Tom had fetched her a glass of water, which she accepted with a grateful smile. In a few moments, she stubbornly continued her tale, with Robert holding her hand.

'Olga once attempted to blackmail me when she came on that visit before the war, but I refused to play ball so she took my daughter instead, turning her against me. Fortunately, Kate was intelligent enough to see through her scheming in the end, and returned home. It left a certain awkwardness between us, each of us cautious of upsetting the other, although this gradually eased over time. At least the Countess failed in her attempt to steal her from me.'

'But having abandoned her as a child, why would she want to?' Abbie asked.

'For the money, for the trust fund generously set up in Kate's name by the Count.' Millie's tone was pragmatic. 'Olga's desire for money was always paramount.'

'If you want my opinion, Gran, I suspect that the reason Mum was nearly bankrupt was because the Countess was blackmailing her, milking her dry of funds she felt she had a greater right to. According to this Ivan, she also resented the fact Kate was given Carreck Place.'

Robert interrupted, revealing a startling piece of information. 'I wonder if he was the person who wrote that letter, Dad, insisting that he had a claim on the house, and that he'd make sure we were evicted.'

'Ah, yes, I vaguely remember you mentioning that' Abbie said. 'If only I'd paid more attention.'

'I did investigate the matter further,' Tom pointed out. 'But I failed to discover anything as it was hand delivered and I couldn't even read the signature.'

'Hm. It sounds very likely, though. Ivan, or whatever his name is, is not a pleasant man, I can assure you of that,' Abbie said. A shudder ran through her at recollection of the dark threat in his eyes.

Millie agreed. 'I'm quite certain the Countess did covet the house, since she'd recklessly spent all her own money on high living, or used it to pay her lovers. I never trusted the woman, and it seems that I was proved right. Despite my care, somehow or other she worked out where we were and came looking to exploit us for every penny she could. I'm afraid I let slip about the trust fund, a bad mistake on my part as it made her more determined than ever to get her hands on the money.'

Robert gently patted her hand. 'Don't blame yourself, Gran. We all make mistakes in life. It won't be your fault if we lose Carreck Place.'

Meeting his tender gaze, Abbie smiled in quiet acknowledgement of his care, brother and sister for the first time silently accepting that they were in agreement for once. 'I reckon that after she died, this Ivan continued to make demands upon Mum.'

Millie closed her eyes in helpless agony. 'Oh, Abbie, I do not claim to regret that dreadful woman's passing but you could well be right. Ivan is a nasty piece of work. There is no one else to lay claim to the house, if the Countess really is dead. The Count would never take it from me, nor would Serge, assuming they both survived, which is something we'll never know.'

'If Abbie is right,' Tom said, 'then the police should be informed. Blackmail is a crime.'

'Not only that,' Abbie interrupted, 'but all of this only increases the suspicion that Mum did not commit suicide at all. She was saving for a trip to Russia, after all, a long-held dream of hers. So why would she? And how did this Ivan know that we had a "beautiful panelled drawing room" unless he'd been in the house?'

A shocked silence fell upon them all as they considered the horrifying possibility of why Kate was found hanged. Fay was the first to find her voice, if barely above a whisper. 'Oh, my goodness Abbie, are you suggesting that this Ivan was responsible for her death?'

'I am. What if Mum refused to pay him any more money and he killed her?'

The three of them stared at each other in dawning dismay for several more silent moments. Then Tom picked up the receiver and began to dial the police station.

It proved remarkably easy to set him up. Ivan arrived, as he'd said he would, at the appointed hour seven days later, demanding payment. Abbie had felt quite confident as they'd made their plans. Now, she felt far less so.

'I hope this will be the end of it,' she said, smoothing the notes out on the counter top, striving to prevent her fingers from shaking too much as tension was high in her.

Ivan gave a low chuckle, seeming to find the remark amusing. 'We shall have to see about that, won't we? And there are, of course, the monthly payments too, don't forget.'

'Remind me how much you asked for? I was too much in shock at the time to take in the details properly.' The plan was to persuade him to repeat his threat, but Abbie wasn't finding this easy, her instinct being to turn and run away as fast as she could.

He leaned closer, that all-too-familiar smirk on his fat wrinkled face revealing those dreadful chipped yellow teeth. She smelled the foul stink of his breath. 'Four hundred a month, every month, or maybe five hundred would be better. Yes, let's say five hundred and make sure you never miss a payment.'

'Why would I agree to such a demand?' Abbie said, her heart beating so loud with fear she felt certain he must hear it.

'Oh, you'll agree all right, unless you wish to end up like your mother.'

A chill crawled down her spine at this remark, even though she had been hoping for him to actually confess to what he'd done. 'How could that happen? What are you saying?'

There was a dangerous glint in his eye now. Then one fat hand snaked out to grasp her by the hair and drag her half across the counter. The pain of his grip caused Abbie to let out a little cry of alarm as he spat his next words right in her face.

'You don't really imagine that selfish bitch would have had the nerve to take her own life, do you? It need never have happened.

But she wouldn't listen. Absolutely refused to cooperate. Claimed she was near bankrupt, that the Countess had already bled her dry. What nonsense! She still owned that bleeding house, didn't she? And she owed *me* for the years I'd spent searching for her, just as she owed a huge debt to the Countess for stealing what was rightly hers.'

'You have no right to our home. It was left in trust by the Count to *my mother*.'

'So how do you propose to stop me? Much safer to simply hand over the property. Otherwise, I might very well choose to take my revenge upon your own daughter in lieu of the one your grandmother stole from the Countess.'

It was at that moment that the entire world seemed to explode as doors flew open and policemen stormed in from every direction. They'd heard every word, of course – the threats and the confession – from Ivan's own mouth. And strangely it was Robert, who'd been hiding with them, who was the first to take Abbie's trembling body in his arms. 'Well done, sis. You were very brave.'

Following hours of questioning, the Myers family were informed that Ivan Lytkin had been charged with murder. Now the family were sitting together over lunch in the conservatory, celebrating their victory while each privately struggled to come to terms with old wounds that had been reopened, and the dreadful truth of Kate's death. The children were also present, so they were careful of what they said. Fortunately, Jonathon and Aimée were paying no attention to the grown-ups, happily giggling together in the corner, as always, while baby Carrie spread chocolate all over her chubby face as she tucked into an ice cream.

'At least we know now that she didn't deliberately leave you, Dad,' Abbie softly remarked. 'She was happy with you right to the end, and planning a wonderful holiday for you both.'

There were tears in his eyes as he nodded. 'Not a great deal of comfort, but it's something, I suppose. And we have you to thank, Abigail, for getting to the truth.'

'I asked a lot of questions, yes, of the orphanage, her friends, and poor old Gran, but that dreadful man's own arrogance and greed did for him in the end.' Abbie was unable to disguise the bitterness in her tone.

'I think your brother might have something he'd like to say to you,' Fay quietly put in, a wry smile on her face as she glanced across at her husband.

Robert cleared his throat before mumbling an apology.

'Sorry, didn't quite catch that.'

He took a breath. 'I'm sorry if I came down hard on you by blaming you for Mum's death. I was a bit screwed up with grief.'

'We all were,' Abbie quietly agreed.

'Then there were the financial problems, and I confess I was always a bit jealous of the way Mum fretted and fussed over you, as if you were special.'

'Of course I'm special. I'm a real hot chick.' Abbie laughed, exchanging a smile with her sister-in-law, who put a hand over her mouth to stop herself from giggling.

Abbie put out her arms and gave her brother a big hug. 'Don't worry. I was a bit on my high horse too, so we'll call it quits, shall we, and agree a truce?' They both grinned and slapped hands.

Tom shook his head with a resigned sigh. 'Just as they used to do when they were kids. Falling out and falling in the whole darned time. No doubt they'll be at each other's throats over something else next week.'

'Why do they do that?' little Aimée wanted to know, coming over to see what was going on.

'Because they aren't as clever as you, sweetie,' her Grandpa said, lifting her onto his lap for a kiss and a cuddle.

Abbie smiled, her heart warming to see them so happy together. 'I suggest we put all of this behind us now, and remember Mum for the life she led and not the manner of her death.' And as they all lifted their glasses in a toast to her memory, for the first time in years Abbie felt content to be here where she belonged, a part of her family at last.

THIRTY-FIVE

Summer was at its height, the steamer ferrying trippers back and forth across the lake, children fishing for trout and char, families picnicking on the tiny pebble beaches or sailing their dinghies and rowboats. Everyone was enjoying the sunny weather and having a good time. 'Families are such an important part of life,' Millie said as the two women walked along arm in arm. 'Don't you think?'

'Indeed they are. I intend to take on another assistant as soon as I can, to allow myself to spend more time with my daughter, perhaps when she comes back from a couple of weeks' break in France.' Then after a short pause, Abbie said, 'I shall have to explain all of this dreadful stuff to her eventually, but hopefully not until she's old enough to understand and able to deal with it. However, I will be entirely honest with her as I don't think secrets are a good thing,' she added, slanting a sideways glance at her grandmother.

Millie had the grace to chuckle. 'You may well be right. However, it very much depends upon the circumstances. As advised by the Count I opted for silence for safety's sake. I kept the truth of Kate's birth a secret because I was always afraid the Countess might come looking for her, as ultimately she did. I was terrified not only of losing my precious daughter, but of what the Countess might do to her. Just as Kate never told me that Olga was subjecting her to blackmail, in case she might intrude upon my life too.'

'I understand now why Mum was against my joining the business. She was trying to protect me.' Abbie was thoughtful for some minutes as she considered this quite different viewpoint, and how these fears must have affected their relationship. 'I'm glad it's all out in the open now. Whether openness and honesty would have saved Mum, had all of this been known earlier, is impossible to say.'

'Best not to think about it.'

Giving her grandmother's hand a gentle squeeze, she asked, 'So how did you get out of prison?'

'*Babushka* rescued me, of course, by paying a huge fine, or perhaps *bribe* is a more appropriate word. *Nyanushki* wasn't well, and both women were suffering badly from hunger. I took over the care of the old dowager, explaining that I'd sent Katya to my home in England to be safe. It was easier to allow her to continue to think the baby was mine, rather than upset her further by telling the truth. She didn't even know if her daughter was dead or alive. People frequently vanished at that time and were never heard of again, and she'd suffered enough.

'After the old lady finally passed away from starvation and grief, sometime in 1919, I decided to make a bid to escape over the mountains. *Nyanushki* planned to join the Count, who remained at his country estate. But she helped, making enormous sacrifices to find me food and get new papers drawn up, and in persuading the bank to allow me to draw sufficient money from the fund set up by the Count to see me safely on my way. We made yet another fond farewell, both of us in tears as we knew we'd be unlikely to ever meet again.

'I again took a train, then paid a guide to take me over the mountains. We trekked for days through the snow and ice, finally taking shelter in a cave. Despite my best efforts I must have fallen asleep one night out of sheer exhaustion, as I knew nothing more till I woke at dawn, when some strange sound alerted me. I looked around for the guide but he was nowhere to be seen. The man to whom I'd paid an exorbitant sum, almost every last kopek I possessed, had deserted me, and I was quite alone.'

'Oh Gran, how dreadful, and after all you'd suffered.'

'I realised that it was the sound of horses' hooves clattering over rocks that had penetrated my befuddled brain, which indicated I was about to receive some unwelcome company. I fully expected to be set upon by bandits, sat cringing and shivering in my shoes as they marched in. Then a voice said, "What, not even a kiss of welcome?"

'My eyes shot open in disbelief, and for a moment I thought I was dreaming, or had died and gone to heaven. But there he stood before me, alive and well, my darling Stefan.'

'Oh, Gran, I don't believe it! How did that happen? I thought he was dead.'

'That was yet another of the Countess's lies. I should have guessed. I doubt she has ever told the truth in her entire life. Stefan had indeed been arrested and put in prison, but he was not executed as the Countess had claimed. Thanks to *Nyanushki*, who had secretly been making enquiries, she finally found him, managed to convince the guard that he was innocent of the charge, and a further bribe was paid. Stefan was released and then followed my trail as described to him by *Nyanushki*.'

'What a good friend she was to you, an absolute treasure.'

Millie kissed her granddaughter's cheek. 'She was indeed. Our reunion was exquisite, and very private, so I shall say no more on that score, but freedom was at last in sight. We crossed the Caucasus Mountains, bribing a boatman to take us over the Black Sea. The journey took weeks, months, but we slowly made our way to good old England.'

Abbie looked troubled. 'So what happened to Stefan after that?'

Now her grandmother's face was radiant. 'He deemed it wise to change his name, just to be safe in case the Bolsheviks should come looking for him over that bomb he'd supposedly planted. He took his maternal grandfather's name of Anton Nabokov.'

'That's my grandfather!'

Millie laughed. 'It is indeed. Our love had been torn apart by a woman who had done us greater harm than the revolution itself. But we went on to enjoy a happy life together until he sadly passed away in 1950, aged sixty-two. He was just four years older than me and we should have had much longer, but he suffered far worse than I did in that prison, so I'm thankful for the blessing of the years we did enjoy together.'

There were tears in Abbie's eyes as she hugged her grandmother close. 'You were so very fortunate to have him. He was a lovely man.'

As they made their way back to the lodge house, Abbie said, 'So what about your friend Ruth? Did you ever meet her again?'

Millie shook her head. 'I know from her last letter, which I received just before leaving Russia, that she placed Kate in the orphanage at Stepney because she was about to be married and her new husband was not prepared to take on the responsibility for someone else's child. Money was tight, so it was perfectly reasonable.'

'So that's the reason you went all the way to London to adopt a child.'

Millie nodded. 'I went to find her, yes. And what a joy it was when I did. I just gathered her into my arms and wanted to rush off with her there and then, but of course we needed to make it all legal. That's the reason Ruth anglicised her name – to keep her safe. I never wanted Kate to know the full story, for reasons I've explained. However, she made her own enquiries when she was old enough. Secrets, as you say, are hard to keep forever.'

As she reached the door of the lodge, Abbie paused for a moment before allowing her grandmother to enter. 'Oh, I forgot to mention that I have a little surprise for you. A secret of my own I've been keeping.'

Millie frowned. 'What sort of secret might that be?'

'A good one, Millie Dowthwaite, or so I hope.'

Millie looked wide-eyed at the woman walking towards her, then with tears of joy already rolling down her cheeks, she allowed herself to be gathered up in one of Ruth's famous hugs.

~

'So what of my own love life?' Abbie asked herself the next day as she sat at her work bench trying her hand at carving a piece of amber. She was practising on a rough chunk, hoping to gain the necessary skills so that she could later work on more valuable pieces. Learning her craft was becoming a real joy to her. She'd slowly fed the piece into a newly purchased diamond-tipped circular saw mounted on the work bench. Now she was sanding it by hand, careful to take her time over the task, as amber is soft and easily scratched or damaged.

Had she been right not to trust Andrew Baxter, or did that reveal a flaw in her own nature, born of her experience with Eduard? Abbie had really no wish to think of Drew right now, but he seemed to be ever-present in her thoughts.

He was no doubt with his alleged ex-wife this very moment.

'Stop tormenting yourself, girl,' she scolded, and began to polish the amber on a special buffing wheel, keeping a firm hold to prevent the piece from flipping from her hand. Work was the only thing keeping her sane right now. 'Who cares where he is, or who he's sleeping with?'

'Were you speaking to me?'

The voice startled her so much that Abbie jerked and dropped the piece of amber, watching in dismay as it fell from her hands. Stepping quickly forward, Drew caught it before it rolled off the bench and on to the floor. She looked up at his grinning face, all too aware of the vulnerability in her own. 'Drew, I thought you were in Scotland.'

Coming to perch on the stool beside her, he set the amber safely to one side. 'But you knew I was coming back, and here I am, duty done.'

'What duty would that be?' she asked, not quite able to keep the caustic note out of her voice.

He pulled a wry face. 'Attending my wife's wedding.'

'What?'

'Didn't I mention that was the reason I was going back? I certainly meant to, although maybe I didn't get the chance as we were both so busy at the time, you with all the orders resulting from the official opening of Precious Dreams, and me working on fitting out the shop next door. But yes, she's now married to someone else, thank goodness. Happily, I hope. And all the legalities over the property split are signed and dealt with, so I shan't ever have to go back. I can now focus entirely upon my new life, and my new friends.' His eyes were twinkling rather attractively as they gazed challengingly at her.

Abbie's heart was racing, along with the thoughts rattling through her brain. What did all this mean? What was he trying to tell her? 'Do you have many new friends here?' she asked, a smile twitching at the corners of her mouth.

'I'm sure I will have in time. Right now I'm only really interested in one.' His grey eyes darkened as he edged closer, his breath warm against her cheek as he whispered sadly to her. 'Unfortunately I feel I may have ruined my chances with her.'

'How so?'

'I clumsily made a suggestion at absolutely the wrong moment, thinking I'd already won her round when I hadn't at all. What an idiot I was.'

'And what was her reaction to this clumsy suggestion?'

'She blew me out, quite rightly. So, advise me: what should I do now? Apologise, or simply tell the truth that I adore her, love her to bits and would be content with a partnership of any sort, business or personal, whatever would make her most happy? So long as it's a life-long commitment. So what do you recommend?'

Abbie could scarcely breathe, let alone answer the question, however artfully worded. 'I'm not sure she would wish to hear any more apologies.'

'OK. So were I to kiss her, do you reckon she'd slap me over the head?'

'Maybe you should try it and see,' she murmured, her eyes riveted upon his beautifully sculpted mouth, and as his arms came about her and his lips closed over hers, her heart was singing. How long she remained there Abbie couldn't afterwards rightly say; she made no protest at all as his kisses deepened. But then she was in no hurry to release herself – she wanted to stay there forever. Maybe she would.

AUTHOR'S NOTE

Dear Friends,

Thank you for all your kind messages telling me how much you enjoy my books. Your comments and your reviews are very important to me. I listen and take note. Many of you have been with me since my career first took off back in the early nineties with my sagas, and I do appreciate your loyalty.

The idea for *The Amber Keeper* came when my husband and I took a Baltic cruise (yes, we've reached that age and absolutely love cruising) and visited St Petersburg. It's an amazing city, beautiful and cosmopolitan. We saw Catherine's Palace and the amber room, sailed along the River Neva, and visited the Fortress of Saints Peter and Paul where prisoners were held during the revolution and which features in my book. I just had to find out more. I began by reading lots of books about the Russian Tsar and his family. *The Three Emperors* by Miranda Carter and *From Splendor to Revolution* by Julia P. Gelardi were my favourites. Then quite by chance, I found *Six Years at the Russian Court* by Margaret Eager, about a governess who went out to Russia at the turn of the century and my creative mind kicked into action.

So although this is a work of fiction, I've set it against a true historical background, a time of great change in the Russian Empire.

My sincere thanks to my editors Emilie Marneur and Victoria Pepe, and all the team at Amazon. Also special thanks to my agent Amanda Preston of the LBA Agency for her support and her faith in me.

Much love to you all,
Freda

ABOUT THE AUTHOR

Photo © 2014 Roger Moore

Born in Lancashire, Freda Lightfoot has been a teacher and a bookseller, and in a mad moment even tried her hand at the 'good life.'

Inspired by this tough life on the fells, memories of her Lancashire childhood, and her passion for history, she has published forty family sagas and historical novels including *Daisy's Secret* and *Watch for the Talleyman*.

Freda has lived in the Lake District, in Cornwall, but now spends her winters in Spain and the rainy summers in the UK.

For more information about Freda, visit her website: www.fredalightfoot.co.uk.